THE

SELAH

BRANCH

BY TED NEILL

All proceeds from *The Selah Branch* are donated to organizations and programs that work in support of social justice, education, as well as racial reconciliation and restoration. For more information check the back of the book.

This book is dedicated to all the women of color whom I have been privileged to know and love. You have been friends, teachers, mentors, allies, and partners and I am a better person for it. To you I can only paraphrase what James Baldwin said so much better than I ever could: the individual who is forced each day to snatch her personhood, her identity out of the fire of human cruelty that rages to destroy it, knows that if she survives her effort, she learns something no school on earth can teach. She achieves her own authority and that is unshakable.

I also want to express special thanks, my admiration, and love for Dr. Leslie Clapp and her late husband Mr. Michael Ezie, whom I wish I could have had the opportunity to meet in this life. May the fruits of your love continue to bless this world, making it a dynamic, more just, and more beautiful place.

Chapter 1

Trellis

A train whistle woke Kenia. A pain behind her neck told her that she was no longer reclined on a pillow. She rocked her head and opened her eyes. I-beams had replaced the slats of her dorm room's bunk bed. The texture and scent of the air was unexpected. Gone was the stale industrial cold of the dorm's AC, along with the manufactured scents of what the detergent company considered "sun-dried linen" that usually clung to her sheets. Also absent were the hints of shea butter, hair conditioner, and scented candles that tended to linger in the room she shared with Audre. Instead the air was warm and dense with humidity, laden with the odors of wood, petroleum preservative, and rusting metal. It immediately brought to mind a rail yard.

The I-beams overhead created tessellations of the night sky beyond them: trapezoids, triangles, and rectangles filled in with satin blackness dusted with stars. The brightest stars she had seen since Nigeria. Her blankets were gone, as was her mattress. She looked left, to where her phone should have been to check the time, and started to fall.

The edge of her bed was not where it was supposed to be. There was nothing beside her but a breeze and a drop. She would have screamed if her balance had not been so precarious and a gasp had not choked her voice. Her hand seized something smooth and metal, like a rail but definitely not her bed. A picture of a train trellis was coming together in her head, but how she had arrived there was a complete mystery. Yet in the disconnected logic of sleepwalking or dreaming, perhaps it was not so strange.

She pressed her leg against one of the ties and pushed herself up, brushing aside debris that had the texture of crumbled charcoal. After a long series of seconds, the rocks made a sound of striking water, like a scattering of raindrops. She settled herself, balanced on the tie. What did they sometimes call these things . . . sleepers? Nothing sleep-inducing about balancing on one over a river gorge. Kenia felt like a cat stranded in a tree, or an unlucky lumberjack holding on to a floating log.

The train whistle that had awoken her sounded again. The bridge started to throb.

So this is one of those dreams.

She got to her hands and knees, words like "lucid" and "anxiety dreams" floating through her mind, for this all felt so real. Looking down, the irregular shapes of the night sky between the I-beams were replaced by uniform squares of space between the sleepers, framing the river below, a glistening black answer to the stretch of galaxies above.

Could she *will* herself awake? What horror would it take to do so?

The train whistle blew again, closer this time, the vibrations reverberating through her bare feet as she determined the direction of the sound. It was difficult, as the wail echoed from all around, bouncing from one side of the gorge to the other. A dusting of rust began to rain on her, a tremor passing through the beams above. The train whistle pierced the air again, this time accompanied by the flash of the locomotive's headlamp blinking between the silhouette of trees. It was not long before the engine itself rounded the bend, a floating cone of light at its nose, the flare hiding the thundering beast of cranking, hammering metal that nonetheless announced itself with a loud hiss of steam.

Kenia considered her surroundings. A traffic and pedestrian bridge ran parallel to the trellis, lit by antique streetlamps. It was much too far away to offer any hope of escape in the form of jumping—unless this was a dream wherein she had superpowers, of course. But since none had manifested yet she refrained, her mind registering the mid-century cars passing by with wide grills, starched roofs, vintage decals, and whitewall tires. She even noted a tailfin lined with glowing brake lights before she turned to flee, the tremors of the beams impossible to ignore.

She stepped from one sleeper-tie to the next, placing each step carefully since failure to land her foot properly would send her plunging into the darkness below. Her progress was inadequate, the locomotive lumbering and closing with mechanized, implacable, efficiency. The end of the bridge, where she could see the floodlights of an industrial space with steel towers and glistening slopes of coal, might as well have been miles away. The sides of the bridge would offer too little room for her to stand while the train passed. The locomotive neared, the heat pumping out of its venting made the girders and stars beyond shimmer. The *kachunck-kachunk kachunk-kachunk* of wheelsets rolling from rail to rail drowned out all other sound but the whistle. All was noise. All was vibration. Rust was tumbling down in a blizzard now, falling in her hair, in her mouth, in her eyes. She could not see the ties now, her eyes watering too much. It was too far to the end of the bridge. The train was closing, the light upon her, illuminating the wood grain of the ties and her own stumbling shadow across them. It wasn't a choice any longer. She pressed her arms against her side and dropped between the rails.

Steel thunder rumbled overhead, the sound diminishing as she fell. The whistle cut the air again, this time its frequency warbling as her body accelerated in its fall. The rush of air lifted her shirt up to her bra, cold passing around her torso. She tried to hold her feet together, to brace herself for the shock of the cold water below.

Chapter 2

Black Lives Matter

"I heard some snowflake-Barbie doll spokesperson on Fox News say Black Lives Matter was analogous to the Klan," Kenia said.

"Doesn't seem like she understands Black Lives Matter," Audre said.

"Doesn't seem like she understands the Klan."

Audre, her eyelids shaded with cobalt, focused her gaze on the space beyond the mass of Black Lives Matters protesters to the stage where the president of the Georgetown African American Student Association, a senior named Breanna Williams, was speaking. Breanna was flanked by other somber-looking black student leaders. Breanna wore her hair natural, its curls piled up on her head, somehow reminiscent of a flower blooming, which felt appropriate this sunny spring morning. Kenia sipped her tea, taking in the backdrop of cherry trees, their flower blossoms rising in the breeze before settling on the lawn of the campus quad. It would have been idyllic if it were not for the protests.

"I'm scared, Re-Re" Kenia said, her lipstick leaving a terra cotta smooch on the plastic lid of her green tea.

"To be a black woman in the age of Trump is to be scared," Audre replied.

"Aren't we supposed to be angry?"

"Oh that too," Audre said. "There are so many ways to be black these days."

Kenia puffed out her cheeks, letting out a long sigh. Her eyes roved across the protesters. They were mostly students, mostly black, but there were whites, Asians, and Latinos mixed in, as well as a good showing of professors, administrative staff, and a few bleary-eyed men and women in scrubs from the hospital on the northeast corner of campus. One woman of color had brought her children, who would have otherwise been in school. "It's like we've been going backwards."

Audre twisted her mouth and crossed her arms across her lap, leaning forward. "There has always been pushback: emancipation—Jim Crow; civil rights—the War on Drugs, mass incarceration; black president—President Cheeto."

Kenia became distracted by a tall black man, too mature to be a student, moving from one clutch of protesters to the next. His locks were piled beneath a red, yellow, black, and green Rasta hat. He wore an oversized Black Lives Matter T-shirt with stark white lettering, a stuffed duffle bag slung over his left shoulder, and dozens of Black Lives Matter bracelets ringing his forearms like sleeves. He unfolded a "White Silence Equals Consent" shirt to a white nursing student—Kenia recognized her from the Nursing and Health Studies Building, but did not know her name. She reached into her JanSport backpack, pulled out a billfold, unfolded a twenty, and exchanged it for the shirt. The Rasta man gave her a dab and moved on.

His eyes met Kenia's and he walked over. She smiled briefly then returned her attention to the speaker to indicate she was not interested in a shirt. He did not pick up on her signal, or rather, he chose not to.

"Morning sisters. Interested in a shirt or a bracelet?" he asked, with the accompanying gestures of display.

"No, thank you," Kenia said.

"How much?" Audre asked.

"Twenty."

Kenia raised an eyebrow.

Audre made a *tsk* noise. "That's too much, we're just students."

"At Georgetown," he countered. "What's tuition here, 60K, seventy?"

"Sixty-seven," Audre said.

"But we're on financial aid," Kenia was quick to add.

He waved his arms like a magician, running his hand along his forearm as if stroking an invisible harp. "Want to show your solidarity with a bracelet instead, then? Just five dollars."

"For five, right?" Kenia asked.

"Two, but I'll make it three for you all."

Audre reached into her bag for her wallet. Kenia stopped her. "That's too much."

"How are you going to support the cause?" he asked.

"I've got the skin God gave me, that shows my solidarity."

"That just tells me that you support yourself," he said, pulling one, two, then three bracelets from his arm then holding them out before Audre.

"I need someone to support my cause of getting through school debt free," Kenia said.

"I hear you," he said, slapping the zipper pouch slung diagonally across his chest. A cameraman moved past them a large number five emblazoned on the side of the camera. A smartly dressed Filipina correspondent in a miniskirt, blazer, and heels clicked alongside him.

"How is it you all got the media to show up to this one?" the Rasta man asked. "I've been to a lot of these, but the media does not show."

"You're obviously not a student," Audre said. "Or you'd know."

"Do I look like a student?" he laughed. "I'm a business man. I go where the customers are. If that means showing up at a Blue Lives Matter rally with the blue shirts and blue bracelets, I'm there."

"You've got to be kidding me," Kenia said.

"Got to respect the hustle," Audre said, handing the man five dollars and taking the bracelets.

Kenia took another sip of her green tea and decided to put the transaction out of mind. She watched Breanna Williams hand the microphone over to Lawrence Crockett, a black professor from the law school who began to speak about the importance of the student activism and civil disobedience.

"So what brought all the folks out today?" the Rasta man asked again.

"Some bozo spray painted the N-word on one of the Black Lives Matter signs in the square here last week," Audre said. "That has made this a bigger story."

"Some people," the Rasta man said.

"Yeah," Audre added automatically, pulled in by the words of solidarity from Professor Crockett.

"Well, you ladies stay strong, smart, and beautiful," the Rasta man said, folding the shirts over his arm and floating off into the crowd to hawk his wares.

They both wordlessly tuned in as another professor, Yesha Jordan, the only woman of color in the English department, spoke for a few minutes. She was accompanied by Dean Aldrich Xavier, the dean of students, who was the picture of whiteness in his gray slacks and blazer, button down Brooks Brothers shirt and tie. Eventually Professor Jordan handed the microphone to Dean Xavier. He licked his lips, lifting his arm in an abrupt, aborted wave before he looked down at his feet, unsure exactly how to acknowledge the crowd before he began to speak.

Audre slipped her phone out of her bag, looked at the time, and said, "We don't have time for this milquetoast."

◊

They fell into the flow of students channeled between the Reiss Science Building and Arrupe Hall, the former a fifty-year-old building with a pea green tile entryway that stood up well to the latter, an upperclassman dorm with a brick-and-fieldstone façade accented by a soaring glass tower that provided a well-lit reading and study lounge on every floor.

"Do you know who Father Arrupe was?" Kenia asked, noting a white undergraduate girl in the reading lounge, wearing pajama bottoms and staring at the laptop on her legs, her head tilted to the side where she supported it with her half folded fingers.

"Some white dude from Hispania who came over to commit cultural genocide on the indigenous people of North and South America, like so many other Jesuits?"

"The padre was legit, Audre. He was in Hiroshima when the bomb dropped. Survived, tended to the wounded, founded the Jesuit Relief Service in response to the Vietnamese Boat People, and went on to work in El Salvador where he was associated with the founding of Liberation Theology."

"Okay. Respect," she said, nodding to the dorm and raising her paper cup of coffee as if in salute. "But for every Arrupe there was some other repressed, over-educated white dude who beat some indigenous children with a belt for speaking their native tongue—or raped them."

"Touché. The tour guides like to remind us here that the clock tower is named after Patrick Healy. He was black and elected president of the university during Reconstruction."

"Healy's mother was bi-racial. Brother was passing."

Kenia laughed, "Probably."

"Let's not forget the 272 slaves that *paid* for the Healy clock tower when Father Mulledy sold them in the 1830s."

"Right, that's more than awkward," Kenia sighed, stepping around a student walking slowly while he texted.

"Shifting gears, Kenia: what was that you said about being on fin-aid back there? You don't qualify."

"He didn't need to know that," Kenia said, adjusting the Black Lives Matter bracelet Audre had given to her so that it was visible among her other bangles.

"You're either a shrewd negotiator—"

"You learn to be in those Nigerian markets."

"—Or you're a bourgeois poser trying to slum it with students on work study, like me."

"Hey!" Kenia said, pinching her friend's bare arm. "If I recall, this bougie poser paid for your textbooks and meal plan last semester," Kenia said, studying a statuesque south Asian girl with a brushed-copper nose ring and a pair of espadrilles that matched her skin tone—and Kenia's—nicely.

"For which I am grateful," Audre said, framing a smile with her hands and blowing her a kiss.

"You are ridiculous."

"And you love me."

"One of my many flaws."

They walked past the student center, weaving in with the foot traffic bottlenecked alongside the bus stops. They had moved from the section of campus dominated by students to that part in the orbit of the hospital with its own flow of staff, patients, and visitors. They reached St. Mary's, a functional mid-century brick building with a steel-and-glass portico added during more recent renovations. They pushed through the glass doors and entered the atrium. It was in this space that the faces of the students and professors became familiar: acquaintances, friends, and mentors. Kenia and Audre greeted the other women—and few men, since the health sciences and nursing schools were still gender imbalanced—and made their way to the Department of International Health and walked down a hall of faculty offices.

They stopped outside a half-open door with postcards from the Dominican Republic, Costa Rica, El Salvador, and Guatemala taped up alongside quotes from Paulo Freire, Frantz Fanon, and Frida Kahlo.

"Dr. Quientela?" Audre said, peering around the door.

"Audre, Kenia, come in."

They stepped into the narrow office. The back wall was given over to a window that looked out on a cherry tree in full bloom. A pink "pussyhat" hung on the coatrack next to a poster that read, "If you are not outraged, you are not paying attention." The walls were lined with textbooks such as *Health Behavior and Health Education, Biostatistics, Educacion para la Salud, El Control de las enfermedades Transmisibles.* These were accompanied by paperbacks, worn and creased with use, that sat closer to Dr. Quientela's reach: *Pedagogy of the Oppressed, Death Without Weeping, The Spirit Catches You and You Fall Down,* and *Infections and Inequalities.*

"How are you ladies this morning?" Dr. Quientela asked as they sat down, the trace of an elegant accent in her voice. Originally from Bolivia, her face was distinguished by striking cheekbones, framed this morning by graceful lengths of hair curving to razored points, the rest of her hair pulled back into a bun with a faux pencil hair pin.

"Honestly?" Audre asked, setting her cup on the professor's desk and her notebook on her knee.

"Of course."

Audre looked to Kenia and shrugged. In the first class they had ever had with Dr. Quientela, she had shared her experiences fighting the cholera outbreak in Haiti after the 2010 earthquake. The professor had described her struggle to learn Creole in an emergency shelter while conducting verbal autopsies, her voice trembling with emotion as she recalled the human suffering she had witnessed.

Kenia and Audre had been the first two students at her door come office hours that semester, resumes and writing samples in hand, ready to volunteer as her research assistants.

"We were at the rally in Red Square," Audre said, holding up her new bracelets.

"That's right. I wanted to go. Was it well attended?"

"Yes," Kenia said. "Bummer we needed it though."

"True," Dr. Quientela said, pursing her lips.

There was a shadow of concern in her face that Kenia attributed to something more immediate than Black Lives Matter rallies, but she could not guess what. She did not have to wait long for an explanation.

Dr. Quientela rocked forward in her seat. "Ladies, I'm afraid I have less than encouraging news about the Haiti grant."

Kenia's chair creaked as she sat up straighter, the pads of her fingers pressing down on her nail beds. Audre began to tap her tablet with her pen.

Dr. Quientela exhaled, "I got an email from Brookings last night. Because of a budget shortfall for the year they have had to reduce the tranches for some of the grants, including for Haiti."

Kenia and Audre were silent as the news set in, each waiting for Dr. Quientela to continue, Audre's pen still tapping.

"The research is still happening," their professor said in a rush, responding to the look on their faces. "But I can only send one of you." She paused only a beat before she added, as if to dispel the tension without delay, "And I've decided it makes sense for it to be Audre."

Kenia wanted to drop her head down, her chin to her chest, but her mother's voice—always urging poise in the face of setbacks—was stronger in her mind. "That makes sense," she said, meeting Dr. Quientela and then Audre's gazes one after the other. "Audre speaks French and has picked up Creole more quickly than I have."

"Kenia, I'm sorry," Audre said, reaching over the gap between the chairs and touching her arm.

"I know you are disappointed," Dr. Quientela said.

"I am," was all Kenia could muster.

"I don't want to leave you without options for your practicum, however," Dr. Quientela said, as if to rally. "I am a PI on another study, a pilot for a smartphone app targeted to low income families in rural settings, helping them to make healthier dietary choices to reduce morbidity and mortality related to diabetes, obesity, and high blood pressure."

Chronic disease, Kenia thought. *Diseases of affluence.* As she let go of visions of working alongside her best friend in Haiti—building solidarity with other members of the African diaspora, and cutting her teeth in one of the most disaster-prone regions of the world—she took a deep breath. Dr. Quientela had projects in Rwanda, Zambia, even Zanzibar . . .

God closes one door and opens another.

"So where is the other study?"

"Selah Station," Dr. Quientela said.

"Selah Station . . . Is that a township in Joburg?"

"Not exactly."

"Selah Station, that's in Grenada, right?" Audre said, hope building in her voice.

"Actually," Dr. Quientela grimaced, "this Selah Station is in West Virginia."

Chapter 3

Wypipo

"West Virginia," Kenia said. This time her head was cradled in her hands, her elbows propped on the ledge of the esplanade on the roof of the Leavey Student Center. They had retreated there among the gentle grassy slopes and cherry trees after the meeting with Dr. Quientela. Kenia stared west, past the business school just below them, over the Potomac to where high-rises lifted to the sky on the Virginia side of the river.

Audre sat at her feet, her back against the same wall, her wrists resting on her knees, her hands dangling. "We were supposed to go together," she said.

"I know, it almost seemed pre-destined."

"I remember that first day in Professor Murphy's 'Religions of the African Diaspora' class," Kenia said. "It was my first college class. I was so nervous. I got there fifteen minutes early."

"I know. And I got there late."

"And the only empty seat was in front, with nerds like me."

Audre laughed, "There were other seats, you know, but I chose yours 'cause I was excited to sit next to a girl with natural hair."

"Really? You never told me that."

"You think I wanted to sit next to Jane Hoya for that class?"

"Figures. Little did you know how bougie I was."

They both laughed, but Kenia felt the disappointment quickly settle into her chest again.

"I knew we would be friends," Audre continued.

"You knew what my name meant. When Professor Murphy called it, you turned and said, 'As it pleased God.'"

"You remember."

"I do. And I remember your *Gye Nyame* necklace. I thought, "Whoa this girl is really African, she's gonna ace this shit.'"

Another laugh. "Yeah, then you learned I was from Philly."

"We're all Halfrican," Kenia said.

Audre had no idea where her roots were, so she had adopted Ghana. She had awoken a dormant interest in all things diaspora in Kenia in the two years since, introducing her to Kofi Awoonor, Chimamanda Ngozi Adichie, and Chinelo Okparanta.

And together they were to journey to Haiti, to see the culture of the first country founded out of a slave revolt, to learn from the Haitians' resilience and bear witness to their suffering.

Now Audre would be alone.

Kenia watched as the crowd from the Black Lives Matter rally was dispersing, a sea of black T-shirts flowing down staircases and along walkways leading from Red Square, that solidarity diluted in the majority white student body, the oblivious, biased, majority. She thought of Trump and looked across the Potomac again, realizing that the shoreline in view was once a foreign country, one committed to the right to enslave people like herself, her friends, her family. She blinked back to the protesters: so many shirts. Their friend the Rasta man had done a good business. *Good for him,* she thought. She should have bought a shirt too; a bracelet was not enough.

"It all feels so damn *present*," Kenia said, looking again at the Virginia side of the Potomac and the state that had once been home to the capital of the Confederate States of America. West Virginia felt like a foreign country itself, like Idaho or Montana. These were places black people didn't really go. She rubbed her temple, a pressure band forming like a wire being twisted around her skull.

"Headache?" Audre asked, rising to her feet.

"Yeah, haven't been sleeping well."

"Still all those weird dreams?"

"Yep."

Audre turned on the ball of her foot to consider the business school. "Ever wonder if they know something we don't?"

"The B-school?"

"Yeah," Audre said, mirroring Kenia, adjusting the strap of her backpack and perching her elbows on the ledge. "Maybe we're just being naïve, trying to make the world a better place, relying on the scraps we get from donors. Maybe we should just make our paper, get in-the-room-where-it-happens, and then direct the cash where we want it. Rewrite the rules from the top."

"Cause the *Man* will be so willing to let you do that. Shit, maybe I should have just gone pre-med like my 'rents."

"Still could. Doesn't hurt to have an undergrad in Public Health."

"I still don't like the science and math though. I wouldn't have gotten through biostats one or two without you."

"Oh, that's true."

"You don't have to agree so readily."

"No, I do."

They shared a laugh while a pair of hospital types walked by, followed by two girls with lacrosse sticks headed to the playing fields. Kenia blew a stream of air out between her lips. "You're going to have a great time in Haiti, Audre. You'll have to tell me all about it. Take lots of pictures."

"Sure," her friend said, putting her arm around Kenia. "What about you? You going . . . over there, to the old Confederacy?" she said, nodding towards Virginia.

Kenia snorted. "Don't know," she said, for the first time looking at the manila folder in her hand. She opened it, flipping through the study proposal that, among other things, included a map of the town of Selah Station, West Virginia. It was perched at the confluence of the Shenandoah and Potomac rivers, where the states of Maryland, West Virginia, and Virginia met. She could not bring herself to delve into the details. In her mind's eye all she could see were pickup trucks with gun racks, Dairy Queens, stretch pants, and Make America Great Again hats.

"Diabetes, heart disease, obesity—not really the diseases I came to school to learn how to fight."

"Kenia do you hate fat people, rich people, or both?"

"Not sure how to answer that. There are days I fit into both those categories."

"Stop it. You're not *fat*," Audre said. "Anyway, it's all still basic epidemiology, and the interventions are all about health education and health behaviors. Fundamentals are the same. You still get your practicum requirement checked off. And it's still the folks who have the least who are always affected."

"Yeah, and funny how those folks voted to repeal the Affordable Care Act."

"Still social justice though."

"Is it? Don't know if I'm really giving it to the *Man,* by working in West Virginia though."

"Seen *Coal Miner's Daughter?*"

"No."

"Neither have I, but maybe we should stream it this weekend. Ethnographic research."

"Are there any people of color in West Virginia?"

"Last time I saw data, not many. But there are people. And well, *wypipo* are people too."

Chapter 4

Becky with the Good Hair

"Kenia," her mother said between chops to the carrots for their salad. "It still sounds like a good opportunity, and maybe you can go to Haiti next summer."

Kenia was home, the spring semester finals over, her second year of college complete. Now it was a question of her practicum.

"Is Dr. Quientela still waiting for an answer?"

"Yeah," Kenia said, sitting on a stool at the kitchen island, tracing a pattern in the granite countertop with a fingertip. The kitchen smelled like her mother's chicken marinara baking in the oven. The recessed lighting was warm and soft. Marvin Gaye was playing on the audio system. The kitchen was the centerpiece of the custom home her mother had designed herself—built to raise four children with room for all of them to sit on stools sidled up to the oversized island. "It's just not exactly what I planned to do when I signed up for a degree in global health."

"West Virginia is part of the globe too," her mother said looking up, her eyes large, luminous, and hazel-green. Kenia had her mother's eyes, but she still felt a thrill to look upon them. They could be, by turns, pools of sympathy or lasers of focus. Many an internist had stammered, feeling the weight of them, and many a patient a sense of calm. They epitomized her mother to her, closely followed by the size of her heart—her mother would save the world if she could—and the sharp edge of her intellect, the tool by which she would save it. Kenia had grown up hearing people compliment them. They were what first attracted her father to her mother, and she felt pride in having inherited them.

Her mother chopped the last of the carrots and slid them off the cutting board into the greens, waiting for an answer.

"Audre said something similar," Kenia said.

"Have you spoken with her?"

"Not since she left for Haiti." Kenia felt a pang of remorse as she said so. She missed her friend, but even more so, her absence was confirmation that there would be no last-minute reprieve. The chance to go to Haiti was closed to her.

"What is the name of the town you'd be in again?" her brother, Chiazam, asked from two stools down. He held his phone length-wise with both hands. Chiazam took after their father. He was dark, had large dexterous hands, and an easy smile.

"Selah Station," she said, picking a carrot out of the greens and crunching down on it. Amy Winehouse came up in the rotation and began to insist on not going to rehab.

"Selah Station . . . ." He was quiet for a moment while his eyes scanned back and forth through the Wikipedia entry. "According to this, it was a station on the underground railroad. It was where escaped slaves would cross from Virginia—later West Virginia—to Maryland. The town was founded in the early 1800s by a family from Buffalo. They were business men and abolitionists who wanted to start a town with an economy based on something besides slave labor. It was supposed to be an experiment, an example for southerners, an alternative to the slave-labor-based model they already had."

"Well, we've seen how that caught on," Kenia said.

"Hey, there was even an HBCU there, one of the first historically black colleges in the country," he added.

"Now that is something I did not know," her mother said, opening the oven door to check the chicken. She closed it and returned to the island while Kenia moved over to the stool closest to her brother.

"Why have we never heard of it?" she asked.

Chiazam read from the entry: "Selah Branch University was the first historically black college, although it was open to students of all races and therefore also the first fully integrated university of its time. The school thrived from 1905–1953 when an industrial

21

accident at the Selah Island Coal Processing Plant spread toxic waste throughout the original town center, surrounding neighborhoods, and the university campus. The island has been declared uninhabitable since, with most of the population shifted to the West Virginia shore of the Potomac."

He scrolled through the entry and tapped a few of the photos. "Looks like you can visit the island and the old campus if you wear a hazmat suit."

"I don't want to be living near a superfund site," Kenia said, leaning over the phone. "Click back to the map."

Chiazam did so. The entry showed the confluence of the Potomac and Shenandoah rivers with Maryland to the north, Virginia to the south, and West Virginia on the triangle of land in between. Selah Island held fast in the Potomac, the river channeled into narrow gorges, the river there labeled the Selah Branches, north and south respectively. "Selah Station was the last stop on the underground railroad before escaped slaves reached freedom," her brother continued to read. "It was a center of African American culture until the accident, one of the most environmentally destructive in US history."

"Cheerful," Kenia said. Tired of looking over her brother's shoulder, she pulled out her own phone and looked up Selah Station herself. "Not too many people of color left," she said, scanning the demographics. "Population of African Americans is 4.7 percent, just a bit higher than West Virginia as a whole; 68.7 percent of the population voted for Trump."

"And it says here that it is one of the few states where deaths outnumber births in the last census, so at least they are dying out," Chiazam added.

"Chiazam Iniabasi Dezy!" their mother snapped. "I raised you better than that."

Chiazam made a sheepish apology and continued to scroll in silence.

Kenia offered a modest defense; "Doesn't exactly sell the place though, Mom."

"It certainly highlights the need for public health interventions," her mother said. "I see Trump supporters in the clinic every day and I still treat them. With the textile industry gone overseas there are just as many poor whites here as blacks. We're not about to discriminate who gets services and you won't either."

Kenia wondered if she could simply volunteer at her mother's clinic for the summer and turn it into practicum credit. The only thing holding her back from asking right then was the fact that she would be letting Dr. Quientela down.

The buzzer on the oven interrupted her thoughts. Her mother slipped on a pair of hot pads, removed the chicken from the oven, and set it on the counter.

"Dinner is ready."

◊

Kenia was on the trellis again. The feel of the ties under her hands and bare feet and the stickiness of the tar seeping from their cracks was familiar this time. She anticipated the tremors before they arrived, accompanied by the snow of rust from the girders above. This night was cloudy, the broken clouds racing across the crescent moon so that it looked to be tracking backwards along the horizon. She caught sight of the locomotive's head lamp, the rails gleaming in its light just before the whistle blew.

She had been here before. She knew this dream by now, how it unfolded, how it ended.

It just feels so real.

She noted the approach of the train. She would not run this time. She could never make it to the end of the trellis anyway. Instead she studied the dreamscape conjured by her unconscious. The train made its way out of a bend, its length still concealed by trees. Beyond she could see the land sloping upward in dramatic fashion, dotted with the lights of homes, like some town set in the foothills of the Alps. Beyond, the black shapes of mountains loomed, with bare shoulders of granite outcroppings, treeless and marbled with the moving play of light and shadow from the moon and clouds. The wind was carrying the cinders in a lateral angle from the locomotive like a cloud of fireflies, their light expiring over the gorge.

It's a dream, she thought, so what were the consequences of not running? She had leapt from the bridge in previous episodes, only to wake just before hitting the water. She was determined, this time, to learn. Perhaps there was a reason she kept being called back to this place, this tableau.

She stepped onto the rail, folding the flat of her foot against it. It was cool to the touch, the vibrations of the approaching locomotive growing. Off balance, she stepped onto one of the ties to steady herself. The cone of light would fall on her soon. Then the engineer would blow the whistle. If it was a dream, why not balance on the edge of one of the sleeper-ties and try to jump onto a passing railcar, like a traveling hobo. *The possibilities are endless in a dream,* she reminded herself.

She went to the edge of the sleeper-tie. Would there be room? Her toes curled around the end, the edge rough under her skin. The tremors were tremendous now, the trellis coming alive all around her. The light fell on her, blinding her so that she could no longer see the dimensions of the train. The expected noise of the whistle followed, deafening. She could sense the desperation in the engineer's long sustained blast. It erased her sense of calm as the avalanche of fire, metal, and motion barreled towards her. It awoke a panic in her own body. There was no sense in waiting. She stepped off the trellis and began to fall . . . .

She woke with a gasp, slipping out of her bed to the floor. It took her a moment to remember she was home, in Raleigh, not at school and not on a trellis. The familiar items in her room came into soft focus in the gray light of early morning. Her poster of Janelle

Monae, her debate trophies, the picture of her and her siblings crawling over their father as he smiled on their plaid couch. The couch was hideous. She could not believe her mother had even let it in the house, but the memory was precious to her. She sat up, her back against the bed, her eyes sliding to a more recent picture on her desk: her sisters, her brother, mother, and father at a Sigma Pi Phi event. Kenia, her mother, and Chikmara were all in formal gowns; her brother, father and sister Chinemere in tuxes. It was shortly after her oldest sister had come out. It had been one of the last times they had all been together before her father had vanished.

Despite his professional accomplishments, his intellectual exceptionalism, and his association with so many other professional black families—despite a life lived counter to the stereotypes of black men and broken black families—none of it had protected him from becoming another statistic. Somehow, something sinister had reasserted itself, and he had disappeared. The fact that no one knew what exactly had happened to her father, where he had gone or who was responsible, made it all the worse.

"Kenia?"

The voice was outside her door. Chiazam, although his voice sounded eerily like her father's.

"Yeah, come in."

The door opened, those precise surgeon hands guiding it, followed by his face peering around the edge, his expression serious as he searched the bed then found her on the floor.

"I heard a thud."

"Weird dream. Been having them a lot lately."

He stepped inside. He was wearing a black Batman T-shirt and a pair of Harvard sweatpants. He set himself down on the end of the bed and the two of them remained in silence together. They were two years apart, so often they had paired off, almost like twins. She never really remembered him not being there, in some form. One of her earliest memories was of putting her ear to her mother's tummy

25

to listen for Chiazam, only to be thrown into a spiral of wonder when she had felt his body move through her mother's womb.

She knew what he was asking her now, in this moment, even without words.

"I just keep dreaming I'm on this train trellis and this train is coming at me."

He said nothing, but raised his eyebrows, letting her continue.

"And it's *ultra*-real."

"Is it a place you've been before?"

"No. It's in the mountains. It's weird, the whole setting feels old-timey. Sometimes it's a steam locomotive, but mostly a diesel. Always on a collision course for me."

"What do you think it means?"

She laughed, "It's my future bro. It's the real world coming at me and all I can do is jump."

"I had a dream like that, except I was on a rope bridge. It was right after Dad died."

"Disappeared."

He swallowed, "Yeah. Remember how we had to go to the psychologist after?"

"Oh, I had that old woman, Dr. Cooper. She was all right."

"Well mine, Dr. Monroe, was worried about me. He was afraid it was suicidal ideation."

"What did you think?"

He shrugged, looking down at the Batman seal on his shirt and flattening it out. "I don't know. I think I was scared. I felt like Dad was always there for us. Then he wasn't. Sort of did feel like being over a chasm on a rickety bridge." He was looking at the photo of them at the ball now. "I miss him."

"Me too."

The silence that followed was broken by a vibration in the pocket of his Harvard sweats. He drew out his phone.

"What time is it?" she asked.

"6:49."

"Is that your alarm?"

"No, it's actually a call," he said, turning the screen away from her.

"Who is calling you at this hour?"

"No one. Must be a butt dial," he said, slipping the phone back into his pocket. He could not hide the embarrassment on his face though—she knew him too well.

"Whatever. Don't lie to me. Who is calling you? Is it a girl?"

"A girl, okay, yes, it's a girl I'm seeing."

He got up and made for the door. Kenia was up and following, "What? Does my little brother have a girlfriend?"

He was already in the hallway, making a line for his room, the phone still buzzing and in his hand again now.

"She is a girl . . . and uh . . . *yes* she is a friend."

"Friends don't call friends at six in the morning." She was at his door now but he was closing it in her face.

"I need to answer."

"What's her name?" she said, propping the door open with her leg.

His eyes rolled. "Her last name is Martinique."

"Okay, sounds Cajun or Caribbean. Do you call her by her last name?"

"No," he said, checking the phone again, while it still buzzed, the urgency growing in his eyes. "I need to take this."

"Let me see," she said, reaching for the phone.

"It's Rebecca, all right? Rebecca Martinique. It's a very elegant name," he said, squeezing her out of the door, closing it, then answering the phone, his voice pitched ridiculously low.

"Really?" she said to the shut door. "Rebecca?"

No response came, only his unintelligible voice, straining to sound deep and full of bass, muffled by the door.

She unwrapped her hair and headed back to her room. She paused in the hallway as the sole of her foot stuck to the carpet. She

27

kicked up her heel, as if stretching her quad to examine the underside. *That's a puzzle,* she thought, finding a black smudge that reminded her of driveway sealant. She went to the bathroom, stepping on the edge of her foot so as not to spread whatever the gunk was, and washed it off in the bathtub. It would not come off with water alone, but took soap and vigorous scrubbing to remove.

. Afterwards she slipped on her Georgetown hoodie and made her way downstairs. The lights were on in the kitchen and she found her mother at the kitchen table, still in her own bed clothes: a robe and an oversized T-shirt Kenia and her siblings had given her for Christmas that read "I'm Sort of Big Deal." She was in that communal space, with no breakfast yet, only a cup of coffee, sitting still and silent. Kenia recognized the mood her mother was in. In these quiet hours of the morning it was impossible not to think of her father.

Kenia poured herself a cup of coffee and slid into the booth next to her mother, putting her head on her shoulder and savoring the softness of her mother's body. Her mom wordlessly shifted and touched Kenia's hair, playing gently with the curls as she would only let her mother do.

"Did you know Chiazam has a girlfriend?"

"Oh yes. Our little man is growing up."

"Have you met her?"

"Sure, she is a nice young lady."

"With a name like Becky?"

Her mother gave a small laugh, her shoulder shaking beneath Kenia's head. "I had not thought of that. she goes by Rebecca."

"Aight."

Her mother let out a loud, disapproving sigh and pushed Kenia's head off her shoulder, "Stop that, you know I can't abide poor grammar."

"Sorry."

Her mother shifted, turned to her. "Have you made a decision about this practicum, honey, or am I going to have you around the clinic all summer?"

"The possibility had crossed my mind."

"It would be nice," her mother said, staring out over her cup of coffee as she took a sip, as if looking into the possible future. "Not very many summers left that I'm going to have my kids around."

"True," Kenia said. Chinemere had spent her summers on internships at the Southern Law Poverty Center and Chikmara had headed off to Broadway. Neither ever boomeranged back. "It would be nice to hang out with you."

"But what would Dr. Quientela say?"

Kenia frowned, rubbing the table then tapping it with her nails. "She would be disappointed and I might not ever get to go to Haiti if funding comes around again."

Her mother said no words but made a knowing, lilting "umm hmmm," her inflection rising.

Kenia continued, "So I guess it is decided then."

Her mother hummed again, saying more with her eyebrows this time than her words. Kenia had known that intonation and that look all her life. Her mother placed her arm around her and pulled her in close again, her finger twirling one of Kenia's curls.

"Speaking of 'good hair,'" Kenia said. "If I'm going to be in West Virginia for three months, I better get some braids. Not like I'm going to find a salon there."

"That's my brave girl."

Chapter 5

Junction

The Greyhound bus lurched and shuddered, the engine groaning as the driver negotiated the road leading to the mountain pass. Out the window the trees broke occasionally to reveal a home, each one a picture of rustic simplicity with a low-slung wraparound porch, gravel driveway, and expansive yard shaded by spreading branches of sugar maples and red oaks. More than a few trees were hung with tire swings. Satellite dishes perched on rooftops and aimed south, towards satellites in equatorial orbits beaming HBO, FX, CNN—Kenia corrected herself: what was she thinking, these folks watched Fox. A wave of disdain passed over her, growing to disgust when she noticed a Trump-Pence sign, weather-beaten and faded, but still triumphantly displayed in one of the passing yards.

She turned her attention to the more immediate roadside, where another historical marker went by. These were sturdy iron signs, marking points of historical or scenic significance, mostly from the Civil War, although a few were from the Revolutionary era. But most, Kenia noted, were about patriots of the Confederacy: Stonewall Jackson, Robert E. Lee, John S. Mosby and his Riders.

The Greyhound engine lulled for a moment as they crested through the pass, the Shenandoah Valley spreading out below them. It was hard not to feel a sense of awe at the purple walls of mountains that rose on the horizon in curves nearly indistinguishable from clouds at sunrise and sunset, the slopes enclosing the patchwork of fields and forests, threaded through by rivers steaming in the morning sun, their meandering paths mercurial in their twists and turns. Her brief search for "Shenandoah Valley" in Google Images had shown Kenia apple orchards, wineries, fieldstone mills with waterwheels, and churchyards with gravestones that predated the United States, from days when the frontier was east of the

Mississippi and colonists were just beginning to invade the lands of the Monacan and Cherokee.

For a moment, however, she forgot the tortured history of the past and simply tried to focus on the beauty of the landscape unfolding beyond the guardrail the color of gunmetal. Her forehead tapped the window with a light bump as the bus turned around a bend. One of her newly plaited braids flattened between her head and the glass. She rolled another one in her fingers, still shiny with oil, her scalp still a bit sore from the process of pulling her hair tight to braid it. *Hair*, she thought with a sigh. Was there any group of people in the world whose hair was more political than black women? She'd picked braids because they would be the least work during a summer where she did not expect to find a black hairdresser. She twirled the coarse braid between the pads of her fingers, wondering if they would be viewed as too informal or, the other extreme, too black, incendiary even, as if she were making some political statement. She knew the only statement she was making was one of convenience. If she had wanted to be political, she would have combed out a 'fro, but even that might have been lost on the whites she would be surrounded by, likely they would just want to *touch it* like she was some animal in a petting zoo.

Her view was blocked by a stand of trees as they rounded another bend. When her view cleared again a large estate slid into view. It was situated higher on the hillside, surrounded by terraced lawns, each with their own row of manicured bushes and trees, and outbuildings such as horse stables, multi-car garages, and guest cottages. The grounds had a commanding view of the valley, situated like a castle over feudal lands. She thought of the simpler homes in the hollows they had passed with the tire swings, late model pickup trucks, and gravel driveways. The bus turned again and the mansion moved to the other side of the road, but still it loomed large, the property filling up the windows of the bus, revealing a pool, a driving range, and paved paths just the right width for golf carts.

31

Kenia turned her back on it. The bus was not full and the seat immediately next to her was empty. Across the aisle a woman in a red North Carolina State University sweatshirt pointed out different cars in the opposite lanes and asked her son to name their colors. He had wide blue eyes, a mess of straw-colored hair, and an expressive face. Kenia had exchanged smiles with them both as she had boarded in Raleigh and had decided to sit across from them. When she had started to nod off and let drop her water bottle, sending it rolling down the aisle, the mother had caught and returned it.

Now the bottle was empty. The water had passed through Kenia, and pressure was building in her bladder. She was relieved when the road leveled out on the valley floor and the driver slowed, pulling into a gas station with a decent sized Kwik-E-Mart, and announced a rest stop. Kenia zipped her backpack closed, her laptop computer and tablet nestled inside, slung it on her shoulder, and followed the mother and her son down the aisle and off the bus.

It was bliss to stretch her legs. The station was busy with Saturday morning shoppers who had come to the market, which was part grocery, part gardening center, part hardware store. Men in flannel shirts and baseball caps pumped gas into pickup trucks, the beds converted, with lockers and rails to hold tools, sheetrock, and lumber. She passed by fuchsia, white, and lavender azaleas, their roots encased in potting soil and black plastic pots. Inside, on her way to the ladies' room, Kenia passed through an aisle with locally made salad dressings, salsas, and something she had never heard of: apple butter. But corporate branding was not to be left out: additional aisles were chock full of puffy bags of Lay's potato chips, Slim Jims, Doritos, and Pork Rinds. Another had every candy bar variety imaginable, all sold in supersizes.

The ladies' room was clean and efficient. Kenia waited her turn at the sink while a roundish white woman in mom-jeans washed her hands and rubbed a smudge of lipstick from her teeth, which were yellowed from nicotine. When Kenia came back out, the line at the register had grown long with the passengers from the bus. The teenage girl behind the counter—thin to the point of anorexia—had Deadpool and Hellboy tattoos on her arms and neck, her lips and nose pierced with rings, her left ear with a rod. Kenia grabbed a bag of trail mix with almonds, peanuts, and yogurt-covered raisins and tried not to think about the added sugar content of the yogurt as she selected a bottle of coconut water.

The line stretched down the toiletry aisle. Kenia took her place among the soaps, shampoos, and tampons. Her eyes fixed on a product she had never seen before: a cardboard stand displayed packets of kits containing pills and powders that claimed to mask the trace of drugs in one's urine. "Pass any drug test," the sign proclaimed. She picked one up, turning the box in her hand. It promised to mask traces of amphetamines, opioids, and tetrahydrocannabinol. She returned it to the display, setting it beside a bottle of synthetic urine, also guaranteed to pass any drug screening.

She stepped outside after paying and noticed a few men of retirement age seated at a table drinking coffee, their voices deep but mostly free of the Appalachian twang she had been expecting. The bus engine was running, but the driver was outside smoking a cigarette and texting on his phone. Kenia continued to stretch her legs, walking to the end of the bus where she noticed another one of the iron historical markers. She approached it in order to read the black, raised lettering on the white backing, expecting another commemoration of a Civil War skirmish or fortification. But she was surprised find it dated 1955 and dedicated to Ernest Cunningham.

From Buffalo, New York, Ernest Cunningham was visiting relatives in nearby Stamford Springs, where he spoke to a twenty-three-year-old white woman who was married to the proprietor of a local filling station. Three days later Ernest was abducted and beaten before being dragged several miles. His body was found hanging from a tree along the Stamford River, close to the crossroads

*informally known as the "Junction." His case became a
catalyst in the growing civil rights movement of the time,
exposing the suffering of African Americans and the
limitations of democracy.*

The rest was unreadable for the groupings of bullet holes
punched through the sign. The plastic bottle in her hand popped as
her hand tightened around it. She had seen a number of speed limit
and deer crossing signs similarly pockmarked. Hillbilly target
practice. But as she stepped closer she could see the unmistakable
epitaph scratched into the paint with a car key: *Go Home Nigger.*

She turned, walking at a staccato clip back to the bus where
the other passengers—all white, not a person of color among them
except herself—were trundling on with their snacks, soft drinks,
headphones, and smartphones. The chatter was upbeat. Could it have
been any more oblivious and removed from the sensation roiling her
stomach, even as the mother in the NC State sweatshirt smiled at her
again. The young man in the seat in front of Kenia bobbed his head.
She could hear him listening to Jay-Z, the same epitaph likely being
rapped in his ears.

Kenia tried to get out of her head. This was the language
written across the landscape of the United States, a history she knew
to be soaked in blood from the vicious supplanting of the indigenous
people onwards. She thought yearningly of Audre and Haiti, then
tried to pivot again, not letting her dark mood overtake her,
determined not to let a barely literate, pickup driving, tobacco
swirling, bumpkin ruin her morning. She unzipped her bag, removed
her tablet, and started scanning through article abstracts and their
accompanying charts and captions, losing herself in data.

These were the prevalence and mortality statistics she was
accustomed to, lining up along the familiar fault lines of social-
economic status. The only difference, in this case, was that these
data were coming from U.S. settings, not Zimbabwe, Angola, South
Africa, or the other African countries she was used to studying.

These charts and graphs reflected rates in counties of West Virginia, cross-tabbed by other demographics such as urban/rural, male/female, and date of birth in ten-year intervals.

It was bleak: a 75 percent increase in mortality rates for women—mostly white—between the ages of thirty-five and fifty-nine. This was in contrast to the national mortality trends for men and women of color which had—across the board—improved anywhere from 10 to 20 percent depending on the region. In the context of public health, it was an unprecedented spike in mortality, analogous to the AIDS epidemic in sub-Saharan Africa. Like the first twenty years of the generalized epidemic, the middle generation of parents and breadwinners was hollowed out, leaving grandparents raising grandchildren.

Kenia thought back to the Junction. The people she had seen there had been a representative cross-sample of different ages. She had seen young, middle-aged, and old. But she heard Audre's voice in her head, from their hours of studying biostats and epidemiology—reminding her that the sample at the Junction would have been biased: all those people were shopping, and therefore had money to spend, and were likely working. The men filling up their trucks, indeed, had looked as if they were headed to construction sites.

She scrolled down the causes of death. The numbers painted a grim picture of drug and alcohol overdoses, vehicular accidents—alcohol related—and suicide. It brought to mind the drug-testing kits she had seen at the market. She let the tablet tilt back and lay flat on her legs and leaned her head against the window again. Anthropology classes had taught her to look at cultural trends and historical context, for these macro forces manifested themselves in the microcosm of the human body, from gene expression to allele length. For the past two years she had thought of the forces of colonialism, capitalism, and slavery and their lasting effects on communities of color. But the same forces had left their mark on the oppressing side too. She thought back to her syllabus from her

35

African American History course, a class which had been full of other black students, three Latinos, two Asians, and a white girl trying her hardest to come across as "woke."

She remembered reading about how the slave system in Europe, for millennia, had been one of indentured servitude, where losers of wars and debtors were made servants. The system had been imported to the Americas in the 1600s, where black and white servants were initially viewed equally. Blacks and Irish both were considered a vile, brutish race of sub-humans, Nathaniel Bacon's rebellion at Jamestown in 1676 uniting white and black servants together in solidarity. Much to the horror of the ruling class.

But things changed after that. The rich saw to it, dividing the servant classes against each other. It was a toxic metamorphosis of the entire concept of slavery: one that created a three-tiered caste system, one ostensibly based on ethnicity. Rich white landowners were elevated, but below them were poor uneducated whites, to whom they granted slightly more privileges, slightly more power, and handed down strict guidelines as to how to interact with blacks, to separate them socially and keep the lowest caste in their place.

Poor whites could aspire to the life of the rich master class and have solidarity together because they were not black, even if such social climbing was—in practice—exceedingly unlikely. The boost they received was more psychological than economic. Scientists, academics, and religious leaders conspired to reinforce justification for the racial categorizations: craniologists "documented" differences in skull sizes, and religious leaders cited Biblical verses such as those describing the children of Ham as cursed. It was not unlike the way preachers in recent centuries "justified" discrimination against same-sex marriage, Kenia's sister Chinemere had pointed out.

But it was a feint, a trick played on the poor whites. They were still poor, and it was the fat cats, the landowners, who lived long, healthy, and educated lives. She saw it playing out now in the data at her fingertips, reflecting the lives in the valley while the castle on the hill with the swimming pools, driving ranges, and golf carts simply sat and appreciated in value.

Unfortunately for people of color, the system had been resilient, adaptable, and anything but self-correcting as it pitted poor whites against blacks, instilling the least educated, least privileged whites with municipal powers to enforce control over blacks. She remembered lectures on the Night Riders, pseudo-police who would ride the roads of the south, harassing blacks for their traveling papers, killing runaways, or kidnapping freed slaves and sending them back into bondage. The Klan was only the most organized and infamous, immortalized in the first American film: Birth of a Nation—her brother pointing out to her how Hollywood did not like to admit that the first use of the close-up was in a film about white men "heroically" lynching a black man. No one, at the time, seemed to have been bothered by the irony of the film's name: a nation's birth centered on the oppression and murder of a black man by white supremacists.

It wasn't even subtle.

Some things had changed over the decades, but some things remained, pernicious, even more so for their thin veil of deniability in the age of color blindness. But it was not hard for Kenia to draw the through line from the Night Riders, the Klan Knights, to police shooting any number of unarmed black boys and men: Amadou Diallo, Sean Bell, Tamir Rice, Philando Castile, Terence Crutcher, Alton Sterling, or others who had died by other means in police custody, such as Freddie Gray, Sandra Bland, and Eric Garner. Just the week before a video had trended in which an eighty-four-year-old grandmother was handcuffed while a SWAT team broke into her house looking for her son. Facedown on the floor and non-resisting, the officers pepper sprayed her anyway, her cries over the chaos of the shaky video echoing the cries of so many of her ancestors throughout the centuries:

"Lord, please protect me!"

37

Audre, who had sent her the video, insisted that the cops wouldn't even be needed to enforce racial order in Trump's America, citing the militia movements in the Upper Midwest, the Rockies, and the Pacific Northwest and other rural areas where whites with diminishing opportunities for jobs clung to guns and ethnicity as pseudo tribal markers, blaming immigrants and other "out" groups for their plight, instead of the very politicians who played on their ignorance and prejudice to win their votes. Mix in a bit of toxic masculinity, a dash of xenophobia, and a pinch of sexism, of course, and there you had it, America becoming "great" again.

Kenia sighed. She knew the system could serve everyone better, people of color, people of less privilege—white, black, brown, *everyone.* The prison industrial complex, fed by the War on Drugs, had ensnared a generation of black men, but also white men and women who were jailed and made permanent third-class citizens as felons, whose records never went away, perpetuating an underclass that it was legal to discriminate against, not unlike Jim Crow.

Biggest threat to American values is America itself.

The man who penned the Declaration of Independence, also owned slaves. And therein was the paradox, the contradiction at the heart of the United States.

Kenia let out a long, deep sigh. Race in America—she could see parallels to so many other struggles and systems of oppression, such as Jews in mid-century Germany. But even in that case, the hurt turned back on itself, the oppressed seeing the faces of their oppressors everywhere, so that all conflicts become existential ones, and in the intractable nature of Israel-Palestine, Jews, formerly victims, were now considered persecutors themselves. The oppressed becoming oppressors.

It was James Baldwin who she remembered saying that it's not the just souls of the oppressed as stake, but also the souls of the oppressors—one twisted their own humanity when they denied it in another.

But they never see it that way.

She had become lost in her head again, drawn into an orbit around a jumble of pain she felt little capacity for all of a sudden.

"Your head can be like a bad neighborhood sometimes," Audre used to say to her. "Don't go in there alone."

She resolved, again, to clear her mind, this time putting her tablet away and plugging her headphones into her phone. She scrolled through album covers until she landed on Solange Knowles. She closed her eyes. It was the same music her mother listened to in the kitchen when unwinding from a long day. They were melodies she had associated with family life, playing in the background as her siblings lined up at the kitchen island, half in a book or magazine, half engaged in conversation. These were some of her happiest memories, but she also remembered times when she would not want to share the attention, when she did not want to compete with Chinemere's intellect, Chikmara's flair, or her brother . . . who, as the little brother, was doted upon by the women in his family. She viewed that as her job, and she did not always like sharing it, since she imagined herself to be best at it.

One evening, instead, she remembered slipping down off the stool and wandering down the hall to her father's study. The music still drifted throughout the house on the speakers mounted in each room, but she found her father lost in more physical labor. His frame, over six-feet tall, was stretched up on a stepladder so that he towered over her, his head close to the ceiling. He held two nails in his mouth and had a pencil tucked behind his ear while he measured the wall, a level in one hand. When he was satisfied with the bubbles in the level, he slid the pencil out from behind his ear and made a few light marks on the wall.

"Hey, Kenia honey, what's going on?" he asked, his voice slightly slurred from the nails in his teeth.

"Nothing," she said. "What are you doing?"

"Hanging a picture. You want to help?"

"Yes."

"Hand me that hammer on the desk please, baby."

She stepped around the ladder and picked up a hammer resting on a stack of *The Lancets* piled up next to the latest issues of *The Economist*, its cover folded back to reveal the leaders. She handed the hammer up to her father and he tapped in the nails with a mixture of delicacy and force.

"All right," he said, coming down one step. "Now really carefully, can you hand me that picture?"

This was a much more important task, Kenia knew, because pictures in their frames and glass were fragile. She picked it up—it was heavy and wider than her shoulders—and handed it up to her father. She imagined herself a nurse passing him a scalpel.

"Thanks baby girl," he said, mirroring her care as he took the frame, turned it to the wall, and slid it into place until the braided metal wire caught behind it. He adjusted it slightly, the frame scraping against the drywall, and then he let it go, splaying out his fingers like a magician completing a trick

"Perfect."

The stepladder squeaked as he climbed off, closed it, and set it against his desk. Next he took Kenia up in his arms and held her up so they both could examine the picture on the same level.

It was a large photo cropped closely around two black men. One man, in the background, was handsome, his smile possessing a relaxed, movie-star quality. He wore a fedora and a pressed suit and tie and looked directly into the camera. A second, younger-looking man with broad athletic features and wearing a leather jacket stood closer to the camera. He was the picture of concentration while he tried to sign something in his hand.

"Do you know who these men are?"

"No."

"That's Muhammad Ali and that is Malcolm X. They were very famous in their time. Ali was the greatest boxer that ever lived,

40

some say, and Malcolm was a great leader and speaker. His autobiography is one of my favorites, and you will have to read it when you are old enough."

She nodded, although it sounded boring. But if it made her father happy, she knew she was likely to do it.

"A lot of people think there is something wrong with this picture. Can you guess what?"

"There is no color?"

He laughed. "No, it's supposed to be in black and white."

She shrugged.

"Well, people like this photo, because it's sort of one of a kind. See, Malcolm is smiling and Mohammad looks very serious, doesn't he?"

"He does."

"But those men were known for just the opposite. Mohammad Ali was always saying colorful things; he was always being quoted in the press before and after fights. He was the one who said, 'Float like a butterfly and sting like a bee.'"

She had heard that before and nodded to show it.

"But Malcolm, everyone thought that Malcolm was always very serious and always very angry."

"Was he?"

"He could be. He was a fiery speaker, just like Martin Luther King, Jr., but some people did not like Malcolm X as much. They were scared of him. He channeled a lot of anger—but justified anger."

She examined the picture, scanning back and forth between the handsome man with the horn-rimmed glasses, whose face was open, friendly, and full of delight, and Ali, intent on the task of signing his autograph.

"Malcolm looks nice."

"He was. He could be. He had daughters like you that he loved very much. He was a good father. But this picture tells you something important. Do you know what it is?"

She stared again into the picture, a little helpless, unsure as to what more he wanted her to extract from this lesson. Fortunately, he threw her a lifeline.

"It tells you, Kenia, that no one is just one thing."

The bus stopped and the engine cut. Kenia opened her eyes as the passengers were standing and pulling their belongings from the overhead storage rack. The driver stepped down off the bus and swung open the luggage doors just under the windows.

"There's grandma," the white woman in the NC State sweatshirt said to her son. Kenia caught sight of a woman who, despite her gray hair, appeared quite spry, stretching up to wave, a pair of florescent pink bifocals hanging around her neck. She was eclipsed from view as another luggage door swung open. Beyond, Kenia saw a red brick church with a bell tower, a leafy park with a bandstand, and a street with long rows of low storefronts with picture windows.

"Have a nice day," the mother said to Kenia, as Kenia waited for them to step into the aisle. The boy looked up, a bit wary of her as a stranger, but returned her smile and wave before he began to follow his mother. As she turned, a red and yellow Ironman figurine slipped out of his backpack. Kenia picked it up and called to him.

"Excuse me, I think you dropped Tony Stark," she said.

The boy turned, his eyes growing large, and ran back to retrieve his toy. Somehow, the exchange seemed to alleviate her stranger-danger status. Emboldened, he asked, "Do you like the Avengers?"

"Sure," she said. "Black Panther is my favorite."

"Colton, you are holding people up," his mother said when she found he was not following. He obeyed, although no one seemed to mind the hold up. His mother smiled and thanked Kenia. Kenia smiled in return and followed in their wake, stepping down the stairs onto the cracked tarmac of the parking lot.

The air was fresh, if a bit humid. Her immediate impression of Selah Station was that its buildings were low. The highest was three stories, with the exception of the church bell tower, which was more like four. She noted a lot of not-so-small waistlines, blue jeans, and stretch pants among the white people waiting to greet family members. One man was actually wearing overalls and a green John Deere hat, which she guessed was better than a *Make America Great Again* hat. She wondered if all eyes were on her, the only black girl, one with braids no less. Her mind flashed back to the words scratched into the historical marker: *Go Home Nigger.* The driver pulled her suitcase from the storage bins beneath the bus. She claimed it, her fingernails digging into padding of the handle as she took it and turned to face the town she would be spending the next three months in.

 For better or for worse, this is my country too, she thought.

Chapter 6

Do the Next Right Thing

"You must be staying a while," the driver said with a glance at her large suitcase.

"Three months. Summer practicum."

"Well, you couldn't have picked a better place. Like an Appalachian Switzerland here," he said.

She made a show of scanning the mountains rising on either side of the town, emerald with the trees full of summer leaves. The clouds were marbled in pink and purple as the sun rose, the color of molten iron. It was a quiet Saturday morning, the main street empty of traffic, the shadows long and the shafts of sunlight between them a rosy gold. She could imagine that the soft whisper she heard in the background was from the river gorges on either side of the peninsula.

"It does look nice," she said and tipped him with a five dollar bill.

He seemed a bit surprised at the gesture, tipping his hat and saying, "God bless you, young lady."

She smiled and he turned to help other passengers with their bags. Once she had tapped her code into her phone, she entered the address of the William Bridgewater Medical-Dental Building. While the phone calculated her route, Kenia watched the mother in the NC State sweatshirt, her son Colton, and her family—her mother with the fluorescent bifocals, her father in a Pittsburg Steelers jacket—cross the street to a diner with the name "Selah Spoon" in its window, advertising itself as home of "Selah's Famous Flying Mountain Biscuit."

Mountain of calories, she thought, glancing back at her phone. She was pleasantly surprised that the Med-Dent center was within walking distance, the blue path leading her east two blocks then one block south. She pulled up the handle on the suitcase, tilted the bag, and started pulling.

The sidewalk was cracked and uneven, and she had not made it more than a few feet before her arm was burning from yanking the wheels over places where the concrete had risen like fault lines, pushed up from the pressure of tree roots. She thought back to her Injury Prevention class, imaging how hard the sidewalk would be to negotiate for the elderly or someone with a physical handicap. She had made a similar observation while in an older section of Raleigh with her brother once.

"Man, if Public Health doesn't make you a scold," he had said.

She smiled at the thought of Chiazam just as she stumbled, the wheels catching on another slab. It would have been easier to just pull the suitcase through the street—there was barely any traffic— but she did not want to stand out any more than she already did. She could just imagine people pointing her out and concluding that "Blacks just did not follow rules as simple as staying on the sidewalk and not walking in the street. . . ."

A bait, tackle, and hunting shop came up on her right. A number of old men in caps, with big bellies and shirts with more plaid patterns, talked at the counter over cups of coffee. No one looked like they were actually buying anything. The middle-aged man behind the register wearing a blue vest with pouches all along the front had his hands tucked into his jean pockets as he listened.

The next storefront was a rustic little shop, not yet opened, that sold "Treasures of the Blue Ridge Mountains," including homespun blankets, beeswax candles, lumpy sweaters, and wood carvings. Next was an insurance office—also not yet opened. She rolled her suitcase under a marquee advertising a movie she knew to have come out six months before. The coming attraction had long since arrived and moved on from theaters in D.C. Despite the film choices, the theater had a 1950's charm with an old-fashioned ticket window. She was sure the haze of nostalgia helped patrons see beyond the cracking paint, the door handles worn smooth from decades of use, and the duct tape on the cracking vinyl chair in the ticket window.

She turned the corner, passing a convenience store, the interior lit by fluorescent tubes that had all the warmth of a morgue. The young man behind the counter looked Indian, his attention focused on his phone while a flat screen behind the counter was playing a football match beamed from some other continent in another time zone, the sky beyond the stadium lights dark. The window advertised e-cigarettes, chewing tobacco, lottery tickets, and she even noted more synthetic urine kits.

She rolled on, her heart beating a bit harder than it would have without the suitcase. She felt warm, but her destination was close. A car was pulling out of the parking lot ahead that she imagined was adjacent to the Med-Dent building. Before she reached it, however, the storefronts receded, and she passed a lot with a Catholic Church: St. Anthony's. It was a simple grey stone affair, with a bell tower and a sign with removable lettering announcing Sunday Mass at 5 p.m. Saturday, 9, 10:30, and 12:00 Sunday (Noon Mass in Spanish). Confession was Saturdays at 3 p.m.

The sidewalk in front of St. Anthony's and leading to the Med-Dent building was thankfully even and unbroken. The Med-Dent building itself was squat, beige, and one story, spreading out in a functional manner with narrow windows and anemic-looking bushes along its sides. The tray for cigarette disposal was full with ground-out butts stained with tar and nicotine. Fortunately there was a handicap ramp which she dragged her suitcase up. An intercom for after-hours stared her in the face, but she found the doors unlocked. She swung them wide and entered at a rush, before the doors could close on the bag.

The lobby was like any other medical office, a receptionist in the window—a middle-aged white woman with her hair dyed red wearing a denim top.

"How can I help you?" she asked.

"I'm here to see Jolene Lewis."

"You must be her summer intern."

"I am," she said, relieved that she was expected. The woman looked down at a note on her desk behind the window, her brow furrowed, the corners of her mouth bending downward in a frown. Kenia knew the signs and what was coming.

"Ken-eee-aaa?"

"Kenia, sounds just like the country of Kenya," Kenia said.

"The country? Huh, that is . . . different."

Kenia felt the strain in her own face as she tried to smile. "It's Nigerian."

"Oh," the woman said, brightening. "Is that in the Caribbean?"

"West Africa."

"Oh, Africa. Are you from there? Your English is so good."

"My father was from Nigeria . . . I'm from North Carolina," she answered, now eager to move on. "Is Ms. Lewis' office left or right?"

"Just down that hall there. Take the first right. The door will be on the left. It's the office of Public Health; you can't miss it," the receptionist said, sitting back with a self-congratulatory air that Kenia suspected was not just from doing her job, but having done her job in a helpful way to a black person.

Another opportunity for a white woman to burnish her color blind credentials, she thought, resisting the urge to roll her eyes.

Kenia found the office door open, a carpeted waiting room on the other side. Another receptionist, this one a younger woman closer to Kenia's age.

"Good morning, I am Kenia Dezy, here to see Ms. Lewis."

"Oh, our intern. I'm Thea, nice to meet you," the woman said. She was in scrubs and had wavy brown hair and blue eyes. She was light on the makeup but wore lip gloss. Both ears were pierced, one with multiple rings that climbed up the side and to the ridge on the top. Her badge read Licensed Nurse, and as Kenia moved closer, she could see a place where the piercing in her nose had closed. "Want any coffee, tea?"

Kenia considered the drip coffee maker and the pot of black fluid beneath it. Powdered creamer and packets of sugar sat in the adjacent tray.

"No thanks."

She sat down, realizing she was tired and now sweaty from hauling the suitcase. She had not showered, had slept poorly on the night bus, and felt a bit more disheveled than she would have liked to when meeting her new boss for the first time. Her thoughts were a little blurry, and she was eager to get settled in her accommodations. Dr. Quientela had told her not to expect much, but at this point, as long as there was a bed, she would be happy.

Kenia has been staring at the poster on the wall for some time before she focused her eyes and read it. It listed numbers for suicide hotlines alongside numbers to call in case of an opioid overdose. On the bulletin board was a sheet of loose leaf with the first names and initials of the last of people willing to be Alcoholics Anonymous and Narcotics Anonymous sponsors, followed by their phone numbers. Kenia turned her attention to the coffee table in the center of the room. Among the dated magazines was a stand with flyers on meeting times and brochures on AA and NA, healthy eating, exercise and meditation, how to detect and live with diabetes, and flyers on what to expect when taking anti-depressants, blood pressure medications, flu shots, and birth control.

A woman entered wearing a McDonald's uniform and offered a sheepish smile before stepping up to the window where Thea waited.

"Here for a drug screening," the woman said.

"Okay. Be right with you," Thea said.

The woman sat down across from Kenia. Her name tag read: Janice. It was hard to guess her age: late thirties, forties? Her hair, currently pulled back into a bun, was graying in places, and her face lined with wrinkles that creased and folded while she looked around, elbows propped on her knees, legs bouncing.

"Twenty-one months clean, but I still get nervous at these things," she said, her eyes darting from the floor and catching Kenia staring.

Kenia was not sure how to respond. Janice eyed the suitcase.

"Rehab or shelter?"

"Sorry?"

"You going to rehab or a DV shelter?"

"Oh, uh, neither. I'm here for a summer internship."

Janice nodded a bit too vigorously. "I should have known. You don't look like a junky or like you just got beat up."

Kenia was not sure if she was supposed to thank her for what might have been a compliment.

"Twenty-one months, that's great."

"Yeah, well, I got tired of hating myself, you know? Six times in rehab. I had a stint of five-and-a-half years clean before I relapsed." She shook her head at, what Kenia supposed, were regrets. "One day at a time and trying to do the next right thing and all that now."

Kenia nodded, now a bit too eagerly herself. "Yeah, I guess so."

She felt some relief when Thea called her back to meet Ms. Lewis. "Second door on the right. Janice, you can follow me to the examination room."

"Hope you like Selah," Janice said. "Nice meeting you."

Chapter 7

Not All Skin Folk are Kin Folk

Kenia assumed a self-assured pose as she went down the hall, gathering what poise she could, her lessons in etiquette—formal and informal—coming back to her. Her mother's voice reminded her to present herself in a professional manner, despite having just spent the night on the bus.

I wonder how red my eyes are. I probably look like I've been smoking drugs more than poor Janice.

Kenia turned into the doorway into a windowless office. Ms. Lewis, the public health services director for Selah Station, was a black woman in her fifties. She sat behind her desk with two mismatched office chairs before it. Her swivel chair squeaked as she stood up and offered her hand, her skin cold, her eyes flat. She wore a boxy salmon blouse with shoulder pads and a mandarin collar buttoned up just beneath her chin. Her hair was short, cut almost like a little boy's, which Kenia thought a shame since Ms. Lewis possessed elegant cheekbones that would have been framed nicely by shoulder-length hair.

And she would be beautiful if it were not for that scowl.

Ms. Lewis's fingers were without rings, her ears not pierced, but a large wood cross with metallic caps on its ends bounced on her chest as she shook Kenia's hand.

"Ms. Dezy," she said, pronouncing it Dee-zee.

"Day-say, but you can call me Kenia."

"Ms. Jolene; please sit down."

Kenia noted the "Ms." before settling into the offered chair. She swung her backpack off, setting it down in the adjacent chair. A filing cabinet sat on her left, too close, and anchored to it with a magnet was a calendar with scripture verses and a picture of a cross on a hilltop in silhouette against a caramel sunset. She noted a picture frame on the desk, as well as a second calendar, a tear-away offering a bible quote for each day of the year.

"How was your trip?" Ms. Jolene asked, her voice laced with a courtesy Kenia found distancing rather than warm.

"A bit long," she said.

"From Raleigh?"

"Correct."

"No flights from there to here."

"No," Kenia said. "Are you from here in Selah Station?"

"Yes," she said, straightening. "Born and raised."

"All right," Kenia said, thinking back to the small population of African Americans her brother had mentioned from the Wikipedia entry. "Well I was lucky you were working on a Saturday and that the office is so close to the station."

"Everything is close in Selah. At least in the town proper, that is. It might be trickier to get to some of the homes outside town. There will be more distance to cover."

Kenia nodded. She had been wondering if she might buy a scooter of some sort. She was almost certain there would not be Uber. Again, she was glad for her braids, as they would fit beneath a helmet better than curls would have.

"Seems like a picturesque part of the country."

"It is. It keeps the tourists passing through. We have a bit of history here in town," Jolene said, folding her hands on the desk in front of her, her eyes glancing momentarily at her computer screen. "But we certainly have our struggles."

"Yes, I was reading about the statistics on the ride up."

"Whatever the rates are for rural West Virginia, they are worse here."

"Sorry to hear that."

"Things have been in decline for years. The coal processing plant has been closed since the disaster in '53. And the pharmaceutical plant closed up and went overseas. It's left us with little but tourism and that's just to the bed and breakfasts, if people are here for the disaster tour of the island. But even that is not much of a draw."

"Disaster tour?"

"Yep, one of our own, Octavian Coates, runs tours of Selah Island. You can tour the integrated-town-that-might-have-been. It keeps the history buffs interested, as well as the occasional biologists who like to visit a site that's gone back to nature. You should do it at least once while you are here."

"Sounds interesting."

Ms. Jolene shifted in her seat, laying her arms on the armrests, her hands—a bit ashy—hanging off the ends. "Tell me about your project."

Kenia leaned forward, slipping her tablet out of her bag. "Happy to. I was assigned a bit last minute, but it's a pilot project, really a feasibility trial for a smartphone app that helps users determine costs for a healthier diet."

She slipped her own smartphone out of her pocket, tapped the icon shaped like a paper grocery bag with a lime-green dollar sign on it and a rainbow of fruits and vegetables peeking out the top.

"It's called Healthy-Bytes," she said, raising her eyebrow and waiting for the play on words to register. Ms. Jolene gave no sign. Kenia pushed through. "I'm collecting qualitative data on the usability of the interface and some quantitative data on demographics and food prices." She handed the phone across the desk to Ms. Jolene.

Ms. Jolene tapped through the menu screen, scrolled up, then down, taking just long enough to note some of the icons, designed for free by students in the graphic design classes. It wasn't long before her eyes seemed to lose focus, and she set the phone down with two fingers, as if it was covered in germs.

"You're skeptical," Kenia said, recognizing Ms. Jolene's distaste.

"Hmmm?" Jolene countered, as if she had not heard Kenia across the desk.

"I know it's not exactly glamorous, but it's what the National Institute for Health funded, so Dr. Quientela went with it, and well, I followed," Kenia said, letting her hands fall into her lap.

Ms. Jolene let out another long "Hmmm," a sneer creeping into her lip, then decided to speak her mind. "Always interesting to me, what gets funded."

"Well, it seems like there has been a lot of focus on obesity and type 2 diabetes."

"Nationwide, but when you do your situational analysis you will find that most of Selah Station is a food desert. Folks have to travel far if they want a banana or spinach." She closed her eyes, mumbled something that sounded like "My Lord," then sighed, starting over. "Can I see the list of respondents you would like to contact for an interview?"

"Certainly," Kenia said. She had it on her tablet, but looking around the office at the beige cathode-ray computer monitor, the keyboard with the letters worn off, and listening to the sputtering sound coming from the fan in the CPU, she thought it better to go with paper. She pulled a three-ring binder from her backpack, flipped to her section on demographic information, popped open the rings, and handed the respondent list to Ms. Jolene.

She began to read the names listed. Only a moment passed before she leaned forward to pull a red pen from the cup on her desk and drew a firm line through one of them.

"Josephine Dawson, she killed herself." She crossed off another name and another, moving down the list. "Lonnie Cooper, drank himself to death. Luther and Bonnie Evans, he shot her then shot himself." She paused, flipped to the next page by slapping it aside, and continued to cross out names. "She died . . . she did too— overdose. . . ."

Ms. Jolene reached the last page. Just when Kenia thought she was finished, Ms. Jolene came to the last name on the list and scratched it out with a flourish and a *tsk* of her tongue before handing the pages back. "She committed suicide. Hung herself, livestreamed it. Video circulated on Facebook for weeks afterwards."

Kenia reached out for the pages and slid them back into the folder, closing the rings slowly so they would not snap.

"What . . . what has been going on here?"

"Opioid drugs, alcohol. Since 1999, the mortality rate in Selah for women thirty-five to forty-four is up 170 percent."

"That . . . that's pushing even the worst of the trends."

Jolene shrugged. "It depends on the region being surveyed." She paused a beat, staring down Kenia, her voice with an edge of bitterness. "Seems like more than a nutrition app can fix, doesn't it."

Kenia shifted in her seat and cleared her throat. "I see you have your work cut out for you."

"Don't I know it? My father owned a mortuary before he retired. I grew up there helping him. He retired early. Said the business was too sad. It was not like business wasn't good. It was. But he used to find some pleasure in ensuring folks had a sense of dignity when they passed. He made all the arrangements, wanted folks to have nothing to worry about but their own grief . . . not whether or not the hearse would show up on time or if there would be enough flowers around the casket.

"But in the last decade or so, things changed. The folks dying kept getting younger." She shook her head, looking down at the desk, her eyes focused on something visualized in her mind. "Not enough lotion or makeup to cover up decades of damage from drugs, alcohol, and despair in a forty-year-old looking like she's sixty."

Kenia nodded. She had no other response.

Jolene took in her silence with a narrowing of her eyes. "It's really the story of small town America these days. Jobs are scarce. Plans recede and reality stretches farther and farther and well, we all need a break. Whether it's a mani-pedi, Netflix, HBO, Facebook, porn, a cigarette, a pill to ease you into sleep, a glass of wine, a puff of weed, meth, or something even stronger . . . and then you are hooked, years pass, and you don't recognize yourself anymore."

Kenia thought of Janice in the waiting room. She could hear her leaving now, Thea wishing her a good-day. Kenia assumed Janice had passed the screening and was genuinely happy for her. "Seems like a few are getting by," she offered. "But it sure must seem daunting at times, even overwhelming."

Another sneer followed before Ms. Jolene turned in her chair, opened a drawer, and pulled out a set of keys on a Wild-And-Wonderful-West-Virginia key chain. "I told Dr. Quientela I'd rent you the mother-in-law suite over my garage. It's just about a mile and a half from here. I'll call Harry; he's the local cab driver. He can drive you there. You won't want to drag all that stuff you have there."

"Thanks."

"And you'll want to save Harry's number in your phone. He's got a monopoly on the cab business, but he doesn't overcharge."

"Great. That will be helpful. I have a suitcase in the waiting room as well."

"The place looks over the Shenandoah. It's a nice view."

"Sounds like it."

Jolene drew out a folder, flipped through a few pages with carbon paper between them. "Just need you to sign this lease for the summer."

"Of course. I can pay you now with a check if you would like," Kenia offered, remembering that her practicum stipend had registered in her bank account the week before. Out of due diligence, she scanned the pages and conditions of the agreement, trying not to take too long.

As she did, Ms. Jolene continued speaking, as if to herself. "This whole town has changed. But I am not surprised. No ma'am. When you take God and prayer out of schools, things like this happen."

Now it was Kenia's turn to offer a non-committal "hmmm," trying to divide her attention between listening to her new boss and landlady-to-be and studying the legally binding contract she was about to sign.

"And now with the gays marrying, Lord Jesus, where is this country going to go."

Kenia stopped, her pen hovering just over the line for her signature. The pause drew out into an uncomfortable silence, her eyes fixed on the point of her pen, reluctant as she was to look up. She willed gentleness into her voice to make what she said next sound like a sincere inquiry, but the resentment in her voice was impossible to disguise.

"You are not comfortable with LGBTQ folks having the right to marry?"

"Sister, it's a matter of faith. It's God's word."

Kenia clicked the pen closed and looked up, leaning back into her chair. Her back felt rigid as steel. In her fingers she could feel a faint tremble. "I think it is a matter of civil rights."

"Does man's law supersede God's word?" Jolene asked, leaning forward, her eyes meeting Kenia's. She was poised to lecture. Ready for confrontation.

"Seems to me, religious folks found all sorts of justification in those same scriptures for things like slavery."

"Well, they say even the Devil can quote scripture to serve his needs," Jolene said, drumming the top of her desk.

Kenia took a deep breath and exhaled giving the pages of the lease back.

"Ms. Lewis, my sister is a civil rights attorney. She represents members of the LGBTQ community in civil litigation. Last year she won the Distinguished Alumni Award from Columbia Law School for the work she has done for the trans community. She has been out since she was seventeen and is married to an incredible woman I'm privileged to call my sister-in-law. I'm proud of my sister. I'm proud of her wife. I love them both."

And I'll be damned if I give you a penny of my stipend, she thought.

Ms. Jolene had not reached out to take the lease back. Kenia set it down anyway, next to the daily calendar of scripture quotes.

"I'm eager to work with you to see to the needs of the community members here in Selah Station. We can serve them side by side, but I would not feel that it is appropriate for me to stay under your roof for the summer."

Finally, Jolene Lewis nodded, took the lease, sliding it back in the folder, closing it, and placing the folder back in the drawer of her desk. Then she took the keys, dropped them from the fingers of one hand to the to her palm of the other, pulled opened another drawer, dropped them in with a clank, and closed it.

The room was silent but for the click of the lock on the drawer. Ms. Jolene placed her folded hands back on the center of the desk, the cross on her chest staring back at Kenia like a crosshairs.

"I understand," Ms. Jolene said.

Kenia slipped her binder back into her bag, picked up her phone and stood up, "I guess I will see you Monday. If you'll excuse me, I need to attend to a few things."

"Of course. Thea will see you out."

◊

Outside the Med-Dent building, Kenia set her suitcase upright beside her as she searched on her phone for an Airbnb. As her pulse returned to normal, she noticed the smell of the overflowing cigarette stand, the sand almost invisible from the stained butts that poked upwards like a clutch of mushrooms on a carcass.

What the hell am I doing?

It all seemed to wrong to her. She remembered one of the most impactful things Dr. Quientela had ever shared with them in class: that the most important elements to any public health campaign were not pharmaceuticals, not policy reform, nor informational pamphlets. Those things played a part, but what came first, what was most fundamental were humanization and empathy. Without those things, there could be no progress.

Which was why what she had heard from Ms. Jolene, as the director of public health services here in Selah Station, just made no sense to her.

Guess they must not have a deep talent pool to hire from here in Selah Station.

Kenia needed to get away from this building. She jammed her phone back into her pocket, yanked her suitcase behind her and began walking back to the main street. Her heart was beating hard in her chest, a lifetime of hurts and injustices she had seen visited on her sister Chinemere because of her orientation flashing through her mind. As recently as last year, Chinemere and her wife had been spit upon in the lead-up to the election. Kenia's braids were flopping against her shoulders in an irritating way as she marched, perspiration forming on her temples and neck. She stopped, took out an elastic, and pulled her hair back.

She needed to rest when she got back to the main street. She turned the suitcase on its side, sat down on it, and checked Craigslist.

No Service.

She dropped her head down again. She took long breaths, closed her eyes, and tried to calm herself. Her head hurt. It was the lack of sleep from the overnight bus. Who knew when she would find a place to rest at this point? Maybe the church? She knew she could stay in a hotel if she needed to, but not for the whole summer. She took a few more breaths, trying to fight the pain growing behind her eyes and the tension wrapping around her skull. She tried to focus on the sound of a car passing, the voices of children playing in the park across the street, and behind it all she tried to listen for that susurration of white water and wind in the river gorges that sounded like the whisper of words.

She closed her eyes, remembering a technique her mother had taught her, that she had learned from a team of Navy Seals she had trained in emergency first aid: four by four by four. Breathe in for four seconds; hold for four seconds; breathe out for four seconds; repeat four times. Kenia felt peace returning. A few more breaths, not unlike a yoga class. A bird chirped. She had found her center again.

When she opened her eyes, the street was transformed. She had shifted from daylight to the darkness of night as abruptly as one might in a dream. She stared out, the scene before her incomprehensible.

It was the same street, the same buildings, lit by the glow of streetlamps and passing cars. It must have been a classic car convention of some kind, because all the models were vintage with heavy frames, boat-like bodies, and paint jobs in primary colors, like those of a comic book. The sidewalks were filled with young people, teenagers mostly, the girls with long swinging skirts and the boys with short haircuts. A half-dozen kids passed immediately in front of her, staring at her, perplexed. They were a mix of backgrounds, white and black. She returned their stares, wondering at their vintage 1950s clothes. One of the black girls offered a wave and a tentative, "Hi."

"Hi," Kenia said, self-conscious, wondering if she'd had a fainting spell, passing out only to wake up, the day passed, some sort of 1950s festival taking place in the evening hours. The group of kids passed, moving down the sidewalk towards the movie marquee, dazzling with its bulbs blinking in sequence around lettering that advertised *The House of Wax,* starring Vincent Price. She saw letter jackets and cardigans under the light of the theater. Was that BB King's *Three O'Clock Blues* she heard playing from a passing Studebaker? She squeezed her eyes shut, seized now with a sense of vertigo. When she opened them again, it was day again, the sidewalk empty, jagged with the press of tree roots once more.

Was that a hallucination?

"Excuse me," a voice called out from the street.

Kenia looked up to where a Dodge minivan with faux wood paneling had pulled up to the curb. The passenger side window was rolled down and framed in its place by the door was the woman—the mother in the NC State sweatshirt from the bus.

"Did someone forget to pick you up?"

"Something like that," Kenia said.

"Where you headed?"

Kenia assessed her situation, weighing the discomfort of the street versus the disclosure of her story, and decided on the truth. "Looks like my housing for the summer just fell through."

The mother turned to the driver, her father in the Pittsburg Steelers jacket, exchanged a few words with him, then turned back.

"Why don't you come with us?"

The woman's father had already stepped out and was making his way around the minivan. He offered his hand, "I'm Earl Corrigan."

"Kenia."

"We sat next to each other all the way up from Raleigh. I'm Sandra by the way," Sandra said, getting out and also shaking Kenia's hand. She was not sure what to do with the sudden rush of friendliness.

"Nice to . . . meet you."

"Mom and Dad have a converted garage. Why don't you crash there? I know you just came up from Raleigh and must be tired."

"I'm really touched, but I was thinking I'd stay at a hotel."

"That will cost you," Earl said.

"I don't know what my mother would say, if I imposed on strangers." Kenia tried to force an uncomfortable laugh. "I mean, I don't know you folks."

"Everyone knows everyone in Selah. Who you working for?"

"Jolene Lewis at the Bridgewater Med-Dent center," Kenia said, her inflection rising like a question.

"We know her," Sandra's mother was saying from the back seat of the minivan now. "Earl, look up the Med-Dent number on your phone."

Earl pulled out his phone. "Didn't know I had that number in here."

His wife rolled her eyes. "You do. Thea, Jacob and Mistie's daughter, works there."

"Oh, all right," Earl said, scrolling through his numbers. As his wife had said, he found the number. "Dang-nammit, here it is." He put the phone to his ear, the surprise still plain on his face.

Sandra was poised close to her father, as if ready to take the phone in case some clarification was needed.

Kenia found the spectacle more than endearing.

"Hello Thea, Earl Corrigan here . . . Good, thanks . . . Seems like we have run into your co-worker—"

"Intern," Kenia corrected.

"Intern. She looks like she needs a place to stay."

Earl chuckled and held the phone out to her. "Thea wants to talk to you."

◊

After being rescued by the Corrigans and assured by Thea that yes, indeed, everyone in Selah knew each other, and that the Corrigans were good, God-fearing people who would not be kidnapping her and insert-any-other-terrifying-scenario-her-mother-had-warned-her-about that would have led to her dead in the gutter, chopped into pieces in a freezer, or brainwashed into a cult, Kenia had climbed into the minivan and ridden a short while into a neighborhood of early-twentieth-century Victorians, where they pulled up to a three-story home painted in soft blues, with high gables and navy shutters and trim. Earl let them out in the driveway on the side of the house. Sandra and her son, Colton, who had already introduced Kenia to his Captain America figure—in addition to the Ironman one she had rescued earlier—helped her with her bags.

The garage was a separate building, painted in periwinkle, offsetting the house without clashing. It took both her and Sandra cooperating to carry her bag up the steps to the room above. The door was unlocked. Sandra nudged it open with her foot and stepped inside. Kenia stood in the doorway flabbergasted. It was one room, but spacious, with an updated kitchenette, stovetop, and a miniature refrigerator, its motor humming. Farther in was a sofa, a desk next to the window, and at the opposite end, a full-sized bed next to a window HV/AC unit. The floor and ceiling were done in natural pine.

"This is lovely, and you are sure I can stay the night?" Kenia asked.

"Likely longer. I heard my mother on the phone with Jolene. They just finished updating this place and could use a tenant. But you can let them know in the morning. I'm sure you will want to rest now."

"That is so generous."

Sandra shrugged, touching Colton's mess of curls and mussing them. "Anything for another Tar Heel, right? Just think of it as southern hospitality, transplanted north."

"I guess so."

"Anyway, you are here to help. Selah needs it."

Kenia nodded, a sense of shame building in her, remembering Ms. Jolene's skepticism at her and Healthy-Bytes. "I'll do my best."

Sandra winked, gathered Colton, and left her to rest.

Kenia closed the door after them, made a circuit of the room, noting that the boards squeaked beneath her feet in a pleasant, settled-in way. The bathroom was clean and also recently remodeled. She was already wondering what the Corrigans might charge for rent for the summer. She texted her mother to let her know she had arrived safely, knowing she would not respond immediately, as she would be at the clinic. She texted Chiazam, attaching a picture of the

room, sat down on the bed, leaned back, and was asleep before he
responded.

Chapter 8

Without Sanctuary

Kenia woke just after noon to a knocking at her door. She opened it to find Colton, who had brought his Black Panther this time. He let himself in over the threshold and walked past her into the upstairs room. He stared at her still-unopened bag before becoming distracted by her laptop, tablet, and phone—its light flashing with Chiazam's reply.

"You have a lot of devices. Can you play games on them?" he asked, pulling out a chair at the table but refraining from touching the electronics.

"Uh, not really. I don't have any installed."

"My mom lets me play games on her phone and watch videos."

"Where is your mother?"

"In the kitchen with Grandma and Grandpa."

"Oh yeah? And what are they doing?" she asked, casually picking up her phone to check her brother's response.

"Making lunch. They want to know if you want to join them."

"Is that why they sent you?"

"Yeah, I guess. But I wanted to show you Black Panther. You said he was your favorite."

"He is. That was sweet of you," she said. Kenia realized she was ravenously hungry, so she suggested that she and Colton walk over to the main house.

Over lunch she learned that Sandra was a preschool teacher, and her husband was in the army. Her father, Earl, had served as a Marine. Earl said he had learned to tolerate his daughter being married to an Army man, provided Sandra could put up with him.

Margaret, Sandra's mother, was a retired nurse who worked part time as a school nurse. She kept refilling Kenia's glass of iced tea until the pitcher was empty and asked her a number of questions about her practicum and Healthy-Bytes. She, at least, caught the pun right away, "'Bytes' as computer bytes or bites of food, right?"

"Yes, that was what they meant."

"Clever," she laughed.

The lunch of cold cuts and cheese sandwiches finished, Kenia was suddenly aware of the long hours to fill between now and Monday morning.

"What does one do in Selah Station, on the weekend?"

Earl laughed. "Not much. You can help me woodwork if you like."

"Earl," Margaret said, punching him in the arm. "I'm sure Kenia has other interests."

"You mean *more* interesting than woodworking?"

Sandra rolled her eyes. "There is a library a few blocks away. It is a museum too. It's run by twin brothers, Octavian and Morris Coates. That might be a good place to start, given the history of the town."

"Oh yes," Margaret said. "The Coates have been here for generations. Their grandparents were students at the University— and so were ours actually—before the Selah Island was closed down after the accident in '53."

"What exactly happened?" Kenia asked.

"It was the CPP, the coal processing plant," Earl said with a shake of the head. "Never did make sense to have that thing on the same island as the University and the town center, but that was the Bridgewaters for you. Those two sides of the family could never get out of each other's way."

"Bridgewaters . . . are they who the Med-Dent building is named for?"

"Yes," Margaret said. "Prentice Bridgewater actually, who was the president of the University and died during the fire and explosion at the CPP in '53. He had gone in to help the workers trapped there. Ironically, his relative Crowley Bridgewater, who actually owned the place, was nowhere near it when it blew."

Colton slipped down from his chair making "whooshing" sounds with his Black Panther and Ironman.

"They're an old family," Earl said. "Old as Selah, descended from the founding brothers of Selah Station, Reginald and Leonard. Those two were involved in the Underground Railroad, and during the Restoration years, it was Leonard's son David Solomon Bridgewater who founded the University. Leonard's brother Reginald, his sons owned the mines around here and went on to establish the coal industry here in Selah."

"There was a falling out between the families," Margaret continued. "Really the stuff of Shakespeare. Go to the museum, you can learn all about it. Octavian can even set you up for a tour of the island."

"Hazmat suit and all," Earl said.

◊

Kenia followed the Corrigans' directions, walking down to the end of the street and heading south, back towards the center of town, then turning right on Xavier Street. The day had grown warm. Children played in sprinklers, bounced on backyard trampolines, and raced bikes and razor scooters in the street. The air smelled of cut grass, barbeques, and the Carolina Allspice and rock roses planted alongside the fluffy blooms of hydrangeas and the bushes of potentilla, all alive with clusters of swallowtail butterflies. There were even a few homes with the proverbial white picket fence, which she snapped a picture of and sent to her sisters, brother, and Audre with the caption, "They still do exist! I'm in a Norman Rockwell painting."

When Audre would get the picture, Kenia couldn't guess. She imagined Audre somewhere in Haiti amid palm fronds and banana trees, working in a clinic full of children waiting on their mothers' laps for vaccinations. Or maybe Audre was conducting a focus group in a stone church somewhere with statues of a black Jesus, Mary, and other saints looking on. It felt worlds away from the place she found herself in. When she finally stopped in front of the museum and library she was eager for a distraction from her depressed thoughts.

The museum was also a large Victorian, in the style of the rest on the street. This one was converted into a public space, a large sign in the front declaring it to be the Selah Station Public Library and Museum of African American Heritage. There was a gateless fence, its planks and posts painted—thoughtfully, she imagined—in a coat of burnt sienna. She crossed the front yard, stepped up on the porch, and pushed on the door that read: "Welcome, Please Come In."

The inside foyer was bright with ample sunlight filtering in through tall windows. The air was pleasantly cool, thanks to a window AC unit chugging away. The wood floor announced her presence with loud creaks. She heard an answering sound, a chair sliding across the floor, and a black man came around the corner. He appeared to be in his fifties, his head mostly bald. He wore a pressed button-down shirt with a starched collar and cuff links, but no tie. An elegant fitted blazer hung on his frame. A pair of wire-rimmed glasses gave him the air of a scholar; however, he removed and folded them before slipping them into his breast pocket and offering Kenia his hand.

"Welcome," he said. His features were handsome, but his expression stopped just short of a smile, throwing her off a little bit. "I am Morris Coates. How can I help you?"

"Kenia," she said. "I was hoping to take a look around."

"Kenia," he said her name slowly. "Short for Keniabarido or as in Kenya?"

"Keniabarido. I'm impressed."

Morris shrugged, "I've tried to make sure I know a bit about where we came from. In your case, are you Ogoni?"

"We're Igbo, or at least my father was—like every other Nigerian you meet in the diaspora," she laughed. "All my siblings have Igbo names. I'm the odd one out. My mother just liked the name Keniabarido, but I usually shorten it to Kenia."

"That probably saves you a lot of breath trying to explain to people."

"Completely."

"What brings you to Selah, Kenia?"

"Summer internship at the Med-Dent building. I'm staying with the Corrigans down the street. They said this would be a good place to come to learn about the history of the town and check out a book."

"That was kind of them. I run the museum side of things. My brother Octavian is the librarian. Together we are sort of the informal historians of the city of Selah Station."

"Your brother leads the tours of the old city?"

"When he is not running the library," Morris said, gesturing to the half of the house given over to rooms lined with bookcases. Through the French doors behind her, Kenia noted a librarian's desk with a bar code scanner next to a stack of laminated books waiting to be scanned.

"And this side?" Kenia asked, with a nod to the room that Morris had emerged from.

"Our current exhibit, *Without Sanctuary.* Tours are free. Would you like one while you wait for Octavian to return?"

"That would be lovely."

"Let me show you around."

The wood floor gave way to a beryl-blue carpet that muffled their steps as they entered the exhibit hall. It had a hushed silence to it that reminded Kenia of a funeral home. *Without Sanctuary,* turned out to be a collection of a series of lynching photographs gathered from all over the United States. Kenia could not help an intake of breath at the first photo of three black men in ragged clothes strung up just inches from the ground, their bare feet still dangling in tufts of grass, the tree almost comically small, but sturdy enough to bear the weight of their murders. White folks, men and women, gathered around posing—not unlike she had seen white hunters in pith helmets do over the carcasses of their kills on safari. In the background, a boy Colton's age was caught in mid-swing striking the youngest of the black victims, a young teenage boy. The shutter speed of the old camera had been too slow to capture the swing of the little white boy's stick and arm, so he appeared strangely armless, the weapon itself erased. Otherwise, the expressions of the adults were those one would expect to find on any group of neighbors and townsfolk attending a Sunday picnic.

She swallowed hard, wondering if she could slip out and wait in the foyer without offending Morris. But he was already a silent, waiting presence next to her. She turned to the caption but after a moment realized she was not even reading it.

"Sorry, it's a tough exhibit," Morris said in a gravelly voice.

"No doubt," Kenia said, willing herself to move forward.

"It was a white historian, James Allen, who collected these over the years. A sad, sad testimony, but one we can't forget."

"We can't," she said, because she felt obliged to. They moved to the next display, this one of a crowd of hundreds gathered in a public square, a black man's body hanging from a flag pole; the camera was too distant to capture what was left of his face or features, but the horror was undiminished, the strings of smoke still rising from his flesh.

She moved in shocked silence through the rest, noting a map of the United States; the size and darkness of red dots over each state recorded the number of *reported* lynchings from the early nineteenth century to the mid twentieth. Every state was marked, even ones she did not expect such as California, Oregon, and Washington.

It was the calm, self-satisfied expressions of the whites gathered in the pictures that Kenia found so chilling. These were not masters, these were everyday people: farmers, teachers, bakers, carpenters, really no different than the white people she interacted with now.

Like the Corrigans.

She leaned in close to read one of the exhibit panels. The text explained that some of the pictures were from postcards that were sold to commemorate the lynchings with family and friends. The equivalent of Instagram, Kenia thought. The back of one was displayed in a case, the paper sepia-colored with age, the print faded but unmistakable:

The Dogwood Tree
This is only the branch of the Dogwood tree;
An emblem of WHITE SUPREMACY,
A lesson once taught in the Pioneer school,
That this is a land of WHITE MAN'S RULE.
The Red Man once in an early day,
Was told by the Whites to mind his way.

The negro now, by eternal grace,
Must learn to stay in the negro's place.
In the Sunny South, the Land of the Free,
Let the White SUPREME forever be.
Let this a warning to all negroes be,
Or they'll suffer the fate of the DOGWOOD TREE.

"It was like pest control to them, back then," Morris said, his voice somber and bitter at once.

Kenia felt sick.

In another photo from South Carolina a black woman, a white man, and their son hung from a bridge, their limbs strangely misshapen, their bones broken. The man's pants were dark with blood where the mob had castrated him. The text indicated that they had been killed for getting married in secret. A Confederate flag waved in the background. The next photo showed the charred skull of a man sticking out from the blackened remnants of a large wood fire. The date was 1930.

Kenia thought of what else had been happening in the world at that time and her trip to the Holocaust Museum in Washington D.C. where she had seen other bodies, charred and burnt. But what she saw depicted on the soil of her own country seemed fundamentally different. Even though the engines of mass extermination by the Nazis in mid-century Germany were unparalleled in efficiency, the deed of it was done behind locked gates and brick walls. These lynchings were public, done by everyday citizens, who consented to have their pictures taken in the aftermath.

She thought of the boy with the stick. The fluttering Confederate flag. She remembered the words scratched onto the historical marker at the Junction: *Go Home Nigger,* and felt repulsed at the notion that some Americans still flew the Confederate flag as an expression of "Southern Pride" and "Southern Culture."

"At least Nazi-ism was denounced by Germany. We still see fools flying that damn Confederate flag these days and you know the ruckus people kick up when you just try to take down an old confederate statue. Are there any statues of Hitler still up?" She looked at the display cases again. "Even the Nazi's didn't make postcards like these."

"They did make reading lampshades out of the skin of Jews, though," Morris said, shaking his head. "I don't know if there is much gained in comparison. Evil is evil."

"But the ignoring of it here . . . the will to forget it, or reimagine it . . ." She was not sure how to finish her sentence, or if she could, her stomach was roiling so. Although she felt a measure of relief, followed by guilt, when she neared the end of the exhibit. *Without Sanctuary,* however, had one last gut-punch, left: a photo of the charred body of what she could only assume had been a black man. A white man with a broad-brimmed hat had leaned an arm against the tree supporting the victim. The legs had been burnt into stumps that stopped at the knees. The face was barely human. The heat had curled the skin of the arms, twisting the sinews and pulling the limbs into a gross parody of flexing, as if ironically displaying the prowess of the living that had now been obliterated.

Coon Cooking, read the inscription on the postcard.

"You all right young lady?" Morris asked.

Kenia noticed a room marked "Restroom" with a water fountain next to it, just beyond the exhibit space. "Yeah, I'm just a bit tired from the heat. I think . . . excuse me," she said, heading for the bathroom.

◊

She didn't vomit, although she crouched over the toilet bowl ready to. Perhaps she didn't because it was really not the first time she had seen, heard, listened to, or witnessed such atrocities. She could almost say there was no escaping the truth of it, if white people didn't somehow live in obliviousness each day. "Crimes against humanity" had such a sterile, faintly bureaucratic air to it. Morris had called it what it was.

Evil.

She moved to the sink, washed her face and hands, and stepped towards the exit, thankful to find a bench just inside the door beneath some coat hangers where she could sit down, still in the semi-privacy of the ladies' room.

Four by four by four.

She repeated it more than four times. She lost count, but knew she had done it enough when she felt calm and centered. The front door swung open; fresh sets of footsteps and muffled voices followed as Morris greeted the next band of visitors. The analogy of a funeral parlor came back to her. The victims here, though, would never be at rest.

More footsteps thumped over her head as, she imagined, someone came down the staircase. With so much movement, she did not expect her own pocket of solitude to last much longer, so she gathered her things and stepped outside. She was careful to turn left this time, away from the previous exhibit, and instead into the library. Once past a few signs about no eating or drinking, she found herself in the children's section of the library. A thick foam mat covered in durable industrial carpet rested on the floor in the center of the section, and she found herself sitting down on it, taking in posters of cartoon bookworms promoting reading from the end of child-sized shelves. A display promoted the book of the month: *The Absolutely True Diary of a Part-Time Indian* by Sherman Alexie.

She noted half a dozen oil drums, their sides cut down and lined with carpet in order to repurpose them as reading nooks. The outsides were painted in cheery pastels and she could not deny her desire to regress and climb into one herself, curled up with a Virginia Hamilton or Jacqueline Woodson novel.

"Circle time is not for another two hours," a soft voice said. She could hear the smile in the words. When she looked up she saw a man in a forest green cardigan over a gray Henley and pleat-less slacks. Otherwise he was identical to his more somber brother, even down to the wire-rim glasses.

"You must be Octavian. I just did the *Without Sanctuary* tour with your brother."

Octavian's knees popped as he settled down onto the opposite corner of the mat, his hand on the bookshelves for balance. He slipped a few picture books back into place, but once he had finished replacing them, he did not rise.

"It's a heavy exhibit."

"To say the least."

"You take your time. You can even stay for story circle time if you like," he smiled.

"Thanks," she smiled.

"I can also recommend something light, Roald Dahl or something of the like."

Kenia laughed, "You know my mother used to go through our books, including *James and the Giant Peach,* and color all the characters with a brown pencil so that they looked more like people of color."

"Protagonists of color," Octavian said. "I like that. She wasn't defacing library books though, was she?"

"No, no, of course not." Kenia laughed again despite herself. "They were our own. But I did not realize she had done it until I got in trouble at the school library, getting into an argument with the librarian because I kept insisting that she show me the Matilda books where Matilda was black."

"How old were you?"

"Six or seven."

"You were an early reader."

"Mom saw to that. We all had expansive vocabularies. It helped on the SATs and GREs. I'm not a quantitative whiz like my siblings, but my score on the verbal section was perfect."

"That's commendable."

"Is it?" Kenia thought aloud. "Or is it just a result of more pressure to be twice as good?"

"I guess it can be both now, can't it."

They both were quiet a moment, pondering, until Kenia realized she had not introduced herself.

"Kenia Dezy. I'm a summer intern at the Med-Dent building."

"And, as you already surmised, I'm Octavian Coates."

"Octavian, your brother has got to warn people about that exhibit before they dive in. Needs a graphic image warning or something."

Octavian nodded his head. "I've told him just that. It's a bitter pill to swallow. But here," he pushed his knuckles heavily down into the mat and stood, "follow me. I'll show you some reading that always helps me in such times."

She followed Octavian past the history and sociology sections to the African American section, where he let his finger hover over the spines of the books before stopping over a series of titles by James Baldwin.

"I'm presuming you have read Baldwin."

"Of course, but he did not write much about women of color, did he? Brother didn't raise himself. I was just imagining sitting in that reading barrel with a Virginia Hamilton or Jacqueline Woodson novel."

"That's true about Baldwin," Octavian said, pointing at the ceiling as if rewarding her a point before he returned to scanning the book spines, moving towards the works of young adult fiction by African American writers. "I have just the thing for you, I think."

He tipped out a title by an author named Nnedi Okorafor: *Zahrah the Windseeker.*

Kenia noted the author's name. "She's Nigerian?"

"Nigerian American. You need a good escape, she'll provide it."

Halfrican. Her thoughts flitted to wondering what Audre was doing at that moment.

"Thanks so much."

"Always happy to connect a reader and a book. Feel free to browse some more, you still have time before story circle starts."

Kenia smiled, seeking out a few picture books she thought Colton would like if the opportunity arose. When she was ready, Octavian met her at the checkout desk and asked for her driver's license to fill out a library card application for her. She handed it to him, reading the sign for tours to Selah Island on the desk next to his computer monitor.

"I heard you offer tours of the old town."

"I do," he said, his eyes lighting up behind his spectacles. "Are you interested?"

"Guess I ought to. After all, I'm living here for the next three months."

"Well, this is a rich place for history. We have microfilms of the local newspapers going back nearly two hundred years. But there is nothing like seeing the old town. It's a fascinating history, preserved— our own sort of Pompeii."

It was an ominous comparison, plasters of bodies crawling, choking, on invisible ash flashing through her mind.

"When would you like to go?" Octavian asked, breaking her free of her ruminations.

"How about tomorrow?"

"Certainly, how about eight?"

"That's early for a Sunday morning," she said.

"Well, it's summer and it gets warm in the hazmat suits. We'll want to go when it's still cool."

"So you really have to wear a suit?"

"Afraid so. A mask as well, out of an abundance of caution, of course. We should be fine. But you will have to sign a release," he said, clearing his throat.

Kenia paused a beat before answering, "Well, it will be a good experience for my public health education."

"Great. Be here at seven-fifteen and we'll start getting ready."

Chapter 9

Summer Feet

Sunday morning. The window of her upper room framed a sky already lavender with the coming of the sun, the season giving the days an early start. It was the coolest part of the day, and Kenia wrapped herself in an oversized oxford shirt she liked to lounge in and stepped outside in bare feet and sat with her coffee balanced on her knees. The feel of the grain of wood beneath her the soles of her feet reminded her of summer days and "summer feet," when her callouses grew tough from running along the creek in the woods behind her home, using fallen trees as balance beams, or crouching on cement sidewalks to chalk a finish line for a footrace among her siblings . . . the beginnings and ends of the course staggered in order to make the effort equitable—the beginnings of the social consciousness her parents had instilled in them.

She was grateful for those long afternoons without structure. But the summer mornings in their household had been different. They would be up early to complete their chores, make their own breakfasts, then head to whatever lessons—French, Chinese, piano, drum, violin—that their mother had signed them up for. Chiazam had often taken advanced math classes, so by the time school started he was taking classes two grades ahead of his peers. In junior high he was already tutoring high school students.

At lunchtime she and her siblings would reconvene, Chinemere preparing a meal for them. Without their parents around, they could eat what they wanted, where they wanted, how they wanted: on the couch, slouched in a chair, their shoes on or off, their shirttails untucked. It was their antidote to the structure enforced on them day after day.

Kenia loved those lunchtimes, when the house was their own clubhouse. Once the meal was complete, the afternoon was theirs.

The arrangement was a compromise between their parents: their mother hated the idea of lazy, aimless, desultory summer days doing nothing but forgetting their school lessons and falling behind. She would cite one study after another from peer-reviewed journals demonstrating that children lost many of their academic gains over the long summer break—a tradition tied to a more agrarian America anyway. She wanted them to exercise their minds. It was the only way to success.

But her father, while agreeing, had wanted freedom for them, too. He wanted them to experience the bucolic days he'd had in childhood—a childhood characterized by kola nuts, *fufu,* and kumquats; when shoes were for school and church and optional all other times. He prevailed on their mother, however, only by touting the peer-reviewed studies demonstrating the importance of children learning social-emotional skills through unstructured play. This won her over, but not without a wink from their father.

He knew his wife.

Upon returning home in the evenings, their mother would want to check the progress of their reading by looking to see if their bookmarks had moved in their books and quizzing them on what they had read. By contrast, her father often just took their feet in his hands, running his thumb over their tough-as-wood soles. He would smile with approval and whisper, "Now this is what an African child's foot should feel like."

A woodpecker drilled away at a tree somewhere adjacent to the Corrigans' property. Kenia watched a robin swoop down across the yard and alight on the railing of the back porch. For the first time she noticed Earl sitting there, a mug of coffee cupped in his hands. He lifted his hand in a silent wave, Kenia feeling the mutual, unspoken, understanding between them that they were both here to take in the stillness of Sunday morning, waking up in the company of their thoughts, but not words.

She raised her own mug, as if in a toast to Earl, then turned back to tracking a squirrel's progress onto the branch of an elm and a chipmunk's explorations out from beneath the woodpile while the woodpecker's *tap-tap-tap* continued to echo.

◊

She walked to the Library-Museum, arriving at ten after seven. The sign on the window read "Closed," but when she knocked Octavian answered, opening the door with a smirk.

"Morning, young lady. If you're not five minutes early. . . ."

"You're late," she finished.

Octavian was dressed in what appeared to be cotton painting pants and a short-sleeved shirt that said, "Selah University, Founded 1905." A torch and a sword crossed behind a shield, where a Latin inscription read, *Scientia, sapientia, et fortitudine pugnemus pro libertate.*

"With knowledge, wisdom, and courage let us fight for freedom," she translated, remembering what she could from two years of high school Latin.

"And you translated the subjunctive properly," Octavian said.

"My Latin teacher, Mrs. Jones, would be proud."

"If you look closely, you can see the Ashanti symbols on the sword and torch handle."

On inspection, she realized what she had taken for shading were indeed Andinkra symbols: *boa me na me mmoa*, cooperation and interdependence; *nyan sapo*, wisdom and intelligence; *sankofa*, learn from the past; and *wawa aba,* perseverance and toughness.

"Not bad for founding principles," she said. "Do you get down wearing a shirt for a university that no longer exists?"

"Absolutely not, I'm keeping the spirit alive. Plus I'm advertising. I usually sell a couple at the end of the tour. We should have your size."

"Right on. I'll have to get one for me and one for my friend Audre," she said, following him into the library side of the house. Octavian stepped behind the checkout desk without turning on the computer. Instead he drew out a binder, unlocking the rings and pulling out a series of forms for her to sign. They included a release, acknowledging that she understood the risks of entering a restricted zone and that she could not hold the town of Selah Station, the museum, or the tour guide (Octavian) liable. She signed one after another, as well as a sheet printed front and back listing the symptoms for chlortrofluorine poisoning, for which she should immediately seek medical treatment.

She slid them back. "Not sure if my mother would approve or not."

"It's only out of an abundance of caution," Octavian said, repeating the phrase from the day before, the words themselves incongruous with his light tone.

"Sure."

He tucked the signed pages into a different folder and produced an 11 by 8 ½ printout, this with a map of the Selah Station City Center on one side, and on the other a closer view of the university campus. Octavian set the page down on the counter and drew a line from the Selah Branch Bridge to the cigar-shaped island using a pink highlighter, tracing a path southeast into the area of the campus and around a rectangular section labeled "The Quad."

"Now the fun stuff," he said. "We'll walk to the center of the old town, see the town square, then head over to the campus. Then we'll tour some of the grounds that give us a good view of the buildings. No entering them though; they are not structurally sound. At least that's what the insurance companies think. Then we'll return back the way we came."

She noted the tour did not take them to the site of the coal processing plant on the north end of the island and asked why.

"Too dangerous, wreckage and contaminants. Not much left to see there," he said.

"Can we go there anyway?"

Octavian's eyes behind his wire frames did not meet her own. He capped the highlighter and placed it in the cup, its end tapping the bottom.

"Well, the area was cordoned off right after the disaster. People lost their lives there, but it was always considered too dangerous to even enter for a recovery effort."

Rescue was for survivors; recovery, for corpses.

"Are there still remains?" she asked, her voice low.

"At this point, there is no telling. The place is considered a memorial ground, so to speak. To be honest, years ago I saw a couple varmints, a fox or two, dragging old bones. I chased them off and gave the remains a proper burial. Have not seen anything like that in years. I imagine anything else has been given back to the earth."

Kenia swallowed. She regretted even asking in the first place. "I'm sorry. I'm fine just sticking to the town and campus."

"Plenty to see there," he said, sliding the map across the counter to her. "Let's go then. The hazmat suits are in my car."

Chapter 10

Zone of Alienation

They drove through the quiet Sunday morning streets in Octavian's 2000 Toyota Camry. There was a hole in the floor mat where the heel of his foot rested next to the accelerator, but otherwise he had maintained the car with a meticulous love, the outside waxed and polished as if the paint were still dripping new, the inside dash glossy and smooth—not a single crack despite seventeen years of solar radiation. Even the worn spot in the floor mat was more a testament to his careful, precise nature—having placed his foot in the same place for seventeen years without variance.

The early-twentieth-century buildings slid past through the window, mixed in with nineteenth-century structures, a church, and a few grand Victorians. But with growing frequency, the homes were not well kept like the Corrigans'. Some had boarded up windows, overgrown bushes, and condemned signs in the yards. This did not keep them from being occupied, as many boards had been torn away, and refuse lay scattered in the yards from squatters.

The condemned buildings became more numerous as they neared the north edge of town, property values declining with proximity to the disaster in the old town of Selah Station. The most thriving businesses were liquor stores, same-day check-cashing services, and a Good Will. A small forest grew up between two of the city blocks, large brick warehouses lining either side, the paint on their sides fading, their windows dusty and broken. Octavian provided some explanation. "Before the disaster, most of the residential areas were on the island and the industrial areas here on the West Virginia side. But that changed afterwards as people migrated off the island. For a while folks thought everything would just continue like they had before."

"But that is not what happened?"

Octavian frowned, slowing to take a turn then letting the steering wheel slide through his hands. "Sadly, no. Losing the island, the university, it was like the heart of the community was gone. The administrators tried to reopen the school, but they kept running into red tape from city hall. Didn't help that the university president, Prentice Bridgewater, perished in the blast, along with a lot of the other town leaders. Without them there was no one to take on the city bureaucracy. People lost patience, lost hope, and folks like us moved away."

Octavian slowed as they approached a railroad crossing, the warning lights and traffic gates weathered and inoperable. The tracks themselves ran out onto a trellis that spanned the Potomac River gorge before reaching Selah Island itself. The island was imposing. With no beach to speak of, it met the water with sheer cliff walls, dark eddies of currents swirling at their base. The foliage was thick, but through the trees she could spy buildings hiding, the shingles green with moss or brown with years' worth of fallen leaves. The walls were stained and weather-beaten. She referenced the map Octavian had given her before and looked at the place where she expected to see the campus, but she saw nothing but treetops. How long had it been? Fifty, sixty years? Time enough for the forest to take root.

The northern end was also lost in growth, but the trees were noticeably smaller, as if the area had been clear-cut decades before. In a way, it had been, with the explosion and fire. Like the mast of a shipwreck, a rusted steel tower jutted out at an angle from the trees. Next to it, what looked like the remnants of a catwalk and conveyor belt twisted up into the air, as if leading to some platform that was long destroyed. Perhaps the various sections had been connected at one time, but no more. Jagged metal struts poked out like broken teeth into the gaps now. A crow perched on the ragged remnants of a handrail. Indifferent to the devastation, he shook out his wings, turned his head from side to side, and surveyed his domain, like a raven in a graveyard.

The train trellis was also rotting, the paint peeling in flakes the size of autumn leaves, revealing rusted metal beneath. The sleeper-ties were in different stages of decay. Some had disintegrated completely and fallen into the river below. Others, while intact, had become covered in mushrooms and moss that had proven resistant to the preservatives and tar leeching from their splitting sides. Parallel to the trellis ran a two-way roadway bridge. That was how they would cross, but they would not be driving. The entrance was blocked by jersey walls and two layers of chain-link fence topped with razor wire. Red and white signs barred unauthorized entry in alarming capital letters. Yellow signs with skulls and crossbones announced deadly toxins and carcinogens with smaller black writing listing the legal statutes against trespassing and the accompanying penalties.

"Good thing you got me to sign all those forms before I saw these warning signs. I might not have agreed," Kenia said, only half joking.

"You know lawyers, always overly cautious," Octavian said, opening the Camry door.

A green building with a corrugated tin roof and tin chimney sat next to the gate, its windows facing the roadway. The narrow door in one side opened and an elderly man in blue slacks and a gray jacket with state and city patches sewn on it stepped out as they got out of the Camry. Before the door closed behind the man, Kenia glimpsed a tiny room with a portable television and a seat repaired with packing tape.

"Morning, Buzz," Octavian said, closing his car door.

"Octavian," the man said. He had reached an age of indeterminate number. He could have been in his fifties or seventies. He was an averaged-sized man, a bit bent with age. His face had a hard, chipped look to it, like the edge of an old ax. His skin was sallow and spider-webbed in parts with purple blood vessels. His small colorless eyes looked up and down Kenia's figure, his attention lingering for a moment on her chest, making her wish she had worn something besides a tank top.

"Buzz, this is Kenia. She's interning at the Med-Dent building this summer. I thought I would give her a tour of the old town. Kenia, this is Buzz Grimsby, gateman of Selah Island."

"Morning," Buzz said, unashamed as his eyes dipped from Kenia's face and back to her chest again.

Kenia was relieved when Octavian went to the trunk of the Camry, pulled out the hazmat suits, and handed one to Kenia along with the breathing apparatus, air filter, and bucket-like helmet. She unzipped it without waiting and began to step into it, Buzz still watching her.

"You a student?"

"Yes," she said, taking note of how Octavian sealed his suit. The material was some blend of vinyl and spandex that would keep toxins out but would certainly not breathe. She understood now why Octavian had told her to dress lightly and come early in the morning. It would be hot inside it.

"She sign all the papers?" Buzz asked.

Octavian reassured Buzz that she had, answering with a "Yes, sir," that Kenia found distasteful for some reason, perhaps because it seemed to appease some assumption on Buzz's part regarding his authority. It was nothing spoken, just something that hung in the air, implied. She almost expected the old man to call Octavian "boy."

Buzz Grimsby sniffed, losing interest in her now that her body was concealed by the suit. "No removing any artifacts, no opening your suit, taking off your helmet or gloves," he said with all the indifference of a flight attendant rehearsing a well-worn set of instructions, his demeanor only shifting when he said, "And absolutely no unauthorized visits to the northern end of the island."

Octavian, used to the litany of warnings, said, "Got it," from within his helmet as he checked the seals on Kenia's, then helped her shove her feet into oversized rubber boots.

"Ma'am," Buzz said moving closer, an edge of intimidation in his voice. He was animated now, his pleasure in exercising his authority clear. "I need *verbal* acknowledgement from you that you have heard and understood the restrictions."

"I acknowledge it," Kenia said, waiting for a defiant beat while she pushed her foot into her boot.

"All right," Buzz said, the keys on his belt jingling as he shook the ring until he could pinch the one between his fingers that opened the gate.

"Thanks, Buzz," Octavian said, his tone still light and airy as they passed through the chain-link fence, walked around the jersey walls, and made their way down the middle of the road, the fading double yellow line running between them.

The suit was stuffy and cut Kenia off from the fresh air, the sound of the river rushing below, and the morning birds above. Her own breathing through the respirator was loud. Their voices were strange, Octavian's muffled, her own echoing in her helmet. Then of course there was the constant sound of the suit's material rubbing against itself as she swung her arms and moved one leg in front of the other. She was certain this was what it felt like to walk around in a spacesuit. Out over the expanse of the river gorge and far from old Buzz's hearing Kenia turned to Octavian.

"He always like that?"

"Who?"

"Buzz Grimface back there, the troll of the bridge."

"Buzz Grimsby?" Octavian chuckled. "Pretty much. Takes his job seriously. He's harmless though."

"I'm not so sure," Kenia said, turning to look back at the gate. Buzz was gone, back into his guardhouse. "He sure seemed to feel a bit of privilege back there. Is that representative of most of the white folks in Selah Station?"

She could see Octavian's brow furrow through his visor. "White privilege is just about the only privilege folks around here get. They are salt of the earth people out here. You noticed, the town isn't exactly thriving. Buzz, he's from a different generation, a dying one."

"Still, he was not exactly . . . hospitable."

"This is West Virginia, all the charm of the north and the efficiency of the south."

"JFK said that about Washington, DC."

"And like JFK's, DC, Selah is very much about that space between the ideal and the real," he said, looking into the island, his eyes lifted.

They continued, suits swishing and their boots squeaking. She already felt warm.

"This place is a real passion for you, isn't it?"

"Of course. Selah is an emblem as much as a place, where a community was committed, from early on in this country's history—to integration, black liberation, and education."

"But . . . it was . . . a failure," she said, her words soft and slow. She was unsure how he would react.

"A beautiful failure," Octavian replied, undeterred. "If Edison had stopped because he failed nine hundred and ninety-nine times at the lightbulb, we would not have the illumination that came with the thousandth, successful try."

"You really believe that," Kenia said.

"It's like James Baldwin says, perhaps it is the very struggle in America to come to grips with its imperfections, its injustices, its racial contradictions and conflicts, that will ultimately be valuable, a source of strength, wisdom, resilience—enlightenment even."

"You are one optimistic brother."

"I have to be. Now, I have been remiss; I need to start the tour. What do you know about Selah's founding?"

"That it was founded by some abolitionists from Buffalo who wanted to create an economy that was not based on slave labor."

"Right. The leader of that group was a Reverend, William Bridgewater. The original name of the town was Carder Rock. The model was a moderate success, with mining and river transport being reliable industries here. It led to a more equitable society, but the profits were not necessarily as huge."

"So the southern plantation owners were not persuaded?"

"No, and they of course were reluctant to give up their power. Like Frederick Douglass said, 'Power concedes nothing without demand.'"

"It has to be taken, because it won't be granted without struggle," Kenia said, also paraphrasing Douglass.

"And we still see how an inequitable distribution of power and resources causes problems today. Historically, in the worst cases it leads to nativist demagogues and dictators as people split into factions, almost tribal like."

"Works in African countries," Kenia said, reflecting on what she knew of the politics of many of them. "Then there is of course Le Penn, Duterte, Trump, Brexit, all buoyed by nativist sentiments."

"This is going to be a more interesting tour than I thought. You are well read," Octavian said. "But we digress. So the growth of the original town was disrupted with the outbreak of the Civil War. But even before then, Carder Rock had become a stop on the Underground Railroad. Its proximity to Maryland, the profusion of boats in and out of the docks, and the multiple bridges made for a porous border, excellent for smuggling runaway slaves, conductors, and supplies."

Kenia nodded, stepping over an expansion joint in the bridge, the gap giving her a glimpse of a pylon rising from the water that had become home to a hawk's nest.

"At this point it was no longer William Bridgewater but his sons Reginald and Leonard who were running things. And that was when they met Selah Branch."

"Selah Branch was a person? I thought it was part of the Potomac River."

Octavian nodded, a raconteur who knew he had hooked his audience. "Yes, most people think that. But Selah Branch was a conductor. She was part of the *gens de couleur libres,* free people of color descended from families that had once been part of the French and Spanish colonies in the Caribbean and American south that found themselves part of the United States after the Louisiana Purchase. Selah Branch's own parents in New Orleans were slave owners, as some well-off *gens de couleur* were. Many women of color of her generation in New Orleans could aspire to be business owners or the mistress of a white man. But she turned her back on it all, rebelling against the institution of slavery and her family. Instead she ventured out of New Orleans and became a conductor."

"Why have I never heard of her?"

"Good question. She liberated many people, possibly more than Harriet Tubman, but like so much of Selah Station's history, her story was buried, forgotten." Octavian picked up a few leaves that had blown to the center span of the bridge and leaned over the side to drop them into the long, empty space over the water. "By all accounts, Selah Branch was fierce, courageous, indomitable," he turned to Kenia. "Not to mention beautiful, statuesque, and iron-willed. Reginald and Leonard Bridgewater both fell in love with her, accompanying her on a number of journeys to free slaves, where the brothers would pose as their owners. Many adventures were shared. But in the end, it was Leonard she fell in love with."

Octavian turned, one eyebrow raised. "War came after that, not just in the country, but in the Bridgewater family. Leonard and Selah married—a union that was illegal at the time, of course. Reginald did as well—to some well-to-do heiress—but already the families had become rivals, not friends. During Reconstruction Leonard, Selah, and their children worked for unity and reconciliation. They had a vision of a diverse community, a diverse country, not unlike their own family. It was their son, David Solomon Bridgewater, a mayor, who went on to officially name the city after his mother and found the university."

They neared the end of the bridge, where a second series of signs warned them anew of trespassing violations, carcinogens, and the structural insecurities of old buildings. Octavian paid them no attention, continuing with his story. "Meanwhile, Reginald's children, as if out of spite, established the coal processing plant on the opposite end of the island from the university. They withdrew from the town, establishing that estate on the hill you see there."

Octavian pointed south. From where they stood on the bridge Kenia could see a section of mountainside previously hidden by the buildings of the town. The mansion, its front façade flat and austere, looked more institutional than residential. It was built with stone the color of lead, presenting a stern face to the town below. The expansive slopes around it were clear-cut and a deep green-blue with Kentucky bluegrass. Kenia could see the shapes of additional outbuildings that populated the sprawling grounds.

Octavian continued. "For a long time there seemed to be an uneasy truce between the two branches of the Bridgewater family, represented by the family associated with the university and the side of the family associated with the coal plant. The school and the plant were integrated among black, white, brown, and red folk. Students, whatever their race, could do apprenticeships at the plant or in the company that ran it."

They were making their way onto the island now, Kenia recognizing the time-capsule quality of the place immediately. The first building they passed, an old filling station, was mid-century America preserved, with two antique Esso pumps and a sign advertising "Minute Man Service" and another guaranteeing "New Power and New Discovery" with a tune up of your car. The rubber of the hoses was disintegrated, the window into the pumps' gauges opaque with weathering. A quart oil dispenser lay on its side, its metal rusted to the point of lace. Next to it a Coca-Cola case still contained bottles of the black soft drink.

But if these remnants were important to Octavian's narrative, he did not say so. Instead he pushed onward with the story and down the road. "But all that came to an end with the 1953 disaster. Like I said in the car, after the explosion and the contamination Selah sort of lost its soul. And the only Bridgewaters left were Crowley Bridgewater, the plant owner, and his family, who had been safe up in their mansion the night of the accident. And they did little to help after. Some folks even speculated that it was Crowley who was behind all the resistance in city hall to reestablishing the university on the mainland."

"Why would he do that?"

"Old family rivalries maybe, or just out of spite for losing his plant. But no one ever proved anything. Just talk as far as I'm concerned."

They moved down the road, coming to what had been the original town center until the 1950s, passing hardware stores, hairdressers, diners, and banks. Everything had an abandoned-in-a-hurry air about it, the signs of daily living still evident despite the encroachment of nature. The decaying hulks of 1950s-era cars sat curbside on their rims. Banks of debris—fallen tiles, broken shingles, decomposing leaves—piled against the foundations of buildings.

"There still money left in those banks?" Kenia asked as they passed through a cross street, a stoplight still hanging, creaking in the wind. Their sealed suits, the sense of traveling back in time, the looming presence of an apocalypse: all made her feel like she was in a Hollywood movie.

"Yes, contaminated with chlortrofluorine of course. This is the oldest undisturbed zone of its kind, twice as old as the Chernobyl Zone of Alienation. Great place for biologists and toxicologists to study."

"Zone of Alienation?"

"Most call it the 'Restricted Zone,' but 'alienation' is a closer translation to the Russian."

"Sounds like a novel by Albert Camus."

Octavian turned at the shoulders to look at her through the visor of his suit. "Anyone ever tell you that you sound like an Ivy League undergrad?"

"Anyone ever tell you that you sound like an Ivy League professor?"

"On occasion," he said, his smile flashing through his visor.

They walked without words, the desolation imposing silence. They passed through more intersections, through more empty-but-not-empty streets. Bushes grew out of cracks in the pavement, trees from the roofs, gutters, and drain spouts of buildings. Other roofs had collapsed, leaving a tangle of rafters, shingles, and young foliage sprouting up in what was once a room. When they reached the town square, it was clear to Kenia that at one time it would have been quaint and quintessentially American. The original courthouse had a clock face set up on the frieze over ionic columns. A brick building with lettering over the door that indicated it was the city hall stood catty corner. Bookstores, drug stores, restaurants, a police station, and a tourist bureau filled in the spaces between. In the center of the square was what had once been a grassy park, a statue standing amid a fountain in the center. The fountain had long ago turned into a fetid swamp and the park a meadow choked with summer growth. The marble statue was green with lichen and moss, staring resolutely out into oblivion.

"That is David Solomon Bridgewater, founder of the university," Octavian said, pointing to the statue. "Over there, in front of the mayor's office, you can see where the review stand was set up. The day of the explosion was also the day the people of Selah Station were welcoming home their boys who had fought in Korea. One of the only integrated platoons at the time."

Kenia realized that what she had thought was white bunting hanging on the wreckage of the review stand actually had the faintest remnants of red and blue. A cat walked across a slanted bleacher.

"Watch the cats," Octavian warned. "They are feral. They don't like people, and you don't want them to claw your suit. Chlortrofluorine is not something you want to take home with you."

"Can you see it, the chlortrofluorine?"

"It's colorless and it's absorbed into most of the things around us now. Initial contact of low dosages causes tingling and burning, but the longer-term effects, including cancer, memory impairment, even changes to your personality—increased depression, irritability, aggression—are not too different from mercury poisoning."

"Just worse, if I recall from the warning leaflet you gave me. Where did the cats come from?"

"Left over from the housecats abandoned in the evacuation. Their lifespans are cut short by the poisoning, and they are meaner for it as well. There was even a pack of feral dogs for a while, but they were becoming too aggressive and dangerous. Only about a decade after the evacuation hunters were brought in to trap, poison, or shoot them all."

It was hard not to feel overwhelmed by the ruination. Hotdog, ice cream, and cotton candy stands were still set up on the sidewalks. Her foot kicked a doll, its clothes mere flecks of fabric, its plastic body faded to a sickly shade of alabaster. The weights behind its eyes were still intact, however, moving its eyelids so that it blinked, startling Kenia despite herself.

"Come on," Octavian said. "I'll show you the college."

Chapter 11

Selah University

Octavian turned them in a southeastern direction, following roads that had narrowed on either side from the advance of the forest. Octavian was careful to point out any brambles or thorny weeds to protect the integrity of the suits. He was in his element. Kenia could read the alertness of his body and the extra spring in his step. There were fewer ruins along this stretch of road. In their place was beauty, offered in the untouched forest, the profusion of meadow flowers, and the steady hum of insects and birds. The slow decay of civilization had been replaced by the self-renewing cycles of nature. The interlude of serenity was such a relief that Kenia was actually disappointed when they came upon the buildings of the campus proper.

The brick pathways among the academic buildings were visible, even as weeds had grown between the cracks, displacing the mortar and disrupting the uniformity intended by the masons. Octavian pointed out dorms, lecture halls, and a gymnasium. The campus had less a ghost town feel and more that of an Aztec city, abandoned in the jungle. Absent were the plain lines and unadorned façades of mid-twentieth-century buildings. These academic buildings were constructed with flourishes, detailed cornices, and even the occasional stained glass window. It was not a college built with leftovers for students without futures. The buildings had once displayed all the trappings of grandeur she was used to at Georgetown. The architecture reflected optimism, granting legitimacy to the dreams of the founders, the faculty, and the students; at once grounded in the past and pointing to a future but, most importantly, aspiring to something greater than the school itself.

They stopped on the path at the far end of the quad before a manor house much older than the other buildings. The ceiling had caved in decades before, collapsing the second and third floors below it. In the grass was a toppled statue, ignominiously face down in the dirt, one of the arms broken in two by the fall.

Octavian studied it, sadness creeping into his voice. "This was the house where Leonard and Selah raised their family. It was converted into the first building of the university. This statue is of Leonard Bridgewater."

Kenia took a deep breath. It wasn't that she was unmoved, but she was suddenly uncomfortable. She was not sure if it was the filtered air or the stuffy suit, but she felt dizzy, a pinprick of pain growing between her eyes like the beginnings of a migraine. In her suit she could not rub her temples or even pinch the bridge of her nose; instead she turned her body back around to face towards town. "Shall we make our way back, Octavian? This suit is getting warm."

"Yes, of course," Octavian said. What she could see of his expression looked downcast, as if the melancholy of the place had finally seeped into him as well.

They took a different route back, taking a closer look at some of the classroom buildings and residence halls. Octavian pointed out a charming chapel, the old school well, and a greenhouse that had morphed into a profusion of life, literally bursting, the interior plants pushing the windows outward as the year-round warmth and moisture had allowed the non-native species abandoned there to flourish over the decades. Octavian was explaining how the biologists who came to visit the island found this greenhouse fascinating and had published numerous papers on it, but Kenia found it difficult to focus on his words. The sensation in her forehead was growing so that her thoughts felt scattered, her ability to process what he was saying impaired.

They were slowed further where the path skirted a creek that had eroded into a ravine and taken a portion of the trail with it. Kenia tried to keep up and did her best not to come across rude or uninterested, but at this point her anxiety to leave, the pain between her eyes, and the claustrophobia driving her to shed her suit were all growing unbearable. When they finally returned to the town square, she was sweating so much that her visor was beginning to fog. She walked alongside Octavian, trying to be subtle as she picked up her pace, but Octavian had recovered his enthusiasm as historian and seemed to be finding a point of interest to stop and examine every few steps. Kenia could no longer even understand his words for the ringing in her ears. She tried to remember the symptoms of chlortrofluorine poisoning but could not recall a single one.

Then it happened: a sudden rush like her body was being squeezed all around and then flung as if out of a giant slingshot. The pressure behind her eyes seemed to snap and disappeared. She staggered, braced as if for an impact, her eyes clenched shut, but none came. Her head cleared and she opened her eyes.

The shade of the forest was gone. She stood in unencumbered sunlight, the heat of it radiating through the suit. She could hear her heavy breathing, loud in her helmet, but alongside it the serenity of the woods was broken with the sound of . . . a marching band? Accompanying the band were cheers, applause, and the honking of car horns.

This is a dream. I'm hallucinating again.

She looked around, unbelieving, at an implausible scene: a marching band, brass instruments shining in the sun, the skin of huge drums gleaming white, while the players moved in step before a reviewing stand that had seconds ago been derelict. Now it was full of people and surrounded on all sides by a crowd, a mixture of black, white, and all hues in between. A man in a gray suit and a *café-au-lait* complexion stood at the podium, a darker, comely woman in a white blouse, blue skirt, and red sash stood next to him wearing white gloves and a box hat. They waved arms and clapped their hands as a regiment of uniformed men—colored and white—marched after the band in lock-step unity, saluting as they passed.

The sign hanging over the bright, un-faded bunting read: *Welcome Home 132nd Infantry. Selah Station Salutes its Korean War Heroes.*

American flags fluttered in the breeze blowing down from the mountains and across the town square. As the measured squares of marching soldiers passed, the townspeople threw flowers and confetti. Closer by, the youngest children ran about the square while wives and mothers looked on proudly at their sons in uniform. The cars, the stores, the statues, the park benches, and the food carts she had just seen rotting were restored, as if untouched by time. It was a hallucination, she was certain, conjured by hypoxia caused by her suit. But it seemed so undeniably real. Four tiny children, their shoes off, their pants rolled to their knees, were wading into the water of the fountain—that moments before had been a fetid pool. The children were all different shades of brown and olive, with one white child who was turning pink with sunburn.

Kenia lost her balance, her foot splashing down into the water and attracting the attention of the children. They stared at her, in her suit, wide-eyed. The youngest began to cry in terror. And why not, she must have looked like a monster. She stumbled out of the fountain, sloshing her feet through the water, turning to where she had last seen Octavian.

The hallucination robbed him from her sight as well. Instead, she saw a wall of people, their backs turned as they cheered on the passing of another phalanx of soldiers. It could have been Atlanta or New York for the mixture of black and white people next to one another, cheek to jowl. One man, however, alerted by the sound of the children's cries, turned and spotted her. He wore red suspenders holding up cotton pants. His sleeves were rolled to his elbows, and a derby hat rested at an angle on his head. A white press pass poked out of the ribbon around the crown. In his hands was an antique Kodak camera. He held it up to his face and the aperture clicked.

Then it was quiet again. The rush of the fountain, the cries of the children, the voices of the crowd—all gone. The shade and silence of the woods had returned, and she heard the blessed sound of Octavian's muffled voice droning on. He stopped and began calling her name.

She was disoriented, standing a stone's throw from where she had been before. Octavian was turned away from her but found her quickly enough.

"There you are. I lost track of you there for a minute. The peripheral vision on these things is terrible."

Her breathing was still heavy. She looked back at the swamp that was the fountain, the surface of the water covered in lily pads. A frog leapt and plopped into the muck. The grandstand was in ruin and abandoned, not a person, or even a cat, on its planks. No children. No soldiers. No families.

"Kenia, you all right there?"

"I think I'm overheating. I need to get out of this suit."

◊

Back at the library, she took a tall glass of water from Octavian and drank it down in a series of gulps, then asked for another. They had driven back in silence, the suits returned to the trunk. Octavian was solicitous, his expression grave, his voice gentle. As she had recovered, Kenia had taken to reassuring him.

"It was just the heat," she said, taking another glass of water. "And a headache. I'm still running a sleep deficit from the bus ride up, I suppose."

"Have you had spells like this before?" he asked.

She thought of her previous experience outside the Med-Dent building the day before, even her particularly vivid dreams of late, but what could she really say about them? What did she want to share?

"No, well, not really." She bought time by taking another long drink.

Octavian was not ready to break off his attention, his piercing scholarly stare studying her. She had nearly finished the second glass when she was saved by a knocking at the door. A clutch of children in their church clothes pressed at the door.

"Oh, I didn't realize how late it was," Octavian said.

"You're open on Sundays?"

"Just after church, to catch some of the lunch, brunch, and church bunch."

He hurried to the door, greeting the children by their names. The children would never guess at his concern just moments before, but she could still hear the heaviness in his voice. Once the kids had disappeared into the aisles of the children's section, he returned to her. She handed him the glass and thanked him.

"Do you need anything else, something to eat?"

"No thanks," she said, her mind shifting to another thought. "Octavian, you said yesterday you had microfilm of newspapers going back decades."

"To antebellum days, yes."

"Would you have copies from the day of the incident at the coal plant?"

"Sure," he said, his eyes narrowing in a question. "Are you sure you want to look at them now?"

"What can I say, you piqued my curiosity."

"All right, follow me."

He set her up at the machine that looked like an old-school computer monitor but was actually a projector screen for microfilms. She had used them in the school library, taking pleasure in how the old newspaper pages flew past in a rapid blur with only a minute motion of her hands on the knobs.

Octavian loaded a canister from 1953, dialing the knob to August while headlines scrolled past, declaring the end of the war, the partitioning of Korea into North and South, as well as local news stories, the name Bridgewater showing up more than a few times. Finally he slowed when he came to Saturday, August 22nd.

"Here you go," he said, and he went to attend to the children calling for him from across the library. He brought his finger to his lips and shushed them, reminding them it was a library.

Kenia turned to the newspaper, the Selah Station Picayune, the pictures of people, the cut of their clothes, the hairstyles, the cars, all so eerily familiar.

The children's parents caught up to them in the library. They were also in their church clothes. Kenia felt self-conscious. She simply hoped they would not notice the black girl with braids and a sweaty tank top, her eyes unblinking as she slowed the scroll of the passing editions. The evening edition had not even featured the explosion, but the next day's front page was plastered with images of smoke and flames, DEVASTATION AND EVACUATION in tall, screaming letters.

That was already too late. She dialed back to the evening edition from the day before, the back page coming first. There, in a little afterthought, space-filling column called "Unexplained Events," she found what she was looking for: a fuzzy picture of a figure next to a fountain, dressed in a twenty-first-century industrial hazmat suit. The visor obscured the identity of the person inside, but she recognized the scene, down to the faces of the children looking up in horror. The caption below read: "An unknown person appeared to scare a few children at the victory celebration. According to reports, the prankster disappeared without a trace. 'He was there and then he wasn't,' said Sebastian Andersen, the photographer for the Picayune who took the photo. 'Strangest thing.'"

Strange indeed, she thought, confusion and horror rising up in her own gut until she realized she had to run to the library bathroom for the second time in two days.

This time she did vomit.

Chapter 12

Motocross and Microaggressions

"Kenia, meet Kermit," Thea said as they turned the corner to the backlot of the Med-Dent building. "Kermit" was concealed beneath a blue plastic tarp which Thea unhooked and snapped off with a flourish, revealing a two-wheeled dirt bike with a sweeping frame, fluorescent green paneling, and an expansive mud flap, also fluorescent green, set nearly a foot above the knobby front tire.

"Kermit . . ." was all Kenia could muster in response.

"I call him that because he's green and he definitely likes to get muddy."

"Ok, a Kermit is a motorcycle," Kenia said, wondering how stupid she sounded as she stated the obvious.

"Well, an off-road motorcycle," Thea corrected. "It is what you will need to get to some of the places in our catchment area."

Kenia nodded, adjusting the strap on her backpack.

Thea, for the first time, detected her apprehension. "You, uh, ever ride a motocross bike before?"

"Only bikes I've ridden had pedals."

"Oh, well, this is a Kawasaki KX450F," Thea said by way of an explanation. "It's a 2009, so its five speed and fuel injected." She used a key on her chain to open a heavy windowless door into a storage closet, entered, then emerged with a green helmet that matched the color of the bike and a pair of black nylon zipper bags that she slung on either side of the seat. "It's a good model as Kawasakis go. My brother and I have kept it running pretty good."

"You ride it?"

"Of course. For all my house visits."

"Huh, I guess I was expecting a government vehicle."

"This is our government vehicle."

"I meant a car."

"You mean some late-model, gray, boring, domestic four-door sedan that would get stuck in the mud? This is much more practical and fun. I guess we could always ask Ms. Jolene to use her car, but with her at the conference this week, I think you are stuck with Kermit."

Kenia did not want to ask Ms. Jolene for any favors.

"I guess I will have to use Kermit, then."

"That's the spirit. We've suped it up, adjusting the swing arm so it's a bit more rigid. Makes for a bumpier ride, but the trade-off is better traction."

"You work on it, too?" Kenia asked, taking a tentative step closer to Kermit as Thea rolled it forward, looking incongruous next to it in her lavender scrubs.

"What, you think a girl can't fix things? You are worse than some men," she said, shaking her fist in exasperation.

"No, I'm sorry—"

"I'm just messing with you. But you do know how to ride, right?"

"I know fatalities are thirty-seven times higher per mile on a motorcycle than a car and that ER nurses refer to them as 'donorcycles.'"

"Huh," Thea said, wrinkling her nose. "I'll take that as a no. Well balancing is just like a pedal bike. Accelerator is here in the grip—it's your gas pedal. Transmission is worked through this foot lever. You can move from neutral to first or second, like a stick shift in a car, but higher gears have to be engaged in order. It's one down, four up action. Neutral is half a click up or down, so you can go from first to second in one motion. Got it?"

Kenia offered a flat, "No."

They spent the better part of the next hour on the finer points of motorcycle mechanics, riding, and control. Kenia flinched when Thea mounted the bike, jumped down on the pedal, and revved it to life with a sputtering roar.

"It's got a loud exhaust," Thea yelled, her wrist flexing as she gunned the engine, a cloud of exhaust dispersing from the rear. "But it's got good power right off the bottom and continues into the top range."

Eventually Kenia graduated from passenger, riding behind Thea and holding onto her waist, to taking a test ride around the block solo. She knew she was going painfully slow, the engine coughing and sputtering and choking on numerous occasions. But by midmorning she was feeling more confident, going as fast as twenty miles an hour, even learning to enjoy the quickness of the acceleration and the surprising backwards tug of inertia that came in response. It felt reckless and freeing at once. Although she did feel conspicuous riding through the city streets, the loud exhaust heralding her approach from blocks away. But she grew used to it, since the folks she passed were unperturbed. Some even waved. In the helmet she guessed they took her for Thea.

In the days that followed, Kenia grew more confident. Thea showed her how to lock her phone in the mount on the handlebars so that she could use her GPS to navigate in and around Selah Station. Before long, Kenia was making home visits and initiating the first of her interviews on Healthy-Bytes. The days with respondents in town were easy. Some of their homes were close enough to walk to, but Thea encouraged her to ride for the practice.

In sessions, Kenia ran through demographic questions quickly. Social-economic status was measured by proxy items such as whether or not the respondent owned big-ticket items such as televisions, cars, washer-dryers, HV/AC. She was surprised how many homes did not have these, or if they did, chose to not use them in order to reduce utility bills. Clotheslines were used often in place of dryers. ACs were frequently not even turned on, leaving her to swelter at the kitchen table while she interviewed housewives, retirees, and the unemployed. Those who had jobs weren't home—two-income households were rare—and many were recipients of welfare and/or disability.

The data did not lie. Through verbal autopsies—asking what close, recently deceased relatives had died of, Kenia tallied up figures that matched her pre-readings. High rates of heart disease, alcohol and drug related deaths, not to mention startling numbers of suicides. Ms. Jolene had not exaggerated the dire picture of poor health and endemic poverty in Selah Station. Kenia determined that the closest hospital in the next county was the largest employer in the region, and nearly half the visits from the residents of Selah Station were to the ER, as a substitute for regular care. The next largest employer after the hospital was road construction, but that was seasonal and inconsistent.

Kermit took her out of downtown into the surrounding "hills and hallows," as Thea called the outskirts. Kenia followed her GPS off state roads onto unpaved one-lane drives that climbed into the mountains on switchbacks. She learned how to downshift for going downhill in order to save the brakes from overheating. The dirt roads were enclosed by trees, the roads' surface alternating between gravel, hard-packed earth, and mud. The homes she visited were modest, some only trailers, all without manicured lawns, distinct property lines marked by fences or hedges. Yards blurred with the edge of the woods and driveways with the lawns, as cars sat parked on grass as often as driveways. Nothing was new: old model cars, old rusting swing sets, old lawn furniture, and old lawn mowers populated the yards. Plastic kiddie pools were lined with dead leaves and filled with greenish rainwater. Some houses were foreclosed upon and abandoned, others had foreclosured and condemned signs but were still occupied. A couple were burnt down.

"A lot of fires," she remarked to Thea one afternoon while she collated her notes from the day.

"Burn your house down then collect the insurance money," Thea said, as she typed up her own notes from office visits from that day. She was unfazed at the decay and blight that Kenia reported from her trips. Thea knew the neighborhoods and had seen it all before. Each morning she would check Kenia's list of homes to visit, warning her away from the homes that were known meth labs.

"How do you know they are meth labs? Have you been inside?"

"Oh yeah. I'm the only medical care a lot of them get. But I wouldn't advise you to go in there alone."

Kenia considered Thea, this medium-sized woman with girl-next-door looks, reassessing her.

"Why you staring at me like that?"

"Nothing, I just like your earrings."

"Thanks," Thea said, touching them to remember which she was wearing. They were actually studs, made from turquoise. "Got them from a local Native American woman, one of my patients," Thea said. "She gets the turquoise from her people living on reservations out west."

Kenia slid her tablet into her bag and began to tie her hair back with a bandana, the helmet resting on the floor between her feet.

"You are starting to get used to that bike," Thea said.

"Yeah, I had to get over the idea that it's not something black people do."

"Why not?"

Kenia paused, realizing that Thea, trying something for the first time, likely had never had to ask herself the question "Is this something *white* people do?"

"Well, I just have never seen a black person on a dirt bike before. Sort of like, we don't do NASCAR, microbrews, acapella groups, LL Bean . . ."

"Kenia, you are funny. That's all I'll say," she laughed, turning to the monitor and checking for the next appointment.

◊

In reality, in those first two weeks of interviews, it was riding Kermit that had been Kenia's favorite part of what were turning into depressing sessions. She found herself sitting down on living room couches or at kitchen tables, trying to put the Trump-Pence signs in the front yard or Confederate flags hanging next to the doors out of her mind. Fortunately, her questions mostly did not delve into politics, although more than once she found herself biting her lip and trying to fix her expression into something neutral when respondents claimed "not to need Obamacare, 'cause they could get their health insurance from the Affordable Care Act." Or surprise that she was so "well-spoken." Not a few children asked to touch her braids.

Kermit was an easy icebreaker, and Kenia herself benefited from association with Thea, whose home visits and referrals for treatment had saved more than a few lives.

"Thea is the only doc I see," a retired postal worker named Shirley said, tapping her cigarette into an ashtray, her inhaler on the table next to it.

The lifestyle of most of the residents Kenia found to be empty, desultory, pathetic—characterized by long hours of watching television in homes isolated from neighbors and separated by large lots and acres of woods. Men passed out from drinking on the couches by midafternoon. Wives and girlfriends made efforts to hide empty beer cans and bottles when Kenia entered, but oftentimes the trash was overflowing with them, if they made it to the trash at all.

She met Tracy, who lived with a herniated disc and took care of her four children and the neighbor's children too. Her household scored low on Kenia's SES measures, but they were slightly better off than their neighbors since her husband occasionally had work on a road crew. When they talked about the cost of groceries, taking inventory of the pantry, Tracy explained that she did not pay cash for any of her groceries.

"EBT?" Kenia asked.

"No," Tracy said, looking down at her hands then back at Kenia. She took a drag from her cigarette then blew the smoke away to the side of them. "You won't bust me if I tell you?"

"Bust you? For what—I mean, no, of course not, that is not my purpose."

"Well, I have a doctor who writes me prescriptions for oxycontin for my back. I haven't exactly been truthful with him. I'm in constant pain, but I've got more pills than I need. I trade them for groceries."

"Trade them?"

"Yeah, there's a whole market, underground you would call it, I guess. We trade oxycontin for everything here, lawnmowing, groceries, car repair, whatever you need. I try not to take them too much. I've never crushed or snorted them. But people do."

Kenia looked at Tracy's three-year-old boy, who was wearing a faded T-shirt and pull-up diapers. He was sucking on a box of High-C.

"I know it's illegal," Tracy said. "But jobs are scarce here. I need to feed my kids." She picked up her son and set him on her lap. Kenia's eyes traced the strings of cigarette smoke curling around his head. "Diapers are expensive."

"Yeah, I understand," Kenia said, turning off the voice recording on her tablet and erasing the last few minutes of conversation. Tracy's husband remained in the living room, sunk deep into an easy chair, the only indication that he was not asleep the steady progression of one channel on the television to the next: sitcom reruns, Fox News, sports, the hunting and fishing channel . . . . "Have you done any physical therapy for your back injury?"

Tracy snorted, "Where would I do it? Nearest hospital is Mercy General, ninety minutes away." She put her son down, crushed her cigarette in the ashtray, then reached to the pack for another.

Chapter 13

Selah in Sepia Tones

It was the last Friday in June when Kenia finished collecting quantitative data on enough randomized homes, breaking the fifty mark, and shifted to collecting qualitative data through in-depth interviews. Diving into her work had provided a welcome, immersive distraction. After long days of riding Kermit, conducting surveys, and collating data, she was exhausted each night, falling into deep, dreamless slumbers. She had been untroubled by dreams, hallucinations, and fugue states and was ready to chalk it all up to the fatigue and stress from her arrival.

The first respondent in her list was Martha Andersen. The home was in an area Kenia already knew, just a ten-minute ride across town, over the bridge to Maryland, and up state road 521. It was an area of less blight, with some scenic views of the valley from the tree breaks. She packed a lunch and planned to find a peaceful overlook to set herself down, review her notes, and eat, post-interview.

The turn-off was marked by a mailbox with a patina of green lichens growing on it. It was missing the number six in "106," but she knew she had the right address from the other mailboxes along the road. She rolled down the driveway at a slow 5-7 mph. Many of the homes could be set far back in the woods, the farther back the more likely they were used as meth labs. But she was pleasantly surprised to see this home come into view after only riding a few yards. The garage was derelict, leaning off-center. The yard was given over to leaves and deadfall, and one of the trashcans was on its side, crows picking at the remnants stuck to fast-food containers. A Dodge minivan with an apparatus for a wheelchair was parked in the driveway. Folks running a meth lab would not be receiving disability checks, she reassured herself. On the other hand, she remembered a story Thea had told her the week before of a son who had buried his mother in the backyard while collecting her welfare and disability checks for two-and-a-half years before he was caught.

A dog barked as she approached the front door. She knocked. She waited a long while for the door to open. The woman who stood on the other side was her own height but easily two hundred pounds heavier than Kenia. She had deep folds of skin on her neck and a sallow complexion that betrayed long years of tobacco use. Her eyes looked drowsy, the rims red, the skin around them gray, and the whites jaundiced. She was breathing heavily, as if the walk to the door had taxed her. Her hair was a greasy blond with exposed gray roots.

"Good morning, are you Ms. Andersen?"

"Yes, yes I am," she said, friendly enough.

"I am Kenia Dezy, a student intern from the Med-Dent building downtown. You might have received a phone call or a questionnaire in the mail describing a study—"

"Oh yes, Ms. Jolene from downtown called me," Martha said, her voice hearty over her panting. "She said you would be coming up. Come in."

Kenia made note that, for once, Jolene had done something to help her. Since returning from her conference, her attitude towards Kenia could have been categorized as benign neglect, Thea having been the one to provide her with guidance and support. Kenia didn't mind.

Martha swung the door open. The dog, a gray brown mutt, wagged its tail and sniffed her. "That's Mocha. Don't mind him, he's friendly. Likes visitors," Martha said.

The house was cluttered, the air stale with the scent of cigarettes, litter boxes, and the smoke from burners on the stove, which were in need of a good scrubbing. The television was blaring the history channel, as a baritone voiceover narrated black and white footage from World War II. The audience consisted of a young man in his twenties wearing jean shorts and a gray hoodie. He was sunk in a leather recliner and made no effort to rise and greet Kenia, nor to hide the bottle of Smirnoff tucked between his thigh and the arm of the chair. Martha sat herself down on an adjacent recliner, the cushion beneath her worn into a deep groove from frequent use. She gestured to a couch across from them where the dog, Mocha, was already sitting, his tail swishing back and forth.

Kenia sat down next to Mocha, a cloud of dog and cat hair erupting as she did so. Mocha pressed his nose to her hand and licked her. A cat reclined on the top of the entertainment center, watching with narrowed eyes. Another sat upright on the back of the couch, as if ready to leap to safety if Kenia's next move made it necessary.

"That is Tom and the other cat is also named Tom. This is my son Joel."

Joel lifted the bottle of Smirnoff in a sort of half toast, half salute. "I'm going to detox tomorrow morning."

"Ok then," Kenia said, careful to pick what she hoped were the right words.

"Joel, this is Keen-ya."

Close enough.

"Ms. Andersen, I'm here to ask you a few questions about an app we're developing to help households make," she hesitated at the phrase "healthier choices," choosing instead to say, "more informed choices about their," she hesitated again at the word "diet," and instead chose, "grocery shopping."

She pulled out her tablet and stylus and got ready to take notes.

"You can write on that?" Martha asked.

"Yes," Kenia said, opening a file on Martha.

"It's called *technology*, Mom," Joel said.

"Joel, can you turn down the TV?"

If he heard her, he ignored her.

Kenia began with the warm up questions, moving from close-ended to open: how long had she lived in Selah Station—all her fifty-seven years; what changes had she seen in that time?

"Oh, many. I grew up here, and we lived closer to town. My father was a photographer for the Picayune. Things were different then; people still had jobs, families were intact. Folks still had pride in this place, black and white. We had more folks like you."

"Black?"

"Yep. Most migrated out though, after the island was quarantined and the university closed. Selah is not diverse like it once was," she said with an audible sigh.

"I've heard that from others."

"Now it just seems everyone is white and on welfare or disability or both. And that, well it's sad. When I was growing up, people could look after themselves. It was just a given that you would repair a car, patch a roof, hunt, or grow your own food. You fixed your own pipes, mowed your own lawn, chopped your own firewood for the winter, or shoveled your own coal."

"And where do you go to buy your groceries?"

"Well, there is the mart downtown off main. That's about it. There's some selection at the Gas-n-Go, but when we're going to stock up, we drive over to Martinsburg."

Kenia made further notes, confirming Selah Station's status as a "food desert" and inquired about the time to drive to Martinsburg.

"Forty-five minutes," Martha said. "One way. We go two or three times a year." Martha cut herself off and leaned forward, rocking herself into a standing position. The seat cushion hissed as air seeped back into it. "Let me get you some coffee. Do you take cream or sugar?"

"Neither, thanks."

Kenia waited, her hands wrapping around the edges of the tablet while the television narrator described the heroics of bands of marines on Iwo Jima in tones breathless with import and patriotic reverence. Kenia stared down at her notes, tapping the screen with the stylus.

"I bet you think we're pretty primitive out here," Joel said over the television.

"Uh, no, not really."

"Come on. It's clear as day what Hollywood thinks of us out here in the country. Look at how we're portrayed on *South Park* or *Parks and Recreation*. Folks think we're flyover country, just like the backward folks in *Deliverance*. That sure is a nice tablet you got there."

Kenia swallowed and wished she could turn her wrist away to hide her tech.

"Your flat screen is nice. It's bigger than the one in my dorm."

Joel snorted. "Your 'dorm.' At college. Which one?"

Kenia looked at her feet for a moment before she replied, "Georgetown."

"Georgetown. That's about sixty thousand a year, right?"

"Something like that, but a lot of people are on financial aid."

She was stuck, afraid to ask if he went to college or wanted to. His resentment was palpable. "You, uh, really headed to rehab tomorrow? That's a big step."

He glared at her in silence, blinking as if trying to focus. He ignored her question. "So many sophisticated folks in the city look down on us out here, you know. It's not a red state, blue state thing as much as an urban-rural thing."

Kenia looked over her shoulder to the kitchen where Martha had disappeared to. She could hear dishes and cupboards but did not see any sign of Martha's immediate return. She patted Mocha on the head.

"He's a sweet dog."

"You're ignoring me."

Now Kenia felt a flash of anger and changed tack. "No, actually, I'm not. I'm a guest in your home, and I'm choosing to be polite. I try not to talk politics while on an interview anyway."

"You don't, but what are all these questions about health and shopping? It's all about social-economic status. It's about the distribution of resources and services, and what is politics if not that?"

"You have a point, Joel."

"You think most people in the city know where their food is grown, where the coal and natural gas comes from? Where their trash goes? Or where their monitor, with all its cancer-inducing rare-earth elements, goes when they are finished with it and want to buy the next version that Apple tells them to?"

She remembered her environmental health class lectures where the same topics came up, although she knew for a fact that most electronic waste ended up in third-world dumps where under-aged children hammered it to pieces to salvage the parts, without protection from the toxins released into their bodies and into the environment. She had seen such places on the outskirts of Lagos. But she chose not to argue the point. "No, most people don't know where these things come from or go."

"You know the recovery after 2008, it came mainly to the cities. Out here, we're still getting pummeled. No jobs, no new businesses. Did you know the suicide rate here is five times what it is in the city?"

"I did actually. It's my job to know."

"'It's my job,' she says," he mocked. "We're just statistics to you, aren't we?" He took a pull from his Smirnoff bottle.

Kenia turned to the kitchen. The movement startled Tom the cat from his perch on the back of the couch. "Maybe I'll go in and help your mother."

"Funeral homes are the only growth industry here in Selah, you know. That and Army recruiters."

"Then why haven't you gotten a job there?" she snapped, surprising herself. "Why don't you move to the city?"

He snorted. "There is this wall that surrounds your cities called the 'cost of living.' It's like a system for keeping poor folks like us out."

"Are you really going to claim systematic, institutional discrimination?" she said, indignant. She could not help the incredulous laugh building in her and thought it best to leave before she said something she would regret. "I think I'm going to go see what your mother is doing."

"Jim Crow has been over for more than fifty years," Joel said.

She stopped, halfway to the door to the kitchen, and turned, knowing she could not let his comment go unanswered, even if she knew he had said it just to provoke her. "Sure, and the War on Drugs and mass incarceration has done its best to take its place." She cocked her head, deciding to take the plunge and engage Joel. "Funny how there is so much talk about the opioid epidemic here in your flyover states, where you are fortunate it's treated as a health problem, whereas in urban neighborhoods it's a criminal problem that has led to more blacks being under the control of the penal system than were ever enslaved in this country."

"I've heard that statistic. It's been debunked."

"By which reputable news outlet, Breitbart?"

"Your people are always playing victim."

Kenia felt the blood rush to her face. "And your people are always getting played by the rich. They've been pitting poor whites against poor blacks for four hundred years. That game has been around longer in your 'Merica than democracy. Seems like they can always count on the bigotry and inferiority complexes of poor white folks to do their dirty work, who've been too brainwashed by closed fundamentalist, religious 'revivals' to adopt any type of critical thinking."

Joel took a pull of his Smirnoff, staring at her over the length of his bottle. He lowered it, took a gasp of air, and said, "And you and your liberal friends gave up on us, didn't you? We're irredeemable, with the original sin of being white, aren't we, in a country you think is irredeemable too, that you'd rather tear down than build up. Talk about extreme. You talk about fundamentalists, closed thinking? Those students on college campuses seem pretty zealous and close minded to me, shutting out speakers they don't like, falling over one another to assert who has the most righteous claim to an oppressed identity. It's sanctimony on the highest level, a competition all its own, an obsession with liberal purity. Do they have any practical solutions, or just disgust for anyone with a modicum of 'privilege?'"

"You seem to be a very angry man," was all Kenia could manage to offer in reply.

"I'll say," he said taking another swig from the bottle. "Donald Trump was our trashcan through your skyscraper, luxury apartment window. He's our Watts Riot, a wake-up call to all the elitists who have forgotten us."

"Let me guess, you're not racist, but you don't think Obama cared about you . . . that he just didn't get you?"

"You know, I voted for Obama."

"So that makes you enlightened?"

"No, but it proves I'm not racist."

"But you voted for Trump."

"Proudly."

"I don't know, seems like the very definition of racism to me."

"Come again, how do you see that?"

"Think about how exceptional President Obama had to be to get elected: his education at elite institutions, his perfect family, his scandal-free career as a politician, a bestselling author who wrote his own books. All Trump had to be was rich and white and he could still get away with being racist, assaulting women, mocking the disabled, being a traitor and a crook, and he still got your vote."

"Trump is a jerk, we know it. But we'd rather have him on our side. A rich billionaire with a big mouth. If you put him in a Marvel movie and put him in an iron suit, he could be a hero."

She pictured Colton and his Ironman figurine. "I guess I'm grateful that Captain America kicked Tony Stark's rich ass in Civil War, then," she said, surprising herself that Marvel would inform the retort she would reach for. Chiazam would have been proud, even if she wasn't. She got up and walked to the kitchen. She had nothing left to say.

◊

Kenia found Martha in the kitchen. She was ready to explain that she had to go, but before she could open her mouth she saw Martha working her away across the kitchen, over the peeling linoleum floor to the table where she had set up a chipped coffee and tea set. Martha rubbed at a stain on the table, then another, then another, her face flushed either with embarrassment or effort. Despite her present state of fury, Kenia felt a wave of pity for the woman, who made apologies for the state of the kitchen but had clearly taken pains to prepare a welcome.

Kenia took a deep breath, centering herself, trying to reset her emotions and be grateful.

"So nice to have company. I'm sorry the place is such a mess," Martha said, setting out two mugs. "Please sit down."

Kenia did so. Martha followed, grimacing as she squeezed into the chair, Kenia experiencing another stab of pity for the shame she could read on the Martha's face for not fitting into her own furniture, for living with the bitter pill of her son, and not being able to offer him a future outside of Selah Station.

Kenia thanked her for the coffee then asked if Martha had a cell phone.

"Yes, I do," she said, drawing out a clamshell flip phone.

Kenia stared. "Oh, the app we're piloting is for smartphones."

"The app?"

"A program," Kenia said, seized with her own growing sense of shame that she truly had nothing to offer this woman for her time. She was simply taking her data, reducing her to a number, when it was clear that Martha just wanted to have coffee and be treated like a human.

Kenia decided to go off-script from the questions she was scripted to ask for the interview. She pulled out her own phone and tapped the Healthy-Bytes icon.

"See, you use this app with the camera feature on your smartphone and scan the UPC codes on the items in your pantry."

"Oh, there is a camera on there?"

"Yes," Kenia said, pushing through with her explanation. She stepped over to the pantry where the folding doors were open. She started to scan items. The usual offenders were all present: chips, packages of cookies, cupcakes, soda, sugary cereals, artificial sweeteners, bagels. She asked if she could go into the fridge, pausing for Martha to consent before she opened the door and scanned the ground beef, hamburger patties, processed cheeses, frozen pizzas, and tubs of ice cream. When she finished she sat back down at the table and let the app process the data, the hourglass icon spinning while she took in the rest of the kitchen.

The dishes were piled in the sink, which Kenia surmised was the source of the foul odor. Nothing was new, the only exception was the Sports Illustrated Swimsuit Calendar. It's glossy pages hung in a prominent position over the kitchen table. An impossibly curvy, olive-skinned woman in a bikini that seemed made of string and tissue paper was stepping out of the surf on a tropical beach, the tresses of her auburn hair kissed by the sun, the toned muscles of her legs glittering with a sprinkling of white sand. Her lips were full and parted her eyes staring deeply into the camera. Notions of patriarchy, the male gaze, and the objectification of women floated to mind from Kenia's class the previous semester in women's studies. She felt a new surge of dislike for Joel as he sat stewing in the next room.

She was rescued from her thoughts by the app, which beeped, announcing that its calculations were complete. "All right, it has now estimated what it will cost to choose healthier alternatives and listed where you can buy them, factoring in costs to drive to the nearest stores."

"Well, I'll be!" Martha said, astounded.

The answers came up on the screen with links to maps to stores with healthy selections—the nearest being sixty miles away. Kenia scrolled past them and instead looked at the budget results. "Looks like you could shift to a healthier grocery list for just $4.75 more per day."

"That's not bad."

"No," Kenia said, working out the yearly budget, grimacing when she came to the result. "Oh," was all she could say.

"What's wrong?"

"Well, it comes to $1,733.75 more per year."

Martha let out a hearty laugh. "Well we can't afford that! Not with my disability and Joel's unemployment checks."

"No, no you can't," Kenia said, crestfallen.

What am I doing here?

She swiped the screen closed in a hurry, as if she had stumbled across a porn site. It suddenly did seem absurd to the point of obscene. Martha could see it in her face.

"You are a sweet young lady. Your heart is in the right place."

"But . . . I don't know what an app will really do here."

Martha laughed again, her voice going soft, shifting into some maternal mode. "Wait here a moment," she said, before using the end of the table to lift herself up. She went into the next room and returned with an ancient photo album, the vinyl cover peeling. It creaked as she opened it and began to flip through the pages. In sepia-stained black and white photos Kenia saw a town she knew and didn't. It was Selah Station mid-century, without the boarded-up businesses, abandoned college buildings, and burnt-out factory ruins.

The Selah Station she had seen in her visions.

"This was the place I grew up," Martha said. "These are my pop's photos. You always hear folks going on about the good old days. Those of us who remember old Selah, we know the good old days were not good for all. We know that this country was founded on genocide and slavery. America has not always lived up to its ideals."

"Sounds familiar."

Kenia watched the pictures of people at lunch counters and drive-ins pass by. Girls wore pleated skirts, oxfords, and blouses without frills, identical to the young women she had seen walking down the street to the movie theater. Here, as then, the groups of people were mixed, black, brown, white, and every shade in between.

"But Selah, it always seemed, was different. We sort of felt like we were living up to those ideals better than other places. It was not a bad way of life," Martha said.

"Yeah, it seems like it was a real loss."

"It was." Martha slowed towards the back of the album. "Here are the pictures my father took the day of the blast, at the celebration just a few hours before."

Celebration. The welcome home. Sebastian Andersen.

Kenia realized with a start that she had seen Martha's father. He was the Picayune photographer who had—

Kenia scanned the photos more closely now. They were well framed, each with good contrast and focus. She did not see the picture of the "prankster" in the space suit. Out of focus and blurry, Sebastian likely had decided not to include it in his personal album. Her eyes did fall, and remain, on one photo, taken at night, that seemed to show a hazy image of a tanker truck with a square cab barreling around a corner, tipped on its wheels as it took a turn at a reckless speed. The driver was engaged in what looked like a struggle with a white man hanging onto the outside by the side-view mirror.

Kenia blinked and the photo was gone, replaced by children playing in water spouting from a fire hydrant on a hot day.

"Wait," she asked Martha. "Can you flip back?"

Martha did so and did again. Kenia could not find the photo of the truck again. "So strange . . ." she said.

"What is that?"

"Oh, nothing," Kenia said, a sinking feeling she had not felt in weeks returning.

Martha continued to the end of the album. The last photos were of the long lines of cars on the traffic bridge over the river gorges as families evacuated. Black and white children leaned out the windows, some even in the same cars together, looking back at the smoke clouds rising from the north end of the island, the prevailing winds pushing the fallout in slanting shafts over the neighborhoods and homes they would never be able to return to.

Martha closed the album. "Happier times then. But we can't forget. That would mean giving up on the future."

"Uh, yeah," Kenia said, not sure at all what Martha meant.

Chapter 14

Do the Right Thing

Kenia thanked Martha, a note of near apology in her voice, as she better understood Ms. Jolene's own skepticism towards her app and her internship. Despite that, Martha stood in the doorway holding Mocha in her arms and waving goodbye with his paw.

Joel did not look up from the television as Kenia left. She was glad for it.

Kenia kicked started Kermit and rolled down the drive to the main road. She found a bend just a little ways down state road 521 that presented a good view of the valley below and ate her lunch of baby carrots, pretzel chips, and hummus while sitting on a warm rock and listening to the buzz of cicadas and the wind in the trees. Not a single car passed.

When she finished she pulled out her tablet. The next home was already close, really the next driveway—an unexpected surprise that it was so close. She revved Kermit's engine, the barking exhaust disturbing the summer afternoon silence. She looked both ways for traffic that wasn't there and shifted to first, riding just a few yards uphill until she saw a driveway marked with a mailbox with the name "Pennel" on the top, carved from a sanded wood block frame.

The driveway was an emerald tunnel broken occasionally by shafts of dappled sunlight. The house that came into view was a grand, rustic farmhouse, its façade was well cared for, the wood freshly painted in white, with blues on the friezes, gables, and shutters to accent. The shingles were in good repair, the air just above them shimmering with heat haze. The brick chimney and foundation were protected in a glossy shellac, and the front porch was free of the clutter she had noted on so many other galleries. Instead of the milk crates, car parts, and moldy furniture, a few straight-backed rocking chairs sat at attention, equidistant from one another while a porch swing rocked in the breeze.

It was a refreshing sight after so many decrepit homesteads, but as she rounded the driveway she was forced to reconsider. The front yard was chaos: three rusty car hulks rested on cinderblocks without wheels or windows. Weeds grew up through the frames where the engines should have been. Each was in a further state of disrepair than the last, the oldest easily dating back to the 1930s. Their guts and interiors were strewn over the ground in haphazard piles, the grass worn into dirt footpaths between them. A moldering mattress lay half folded, its rusted springs showing through its padding like bones through a rotting corpse. Clay jugs surrounded a moonshine still, its parts gleaming in the sunlight. Close by a string of smoke rose from a dying fire within an oil drum. The backseats from one of the cars sat in the shade of a crepe myrtle, and from the branches, forming a kind of backdrop behind the bench, hung a faded "Don't Tread on Me" sign with a coiled snake and a Confederate flag.

Kenia removed her helmet and set it on the handlebars, Kermit's engine still turning over. She was paralyzed by what she saw: disorder that was such a contrast to the well-loved house, a yard that was a parody of her most slanted stereotypes of the region. A figure rounded the corner of the house. It was a young boy in bare feet and overalls without an undershirt beneath. His head was covered in a wide-brimmed straw hat, his face streaked with dirt. In his mouth he chewed a corncob pipe, his lips set in a pensive frown. He was Huck Finn, from central casting, and was followed by a strawberry blond girl, a bit taller, her hair pulled into Pippi Longstocking pigtails, wearing an orange hunting vest over camouflaged fatigues, a rifle nearly as long as she was tall hanging on her shoulder. A third figure, this one a lankly young man in an oversized white robe, came last. In his hands he carried a loop of extension cord. The hood on his head had flaps on either side and rose up into a defiant point twelve inches above his head.

Kenia was not sure she could believe what she was seeing. All three young people stopped around the same time when they heard the idle of Kermit's engine. The girl in between the two boys looked back and forth as if taking a reading of their own reactions. The boys remained frozen. The girl in pigtails looked back to Kenia, but Kenia had already shoved her helmet back down on her head. Kermit's back wheel fired off a barrage of gravel as she spun the bike around and gunned the engine to take her back to the road, to sanity and safety, as quickly as possible.

◊

That night Kenia did not dream as much as she remembered. She was only around nine or ten, creeping down the steps she could see the blue numbers on the digital clock of the VHS recorder reading 3:47 a.m. It was a few days before Christmas. The tree with its boxes and presents was resplendent in its tinseled cheer, even if the lights were off for the night. It was Saturday. Kenia was usually awake early, before her siblings, and would come down to watch the earliest of the Saturday morning cartoons. But she knew from the dark of night outside—stars were still visible among the bare treetops—that cartoons were still far off. The television would only be playing infomercials and televangelists, both speaking out earnestly to their listeners while phone numbers scrolled across the screen.

Despite the hour, the light on the oven range was on. She crossed the living room to find her father's shape filling up the overstuffed chair, which they had moved into the corner to make room for the tree. He was taking deep, even breaths as he slept, a Harvard Med School hoodie pulled over his scrubs. His hand held a half-tipped glass of milk, most of the contents having spilled, darkening his sweatshirt. He had fallen asleep before he had even taken a drink.

Kenia retrieved dishtowels from the kitchen and slipped the glass from his hands. *Those hands.* Two days before, a school bus carrying the girls and boys basketball teams from Eleanor Roosevelt High had lost control on a patch of ice and crossed the centerline into an oncoming dump truck.

Her father had been on call, his beeper summoning him from the kitchen table where he had been helping Chinemere with her calculus. He had not been home since, her mother providing them with updates as the most injured children were treated in the OR.

All the children had survived and her father, as chief surgeon, had played an integral role, pushing himself beyond his own physical limitations. Kenia considered those hands as she laid the dishtowels across the spilled milk. She was old enough to know that magic—probably—was not real, but to her, her father's hands were just short of magical. After all, they could put broken people back together, a process that was miraculous to her and as beyond her comprehension as her sister's calculus problems, which had more Greek letters in them than numbers, or the impossible birth of Jesus, who looked up at her from his nativity scene, this one made in Kenya out of banana leaves and yarn with black faces.

Her father did not stir. She carried the glass of the remaining milk to the kitchen, pulled up a chair, dumped it, and washed it in the sink before placing it in the dishrack to dry with a faint clink. Then she returned to the living room, considering the darkness outside before plugging in the lights of the tree. It didn't actually warm the room, but it still felt like it to her. To that end, she pulled the throw blankets from the back of the couch where her mother had folded them—she could not help it, her obsessive need for order overriding her patience with her brood of children, who only folded them when asked. Kenia climbed onto the arm of the chair and pulled the blankets over her father and herself before falling back asleep.

She was not sure how long she had been lying in bed crying, but when Kenia came to herself, snapped back to the present day by her thoughts, she checked the time on her phone. A little before five in the morning. Her alarm would not go off for another hour and a half. It was Saturday again. She closed her eyes, but sleep was out of reach, her mind a nest of competing anxieties and imperatives. She finally settled on one.

Dad helped people who needed it.

She knew what she had to do.

◊

It was close to eleven a.m. when Kenia rolled back up to Martha Andersen's house. It looked the same as the day before; perhaps some of the fast food containers and pizza boxes had been dragged further away from the trashcan by raccoons or whatever vermin visited during the night. She pulled the grocery bags from the side saddles on Kermit, her footsteps heavy with the weight of her purchases. Her backpack was also full to bursting.

Martha opened the door, surprised. "Ms. Kenia, you're back!"

Mocha jumped up, placing his paws on her thighs. Kenia stammered for just a moment, last second reservations about violating study protocol and even simple boundaries of etiquette making her hesitate. But she pushed past her discomfort.

"Ms. Andersen, you were so gracious in hosting me yesterday and showing me that photo album, I wanted to repay the kindness and make you lunch."

"Oh Kenia," Martha said, her hand on her ample bosom. "You don't need to."

"I insist," Kenia said, surprising herself by pulling open the swinging screen door, trying to soften the intrusion with a gracious smile. Mocha danced around her, his claws tapping on the floor. The television was on but the volume low. She was relieved not to see Joel as she crossed to the kitchen. The sour smell of garbage and the refuse in the sink hit her fresh in the face. She did her best to breathe through her mouth, but even then she could taste it.

There was not a clear space on the countertop with so many dishes stacked there. One end, however, was covered in a flurry of mail. Envelopes for utilities, loan consolidation offers, and Publishers Clearinghouse waited in different stages of being opened and read. Kenia set the grocery bags down on them, pulled out a new set of dish gloves, dish soap, and spray disinfectant.

"My, you've come on a mission," Martha said.

She had. She couldn't quite explain it even to herself, but Kenia had been seized by a desperate, impatient urge to be useful, to do something . . . effective, impactful, practical. Maybe it was a delayed reaction to the long weeks of data collection, consisting of talk without action. Maybe it was because Martha had shown her kindness, reacting to a sadness she had detected in Kenia, and had acted as a mother might. Maybe Kenia just missed her own mother.

"What can I do?" Martha asked, a bit dumbfounded, twisting her fingers together in front of her belly.

"You sit there in that chair and tell me stories of how Selah Station used to be," Kenia said over the clank of plates and bowls.

And so she did. Martha sipped her tea while Kenia attacked the dishes in the sink first. Some of the dishes were well beyond saving, and she tossed them in the trashcan—there were no recycling bins in Selah Station that she had noticed. The trash was already close to full, and even stomping on its contents didn't help much. So she pulled out the bag, tied it off, and carried it outside with a box of additional black trash bags she had also purchased. She righted the overturned trashcan, did a quick cleanup of the scattered to-go and delivery boxes, then returned to the kitchen where Martha had made fresh tea.

Kenia thanked her. She had already worked up a sweat and preferred cold water, but she took some of Martha's offered tea before turning back to the dishes. Forty-five minutes later the sink was clear, the water running through over the freshly scrubbed stainless steel basin. The counters were clear and clean, even if they were old, chipped and cracked by wear and tear. In the meantime, Kenia had learned that Martha had grown up quite the tomboy, rambling in the creeks—"cricks" as she called them—catching frogs, climbing trees, and playing with children of all colors.

"Back then, it didn't matter, at least not here in Selah," Martha said.

Kenia learned that Martha's favorite childhood friend had been named Mable, who she had been as close to as a "sister." They would sleep next to each other on summer nights when they would inevitably spend the night at one or the other's house.

"We were inseparable; Mable and Martha, Martha and Mable," she said.

"What happened to her?" Kenia asked, pulling out a pot to cook quinoa in—she had ridden Kermit the ninety minutes to Martinsburg and back that morning to buy it and the other groceries. Introducing Martha to options other than pasta and white rice was part of her goal for that day. It might have been presumptuous, arrogant even, but she justified it to herself that she needed to know how hard it was to actually prepare the recipes recommended by Healthy-Bytes.

This is community-based participatory research, she told herself.

Plus Martha reveled in reminiscing, her delight in having an audience again and her curiosity about the dish Kenia was preparing growing. But she became downcast when she returned to the subject of Mable. "Her family moved away. They didn't feel comfortable here after the university closed and attitudes in Selah started to shift."

"Mable was black?"

"Yes, sorry I didn't mention that."

Kenia shrugged and added water to the quinoa.

Joel was still sleeping. Martha told her he did not get up until three p.m. most days.

"I figure the more he sleeps, the less he drinks and smokes," Martha said, the sadness of her resignation heavy in her voice.

"So he didn't make it to rehab this morning?" Kenia asked, lighting the stove to heat the water before she pulled out the cucumbers, red peppers, and carrots she had bought from local farmers selling produce on the side of the road.

"He says that hooey about sobering up every day. Still doesn't." Martha sighed and grew quiet and downcast.

Kenia chopped the vegetables as the water warmed. "Tell me about Christmas here. What was that like?"

Martha picked up the thread of her childhood memories where she had left off, recalling one Christmas after another, when Mable was still a part of her life. The kitchen grew warm and fragrant. Kenia seasoned the skinless chicken breasts she had brought with Greek spices and slid them into the oven to bake. While they cooked, she washed the arugula and baby spinach salad, tossed it with the vegetables, cranberries, crumbled goat cheese, and with virgin olive oil and balsamic vinaigrette. A wave of heat hit her in the face when she checked on the chicken. When it was done, she slid it out, diced it into cubes, drizzled them in a chipotle reduction and filled a set of plates, placing the salad on a bed of quinoa and topping it with the chicken. She set the plates down on the table and pulled out a chair next to Martha.

"Let's eat."

◊

They put the leftovers in Tupperware and sipped green tea, which Martha was surprised Kenia served without sugar.

"A bit plain, isn't it?" Martha said taking a tentative sip.

"You'll get used to it, if you drink enough."

Martha flipped through the recipes Kenia had printed up for her, reading some aloud. "Spaghetti made out of squash! What will they think of next?"

Kenia shrugged, staring into her mug. "I've realized that some of them just aren't practical. This whole app might not be practical, but it's good to know if you like them."

"Like them, dear, that was *restaurant* food, gourmet. I want to try to make some on my own."

"Great. Let me know how it goes; it will be useful for feedback for my professor," Kenia said, trying to explain away her imposition as part of the practicum, wondering if helping Martha had been as much for herself as for Martha. Kenia looked at the clock on the wall and Ms. July, her tissue paper bikini barely containing her breasts, as she glanced back from her tropical photoshoot with a contrived come-hither look. The afternoon was wearing on. Martha offered to show her more photos albums but Kenia declined, eager to be going before Joel woke up.

Martha and Mocha walked her out to Kermit, Martha giving Kenia a tight, enveloping hug that squeezed the breath out of her. Then she hooked her leg over Kermit, started the engine and rolled away, Mocha barking and chasing her, tail wagging, until she twisted the handle grip and accelerated with a wave of her gloved hand.

Where the driveway met the road she hit the brakes. A dark blue police cruiser was parked behind a Jeep Cherokee, lights flashing. The driver of the Cherokee was a young white man in sunglasses and no shirt, and his female companion was in jean shorts and a bikini top. Kenia was glad for the helmet, hoping to hide her skin color from the police. In an effort to slide past unnoticed, she coasted, as quietly as the motor could allow her to. But then two things happened that surprised her. She realized the police officer, who was waving on the driver, was black. Second, seeing her, the officer smiled and walked over.

"Thea, how are you?"

He was middle-aged, cutting an impressive figure in his uniform, his stiff Smokey the Bear hat tipped forward on his head in a slightly menacing way. But this was belied by the wide smile on his face. To correct for the mistaken identity Kenia pulled off the helmet and cut the engine. The officer stopped for a moment in his tracks, registering his surprise and confusion.

"I'm sorry, I thought you were Thea Ferguson."

"I'm Kenia Dezy. I'm an intern working with her and Ms. Jolene down at the Med-Dent building."

"Kenia," he said, closing the distance between them and shaking her hand. She took it, realizing she had never actually *touched* an officer of the law—ever. "Am I saying that right?"

"Yes, nice job."

"I'm Officer Farrcroft, but most everyone knows me as Keith."

"Pleasure," Kenia said, processing.

"You looked perplexed."

"Sorry, I need to fix my face," she laughed. "I guess I'm just surprised, and a little relieved, to see a brother in uniform out here."

Officer Farrcroft flashed a relaxed smile. It was hard not to like him, she realized, despite his profession. He carried his authority with a lightness that was refreshing. His nightstick, mace, and pistol all seemed more like inert decorations than threats to her. "Well, Selah can still surprise you."

"It can."

"What are you doing up here?"

"I interviewed Ms. Andersen yesterday. Came back to try out a few recipes with her."

"She's a very sweet lady."

"She is. Her son was not quite as welcoming."

Officer Farrcroft grimaced. "Yep, he's a bitter one. But don't let him get under your skin."

"Might be too late."

"His bark is worse than his bite. Sad case really. He is a bright kid. Just not a lot of opportunities for young people in these parts."

"Yeah, I've been hearing that a lot. By the way, what do you know about the folks the next lot over, the Pennels?"

Keith's smile returned. "Great family. You met them yet?"

"Uh, I did . . . I rode up yesterday. House was nice and all, but well . . . I don't know what I saw, but one of those kids came around the corner in a grand wizard robe. I got the hell out of there."

Officer Farrcroft laughed so hard Kenia wondered if he had actually understood her.

"I don't mean grand wizard as in Gandalf, I mean as in the Klan."

He wiped a tear from the corner of his eye. "Oh I know. I guarantee it was a misunderstanding. You probably stumbled into one of their shoots."

"Shoots?"

"Their whole yard is a set. Never heard of Redneck Manor, the YouTube show?"

"No."

"Well, we'll remedy that. Come on, I'll introduce you to them. Those kids are putting Selah back on the map."

Chapter 15

The Pennels

Kenia followed the police cruiser at a slow roll up the driveway, back to the Pennel place. It was as she remembered it, a tunnel of green broken by pleasant shafts of sunlight leading to a picturesque home with a front yard that resembled a junk heap from a documentary on the Great Depression. Kenia pulled up beside Officer Farrcroft as he stepped out of the cruiser, studying him and his reactions as he scanned the automotive wreckage, the overgrown weeds, and most of all, the flags hanging from the branches of crepe myrtle.

He looked at her askance before nodding at the flags. "It's not what you think."

She had nothing to say. Instead the image of the hunting rifle on the shoulder of the girl from the day before flashed through her mind, and she wondered if his badge was enough to protect them both.

Officer Farrcroft began walking towards the porch steps, his thumbs hooked in his gun belt, but stopped short when he realized she was not behind him. "Come on young lady, I wouldn't put you in danger."

She set her helmet down on the seat of the motorcycle and followed. She rounded the wreck of a pickup truck. Now that they were approaching the house, Kenia stuck close to her escort, nearly bumping into him when he turned to check if she was indeed coming along.

"Officer Farrcroft," a voice said from the shade of the porch.

Kenia's stomach clenched in surprise and she stepped backwards without meaning to. She had not noticed the white man sitting back in one of the rocking chairs. He looked to be in his early thirties and was wearing a button-down cotton shirt, the material worn with many washings, the sleeves rolled up to reveal forearms marked by ridges of muscle and a USMC tattoo.

"Captain Pennel," Officer Farrcroft said, tapping the brim of his hat. "How are you this afternoon?"

"Can't complain," the man addressed as Captain said, rocking forward to stand up out of the chair and setting a sweating glass of iced tea down on the porch rail. As he moved out of the shade Kenia could see his expression was guarded. His hair was cut short, in the manner of a man recently enlisted, yet his jaw was unshaved, in a sort of fashionable magazine model sort of way. He looked at Kenia with iron-colored eyes and nodded, giving her a short, "Ma'am."

Officer Farrcroft continued. "This is Kenia Dezy, and Kenia, this is Captain Austin Pennel, US Marine Corps."

"Retired," the captain added.

"Once a Marine . . ." Officer Farrcroft said. "The Captain here served in Iraq and Afghanistan."

Austin Pennel's eyes floated downward, as if he was unsure or unused to such deference for his service.

"Austin, Kenia is working as an intern at the Med-Dent building with Ms. Jolene Lewis and Thea Ferguson this summer, conducting home visits for surveys and such. Anyway, I think she stumbled into your siblings doing one of their films yesterday, and it gave her a . . . a mistaken impression."

Austin ran his hand over his face, his palm brushing against his whiskers. His expression was more open now, one Kenia read as tired and a bit embarrassed.

"Those kids," he shook his head then turned to Kenia. "I'm so sorry, ma'am. They have this crazy show they do for YouTube, Redneck Manor. I'll get them and they can explain."

He turned to the house and swung open the screen door. "Can I get you all some iced tea or lemonade?"

Kenia was not sure if she should accept or not.

Officer Farrcroft did not hesitate. "I'll take a little of both. So will Kenia."

"Coming up," Austin said.

The door eased shut after Austin while he called out, "Shane, Hailey, Stan, get out here, front and center."

Keith took the steps two at a time then settled into one of the rocking chairs with a sigh, his gun belt squeaking as he bent at the waist. He offered no explanation, but he was the picture of relaxation, as much as he could be while on duty. A thundering of footsteps preceded the screen door bursting open again.

The first to emerge was the youngest, a boy of about thirteen. The Huck Finn look was gone, replaced by more conventional shorts, flip-flops, and a T-shirt that had a cat's face on a Wanted sign. Kenia did a double take to make sure she was reading it correctly, "Schrödinger's Cat, Wanted Dead and Alive."

There was no time to process the paradox as he had recognized her from the day before and glanced to take in Officer Farrcroft as well and mumbled, "Oh, no."

"Afternoon, Stan."

"Hi Officer Keith, are we in trouble?"

"No, I wouldn't say that," he said. "Just clearing up a misunderstanding and bringing good people together."

Next to emerge was the young lady, who Kenia took for Stan's sister. She looked about fifteen or sixteen. Her strawberry blond hair was let down onto her shoulders. She stepped onto the porch with the same expression of surprise, shame, and embarrassment that her brother wore. Her shoulders shrugged high, close to her ears, as she offered an awkward wave to Kenia. "Uh, hi. I'm Hailey," she said, then bit her lip and stared down, as if she were counting the planks of the porch, or hoping a hole in the earth would open and swallow her up.

Shane, the young man who had been in the Klan robe, emerged last from the shade of the house. He appeared to be between Stan and Hailey in age and looked most guilty of them all. He took a hard swallow, recognizing Kenia immediately.

"Well, this is embarrassing," he said.

Austin opened the screen door with his foot, two glasses of lemonade and iced tea in his hands. Officer Farrcroft thanked him and took a long swig. Kenia was not thirsty, but she felt it would be rude not to take a sip, and if nothing else, it helped to counter the dry feeling in her mouth.

Austin crossed his arms over his full chest and prodded his younger siblings. "This is Ms. Kenia Dezy. She is a college intern at the Med-Dent building this summer. She has been doing house visits, and I think you owe her a bit of an explanation."

"We're, like, so sorry," Hailey said, drawing out the "so" and "sorry."

"Yeah, we were in costume when you saw us yesterday," Shane said in a rush. "See, we have this channel on YouTube where we have these shows. We were in costume. We figured we gave you, really, the wrong impression. The shows, they're satires. We're peddling an ironic take on . . . well . . . a sort of commentary on wealthy and poor dichotomies and the ongoing cultural dialectic in the US. We sort of juxtapose stock characters and tropes of different demographics against one another in an effort to—"

"Shut up, Shane," Hailey said, rolling her eyes. "It's probably easier if we just show you."

◊

The interior of the house was what Kenia would have expected after seeing the outside: gleaming wood floors, pine paneling, and redwood banisters, all finely sanded and freshly coated in varnish. The kitchen was a recent renovation with granite countertops and glass cabinets which revealed dishes placed inside, stacked with careful meticulousness. Like the exterior, the inside of the home was maintained with an eye for detail and almost military precision.

The back rooms held the surprise. The rear of the house was nothing short of a broadcast studio, with dozens of set lights on stands and hanging from movable tracks on the ceiling. The walls were dark, covered with acoustic foam except for the one wall, which served as the backdrop to a news anchor's desk, the name "Folks News" written in lettering and styling reminiscent of Fox News. Tripods with expensive-looking digital cameras and light meters were placed throughout the room, their feet set on x's of glow-in-the-dark gaffer tape.

The adjacent room had been converted into a control room with half a dozen flat-screen monitors mounted on the walls. Tablets and Bluetooth keyboards were scattered on different surfaces throughout the room. A server tower blinked in the corner with a series of green, yellow, and red lights, its fans giving off a steady hum. The room, although crowded, bore the same signs of meticulous order as the rest of the house: cords that ran across the floor were bundled beneath covers with alternating yellow and black stripes, and a stack of transparent plastic drawers held additional equipment—cords curled and twist tied, logbooks arranged by date, and collapsed tripods labeled by minimum and maximum height.

The only exception to the order were the three workstations. Each bore all the signs and distinctions one might expect in an office setting. One station's flat screen was larger than the others, the borders a mess of post-it notes that had extended to the arm of the overhead lamp and the keyboard as well. The next work station, more orderly, had postcards of landscapes, famous buildings, and what looked like a corkboard of index cards storyboarding a series of scenes. The final workspace was notable for the small army of classic transformer figures in various states of robot or vehicle form.

"And this is where we do the creating, editing, and social media posting to keep up with our fans," Shane said.

"Fans . . . " Kenia repeated. "Do you have an idea of how many?"

Oh, that's easy," Stan said. "We have over three million subscribers and 7.2 million followers on Facebook, Twitter, and the 'Gram, although some of those are double counts."

"We hit a billion views on YouTube last year," Hailey said.

"A billion?" Kenia asked, slack jawed.

Officer Farrcroft, standing in the doorway with Austin, sucked at his teeth then whistled, "Not bad, you all. Not bad at all."

"All this is just talk. You want to see some of our videos?" Stan asked.

"Sure." Kenia settled down in front of one of the larger flat screens, the Pennel children wheeling over swivel chairs.

Officer Farrcroft announced that he would be going, but not before putting his hand on Kenia's shoulder. "You all right?" he asked into her ear.

"Yeah, I think."

While Austin walked with the officer to the door, the blitzkrieg of videos began. They started chronologically with a faux newscast. This first video had no backdrop and only an ill-fitting secondhand suit and hair gel to sell Shane as a reporter. The story was invented, focusing on a local man who had claimed to have seen Bigfoot. Stan played the witness in fairly convincing makeup, standing on a milk crate for extra height, that Hailey, behind the camera, was mostly successful in keeping out of the frame. The timing between the brothers was quite good and made up for the amateurish production value. They were natural actors and comedians. Kenia knew her sister Chikmara would find a lot to praise in their technique.

From that first newscast the videos evolved into a wider cast of characters and settings. These grew into new shows, each with some sort of countrified theme. A Redneck DYI show demonstrated how to build a birdfeeder by sticking a toilet plunger handle-first into the ground; how to build a toilet out of an upended traffic cone;

and how to trim hedges by putting a chainsaw on a rope and swinging it overhead. A cooking show shared recipes for roadkill. The sports channel featured ATV and tractor races, each staged with ever-evolving storylines, punctuated by wrecks, arguments, and fistfights among the racers—many of them involved in complex storylines with cheating wives and girlfriends, some of which, uncomfortably but sticking to type, were also siblings. Hailey played some of the roles, but other local residents had joined to play the growing cast of recurring characters and increasingly elaborate plots.

As the videos progressed, the production quality improved. The Pennels explained how they had created additional channels on YouTube for the different shows as well as vlogs for many of the characters who would comment on current events. In between the videos, and sometimes during them, YouTube played commercials and flashed banner ads for feature films, smoking cessation programs, and video games.

"And this is how we pay the bills," Stan said, pointing to one of the ads.

"Bills?" Kenia asked.

"Well, we're doing better than breaking even now, obviously," Shane volunteered, gesturing at the equipment and the recording space. "Otherwise we couldn't pay all the extras or refurbish the house or pay for all the junk we had hauled into the front yard."

"Wait, you *paid* to have that stuff brought here?"

"Well sure we did," Shane laughed. "It's all part of the set for our 'reality show,' Redneck Manor. It's our most popular show yet. You saw some of the characters yesterday."

"Those flags are part of their own homemade news, commentary, and opinion show," Stan said.

Kenia sat back in her seat, her eyes glazing over as another ad played, followed by another video. "Let me get this straight," she said during a subsequent ad break. "You started out with a fake news show that gave rise to fake TV shows, fake TV channels, and a fake 'reality' series wherein the characters have their own fake news show?"

"Well, it's not fake to them," Shane pointed out.

"I guess, when you say it that way, it all sounds quite meta," Stan said.

"I'll say. You three have your own little media empire up here. Who watches this?"

"Our demos skew young, but it's really across income, racial, and education brackets."

"Huh," Kenia said, contemplating the jokes, the outlandish scenarios, and the characters she had just seen—each a take on stereotypes and tropes of fat, racist, ignorant, and bigoted rural white Americans with poor dental hygiene, thick accents, and bad hair.

"Some people watch it for laughs, but there are others who take it all pretty seriously. You can tell in the comments they actually agree with some of the racist attitudes we're trying to parody," Hailey said.

Kenia was still quiet, not sure what to say. She thought of Chikmara sitting in her poorly lit apartment in North Hollywood, studying her lines while still wearing her barista uniform from Starbucks, where she worked to pay her bills. How often Chikmara had complained about the limited parts for black actresses: "They just want us to play hookers, junkies, or angry black women," she had said so many times over the years.

Kenia had always sympathized with Chikmara in a powerful way. Growing up surrounded by educated, professional, successful people of color, Kenia had often wondered why she didn't see those people represented on television. BET was the only channel on which she would see people of color regularly, but the depictions were so narrow: rappers brandishing bling and pistols surrounded by the omnipresent indistinguishable video hos. And, to her surprise, she felt that same discomfort in some of the stereotypes she saw in the Pennel's videos. As much as she wanted to laugh at them, Kenia also kept thinking of the sad, real people she had met in the past weeks: Shirley alternating between her cigarettes and inhalers; Tracy trading in an oxycontin economy; Martha, so sweet and so lonely, stuck in that house with a bitter alcoholic son; and how they were not living lives to laugh at.

She wanted to ask the Pennels about it, start a conversation with them. They were all clearly brilliant kids, well read, deeply informed, and talented. Stan was explaining how their subscriptions had exploded during the election and the weeks and months that followed. How Trump terrified them but provided them with endless material to parody. The administration's incompetence and controversy had been growing their audience, their advertisers, and as a result, their income. Kenia tried to concentrate on what he was saying, but she felt a blinding pain building behind her eyes that came on so fast that, by the time she pinched the bridge of her nose in a futile effort to stop the pressure, everything—the computers, equipment, the Pennels themselves—had disappeared.

Chapter 16

Trailways and Runaways

Kenia stumbled, finding herself on her feet, her head still spinning. She lost the battle to stand and crouched down, a knee to the ground, one hand next to it, the other to the crown of her head. She clenched her eyes shut until the flash of pain and disorientation passed. She became aware of sound before sight. The sounds were . . . familiar, the buzz of insects, the whisper of wind in trees, the songs of birds.

She opened her eyes. She was along the roadside. A break in the trees allowed for her to see down into the river valley. It was a view of Selah Station she recognized.

The confusion began to resolve. She knew this place. It was where she had stopped to have lunch the day before. She approached the break in the trees and found the same spot where she had sat— the same but different, just as the trees and bushes were not quite as she remembered them, even if she could not put her finger on why.

The town waited in the valley below. The island, instead of being an overgrown forest with the wreckage of an industrial disaster, was marked by buildings and streets that were visible, even occupied. The trees of the avenues were under-pruned and evenly spaced. Traffic moved, the sun reflecting off the windows and fenders of cars moving along the roadways. Even the buildings of the college were visible. Farther to the northwest, white clouds of steam rose from the chimney stacks at the coal processing plant and evaporated in the breeze rolling down the changeless faces of the Blue Ridge Mountains.

The groan of a diesel engine drew her back to the shoulder. A bus was chugging up the hill. It was a Trailways, a cherry red model she would have called "vintage," with gleaming aluminum sides, sliding windows tilted forward air-stream style, and "Trailways" written on the side in eggshell white. The destination roller on the front read "Selah Station," and as it passed she caught glimpses of young black faces staring back at her. These were college-aged men and women, their shirts and blouses buttoned to their necks. They were not looking at her so much as they were looking at the valley beyond, their eyes wide, full of hope and apprehension. Only as the bus rumbled past did some of them take note of her, those that did wearing quizzical expressions, as if she were something exotic and out of place.

The bus rolled on, the engine rumbling as the driver downshifted to use the compression brake. She was left staring through the empty space left behind. A mailbox stood on the far side of the road. It was built in the shape of a red barn, complete with a miniature barn door where the mail would go through. What caught her eye was the name.

Pennel.

She swallowed and crossed the road, noticing that the asphalt was old and faded, its face crisscrossed with swaths of tar painted over cracks. As she walked up the gravel driveway, she noted that the day was not particularly different from how it had been: it was summer and hot. The sun was sinking behind the trees. She tried to remember when it had gotten so late, but couldn't. She checked her phone. It read 2:37 p.m., but it certainly did not look like 2:37 in the afternoon. The long shadows and haze in the air told her it was closer to four p.m.

Then she noticed she had no reception.

She slipped the phone back and walked a bit faster. A squirrel danced on a limb overhead, startling a cardinal that swooped across her path with a series of staccato chirps. She could smell honeysuckle and sassafras and, somewhere more distant, a wood fire. The Pennel house came into view, and like so many other things, it was the same but different. The arrangement of bushes along the front walk was new. She did not remember flowerboxes at the windows, but there they were now, their blooms and leaves hanging over the side in fecund and cheery displays.

Then she stopped short. The yard was empty of car carcasses, bathtubs, and rotting mattresses. The distillery was missing, the grass where it had been not even flattened. No flags fluttered in the breeze except for an American flag that hung from the porch. The crepe myrtle trees that had held the other flags were nothing more than knee-high bushes.

She climbed the steps to the front door and, before knocking, slowed, wondering if this was indeed the right house. The timbers of the porch showed their age, cracks having opened along their lengths. The house paint was thin and without the luster that had characterized it earlier. This house had a weathered but comfortable, lived-in feel. The doorbell was missing but the front door was open, only the screen door shut across the empty space of the door frame allowing her to see all the way back to the kitchen.

The cupboards were no longer glass, but the more traditional wood.

"Hello?" she said, rapping on the door.

"Coming," a voice answered back.

She could hear footsteps climbing up a set of basement stairs before the silhouette of a man came into view. At first she was certain it was Austin and was relieved that something—someone—was as she remembered it. But as he neared, she could tell this man only *resembled* Austin. This figure was a stranger. He was younger than Austin, by a decade or more. He had the same handsome features, except the haunted look in Austin's eyes was gone. This young man's expression was an open one, his face clean shaven even if his hair was a bit longer, his bangs in a tousle at the top of his head.

His eyes were most striking. They were an electric blue, and once he looked at her she felt her heart skip a beat. She could not quite find her words as he opened the screen door with a gracious smile of greeting. She was seized with a sense of self-consciousness.

It was a familiar feeling, one she felt around some of Chikmara's actor friends, who with their movie-star looks, smooth voices, and self-assured poise made her feel at once giddy and ordinary. This young man, however, wore his attractiveness lightly, as if unaware of it. His demeanor was relaxed and kind, his expression so humble she would have thought he was the one trespassing.

She took a deep breath and searched for how to start, how to explain that she was lost but not lost, that she had never been there before, and yet, had been—at least she thought she had been. She opened her mouth to speak, but nothing came out. Instead the pain slapped her between the eyes again, and her world started to spin.

All she managed before it all disappeared was, "Oh, no."

◊

Kenia came to in the yard of automotive wreckage again, facedown, next to the distillery, a snail leaving a silver trail as it inched up one of the serpentine copper tubes. She looked up, propping herself up on her elbows. *This* Pennel house was as she remembered: the fresh paint, the double-paned energy efficient windows, their sills free of flower boxes, the timbers of the porch new, the stone and brickwork lacquered with shellac.

It was Hailey who saw her first, crying out, "She's in the yard."

The screen door opened and shut as Hailey rushed out to her. But Kenia was already up and running to Kermit. She kicked the engine to life, twisted the grip, and for the second time in so many days, fled from the Pennel household.

Chapter 17

Schrödinger's Cat: Wanted Dead and Alive.

Kenia was still tearful when she called her mother. She knew she was blabbering, sniffling and sobbing between her breathless retelling of the past few weeks, her episodes relayed in gasps of breath and desperate inquiries of "am I going crazy?" or "have I lost my mind?" and "what is happening to me?"

Her mother, her voice composed, if not calm, replied simply, "Kenia, get out your computer, log in, and call me. I need to see your face while we talk and I tell you what I need to tell you."

Ominous words, but at least her mother didn't seem to think she was going crazy—at least not yet. Kenia braced herself as the computer booted, anticipating disclosure of some history of mental illness in the family—bipolar, schizophrenia, something resulting in complete psychosis.

"Mom, I don't want to be sick," she said into the phone.

"You're not. You're not. You're all right baby. Just let me explain," her mother said, in measured tones.

"Don't hang up," Kenia said sniffling, afraid to break the connection.

"Baby, I'm holding on. I'm not going anywhere. I'm right here."

Then she was. Her mother's face, Kenia's own eyes staring back at her, her childhood home in the background. It was so familiar, so comforting, that Kenia sobbed anew. Her mother's expression looked fraught, despite the tone of her voice. Her hand trembled as she wiped away her own tears. She clicked off the phone now that they were face to face. Kenia did the same.

"Momma, what is happening to me?"

Her mother took a deep breath under closed eyes. It was the same mastering of herself she had done just before telling the four of them that their father was gone. It was the same expression she pictured her mother taking on in the privacy of a backroom before going out to tell the family of a patient that, despite all available resources and best efforts on the part of the hospital, their son, daughter, father, mother, brother, sister, husband, or wife had passed.

It could not be good news.

"I guess the best place to start is your father."

"What does this have to do with Dad?"

"Everything, Kenia. Everything. Remember how your father disappeared? There was never a body."

She did. She remembered how she had held on to the hope that it was some sign he was still alive. But after a time, it was just another source of uncertainty that turned to pain. She had never understood those families who described themselves as "at peace" once their loved one's remains had been recovered, be it from a plane crash, a battlefield, or a murder scene, sometimes long after the disappearance, until she herself had lost someone important, with no answers, no leads, just a void left filled with questions.

"Yes," she said.

"Well, in truth, I told you Daddy was dead, but the truth of it is, I don't know."

"What?"

Another deep breath on her mother's part as Kenia felt her heart beating rapidly in her chest, driven by anxiety, or hope, she was not sure.

"It's so complicated, Kenia, and when I finish you will understand why I didn't tell you—or anyone for that matter. It was always a secret. Donovan wanted it that way."

Kenia was silent, waiting for her mother to continue.

"Kenia, honey, what I'm going to tell you is hard to believe, and I would not believe it if I had not seen it with my own eyes. But your father . . . your father was a . . . a time traveler."

It would have seemed like a joke if Kenia had not had her own inexplicable experiences. She asked her mother to go on.

"I'm a scientist, Kenia. So was your father. So you've got to understand that neither of us believed it at first. We explored all the scientific, medical, psychological explanations we could: hysteria, psychosis, schizophrenia, just like I'm sure you are already thinking. But none of it fit, and then . . . then I saw it with my own eyes. I watched your father disappear. One minute he was there, then he was gone. I panicked. I thought *I* was losing my mind. Then, after I had searched the house, the yard, the garage, and I was about to call 911, he reappeared out of nowhere. Right there on the back deck."

"Mom, is that what has been happening to me?"

"Oh baby girl, I'm so sorry I never told you. I couldn't tell you, you see?"

"Where would he go?"

"The past, always the past. But they were always crucial moments, turning points in history. He had no control of when he would leave, the *when* he would journey to, but he was certain there was always some change he was supposed to make, a correction to a mistake, a historical injustice of some sort."

"He changed history?"

"Yes. In little ways but always for some greater affect."

"But how do you know once it's happened?"

"It's hard to explain, but he learned to live with it, with the possibility of more than one timeline. He could sense when the *jump* was coming, so he would try to make sure no one would see him disappear and be alarmed. Once I knew, I would help cover for his absences. Over time we both came to accept it. He looked for explanations, studying physics, space-time, and history. But the only tangible explanation came from his ancestry."

"In Africa?"

"Yes. You see, your father came from a line of shamans. They were called *Dibia* in Igbo culture."

"*Dibia?*"

"Yes, the religion was called Odinani; the supreme creator god, Chineka—*chi* being the spiritual connection with the supreme

147

God and that connection being stronger in some than others. For shamans it could be so strong that they worked with Chineka to help determine the course of history."

"Chi . . . I thought that was a Chinese word?"

"It means God in Igbo. It's right there in all of your names, Chiazam, Chikmara, Chinemere: God has answered my prayers, God is Wisdom, God is doing. Your name, Keniabarido, even if it is Ogoni and not Igbo, means 'as it pleased God.'" Her mother sighed. "You and your friend Audre took so much to Ashanti theology, I never really told you about your own Igbo people."

"But Mom, we're Catholic!"

"And so is sixty percent of Haiti, while a hundred percent practice Voodoo. Your friend Audre told me that." She leaned closer to the screen. "Kenia, you have to remember, no one is just one thing."

Kenia sniffed. She remembered her father saying the same to her so long ago. She breathed, composing herself as best she could.

"That's my girl."

"But Mom, what happened to Dad?"

Her mother's throat fluttered as she struggled with her own emotions. "He disappeared. He journeyed back, to somewhere, to some *when*, but did not return."

Kenia covered her face. Was that her fate, too? She felt the tears returning.

"Kenia, Kenia honey, you need to be strong. I'm so sorry that this thing . . . this burden has come to you. It's a curse, but it's also a gift. You are called. You are called to help, to go back, to make things right."

"I don't want to make things right. I want to live a regular life. I want Dad back."

Her mother was rendered silent while Kenia cried out five years of yearning, loss, and sadness. When she was finished, her body exhausted from the spell, her mother was still there and said in an iron voice, "I did not raise you to be *regular*, Kenia. I did not raise any of you to be regular. And you are not. None of you. I raised you to be extraordinary, to be resilient, to fight, and to thrive, despite the headwinds you will face. Every night your father prayed that same prayer by W.E.B. Dubois, the one that says, 'Mighty causes are calling us . . . and they call with voices that mean work and sacrifices and death. Mercifully grant us, O God, the spirit of Esther, that we say: I will go unto the King and if I perish, I perish.'"

"I perish," Kenia repeated the last words, contemplating the father-shaped hole in her own life.

"He was willing to serve, Kenia," her mother said, the growing fear in her voice making it tremble. "But you don't have to perish. Be smart. Be strong. Be resourceful. Find friends whom you can trust. Learn about wherever, *when*ever you are being called to. And most of all, you come back to me. You hear me? You come back."

◊

There had been a fight at school. Not the typical scuffle between young men too full of testosterone and themselves, the type of fight that opened with a prolonged period of shouting and posturing, followed by the exchange of a few strikes and blows before the combatants tumbled to the ground and grappled, so close that neither could do much harm to the other, and both secretly relieved when bystanders stepped in to break it up.

No, this had been a fight between two girls, over a boy. It had spilled out of the girls' bathroom, into the hallways, down a set of stairs, and onto a landing where one girl, Jennifer Retnash, was kicking at the other, Susan Howland, who was curled into a fetal shape, having given up even if her attacker had failed to acknowledge it.

That had been when Chikmara had come upon them. She was halfway up the steps, on her way to Trigonometry, when Jennifer cornered Susan. The *thud* of each kick on Susan's torso was terrible.

For a moment all the witnesses stood frozen until Chikmara, disgusted by the violence and failure to help, stepped in. She had tried to protect Susan, throwing herself over her.

Jennifer Retnash didn't like that. She grabbed a fistful of Chikmara's hair and dragged her off. Chikmara resisted, and that was the point that Mr. Miller, the Civics teacher, rushed in, drawn by the screams and chaos. Arriving when he did, without context, he read the main fighters as Jennifer and Chikmara and tried to force the two of them apart. Jennifer reached past him to grab another fistful of Chikmara's hair, pulling her closer to knee her in the stomach. Mr. Miller, feeling Chikmara pulled towards him, mistook her movement as the lunge of an attack. He reached out with his arm and tried to brace her away.

That was when the tufts of hair ripped out of her scalp and Jennifer's hand went free. Chikmara was thrown off balance. Mr. Miller's arm sent her flying backwards. There was nothing for her to catch herself on, as they were still on the landing of the stairs. Chikmara floundered, as if into a "trust fall," without anyone to catch her but the descending stairs. She struck her head on the banister first and continued to fall until she landed, splayed out on the tile floor at the bottom.

By then, the other teachers had arrived. Jennifer was restrained, a tuft of Chikmara's hair still in her fist. Susan Howland was tearful, bruised, but intact. It was Chikmara who had suffered the worst of it, the banister splitting open her head. It being a head wound, the stairs were covered in bright, oxygen-rich, almost fuchsia-colored blood.

They carried Chikmara away on a stretcher and took her to the ER as a precaution. The truth of the incident eventually came to light as witnesses explained what had happened. Kenia had heard bits and pieces of the story all day long and was relieved when her father showed up at the door of her sixth period Geometry class, a visitor badge on his chest, and called her into the hallway.

Her first question was about her older sister, and she barely had it out of her mouth before her father reassured her.

"Chikmara is fine. She got a couple of stitches. Her biggest concern is whether or not people will be able to see the missing patch of hair in the play next week."

Kenia remembered her sister was the lead in the Color Purple. She knew her sister. She had been in scraps with all her siblings at one time or another, and Chikmara was made of stern stuff. She would be fine. Of course her sister was more concerned about the play. Theater was her life.

"But we have something to do first," her father said. "Come with me."

The period was almost over, so Kenia went back into the classroom, gathered her things, then followed her father. He walked the halls, lined with forest green lockers, as if he knew just where he was going. She realized that, of course, he knew the school; she was the third of four children who attended. There were debate trophies at the front entrance that Chinemere had won over the years. Her Dad had also been there for his share of parent-teacher conferences. But it was still incongruous to see him there in this space of teenagers and teachers. It was not the place for her surgeon father and was about as strange as those occasions when she would see her teachers out in the "real world" of the supermarket or the movie theater, living a seemingly "real life." Her father, for his part, belonged in a hospital, in scrubs, or at the kitchen table or in the pew next to her in church. It was simply weird and unnatural to have her worlds collide so, the boundaries and distinctions, so resolute in her teenage mind, blurred. Only something significant and unsettling could bring such a disruption about, and she didn't like it.

A tremor of unease started in her chest when she realized where they were going: Mr. Miller's classroom. The stairwell at the end of the hall was still blocked off with yellow wet floor, *piso mojado* signs as the custodian, a friendly brother named Reggie,

151

cleaned up her sister's blood. Her father knew Reggie from pickup basketball games at the gym.

"How you doing, Reggie?"

"Good, Dr. Donovan; how is Chikmara?"

"She'll be fine."

"God is good."

Her father stopped before the open door to Mr. Miller's classroom. Mr. Miller was standing before the chalkboard. Posters depicting the presidents, the three branches of government, bicameral versus unicameral legislatures, as well as movie posters from historical dramas such as The Patriot, Gettysburg, Amistad, and Pearl Harbor were on the walls. Mr. Miller was a thirty-something white man with a wife and two kids, three and eighteen months. By all appearances he was a decent guy doing a decent job. He was one of the more popular teachers.

At the moment her father appeared, Mr. Miller was reviewing a quiz. When he noticed them waiting in the hall, he had a student from the front row take his place at the lectern and continue to read out from the answer sheet while students graded their neighbor's papers. Mr. Miller showed no surprise, his expression somber when Kenia's father introduced himself.

Her father started right in, his voice low enough that their conversation could not be overheard by the students, but firm nonetheless. He did not ask about the fight, Chikmara's word having been enough for him. Kenia and her siblings knew better than to lie to their parents. Instead her father spoke as if he had known what he would say long before.

"There are a lot of kids in this school. Lots in your class there," he said with a nod to the students just over Mr. Miller's shoulder. "I have just four, and that is all I can handle most days."

Mr. Miller nodded. Kenia could read the uncertainly in his face. He was not sure where her father was going. She had no idea, and listened, rooted in place. Mr. Miller was the soccer coach and had an athletic, if slender, build, but he looked slight and undersized next to her father. Kenia was not sure why, but she felt an underlying current of tension building between the two men. Her father reached across the space between the two men and let his big hand settle on Mr. Miller's shoulder.

"I never raise a hand to my children. Neither does my wife. No one does. Not today. Not tomorrow. Not ever. There has been enough of that in this world."

Kenia was not sure what her father meant by "enough of that," but she recognized that her father's touch was not friendly in this instance, but controlling. For the first time in her life, she saw that those hands that could put broken people back together could . . . threaten to do the opposite, too. They could be menacing; her father, threatening.

"I have two more children who will come through this school. This here is one of them. The other is in junior high. Take a good look at her, because you will never need to lay a hand on a child with the last name of Dezy in any way other than to protect them from harm." He turned to Kenia, surprising her. "Did you hear that Kenia? You won't ever be in a fight where Mr. Miller needs to restrain you, will you?"

'No, sir," she said without hesitation.

"Dr. Dezy, I certainly did not mean—"

"Mr. Miller, I *certainly* was not finished," her father said, his voice a low rumble. "I'll remind you, we are men. We are just as good as our sisters, just as smart, just as deserving, but nature has seen to it that we are stronger. It's our job to use that strength to protect, nothing else." Her father's voice softened, almost to a plea. "Do you understand?"

"I do," Mr. Miller said.

"Good," her father said, clapping the younger man on the shoulder then shaking his hand. "Keep doing what you are doing; yours is an honorable profession. I'd be nowhere without my teachers. But these children need us to rise above ourselves, to do our best."

Her father's countenance changed back to the father she knew, genial and gentle, as he turned and smiled at her. "Come on, Kenia, everything is going to be all right."

◊

"And so, apparently, I'm a time traveler," Kenia said in finality. She was at the kitchen table in the Pennels' home. After all, they had been the only ones to *see* the phenomenon firsthand. She owed them *some* explanation, and her mother had urged her to find allies. But after sharing what she knew, and sitting in the pregnant silence that followed, she felt like a fool, waiting for their reaction and wondering if her own partial explanations were convincing. Why did the backdrop have to be a kitchen of all places, so ridiculously prosaic a setting for a testimony of ancestral gifts, spiritual beliefs, and the violation of the laws of space-time.

But whether they thought Kenia a fool or credible, the Pennels didn't show it. Austin was impossible to read. Kenia imagined he was already contemplating where the nearest mental hospital might be. Shane looked straight out the window, his eyes unfocused. Stan's head was down, his brow furrowed as if in the throes of a difficult math problem. Hailey alone was looking at her with a measure of compassion. She reached out across the table for Kenia's hand, took it in a firm grip, and showed no sign of letting go.

"Please, somebody, say *something,*" Kenia pleaded.

Stan spoke first. "I . . . I can't explain it, but then again, if I could, I'd have a Nobel Prize. But I can offer theories."

"Wave function?" Shane turned to him, a questioning look on his face.

"Yeah, it's the only sort of explanation I can think of that makes any sense, but there is still so much we don't know. So much of the physics are still being worked out, even now."

"So you believe me?" Kenia asked, hope and relief mingling in her chest. Her stomach felt light.

"Yeah, of course. I mean, we all saw you disappear, Kenia. That doesn't just happen," Stan said.

A tear escaped from Kenia's eye. "I thought I was crazy."

"We didn't think you were," Hailey said. "Then we all would be."

"No, not crazy," Stan said. "Not crazy at all. It's actually . . . well you have to make a couple of assumptions that have yet to be proven in physics . . . but considering what we observed, such assumptions might be in order. It would appear that for some unexplained reason, Kenia, you are jumping among different possible realities, different timelines."

"Or different points on the same timeline before it diverges with others," Shane offered.

"We'd have no way to know that," Stan countered.

Kenia tried to remember what she could of physics, but it was not much more than force was equal to mass times acceleration, Newton having three laws, and the relativity of time —but that was knowledge gained more from watching sci-fi movies than Mr. Edmond's high school Physics class. Her AP classes had been in chemistry and biology, things she thought would help her with a major in public health. "I know time is perceived differently depending on your speed, that's an old sci-fi movie staple. I do remember my high school physics teacher saying nothing can move faster than light."

"Correct," Stan said. "That's all based on relativity, but what you are experiencing has more to do with what happens on an even smaller, subatomic level. This is where scientists turn to quantum mechanics, which is still being reconciled with relativity. But in quantum mechanics, it's not about the fixed position of a particle or the energy level of a wave, but rather, the probabilities."

"Like statistics?" Kenia asked.

155

"Sort of," Stan said, setting his hands on the table. "You know the model of the hydrogen atom, the nucleus with the proton and neutron and the electron orbiting around it?"

"Sure."

"And if the nucleus was blown up to the size of an apple, the diameter of the electrons orbit would be the size of Manhattan Island?"

"The *Big* Apple," Shane said, a wry smile lifting the corner of his mouth. Hailey rolled her eyes before he apologized. "Sorry, serious time now. No more puns, I promise."

"It's all right, I could use some levity," Kenia said. "Go on, Stan."

"Well, quantum mechanics says there is no real point that the electron is at, at any one time. There is just a region of *probable* locations, none of them fixed until observed. That region of probable locations is a sort of cloud of probabilities."

"And that has all sorts of implications for the nature of reality," Shane said.

"How so?" Austin asked, displaying more curiosity than he had before.

Stan continued, "Well, the most famous thought experiment was Erwin Schrödinger's cat-in-a-box scenario."

"Not to be confused with Seuss's Cat-in-a-Hat," Shane said.

"Shane, I'm going to murder you," Hailey said.

"Sorry, I promise I'll stop," Shane said with a smirk, which he wiped from his face, mime-like, after another scowl from Hailey.

Stan tried to start again. "See, Schrödinger hypothesized that if you put a cat in a box with a radioactive element with a half-life, let's say of sixty minutes, that means it would have a fifty-fifty chance of breaking down and releasing enough radiation to kill the cat in the span of thirty minutes or so. But at the thirty-minute mark, before we open the box to check on the cat, in theory, both realities, the cat being dead and the cat being alive, exist in equal probability.

Until we observe the state of the cat, Schrödinger would argue that the cat is both dead *and* alive."

"Your shirt from yesterday," Kenia said.

Stan pointed at her, as if rewarding a point just scored. "Yes, I'm a bit of a physics nerd, if you didn't notice."

"We noticed," Hailey said.

"I'm not following," Austin said. "What does that have to do with Kenia?"

"Well, if the probability of where particles are and what they do determines reality," Stan said, "We can extrapolate that there are nearly infinite possibilities for the trajectory of reality at every moment. Where science is split right now is whether or not all those possible realities collapse into one—the one we experience—or if they split off into different ones, different timelines, different universes."

"It's where the theory of the multiverse comes from," Shane added, finally serious. "There is scientific evidence that these possible universes *do* interact and that somehow governs the expression of the energy levels of particles or their wave function. But like Stan said, no one knows yet if they collapse into one observable universe or if they split off."

"How do you know all this?" Kenia asked.

"Shane and Stan are geeks; it's genetic, chronic, and incurable," Hailey sighed.

"It's sort of a hobby of ours," Stan said, bright-eyed and undeterred. "You can learn a lot from YouTube science lectures and MOOCs."

"MOOCs?" Austin asked.

"Massive Open Online Courses," Hailey said. "It's actually where I learned a lot about camera work, lighting, and editing."

"And I thought the Marine Corps had too many acronyms."

"See Kenia, we're not just pretty faces," Shane said, framing his face in a square made of his fingers. It reminded Kenia of Audre, and this time she did laugh at his antics. Stan cleared his throat and brought them back to the subject at hand.

"Perhaps, after what Kenia said about her father, how he was always called back to critical points in the past, one could theorize that these points are nodes, where a number of possible realities converge and branch off again. They could be important. So important that some force, be it scientific, or something more metaphysical that we don't understand, a force of will, a force of wanting, an 'arc towards justice' for all we know, is drawing Kenia, like her father, to go back, to make something different."

"To make something right," Hailey said.

"How do we learn more?" Kenia asked.

"Yeah, that is what I'd like to know," Austin added.

Stan and Shane shared a look between them before Shane shrugged his shoulders and said, "We do what any good scientists would do . . . ."

Stan finished his brother's sentence, "We observe."

Chapter 18

A Lesson Before Dying

Hailey or Stan accompanied Kenia on her remaining interviews that week. She explained their presence to the respondents by introducing them as her assistants. The residents of Selah Station whom they interviewed did not mind. Some were actually eager to meet young people, and more than a few had heard of their YouTube channel, even if they did not know what exactly YouTube was. Hal Olson, a ninety-two-year-old widower whose gas station had stopped pumping gas in 1997, spent more time asking Stan about the internet and how it worked than he did answering Kenia's questions. He was in no hurry to do anything else. His days consisted of waking up at 6 a.m. and heading across the street to his station where he put on his mechanic's hat and read the paper to kill time.

As Kenia and Stan left, walking out to Kermit, Stan was sober. "He just reads the paper all day to pass the time. The same articles over and over. The man doesn't even have a flip phone. What kind of existence is that?"

"It's not much of one. But I've realized it's sort of common up here where there are no jobs. It's good he's not turning to drugs or alcohol."

"Coal is not coming back," Stan said. "People need to stop talking about jobs and start paying attention to workers and their skills," he said, staring up at the ridge of Manahoac Mountain looming over them.

"But how is he going to learn new skills? How is a MOOC supposed to reach Hal when he doesn't even have a flip phone, much less dial-up?" she said, pulling on her helmet and buckling the strap beneath her chin.

"I don't know. I'm not a politician."

"You are an educator of sorts though," she said.

"Yeah," he replied, looking off into space. He put his arms around her waist as she kick-started the engine and they accelerated away.

With most of the interviews finished, Kenia set up a station in the Pennels' control room. While Hailey edited their latest videos, Shane made calls organizing extras and emailed them scripts, and Stan posted on social media, Kenia transcribed, reliving the dozens of interviews on porches, in dining rooms, and kitchens all over Selah Station and the surrounding hollows. She checked in with her mother multiple times a day. At night, Hailey came home with her to the Corrigans', sleeping on the couch in the upstairs apartment.

The Fourth of July came and went. There was no grand municipal display of fireworks; the city could not afford it. But under an indigo sky they gathered with the residents of Selah Station to eat barbeque chicken and apple pie, while a *Back to the Future* marathon played out on an outdoor screen. Neighbors set off fountains and children ran about with sparklers, dazzling in the night air that was already full of laughter and patriotic music pumped from speakers on the gazebo.

Kenia could almost see how present-day Selah Station resembled the old one—families still had children and children still played the way they always had. But it did not take much further reflection to realize the crowds of today were so much smaller and far less diverse than the ones she had seen in the decades before. And even this crowd did not account for many of the residents of the city and its environs. Few of the people she had interviewed were actually there in the downtown square, unable, unwilling, or uninterested in joining in the community spirit.

The days of transcribing wore on. When Kenia needed a break from the dark control room, she would take her laptop and station herself on the porch. Austin had set up two of his sawhorses there and was planing the wood siding he had decided to replace. After transcribing a particularly tedious and depressing session, an interview with a woman who had lost her last job fifteen years before when the last mines had shut down and now made her living scavenging aluminum cans from the side of the road, recycling them for forty-five cents a pound, Kenia looked up at Austin, studying him and his work. She envied the straight-forward nature of his task. He paused to run his hand along a board, closing one eye and studying its face.

"You are quite precise," Kenia said.

"Yeah, I guess I am," he said, without looking up from the grain of wood. "Always have been a fan of order, ever since I was little. My mother said I used to stack the soup cans in the grocery cart, even as young as two, labels out, and according to color."

"A little OCD?"

"Maybe," he said without a smile. "Got worse after our parents died."

Kenia waited a moment before she asked, "What happened?"

"Car accident. Drunk driver crossed the center line. They died instantly; he walked away."

"I'm sorry."

Austin blew the wood shavings off the face of the board. "Yeah, so were we. They were good people."

"Who took care of you all growing up?"

"Our Uncle Mike, actually. He lives up in that house on the back of the lot with his wife Rochelle. They didn't have kids of their own, took us in. Uncle Mike owned this place, but turned it over to us as we got older."

"Austin, do you think he was the person I saw when, you know, I jumped back last time?"

"I had been thinking that myself," he said, laconic.

"Could I meet him?"

"Not unless you go to the Florida Keys. He's down there with Rochelle, brushing up on their scuba diving skills."

"Scuba diving . . . how old is he?"

"In his eighties, but he's well preserved, him and Rochelle both. Iron Mike, they call him around here."

He returned to planing the wood.

"So you've done all the renovations here?" Kenia asked.

"Yep. It's the kids that bring the money in. I sort of work for them." He brushed shavings from the hair on his forearms. "Not sure what else I would do around here. I'm good with my hands. I'm organized. The Marine Corps taught me how to kill people and disable IEDs, but those are not marketable skills in Selah."

"All this stuff in the yard must make you a bit crazy."

"Like you wouldn't believe," he said, chuckling for only the second time since she had met him. "But it keeps them out of trouble. There are worse things they could be doing in these parts." He stopped, balancing the plane on its corner as he spoke. "It's funny, how folks think this is the real America. I served next to guys from downtown Phoenix, the backwoods of Oregon, suburbs of Indianapolis, New York, Newark, and Miami. All those places are just as real as rural West Virginia. Not as white, but just as real. I don't know why places like this are such an obsession."

"Nostalgia?"

"Seems like hooey to me."

Kenia sighed. "At best that picture of the past is ignorant, at worst it's racist."

"I feel like a lot of these folks around here, they have never seen New York City, Miami San Francisco. They need to. Otherwise they'll keep thinking that America is supposed to look like the cast of the Brady Bunch. They need to get out, meet some people like yourself, shake hands with a middle-aged lesbian, have coffee with a Muslim. See that America is a place where all these people can be at home . . . freedom of faith, respect for all, malice towards none, and all that."

Kenia thought back to Joel Andersen and the wall of the cost of living he had described surrounding cities. "Sometimes travel itself is a privilege."

"So are ignorance and indifference, but they shouldn't be. I don't know, seems to be that everyone at once is more lucky than they deserve and more worse off than you can imagine. If we could just realize that about everyone, maybe we could get out of each other's hair."

Austin grew silent after that and lost himself again in his work, Kenia in hers. But it was a companionable silence they shared. Later in the afternoon, when it was too hot to work, Austin went inside, changed shirts, and returned with iced tea lemonades for both of them. He settled into a rocking chair and drifted in and out of sleep, an Ernest J. Gaines novel in his lap.

◊

Stan took over for Austin before dinner, keeping an eye on Kenia while Austin cooked. They set themselves up at the kitchen table. It was late in the day and Kenia was having trouble concentrating. When news broke that a white man had rammed a car into a crowd of anti-white-supremacists marchers in Charlottesville Virginia everyone's phone started to buzz with updates and posts at once. Kenia and Stan stopped all their work and began reading, watching, and listening to reports online. Kenia felt sick, like something putrid was roiling in her gut. Her vision was blurred with tears of outrage.

"This country can't seem to make it through a summer without racial violence," she heard Hailey say from the studio. Apparently she was not getting much work done editing new videos either.

Can't make it through a day is more like it, Kenia thought, bitter.

"The president has notably not condemned the white supremacist protestors. Instead he is calling for the "bigotry, hatred, and violence on many sides, to stop," Stan said, his eyes scanning his laptop screen back and forth, a note of disbelief in his voice.

163

"Seems to me, there's a side that wants peace and justice and a side that doesn't," Austin growled from where he was at the stove. He shook his head. "We all know which side he is on." He knocked a spoon against the side of one of the cooking pots. "You all sure you want to keep reading that stuff?"

Not really. Kenia thought to herself, closing her laptop and putting her phone on silent. She found herself staring at the Decepticon sticker on the back of Stan's laptop. She needed something superfluous to distract herself.

"You really like the transformers," she said.

Stan shrugged. He seemed to understand she needed a change in conversation and obliged her. They all were feeling the frustration and fury of being far away and powerless. He closed his laptop. "It's a bit absurd, but they are my favorite. And in the end our civilization may be one perpetuated by artificially intelligent machines. I get tired of the same mainline Marvel and DC plotlines anyway."

"Yeah, so does my brother," suddenly deeply grateful for Stan and his willingness to indulge her. "Don't get him started on how superior Dark Horse is."

"He's right, you know."

Kenia, trying to avoid a lecture similar to ones she had heard before from Chiazam, shifted. "I noticed you had a lot of the classic toys from the '80s at your workstation."

"Yeah, Austin had a bunch and I got the others from collectors on the internet."

"My older sister had lots."

"Really, she wasn't playing with Barbies, My Little Ponies, or Strawberry Shortcake back in the '80s?"

"No . . . Chinemere wasn't really the type who was into dolls."

"I like her already."

"She passed them down to my brother. He was into the comics too, but I couldn't get into them and how they kept going

164

back with different series and making the origins of the Autobots and Decepticons different."

"I know what you mean," he said, sitting up. "But they were all variations on the same themes, some better than others. They got more interesting the more Megatron's principles of freedom, equality, and revolution evolved and with how they informed Optimus Prime's own ethics. Tied together more closely, learning from one another, it made the story better."

"Did you like the new variations, post Michael Bay?"

"Hated them!" he said, putting his hands up over his head. "Oversimplified it. Just all good versus all evil."

"So how do you know what storyline to invest in?" she asked, as Austin began to set the table around them.

"Well, it happens all the time, doesn't it, with rebooted origin stories," Stan said with a shrug. "But all the best myths get recycled, and nothing is new under the sun, right? Shakespeare was right and so was Joseph Campbell when he said it again. Even the Gospels had four versions."

It was Kenia's turn to shrug. "I guess you're right."

◊

Austin served dinner. They tried to avoid talking about the news. Afterwards Kenia headed back to the Corrigans' with Hailey on the back of Kermit. Colton came by the apartment and they read to him until Sandra retrieved him to put him to bed. It was a calming relief to lose herself in a children's book. As she and Hailey got ready for bed Kenia was starting to wonder if all the precautions they were taking to observe her were necessary. Had they overreacted? She worried the Pennels might even begin to doubt her story, the longer they went without an incident. She had to admit, however, she slept better knowing Hailey was there. Hailey, for her part, relished the time away from her brothers. Together they painted their nails and flipped through issues of Ebony. It was the first time Hailey had looked at a "black" magazine.

"I never realized hair was so complicated," she said. "I mean, this classification system with letters and numbers, it's surreal."

Kenia drifted off, Hailey still flipping through back issues. It was not until 1:12 a.m. that Kenia sat up in bed, the sensation growing in the space just behind her eyes. She pressed the pads of her fingers to her forehead and reached to shake Hailey, but she was already awake, clicking on the lights and flipping on her phone's camera.

"It's happening, isn't it?"

"Yeah," Kenia said.

"Here." Hailey tossed Kenia a pair of jeans and a button-down plaid shirt. "You don't want to show up pre-sexual revolution in your Victoria's Secret shorts. Everyone will be wondering why your ass says 'I love pink.'"

"Or why my ass says anything at all," Kenia said, changing quickly, sliding into the jeans and pulling on shoes. She looked up to thank Hailey, but she was already gone.

Chapter 19

The Latest in Smartphone Technology

The bedroom had been replaced by the darkness of night, the familiar sound of crickets and cicadas closing in on her like a wave. Kenia had "appeared" outside, standing in a street.

Thank goodness there's no traffic.

The time of night she had jumped to lined up with the time she had left. The quiet of the street and the darkness of the windows told her it was late at night, likely past midnight. The sound of insects was distinct, but soft, as in the small hours of the morning. For that reason, she imagined it would not be a good idea to knock on any doors to ask for help. Instead, she decided to use the cover of darkness and the relative quiet of night to explore, at least until she jumped back.

She noted that she was less panicked during this episode. Perhaps, having heard an explanation from her mother and the affirmation from the Pennels gave her some security that her sanity was not completely lost. If she ignored the cars and the yards, the neighborhood was unchanged: the houses appearing as they did sixty years in the future. They provided familiar and helpful landmarks. The three-story Victorian on the corner of Delaney and Harper was recognizable. The Lutheran church on Gardner Street was nearly identical to its 2017 version. She noted the parked cars she passed: Chevys, Fords, Oldsmobiles, Pontiacs, even a Studebaker and a Packard. No imports of course. The hum of AC units was noticeably absent. Windows were open. While passing a few houses she could hear the snores of sleepers inside.

The sidewalks remained empty and her confidence grew. She moved towards downtown, passing quietly under the streetlamps surrounded by clouds of night insects tapping against the glass. At the intersection of Craft and Meachum, the red-yellow-green traffic lights had yet to be put in place. Only a single flashing red blinked into the empty streets on all four sides. She jay-walked from one corner to another. When she saw a newspaper stand outside Dawson's Hardware she sped up. The tools in the window of the hardware store were not electric or especially sleek, but the wrenches, hammers, and screwdrivers had a solidness to their heft. She directed her attention to the newspaper dispenser and was rewarded: a single issue from the day before remained, although in the light she could not read it. She reached for her cellphone and stared at it with more than a little disbelief, recognizing that it was, without doubt, the most sophisticated piece of technology on the planet at that moment in time.

She used the flashlight app to shine it into the stand.

Saturday, August 15, 1953.

President Eisenhower rebuked senators for the time they were taking to debate a bill already approved by the House. There was an ongoing strike in France to protest austerity measures. Unrest in Iran. Locally, a youth group had set a record for collected donations for canned goods. Preparations were ongoing for the celebration in honor of the Selah Station troops returning home from Korea.

She took a picture of the edition, feeling suddenly vulnerable and exposed after the bright flash. She scanned the street. No movement, no change, save for the blink of the stoplight. She moved quickly anyhow. This was the longest any jump had lasted, and she was grateful for the opportunity to gather information, while at the same time, her heart fluttered with panic at the thought of being trapped in this time, pre-civil rights, pre-women's liberation.

The fifties were hardly halcyon days for everyone.

Yet Selah Station had prospered. At that very thought she took her bearings and turned towards the island proper, the idea of exploring downtown in its prime drawing her. As she moved block by block, she realized that *this* Selah Station on the mainland was indeed only the outskirts. The park that would become the heart of downtown in the twenty-first century, where they would watch Back-to-the-Future, was still just a wooded lot. In this period, the buildings became more distinguished the closer she moved to the Selah Branch Bridge. A train whistle sounded off in the hollows, and in the silence that followed she could hear the sound of the rapids and currents swirling at the bottom of the river gorge.

No roadblock, no guardhouse, waited for her at the crossing, only the bridge, its girders freshly painted. This truly was a sleepy town, as there was no late night traffic. She was able to cross walking down the centerline. When she was halfway to the island, the train whistle echoed through the hills again, this time closer. Kenia realized the train was rumbling along the bend in the river to the north. With another blast of the whistle, its headlamp blinked into view as it made the turn upriver and chugged towards the bridge. She recognized the scene with a rush.

I've been on that train trellis in previous jumps.

Grateful not to be racing away from an oncoming locomotive this time, she continued on the Selah Branch Bridge, taking in the surroundings. She turned back to note the Bridgewater Estate, anchored up on the hill, looking down like a feudal castle even in this time. The outline of the mansion was indistinct in the darkness, but she could make out the lights of a few windows, dim but sleepless eyes.

Two headlights appeared at the start of the bridge just as she was crossing to the island. Out of instinct, she scrambled off the road and waited. She had not been sighted yet but preferred the anonymity of invisibility. She pushed through a thicket of bushes, experiencing a sort of frisson to think that she was actually on Selah Island without a suit, followed by a sadness that this place, so tranquil, would soon be rendered uninhabitable. The peace of this night taken for granted by the sleeping residents: students, faculty, and families ensconced in their bedrooms.

The university, she knew, would be a place she might fit in, if she still remained after sunup. She might be able to pass as a student on the integrated campus. But first she would have to wait for this truck on the bridge to overtake her. It was moving with painful slowness, so slow in fact that she could see men, evenly spaced, walking beside it.

Strange.

She could not afford to squander time in the bushes when she did not know how long she had before she jumped back, but the growing presence of the machines of industry—the slow-moving truck with its escort of men; the train rattling its way onto the trellis, its light blinking between the struts—gave her a new idea. She needed to see the plant. It was a place off-limits in the future, but now, tragedy had yet to strike. She had a growing sense that whatever was drawing her back to this time, this place, had to do with what would happen there in the coming days.

She shuffled out of the bushes and sidled down the shoulder of the road until she was certain she was lost in the shadows, beyond the reach of the truck's headlights. She darted to the opposite side, jogging north until she came to an intersection. She had been to this place with Octavian. In the future the turn was sealed off. But now, this night in 1953, the road was as open as any other. A sign indicating that the SSCPP, the Selah Station Coal Processing Plant, was .25 miles distant helpfully pointed the way.

◊

The gate to the plant was nothing more than a booth, the lights off, and a traffic barrier, which was down. The barrier looked as if it was raised just by hand. She was fairly certain she heard the faint sound of someone snoring in the booth. There was no fence surrounding the plant, however, so she took to the woods and approached the perimeter. Despite the hour the plant was alive with activity, the noise of machinery drowning out the sound of her footsteps crunching through the deadfall. Floodlights illuminated the conveyer booms of the stackers as they piled up mountains of coal, which rolled out of the roaring machinery housed in the white, windowless plant. A tippler and a reclaimer crane moved the coal from the mountainous stacks to a row of freight cars likely pulled into place by the same locomotive she had seen crossing the trellis.

In a few days this will all be a smoking ruin.

Could she warn them? Could she avert disaster? Should she? What would it mean to change history?

She had no idea what to do, so instead she watched, noting men and even a few women moving about the grounds in coveralls and hardhats. When they walked close to the lights, she could indeed see that they were of all skin colors. She had no idea how much time had passed until the truck from the bridge rolled up to the gate, having finally covered the distance from the bridge to the plant at its slow crawl.

One of the men escorting the truck knocked on the window of the booth. A light flicked on outside, shining on the truck, its escort, and its trailer. A short, thin man, could have been just a teenager really, stepped out of the side door of the booth, adjusting the oversized hat on his head and rubbing the sleep from his eyes. He and the lead man from the truck's escort exchanged a few words and documents before the guard raised the arm of the gate and waved the truck through.

Just as the truck shuddered into gear, a whistle sounded at the plant. The roar of machinery spun down. Lights began to click off throughout the plant while men and women retired from their posts, their shifts over. Only the reclaimer continued its work, pouring a stream of coal into the waiting train cars. Kenia watched a bus pull up outside one of the outbuildings, which the workers entered in coveralls but exited shortly after in their civilian clothes, toting lunchboxes, the orange tips of cigarettes glowing in their hands and at their mouths. They boarded the bus, their voices indistinct, but the sound of laughter and comradery unmistakable as they hand-rolled more cigarettes while they waited, sharing them with one another. When it was full, the driver cranked the engine, and the bus rolled out of the traffic circle outside the administration block and disappeared towards a gate somewhere at the north end of the plant.

Everything was still and quiet, save for the rumble of the tippler and the hiss from the reclaimer as they filled one coal car after another. Now the truck at the gate nearest Kenia started forward with its escort. The lights of the plant had gone dark, except for a few along the driveway making aprons of light that danced over the long, gleaming tank pulled by the truck. The cab itself, now that she could see it, was a square design that could tip forward to reveal the engine. She had only seen its like in pictures. The driver's compartment looked narrow and cramped compared to the rigs she knew. The tank that followed, however, gleamed with the same silvery exterior and dimensions of modern gas trailers with ExxonMobil, Shell, or BP emblazoned on their sides.

The driver continued to move the delivery with extreme care, the men tracking alongside. The garage opened up to reveal a few workers waiting to meet them. Accompanying the workers were five guards, each with a Doberman pinscher on a short leash. Unlike the workers she had noticed earlier, these men were all white, not a black man among them.

Whatever was being delivered had to be valuable, she decided. Hadn't Octavian and all the warning flyers and legal releases named it? Chlortro—*something* . . . it had exploded during the fire and it was the toxic fallout that rendered the island off-limits. Was Kenia witnessing its fateful arrival? If so, she wondered with new urgency, what was she supposed to do? This burden of time travel was so new. What would her father have done? Had he made the wrong decision at some point and that was why he had never returned?

If nothing else, she knew she should document. She slipped her phone from her pocket and held it up, zooming in on the image with her fingers. Her mind was astir, marveling once more at the mere presence of her smartphone in the current era, while also noting her growing tension, the tightening of her back muscles, and the irritating discomfort of sweat running down her temples into her eyes as she waited for the camera to focus. With so much running through her head, she did not think to turn off the flash.

The dual-color LED flash on her phone, advertised as the most advanced source of lighting available on mobile phones, promising better skin tones for people of all shades, did its job—too well. The guards did not fail to notice the "handy" staggered flashes—a feature to reduce redeye. Nor did they hesitate to release the Dobermans, sending them barking and howling in the direction of the flash.

Kenia cursed, clutched the smartphone in her hand, and went crashing through the bushes and undergrowth. During her approach, the woods had offered plentiful coverage from view, but it was a space bereft of hiding places that would be safe from Dobermans with their canine sense of smell. All she could do was run, but even that was fruitless—she knew—as the noise she was making only made it easier for the dogs to track and gain on her.

Her knowledge of what guard dogs were trained to do to colored interlopers in these times was informed by old stories from the south and black and white photos of dogs set on civil rights protesters. She ran with her heart in her throat, branches whipping her face and body. She was prey without a plan, and her only thought was to run. The river was not far, but the drop from the cliffside might be fatal. Even if she survived the impact on the water, she would have to negotiate rocks and strong currents in the dark. No, jumping was not an option. She stumbled and careened into a tree trunk, hitting her head so hard that she saw a flash of light. Dizzy, she scrambled to her feet and kept running, the dogs shooting through the foliage just over her shoulder.

The inevitability of her capture became clear. She knew it was only a matter of minimizing injury, if she could. She switched tactics, no longer looking for a path of escape. Instead she searched for a tree with limbs low enough and thick enough for her to climb. None of the immediate contenders offered both. The nearest dog was so close that she could see its teeth gleaming in the faint light from the plant. She picked a maple with a low fork just within reach, hoped that her upper arm workouts would pay off, and hopped up, grabbing hold of the branches and pulling. Her time at the gym's climbing wall helped her. She remembered to use her feet, pushing herself just out of reach as the dogs swarmed the base of the tree, their jaws snapping inches short of her shoes.

It was a stalemate, only delaying the inevitable, she knew. But at least she did not have to contend with dog bites. Although what these men might have in store for her made her shudder. She wondered how long she could remain treed? Could she make it to morning? Who were these men anyway? Would they call the police? She ran through scenarios to offer as possible explanations for what she had been doing, her mind working better now that she was no longer fleeing.

I'm a student from the college. An RA even. They will be looking for me at my dorm soon enough.

She considered her phone. Would they search her? How could she explain it? They would search her for a camera, not a phone. She held down the power button and turned it off. At best she could pass it off as . . . what . . . a toy? She slipped it into her bra against her breast. It would look lumpy, but in the darkness perhaps it would go unnoticed. If things progressed so that one of them actually felt it there, she knew she would be in a whole different universe of problems.

The security men came into the clearing, their faces shiny with sweat, and stomped through the fallen branches and bushes, kicking aside thorny vines and sweeping the clearing with the beams of their flashlights. Kenia could see that they were all armed. She realized she might have less time than she thought. They raked the branches of the maple with their lights. Kenia pressed herself against the trunk, even though she knew it was ultimately pointless. Just when she thought all hope was lost, a new avenue of escape opened: a growing pain, which had never been so welcome, just behind her eyes. Could she accelerate it, could she bring on the jump? She closed her eyes and clenched her fists, willing the phenomenon to manifest. One of the men shouted. He had seen her. Her eyelids flashed red with the beam of a flashlight.

"Someone is up there!"

But that was all she heard before the voice was cut short.

Chapter 20

Candles, Cupcakes, and Kerry Park

Kerry Park, Seattle, Spring 1998. Kenia and her family were on the west coast visiting their mother's sister, Henrietta. It was also Chikmara's birthday. To mark the occasion, just after sunset they piled into the rented Ford Taurus station wagon and drove up to Kerry Park.

"Kerry Park, at just 1.26 acres, is one of the smallest parks in Washington State. It was donated to the city of Seattle by the Kerry family in 1927 so that all residents could enjoy the stunning view of city and Mt. Rainier that the park provides from its elevation of 339.83 feet," Chinemere read from the guidebook from where she sat in the foldup seat in the far back of the car. Their father drove the car uphill from downtown, where they had visited the Space Needle, taken a boat ride on Lake Union, and visited the Children's Theater. The climb into the Upper Queen Anne neighborhood was steep. The shops and offices of downtown gave way to brick apartment buildings and homes made in the Queen Anne style, which gave the neighborhood its name.

Their mother was navigating, their Aunt Henrietta providing editorial comments. She lived in the city after all, but being the younger sister still fought with her sibling for dominance. Kenia noted how her father tried his best to heed the instructions from both women, displaying not a small amount of discomfort.

Chiazam was still too young to notice the sibling dynamics, but Kenia was aware, her aunt sharing with her a wry smile and a roll of the eyes, as Kenia's mother pointed out what she was certain was the correct turn.

"Are you sure about that, Leanna?" Henrietta asked.

"Of course I am, I know how to read a map," Kenia's mother said, her words short and clipped.

Henrietta let out a long hum and winked at Kenia.

Kenia giggled uncontrollably, thrilled to find an adult comrade to commiserate with regarding her mother's bossiness. Chikmara, for her part, was oblivious. She was buckled into the same lap belt as Kenia, but her attention was focused on the cellophane window on the to-go box holding the oversized cupcake in her lap. When they finally arrived at the park, they found a patch of green grass bordered by a brick wall and centered around a piece of artwork about fifteen feet high that consisted of two large cubes with circles cut through them. Chiazam immediately began to climb on it. Kenia was old enough to understand, however, that the focus of the park was the view. The city of Seattle was set beneath them. The top saucer of the Space Needle rose to their very height, while downtown sparkled in gold, red, greens, and blues. The expanse of Puget Sound was a mirror of the sky set between misty shores and the jagged Olympic Mountain Range, crowned in spring snow to the west. Far in the south, but still huge and imminent, was Mount Rainier, its white slopes nothing short of celestial, transcending the whole of the Olympic range so that the peaks looked to be but foothills. The dormant volcano loomed with insistency over the region and into the sky, the clouds parting, as if in reverential deference.

No wonder the First Nations People had thought it was a god.

Along with a gaggle of other tourists, the Dezys posed for family pictures, the city, the needle, the mountains in the background. Chikmara posed for a few individual portraits holding her cupcake, her hair decorated with an explosion of twists and ribbons in every color of the rainbow. Their aunt and mother forgot their earlier tension, as sisters were apt to do, and posed together, turning up their collars to the chilly spring wind.

The light faded, pink clouds to the west catching the last flares of color from the sun. Their father announced it was time to sing Happy Birthday. He set Chiazam on the brick wall and pulled out a book of matches and a packet of birthday candles. Chikmara clapped her hands. Chinemere, being the oldest, insisted that she be responsible for lighting the matches. Chikmara, as the birthday girl, did not object, so they watched as Chinemere, with her characteristic focus, stared down a match through her coke-bottle glasses and struck it on the back of the paperback matchbook.

It flared, sputtered, and was extinguished by the wind. She tried again, cupping it with her hand, but the wind on the heights was too strong, snuffing out the flame into a piteous string of smoke.

"Here, let's move closer to the wall," her father suggested.

They placed the to-go box closer to the wall, its top open, the candle poked into the spongy moistness of the cupcake, waiting to be lit. Chinemere tried again; this time the match lit, the flame flickered but failed before she could bring it to touch the wick of the candle. The frustration was building in her face while the smile faded from Chikmara's.

The pile of extinguished matches grew.

"Come on. We need to form a wall," Aunt Henrietta said. So they all moved in, closer to the cupcake, shoulder to shoulder, giggling. Chinemere tried the matches again, her mother issuing a threat that if Chinemere caught her hair on fire, she would not live to see her next birthday.

They all laughed, except for Chinemere, whose status as competent older sister was on the line. She snapped the match against the striking surface. It popped to life, with more flame than any of the previous ones. As a group, they tucked in even closer. Chinemere touched the match to the inert wick and the candle began to glow, the flame a perfect little scalpel of light cutting the darkness and casting their faces in a warm glow. Their mother started the singing, with all the children joining in at various keys and pitches, their father attempting to sing some semblance of a harmony with his deep bass. Even Aunt Henrietta reveled in the absurdity, adding a *"Ba-da-dum"* to the end of each line. They stumbled through the traditional words, the children adding on the coda of "How old are you now, how old are you now . . . ."

It was a joyous cacophony that they concluded with a round of applause for Chikmara, who stood up to take a bow before she settled back down, shoulder-to-shoulder with the rest of her family. Their bodies formed a better shelter for the flame than the brick wall had ever done. The moment of silence stretched into a minute as the molten wax dripped down the candle to form a waxy film on the frosting of the cupcake.

"You can blow it out now," their mother said. But Chikmara hesitated, her eyes flicking up to their faces, then back to the candle.

"I don't want to."

"Why not?" Chinemere asked in a tone of cross-examination. "People are cold."

Chikmara shrugged, unmoved. "Because when I do, this moment will be over."

They looked over the candle at one another, as if noting the nuances of their immediate family's features for the first time: the warm gleam of skin, the curve of cheekbones, the gleaming of piercing eyes. Radiant in the candle light, everyone was beautiful.

Her aunt's mouth was screwed up in that wry smile that was so distinct on her. "Out of the mouths of babes . . . ."

Her father rubbed his hands together and extended his arms around them. They each followed suit. Like campers around a campfire, they gazed wordlessly into the candle. Chikmara was more than happy to let it burn down until the wax had run down over the icing, dripping onto the sidewalk. No one protested. Just before the flame guttered, she closed her eyes, moved her lips in a silent wish, then blew it out.

Chikmara kept the wish to herself, but Kenia, and all of them, knew exactly what it had been.

Chapter 21

Bender

Kenia snapped her eyes open in an alleyway. She was on her side, curled into a ball, staring at the base of a dumpster. The odor of garbage was pungent, and she struggled to sit up, placing her back on the cinderblock wall opposite the source of the foul smell. She slipped her hand into her shirt and sighed with relief when she felt the familiar shape of her phone. She powered it on. The screen was smudged with perspiration. While she wiped it clear, the icon indicating it was looking for the nearest tower spun. The phone registered with the network, the time and date popping up.

"Jesus Christ, thank you," she said, nodding her head back after reading 7:48 a.m., Sunday, August 13, 2017. She had been gone only a few hours. Further news and texts from her friends about the events in Charlottesville popped onto her screen. But she could not deal with that just now. Her life, her reality, was complicated enough at that moment.

She tipped her head back. The sky was bright and the morning sun reached the upper stories of the buildings on either side of the alleyway. She estimated that she had been gone from the present for about the same amount of time she had been in the past.

A door scraped open beside her and a woman in a red apron that read Dawson's Hardware stepped out carrying a bunch of cardboard boxes collapsed, accordion-style, under her arms. She dropped them into a recycling bin next to the dumpster then jumped as she turned and saw Kenia.

"Kenia!"

"Janice . . . Oh, uh, hi." Kenia said with a weak wave, recognizing the woman who had come into the public health office to get a drug test the day Kenia had arrived in Selah Station.

Janice cocked her head to the side, her arms akimbo. "What are you doing out here, girl? You all right? You on a bender or something?"

"A bender . . . ."

"Girl, I'm not going to judge you. You know I've been there myself," Janice said, kneeling next to her, her hand on Kenia's shoulder, voice tender and full of concern. "If you need it, I know a meeting just down the block at the Elk Lodge that starts in ten minutes. You can pick up a white chip . . . ."

"No, thanks, I mean, thanks, but no," Kenia said trying to gather her thoughts. "It's hard to explain. I'm not hungover."

"All right, but what happened? Your face looks like you got in a fight with an angry cat and lost, your arms, too. And you've got . . . stuff in your hair," Janice said, nodding at the scratches all over Kenia from her flight through the forest then pulling a few stray seed pods from Kenia's hair. A quizzical look came over Janice's face. "First time I've touched . . ."

". . . a sister's hair."

"Yeah," she said, and they both sighed. Janice pulled out the last bits of debris, her voice becoming serious. "Kenia, you're a good girl. What happened, someone messing with you? If so, we'll call the cops."

"Had to run through the woods. It's a long story," she took a deep breath, not sure where to start or even what to share. But her train of thought was arrested. "Wait, Janice, I thought you worked at McDonalds."

"I do, but that doesn't pay all the bills. I work here on the weekends and evenings."

"In your free time?"

"What's that?"

Kenia shook her head and rested it against the wall. "That must make for long days."

"It does. Could drive a girl to drinking and drugging."

Kenia stared, speechless.

"Hold on girl, that was a joke."

"Oh, sorry, I'm . . . a bit out of sorts."

"One thing you learn in the recovery community is that we don't take ourselves too seriously. Can't—most of us tried. Didn't get us very far."

"I'll take your word for it."

Janice slapped her knees with her palms, stood up, and offered her hands to Kenia. "Well, come on. It's slow, and my boss likes me. I'll get the rest of the morning off."

"But Janice, I don't want you to get in trouble, or lose your job—"

"Don't you worry. I'll be doing him a favor. You may *say* you are clean, but you look the part of a junkie right now, and he'll be glad to get you out of his alleyway."

Kenia couldn't help but laugh as Janice helped her to her feet.

◊

"You had me scared," Hailey said, her face close to Kenia's as she closed a cut on her face with a butterfly strip.

"You and me both," Kenia said, sitting on the toilet and wincing. Austin appeared in the doorway of the bathroom and leaned against the frame.

"Your friend Janice is nice," he said. "Good thing she found you."

"She head back to—" Kenia started to ask, but Hailey cut her off.

"Don't talk, trying to close another cut here."

"Yes, she went back to work, after I assured her you were in good hands."

Only when Hailey had finished and leaned back against the sink did Kenia dare speak again.

"Good, I don't want her losing her job over this."

Hailey held up a mirror. Kenia groaned. She wasn't winning any beauty contests any time soon. A cut across her cheek was knit together by a set of adhesive Steri-Strips. So was the gash over her eye. Her face was marked with half a dozen other welts where the branches had struck her hard enough to scratch, but not cut, the skin. Hailey gathered the wrappers from the sterile strips, crumpling them and dropping them into the wastebasket. "That was the longest you've been gone so far, right?"

"Yeah," she said, standing up. Austin moved to the side so she could leave the bathroom and cross the room to the sofa where she sat down, her knees pulled up to her chest. "But it was useful, in a sense. I learned more and I didn't panic, at least not until the end."

"I would have panicked at that point, too," Austin said, sitting down across from her and leaning over the coffee table where Hailey and Kenia's phones were set side by side. He pressed the playback button on Hailey's, and Kenia could hear a tinny version of her conversation with Hailey just before she disappeared.

"Gone, just like that," Austin said over the sound of Hailey's own recorded exclamation of, "Oh my God!"

He set his sister's phone down and picked up Kenia's, his fingers and thumbs expanding the image on the screen. Kenia didn't need to see it to know he was studying the photos she had taken.

"The more things change, the more they stay the same," he said, squinting at the newspaper headlines. He swiped to the picture of the truck, zooming in with his fingers on the screen. "They're definitely from that era, no doubt. The guards around the truck, they're trained. They're spread out at regular intervals, military like."

"What do you think it means?" Hailey asked, closing up the first aid kit. Without stopping, she moved to the kitchenette where she opened the fridge and began to remove ingredients for French toast and scrambled eggs.

"Not sure, but it sure is interesting to see the old CPP before the disaster."

"We need to learn more," Kenia said, wrinkling her nose and puffing out her cheeks to get a feel for the bandages on her face.

"Don't do that. You'll make them come off," Hailey said, apparently not so distracted by cooking that she had forgotten her responsibilities as a nurse.

"Sorry," Kenia said, exchanging a knowing smile with Austin. "I'm convinced the jumps have to do with the plant, the school, the disaster. It really was the turning point for Selah Station. I think we need to visit the plant. Today."

"How?" Austin said, leveling a stare at her over the phones.

"Octavian Coates."

◊

Austin drove them in his Jeep to Octavian and Morris' house, which was walking distance from the Library-Museum. Kenia decided on full disclosure with the two men. There was no time for anything else, she argued, and she felt like she could trust them.

Now the twins sat at their kitchen table, wearing identical navy bathrobes except for their initials embroidered on the breasts. They each sat in thoughtful silence, their hands wrapped about their coffee mugs. They had spent the morning listening to coverage about the violence in Charlottesville. Just a few hours away by car, they had been discussing whether or not to go south and join the counter demonstrations for peace and against the white supremacists. Now Kenia and her story had showed up at their doorstep. Although identical, she could see each man absorbing the news in his own distinct way. Morris was less sure. He turned his eyes to his brother, probing him for a reaction. Octavian was taking a third and even fourth look at the footage of Kenia disappearing before Hailey's eyes. Then he set the phone down with care to pick up Kenia's. He considered the photo of the tanker truck a long time before setting down both phones.

"This is quite extraordinary, if true," he said. "Momentous even."

Morris's brow knitted. "This isn't some stunt for your show?" His voice was low and serious.

"No sir. I let these kids get away with a lot of shenanigans, but I wouldn't involve anyone else or waste your time," Austin answered back.

"Where is your uncle? Does he know?" Morris asked.

"Florida Keys with Rochelle. Seemed to feel like he needed to brush up on his scuba diving skills. You know Uncle Mike, he goes where the spirit takes him."

"That he does," Morris sighed, looking back at Octavian. "Well brother?"

Octavian shook his head. "I'd be more skeptical if I had not seen you do it yourself when we were at the old town in June. You were there then you were gone, Kenia. Then you were back. I thought I had just lost track of you in that blasted helmet. But now . . . now I wish it were so simple. I wish you had told me then."

"What would you have said? I didn't even know what was going on," Kenia said.

"True, but you'll show me the photo in the microfilms when we get to the library?"

Kenia nodded. She could see by the light in Octavian's eyes that he was coming to believe her. Morris leaned back in his chair. "But time travel! It calls everything we know into question."

"Not quite," Octavian countered. "It fits with emerging theories of wave function. Waves that interact and form the building blocks that make up matter and energy. Absent observation, the unobserved universe is only a suite of possibilities of various states that those waves can take if that observation occurs. Physicists are still trying to figure out where all these possibilities go. And how they interact—because the single-particle, double-slit experiment shows that they do. It's really been in debate and discussion since the Copenhagen Interpretation was accepted in mainstream physics.

Werner Heisenberg and Niels Bohr were contributors to this line of thinking. It was an American graduate student in the 1950s, Hugh Everett, who took it a step further, suggesting that the possibilities never collapse at all, but split off into full-fledged different realities, resulting in multiple timelines, multiple worlds."

The four of them stared at Octavian in uncomprehending silence before Austin said,
"I feel like I need to go back to school just to understand what you just said."

"Me too," Morris chuckled.

"You sound like Stan and Shane," Hailey said. "They're both into that type of stuff."

Octavian nodded, pushed his chair back to get up and crossed the kitchen to the sink where he washed his cup. "Give them a call. Tell them to meet us at the library, *pronto.* We need as many heads put together on this one as possible."

"Well, all right then. I guess you're on board," Austin said.

"I'll call Shane and Stan," Hailey said, scooping up her phone.

"Morris, give Bernadette over at the Flying Mountain Biscuit a call. I'm going to need some more coffee. Order some muffins and fruit, too. We'll need it to keep us alert. It's going to be a long day."

Chapter 22

After the Fall

Octavian's knack for information management served them well as they set up stations for study throughout the library. Shane, Stan, and Austin poured over any public company records from the now-defunct Bridgewater Coal Company that had operated and owned the plant. Hailey and Octavian combed through information gathered from the town's municipal records while Kenia set herself up with the microfiche machine and scanned through hundreds of editions of old newspapers from the year of the disaster. They poured themselves into the task. In one sense it was an escape from the news of the country that couldn't seem to keep from tearing itself apart. On the other it felt like their own way to engage in some sort of effort towards justice. Octavian put a sign that read "Closed for Renovations" at the door to keep them from being interrupted.

It was Morris, however, with his deep understanding of history and the heritage of Selah Station, who led the investigations. The normally dour-faced brother was attentive and focused, moving among his assistants, a conductor among his musicians, helping them sort useful leads from dead ends. It was Morris who, on a hunch, sent the boys looking into the company records, including tax filings. When Shane thought he had found something, he brought it over to the table where Morris was using a magnifying glass to study aerial photos of the plant taken in the late 1940s.

"Does this make sense Morris?" Shane asked. "The revenue at the plant in these years before the explosion was steady, but the bottom line was all over the place. The only indication that we could think of was that they were heavily leveraged. So we looked to see where the assets were being transferred, and it looks like a lot them were going to a holding company called Drummer Inc. Nearly everything that was liquid was moved to Drummer by the end of the fiscal year, 1952."

"The year before the explosion. That's suspicious," Morris said, taking one of the old balance sheets in his hand.

"We thought so, too. So Austin looked at what we could find on the Bridgewaters, and it turns out that, early in 1953, Crowley Bridgewater took out a second and third insurance policy on the remaining assets of the plant."

Octavian and Hailey joined them around the table full of photos. Kenia turned from the microfiche and set her elbows on the end, listening, while Shane continued.

"Stan looked deeper into Drummer Inc. and found out it was a subsidiary of BMD Associates."

"What are they?"

"No idea."

"A shell corporation most likely," Stan said walking over, his mouth full from a bite of a banana nut muffin. "What they did was less interesting than who owned them."

"And now for the big reveal . . . wait for it . . ." Shane said, a magician taking a bow.

Stan finished chewing and swallowed. "Abigail Davenport."

Morris was unfazed. The name meant nothing.

Kenia turned up her hands. "Did I miss something?"

"Well, Davenport was Abigail's *maiden* name," Shane said with a smile, as if he were about to share a bomb of a secret with them all. "She changed it when she got married."

"To Bridgewater," Stan finished.

"She was married to Crowley?" Austin said, turning one of the chairs around and sliding into it backwards.

Morris set the magnifying glass down on the table. "So overnight, as the result of the accident, they doubled their fortune many times over."

"All inherited by Sterling Bridgewater, up in his mansion on the hill," Stan said.

"Who bequeathed it to his son, Harold Bridgewater, who lives there now, which brings us to the present day," Shane said, dropping his notebook on the table like a mic.

"You are ridiculous," Hailey said to her brother.

"Suddenly doesn't seem like much of an accident anymore," Kenia said.

Austin had picked up one of the aerial photos by the corner. After considering it a moment he tapped it, edge-on, against the table. "Octavian, any chance you can take us over to Selah Island? I think it is time we did some reconnaissance?"

◊

Buzz Grimsby met them at the gate to the Selah Branch Bridge. His eyes were narrow and mean as he looked back and forth between Austin, Octavian, and Kenia.

"Kind of late in the day to venture over to Selah Island," he said, the voices of talk radio murmuring in the guardhouse behind him.

"Meant to get here sooner, but had car trouble," Octavian said, zipping up his suit. His voice was shaky and unconvincing. He was not a practiced liar.

Kenia tried to cover for him. "That's why Austin drove us here."

Buzz's face creased as he looked over at Austin, one white man to another. Kenia was unsure if it was a squint or a smile. "You served in the Corps, didn't you?"

"Yes, sir," Austin said.

"Well, *Semper Fi,*" Buzz said, his voice settling into a deeper register as he turned to unlock the gate. "I'll leave it to you to make sure these two stay out of trouble."

Kenia bit her tongue and double-checked the seals of her suit while Buzz swung the gate open. They filed through one by one, following Octavian, before spreading out again, three abreast, on the other side.

"What did he mean by that comment?" Kenia wondered aloud.

"Not sure," Octavian said, turning his head to look at Austin, who tried to shrug in his suit. Finding the gesture insufficient he said, "Not sure myself."

Kenia checked over her shoulder one more time, feeling some relief as Buzz disappeared back into his guardhouse. She noted, with some foreboding however, that he reached into his pocket as he did so, pulling out his phone to make a call.

"Stop looking back, Kenia. He'll get suspicious," Austin said.

"Might be too late for that."

"This is just a routine trip to the campus," Octavian said, and he made good on the appearance of it, continuing down the road past the old filling station and around the bend towards the campus.

Kenia studied the roadside, searching for the place where she had hidden the night before during her last jump, but the woods were overgrown, the trees and ground cover having engulfed the shoulder. When they passed the turn she had taken to the plant, it was still barred with hazard signs. Unsatisfied that they were completely out of sight from Buzz in the guardhouse, Octavian led them a bit further until the woods offered better cover. From there he cut a trail through the growth to the northwest end of the island.

Kenia and Austin followed, taking care around some of the branches and watching out for thorns and cats.

"We don't want any chlortrofluorine poisoning," Octavian said.

"Well, maybe the fluorine would be good for my teeth," Kenia offered, but neither man laughed.

Octavian cut to the left and they emerged onto the blocked-off road. They moved three abreast again. The road itself was nearly invisible, covered in decades' worth of deadfall. The experience of walking down the same road, half a century apart, in the span of a few hours, was dream-like to Kenia. Octavian, for his part, was also quiet with awe but for a different reason.

"This road has been abandoned for over fifty years. Not a human soul has walked down it." He turned to face Kenia. "You said earlier that the jumps always seem to concentrate around some important point in history. This disaster was really a fulcrum in a lot of stories here in Selah. Do you think you're supposed to do something about it?"

"I don't know. I was wondering about that myself," Kenia said, anxiety followed by a sense of loss welling up in her chest. "I wish my dad was here to ask."

She noticed Austin look askance at her but couldn't read his expression through the suit. His intentions were clear enough as he reached out with his gloved hand and touched her shoulder. He knew what it meant to lose a parent.

The gate was not as she remembered it. The guardhouse was gone. Nothing remained but the cement slab that had been its base. Layers of leaves and crumbly lichens covered it now. The traffic arm was gone, its frame rusting, ivy curled around it like vines around a tombstone. A few more signs stood in the way, their messages warning of hazardous chemicals obscured by weathering. A final sign added, redundantly, "No Trespassing."

Octavian slipped between the blackberry bushes grown up along the shoulder and the barriers with their faded but strident warnings. As Austin followed, Kenia took a closer look at one of the warning signs describing the symptoms of chlortrofluorine poisoning:

Black spots in vision
Diarrhea
Dizziness
Fatigue
Nausea
Heart palpitations and increased heart rate without exertion

Hives, blisters, rash on exposed areas of skin

Smaller print beneath the list of immediate symptoms warned that in addition to contributing, long-term, to arthritis, asthma, blindness, cancer, diabetes, gastrointestinal problems, kidney failure, thyroid disease, and tooth loss, chlortrofluorine exposure could lead to immediate death.

"You coming, Kenia?" Octavian asked from up ahead.

"Yeah," she said, slipping around the warning sign with a sense of foreboding. Here they were, breaking into the inner sanctum of some secret mystery within the history of the town. They walked without speaking, sharing a sense of espionage and trespass.

It did not take long for them to reach the desolation that was once the plant. First there was the ring of fallen trees, blasted down in the explosion. Each tree lay lengthwise, pointing away from the plant. They were rotting and grown over by new trees that had sprouted on the blast radius, but the line of destruction was clear. The fallen trunks, stripped of their limbs, reminded her of photos she had seen of the 1908 Tunguska Event, when a meteoroid exploded over a Siberian forest, flattening eight hundred square miles of forest and knocking down eighty million trees, not to mention incinerating any and all wildlife. Here on Selah Island, the blast had been smaller, but as in the photos she had seen of Tunguska, everything that remained tilted out and away from the center. The trees just at the end of the blast radius, the ones that had survived, were scarred, their surfaces uneven where branches had been torn away and the carbonized bark had regenerated and knit back together.

Closer in, industrial wreckage lay in tangled heaps throughout the grounds. Octavian pointed out the remains of coal breakers, stackers, and reclaimers, but to Kenia the piles of twisted wreckage were indistinguishable from one another. None of it resembled the gleaming and humming machines she had seen in her jump the night before. She would never have believed this was even the same place, the scene was so transformed. Nothing remained of the buildings she had seen except for a few rusting, charred I-beams. Corrugated sheets of blackened steel lay in random intervals, contorted and shriveled like leaves scorched in a fire. The pieces of ejecta became larger as they moved down the service road, and she tried to determine the exact center of the blast, but it was hard with the decades of weeds and trees that had taken root in the blast zone. It was only when they reached the traffic circle that she regained her bearings.

"Now I know where I am. There was a building here where I saw the company bus pick up a bunch of workers at the end of their shift." She looked to the end of an empty field where she could see a few twisted knots of steel. "I think that is where the railroad tracks were."

"That's about right," Octavian said, stepping up to the curb of the traffic circle where three stairs remained, leading up to nowhere.

"So the coal would have been over there?" Kenia asked, pointing to where she had seen the tall mountains of the stuff blocking out the view of the ridges beyond. "They were huge."

"That was the problem," Octavian said, his voice muffled in his suit. "Standard practice now is to create many small piles of coal when sorting out inventory—stacks they are called. The bigger the stack the more pressure on the coal at the bottom and the more heat the stacks retain from daytime sunlight. But Selah, being an island, didn't have land to spare, so they piled the stacks high, too high. Given those conditions, that caused coal stack three to spontaneously combust, and with all the coal dust in the air, it was like lighting a match in a cotton mill. That is what the investigators determined led to the fire."

"Coal burns, but it doesn't explode," Austin said.

"No, that was the chlortrofluorine."

"What is chlortrofluorine, aside from something that will kill me?" Kenia asked as Austin made his way south across the grounds, Octavian following.

"Well, it's a variant made from chlorine trifluoride, CLF3. It was one of the most vigorous fluorinating agents ever known."

"Substance N," Austin called out from ahead of them.

"Yes, indeed. I should have known an explosives man like you would have heard of it," Octavian said, a measure of revelation sounding in his voice.

"It's sort of legendary among sappers like me."

"Sapper?" Kenia asked.

"Old WWII term for experts who diffused bombs," Octavian said.

"That's what you did, Austin? Like *Hurt Locker*?"

"Well, not exactly like that. We never took our suits off like that. It was a bit . . . Hollywood there."

"But you diffused bombs."

"Yeah," Austin said, slowing as he came to a drop off. Before them the ground rolled steeply down, as if a giant tool had scooped the earth away.

"Here is your blast crater," Octavian said.

"It's huge," Kenia marveled. The space was as wide as a football field, not round so much as butterfly shaped. A marshy pond sat at the lowest point, covered over with green duck meal.

"So, what is Substance N?"

Austin slipped over the lip of the crater, wading through the knee-high grasses and reeds. Kenia made no move to follow. Neither did Octavian, but the librarian did provide some sort of explanation.

"Substance N was what the Nazis called it. They developed it during World War II but abandoned it. It was too volatile even to experiment with. It creates such a violent exothermic reaction that it can burn through concrete, bricks, even dirt."

"Dirt can burn?"

"Substance N can burn it."

"What was it doing here?"

"Well fluorine is a better oxidizer then even oxygen. It's all too happy to steal electrons from other chemicals. In the 1950s there was growing concern with the runoff from coal processing plants like Selah's. See, when coal comes out as a raw material, it needs to be processed, liberated from other substances. Waste rock, dirt, and other macro-materials are cast off through thrashing, breaking, and screening them through jigs. Then the coal has to be dewatered. This would usually produce wastewater or black water—coal slurry—but the stuff is toxic and can't be treated. It has to be sequestered, not unlike radioactive waste.

"So dry separation techniques were in vogue at the time. DuPont got their hands on some formulae for Substance N after the war and were successful in developing a more stable version of it that they branded chlortrofluorine. The idea was that chlortrofluorine would mix with the coal and those fluorine atoms would bond with the oxygen atoms in the water molecules and strip them away. The tricky part was collecting the hydrogen that was released. No good if that caught fire, then you'd have a Hindenburg-like explosion."

"Is that what happened here?"

Octavian pried a bolt from where it had been embedded into the crater wall, examined it, then tossed it back into the crater. "They had figured out how to burn off the hydrogen safely, like a flare stack over an oil refinery," Octavian said. He paused, squinting into the crater where Austin was bent down, pulling up tufts of grass to poke at the clods of soil beneath. "No, what they speculate happened here was that the fire spread to the warehouse where the chlortrofluorine was being stored. It ignited, and the rest is history," he said, spreading his gloved hands out to the desolation around them.

Kenia scanned the grounds, judging the distance between the place where she estimated the coal stacks had been and the blast crater. It had to be a quarter of a mile of empty wasteland.

"Must have been a big fire."

"They say it was. Nearly a thousand men and women lost their lives. And it was the chlortrofluorine fallout that made the island uninhabitable. It was a public relations nightmare for DuPont.

They dropped production of the substance, and it was never commercially viable again."

"So you think the tanker truck I saw had the chlortrofluorine in it?"

Octavian shrugged. "Can't be sure, but the model, with its cracker-box cab and that reinforced steel tank, looked about right. I'd expect a substance formally classified by the military to be guarded like it was."

"But Crowley Bridgewater still got his money."

"That he did," Octavian said with a bitter sigh, as he looked to the gray mansion on the mountainside.

Austin returned. Like Octavian, he had picked up a few metal fragments, but upon closer examination from them both, they decided they were insignificant and tossed them back into the crater. It was not like they could take them with them anyway, contaminated as they were.

"It's interesting to be here, but I don't know what we might find," Octavian said.

Kenia felt a growing sense of unease herself. "We should go."

They turned to Austin, who stood looking back and forth from the crater towards where the coal stacks had once stood, his hands on his hips. Finally, his gaze settled on the still, dark water collected at the base of the crater, an open sore on the skin of the earth.

"It just doesn't make sense," he said.

"What doesn't?" Kenia asked. But whatever it was, Austin kept it to himself.

Chapter 23

Bannister

The sun was setting when they returned to the library. Hailey had fallen asleep in one of the reading barrels, a stack of topographical maps next to her and a record of land deeds tipped open on her chest. Shane was on one of the computer stations, his eyes bleary, while Stan and Morris studied more county records seated next to one another. Both young and old man rubbed his temples, unaware of mirroring each other. It made Kenia smile as she came through the French doors from the foyer with Austin and Octavian. Austin, who had maintained his brooding silence during the drive back, went straight to an empty computer station and settled in next to Shane without a word.

"You all find much?" Morris asked.

"Well, it was interesting to see the ruins. The blast radius is impressive," Octavian said. He looked to Austin, as if waiting for him to provide his own comment, but he was already lost to them as he clicked through websites. "But I don't think we found much."

"I learned about explosive agents, but I could have learned that sitting here in the air conditioning, not burning up in that suit," Kenia said, snapping the front of her shirt for air.

"How about you all?" Octavian asked.

Morris and Stan's eyes met before Morris answered, "Other than the fact that Harold Bridgewater is astronomically wealthy, nothing new."

"Heterosexual WASP man owns half the world. Not really breaking news, is it?" Shane said, without looking up from his computer terminal.

"But he's really rich. He's got investments in everything from Lockheed Martin, Halliburton, and ExxonMobil," Stan added.

"And through his shell corporations, he owns more than half of the wealth in this state."

"Don't white men own enough shit?" Kenia asked, settling into a chair.

The twins exchanged a look. Stan shrugged, "Apparently not."

Octavian said he would order a pizza and start taking requests for toppings. Shane turned from his computer with renewed vigor. "Green peppers and olives."

"Noted," Octavian said. "Austin?"

"Whatever, I'll eat whatever," Austin said, without turning from the computer screen.

"What's with him?" Stan asked.

"Don't know," Kenia said. "He's been like that since we visited the blast site."

They ate on the back porch, the topics of Bridgewater, Selah, even time travel exhausted for the day. Instead, they told stories about their families. The Pennel children laughed as Octavian and Morris fought over whose recollection of the time they had set off a coffee can of black powder in their basement was more accurate. They agreed that they had been using a soldering iron next to the can—which had been left open. But it was what they were soldering that was in dispute. Octavian insisted it had been a shortwave radio, while Morris remembered a pinewood derby car.

"But you didn't even like the Boy Scouts," Octavian countered.

"It was your car. You asked me to help!"

"What were you two doing with a can of black powder in the first place?" Stan asked, lifting a slice of pizza from the box while Shane picked up an olive stranded behind in a string of cheese.

"Well, you could order the stuff right out of the back pages of *Boy's Life* magazine back in those days," Octavian said. "Along with sea monkey colonies, X-ray glasses, and solar-powered blimps."

"Those were less litigious days back then," Morris added.

"Austin would flip if we had something like that in the house," Hailey said.

"Well, then the piece of molten sodder popped and landed in the can, and we made for the basement steps. It saved our lives. The explosion was so big, it lifted the house off the foundations," Morris said, his expression caught between mirth and astonishment.

Hailey was looking through the back window into the reading room where Austin was eating his pizza off a paper plate, still in front of the computer, alone except for whomever he had on speakerphone.

"He all right?" Octavian asked.

"Yeah, he gets fixated like this sometimes. Blocks everything else out."

"I guess that helped defusing IEDs," Morris said.

"Probably," Hailey said with a yawn.

Kenia realized what all the Pennels had been through since she had last jumped, Hailey having awoken and alerted them all when Kenia had disappeared. Now that the pizza was in their bellies and the adrenaline worn off, weariness was descending on them all.

"Guys, I'm beat. I think I need to crash," Kenia said, sipping the dregs of her lemonade, the ice cubes clinking together in the empty cup.

"Well, Austin seems too preoccupied to drive you home in the Jeep," Octavian said, dabbing at his mouth with a paper napkin. "I'll give you a ride in the Camry."

◊

It was dark by the time Octavian dropped Kenia off at the Corrigans'. She stopped outside along her walk up the driveway to chat with Earl and Margaret, who were on the front porch watching Colton catch the fireflies lifting up from the lawn in lazy circles. Sandra was out with some old girlfriends, they said, and so they were babysitting. Colton was consumed with his efforts to capture the fireflies, for which Kenia was secretly grateful, for she did not have the energy to read him a story that night. After a sufficient amount of small talk, she made her way back to the apartment over the garage. Her steps on the stairs were slow and plodding, her head thick with fatigue, even while she tried to untangle all they had learned that day, deciphering facts from speculation.

The door popped open as she unlocked it, almost as if it had not been locked properly in the frame. She thought little of it, except to make a note to give it an extra tug the next time she left the house.

Her keys had just landed on the table next to the door and she was reaching for the light switch when she felt someone wrap her forearm in an inescapable grip and twist it behind her back, tugging it hard into the space between her shoulder blades. She flailed with her free arm and elbow, striking her assailant. He was a large, solid man, from what she could gather from her useless counterattack. He clamped a hand covered in a leather glove over her mouth and pulled her head back. In that moment, a second intruder punched her so hard in the gut that her eyes filled with tears and she struggled to breathe. A second punch followed the first so fast that she was not sure she would even be able to remain conscious.

Her assailants realized this, the one behind her yanking on her braids while the other slapped her face. "Oh no, you are not leaving just yet," he said in a cloying voice tinged with a backwoods twang.

She could smell the remnants of ham, onion, and mustard on the breath of one of them. She tried to call for help while her mouth was uncovered, but the air was not in her lungs.

"Ah, ah, ah," the man in front of her said.

Her eyes had adjusted to the dark enough that she could see that his face was hidden behind a black ski mask. He was tall, well over six feet, but he was also top-heavy with shoulders as thick and muscular as a bull's. She heard the unmistakable sound of a strip of duct tape peeling off from its roll. They stretched it across her mouth, allowing the man behind her to restrain her by both arms.

"Now that's a good girl, a good little nigger bitch. Now you want to have some fun with us?"

Thiscan'tbehappeningthiscan'tbehappeningthiscan'tbehappe ning . . . .

The one in front grabbed her jawbone, pinching her face in the vice of his hand, and turned her face from side to side then looked at her straight on. His breath was a hot funk in her face, his lips curled around his barred teeth. "How would you like some *white* in you? Would you like that?"

She tried to resist, but it was utterly useless, her strength insufficient to counter her captors' force. She dragged her feet and tried to kick, but there was nothing she could do to stop the chain of movements leading them to slam her down, face first, on the kitchen table. She felt one of them put a hand on her hip and squeeze. Dazed, she turned her head, craning her neck, only to see one of the men stepping towards the door to lock it.

That was when the door exploded. The frame splintering, the glass panes shattering, the shards falling in a rain from behind the horizontal blinds, which themselves billowed and waved as the door swung open, struck the man in the face, stunning him, and sent him tumbling backwards.

The figure from the other side burst in with—what appeared to be—a post from the bannister along the stairs outside. The wood of the post gave way with a crack after Austin Pennel slammed it down on the crown of the nearest man's head. The man fell back, trying to steady himself against the back of the sofa, reaching for what looked like a Taser of some sort on his belt. Austin wasted no time, closing the distance and punching the man, not in the face, but his left collar bone.

They could all hear a muffled crack before the man let out a groan and dropped the Taser. He reached up with his right hand to protect his left shoulder. With a cold methodology, Austin took the man's right wrist in his hands and folded it back, leveraging the hand down with nothing but the force of his thumbs. When the elbow locked, Austin hammered down on it with a crisp motion, hyperextending it a clean forty-five degrees.

When he let go, the man fell to his knees with a cry. He started to pitch forward, but when he reached out to catch himself, he found both arms immobile and fell flat on his face.

Austin picked up the Taser, cracked open the back and let the battery drop to the floor. The second intruder had let go of Kenia and stepped backwards, his hands raised in supplication, his voice high and tight as fear closed his throat.

"We didn't mean no harm, just trying to scare her. Send her a message. We were just following orders."

Austin answered by splaying out his fingers, before curling them back into fists, his knuckles cracking. He shook out a crick in his neck, watching the injured man scramble across the room and disappear out the door, slipping and crashing into the splintered frame of the door as he did so. The apartment shook as he ran down the steps, leaving his partner behind.

"You want to reassess your options?" Austin asked, his voice laced with menace.

The second man did not hesitate to run to the door himself, Austin and Kenia both listening as his footsteps trampled down the stairs, pounded across the driveway, and were gone.

Chapter 24

Fart, Barf, and Itch

Austin demonstrated a reassuring ability to multitask, taking Kenia in one arm and holding her against his chest while dialing 911 on his phone and calling in a home invasion, reporting that the assailants had fled and that both were armed.

"Did they have guns," Kenia asked when she could muster a moment of calm, her entire body still shaking.

"Not that I saw, but it will bring the cops faster and keep them on their toes, just in case Tweedledee and Tweedledum are stupider than they look." He reached out one arm to flick on the lights in the room. The recessed lighting illuminated a scene of chaos: splinters from the door spread across the floor, the sofa knocked out of place, a kitchen chair overturned.

"Please don't go," Kenia said.

"I'm not going anywhere."

He didn't. Instead he remained seated on the table, holding Kenia against him until the sound of sirens and walkie-talkies neared, and uniformed deputies came up the stairs and into the apartment, guns drawn.

First time in my life I've been glad to see the police.

The third officer in the door was a female, and she radioed in that the property was secure. Austin still did not leave Kenia's side while the female officer sat her down and questioned her. His arm over her shoulders was reassuring, and she reached up and held his hand as she recounted what had happened.

It was not long before the Corrigans were outside trying to figure out what was going on and why a half dozen squad cars had converged on their property. One of the officers asked Kenia if it was all right if they came upstairs.

"Of course, it's their house," she said.

Only when Margaret, and now Sandra, having returned from her girls-night-out, were there, did Austin step aside, allowing the women to gather on either side of Kenia. Officer Farrcroft arrived around the same time, his expression a mix of professional focus and paternal concern.

"You all right, Kenia?" he said, kneeling down next to her. Margaret and Sandra had moved her to the couch and sat close to her.

"Yeah, well, sort of, thanks to Austin."

"I know you are shook up, but did you give a description of the two men?"

"Yes, I did," but she relayed it again to him. Austin repeated his version as well.

Kenia was sure the effort was fruitless until Austin said, "I'd suggest you start with a visit up to Arnold Reynolds and Reed Baxter. They both live up on Manahoac Ridge and do odd jobs for Harold Bridgewater. From the looks of what I saw, they would fit the bill."

"Noted," Officer Farrcroft said, before pulling the walkie-talkie fastened to his shoulder and dispatching units up to the Reynold and Baxter residences.

"How can you be so sure?" Kenia asked.

Sandra laughed. "Honey, it's a small town. We all went to high school together. You tend to know who's who."

"Even if they have a ski mask over their heads," Austin said, sitting on the arm of the couch. He looked ready to say something else, but was distracted by the phone buzzing in his pocket. He checked the caller ID and decided to answer, turning away as he said, "Hailey, we need to talk . . . ."

But if Austin was going to update Hailey, he would have to wait. Kenia could hear the panic in Hailey's voice, even if she could not understand the words.

"Which—wait—what? Hailey, slow down. They said they were from the FBI?" Austin turned to Officer Farrcroft, his face the

204

picture of puzzlement. The officer frowned at the mention of Federal law enforcement. The room grew quiet as Austin listened further before hanging up. "Keith, I think we have a problem."

"What is going on?" Kenia asked, wondering how the FBI had responded so quickly. "What does any of this have to do with the FBI?"

"It doesn't," was Officer Farrcroft's flat-out answer.

Austin shook his head, his knuckles growing white as he clutched his phone. "They're raiding our property. Hailey said they just served a warrant accusing us of distributing child pornography on the internet."

Officer Farrcroft made for the door, calling out to some of the other officers. "Carl, you have any word on the Feds serving a warrant on the Pennel property?"

"What is going on?" Margaret asked, her face blanched.

"I think we might have kicked up one too many rocks today," Austin said. "Kenia, I need to go home."

Kenia stood up. "I'm coming with you."

The Corrigan women made noises of protest, but Kenia had already grabbed her keys and phone and was following Austin out the door.

◊

Austin followed Keith through the neighborhood in his Jeep, but soon fell behind as Officer Farrcroft turned on his siren and lights and sped through red lights and four way stops.

"The way this day is going, I'm not giving anyone anymore reasons to ticket or arrest a Pennel," Austin said letting off the gas and slowing to just five miles above the speed limit, his fingers clutched in a tight fist around the wheel and the gearshift.

"Austin, what were you doing back at my place?" Kenia asked, trying to make sense of all that had happened.

"I came to tell you that I think the explosion at the plant was deliberate, and I had stumbled upon proof."

"What?"

"I didn't want to say anything until I knew more, but it hit me when we were at the plant today. The coal stacks were so far from where the tanker had been parked. I was wondering how the fire could have ever reached it."

"I wondered that myself."

"Then I was thinking: 'well maybe it was just the radiant heat from the flames, maybe the garage where it was parked got hot enough that it would blow.'"

"Sure, that was what I figured the official story would be."

"But that didn't work either," he said, taking a corner with a hard right. Kenia steadied herself on the roll-bar overhead. "I had to check to make sure, but from what I remembered of my training, Chlortrofluorine has a really high flashpoint. It was one of the reasons it was supposed to be so much safer than chlorine-tri-fluoride—Substance N.

"But it's still a controlled substance and that information is classified. So I had to make a couple of calls to my buddies still in the service. One of them got back to me and confirmed my hunch. Chlortrofluorine has a flash point of 1,300 degrees Celsius."

"That's really hot."

"Oh yeah, and here is the thing: coal and coal products, they burn at about half that temperature."

"Could the fire have gotten hot enough at the plant that night in '53 to ignite the chlortrofluorine?"

"It's doubtful. I mean, maybe if you had a kiln and you were trapping all that heat, but that was not the case. It would have been radiating out into the sky. That was why chlortrofluorine was supposed to be such a breakthrough—it was hard to ignite. It was not as volatile as its base chemical compound. DuPont knew what they were doing. You would need a special type of ignition source to set it off and those are hard to come by, even today. Harder even, back then. The technology was still new and tightly controlled."

Austin took another turn. leaving downtown behind. He downshifted to begin climbing state road 521, the road leading to his home.

"Could an electric short, a downed power cable do it?"

"A high voltage line *might* do it, but when I looked at the specs of the plant from back then, the lines ran through transformers and substations first, outside of town, off the island even, so the voltage was already stepped down a notch when it fed into the plant. It was higher than the voltage in a home, but it was not the ultrahigh voltage in powerlines. The lines at the plant in the 1950s could not have produced an arc hot enough. Everything is pointing to the blast being deliberate."

They pulled up to the edge of the Pennel property, but the traffic was stopped in both directions. Special agents had set up roadblocks. Officer Farrcroft and other Selah Station officers were arguing with the them while folks whose cars had been stopped in a long line in front of the roadblocks had gotten out and were making phone calls, or standing and watching the drama unfold. Austin pulled the Jeep to the shoulder of the road, slammed the door behind him, and started into the woods.

Kenia followed. They crossed what she guessed was Martha Andersen's property—Kenia wondering for a moment what Martha would have thought of the flashing lights and commotion outside her home—and followed trails Austin clearly knew well enough to navigate in the dark. They emerged halfway down the Pennel driveway, at which point Austin broke into a jog. Kenia followed as best she could, but discovered she was somewhat sore from her assault. Moving and focusing on something besides the horror of her experience, however, helped keep the flashbacks and anxiety at bay.

The farmhouse was lit up with floodlights from government vehicles. Lights were on in every window of every room, where Kenia could see figures moving back and forth with boxes piled with the Pennels' personal possessions. Red and blue dash lights blazed from the interiors of a dozen black SUVs and sedans with government tags. Men with uniformly short haircuts and blue windbreakers with FBI in yellow letters across their backs marched in and out, carrying the electronics ripped from the Pennels' studio.

Austin came as close as he could before an agent stopped him. He was a mature-looking white man in his fifties, but with a build that indicated he still worked out regularly. A gun was holstered under his arm.

"Get back, this is a crime scene."

"This is my house," Austin said.

Shane, Stan, and Hailey heard his voice and called Austin's name from where they were sequestered, sitting at their fake-news set in the front yard while a Latina agent watched over them, her nose and mouth curled in disgust at the Confederate and Don't-Tread-on-Me flags.

Austin ignored the orders from the other FBI agents and ran over to his siblings. Kenia, a little astounded by his confidence around law enforcement, reminded herself that he was white. She was not. Much more slowly, she followed, keeping her hands visible and at her sides. For all her precautions, she seemed to go unnoticed, approaching the circle of the Pennels and the Latina agent.

Austin wanted to know if any of them were under arrest.

"Are you their legal guardian?" the agent asked.

"I am."

"They are persons of interest, at this time."

"So what does that mean?" Shane asked. He was seated on a log that served as their anchor's chair. Hailey sat next to him, her face the picture of stony defiance. Stan was on the grass, looking pale and scared.

"It means you are free to go, whenever and wherever you choose," Officer Farrcroft said, appearing out of the glare of three Selah Station Police cruisers that were pulling up the driveway. "Who is the agent in charge here?" he asked.

"I am," the Latina woman said. "Agent Saavedra."

Officer Farrcroft did not wait to start in with her. His face was sheened with sweat, the veins in his temples full and pounding. "What kind of investigation is this where you don't contact municipal law enforcement?"

"We had reason to believe the suspects might be notified that a warrant had been issued and would destroy evidence."

"On what grounds?" Officer Farrcroft said.

Kenia could not follow the details of their discussion. She was more interested in her friends. The entire scene, the entire night, had taken a turn into the surreal. Austin gathered up his brothers, his arms around them protectively, as he had done with Kenia earlier. Kenia followed suit and put her arm around Hailey. They all moved into an open space behind the police tape, between cruisers. Stan was crying silently. Shane cursed under his breath as he watched agents dump their cameras, flat screens, and servers into the backs of their SUVs. Hailey was shaking, but her jaw was set and her fists balled in anger. Kenia felt it was more likely she would have to restrain her than comfort her. One of the agents slammed the hatch of the SUV, slapped the back window, and the driver sped off down the road.

Shane collapsed on the bumper of the nearest cruiser, his head in his hands. "What are we going to do?"

Kenia had no answer. Stan looked at his oldest brother. "Austin, who would do this?"

Austin said nothing in reply, but he looked at Kenia. She had the sense he was making some of the same connections in his mind that she was. The timing with her own attack had to be more than coincidental.

Officer Farrcroft stepped into their midst, grinding his jaw. "They can't hold you, not in the least. Unless they find something." He looked down at the ground. "You all think they could find *anything* against you?"

"Who knows at this point," Shane said. "Something could have been planted if we were hacked."

"What my brother is saying, Officer Keith, is that we're being framed," Hailey said.

Farrcroft pressed his lips together hard, rubbed his neck, and shook his head. "This is getting out of control. Fast."

"Can you help, Keith?" Austin said.

Officer Farrcroft sucked a breath in between clenched teeth. "Not in an official capacity. Not as an officer of the law. I can tell you to get a good lawyer."

The Pennels, as a group, drew inward, their faces falling to the ground.

"But as a friend," Officer Farrcroft said, "I'd say that sometimes, when the *Man* is tightening the screws on you, it's worth letting him know that *you* know him and that *you* see him. Look him in the eye. Throw some heat in his face while you still can. These guys are used to sitting behind layers of others who do their dirty work. Maybe he'll rattle if confronted. Maybe he'll make a mistake. He might have already overreached, sending those bozos after Kenia."

"What? Who was after Kenia?" Hailey asked, her voice strident.

"We'll explain on the way," Austin said, starting down the driveway, leaving them staring at his back.

"Where're you going?" Shane asked from the car bumper.

But Austin was already out of earshot. It was Officer Farrcroft who answered. "I think he is on his way to pay Harold Bridgewater a visit. Be a shame if there was a disturbance up at the mansion, with all our units engaged tonight here and at the Corrigan place."

It took a moment for the hint to land. It was Kenia who rallied the Pennels, pulling and pushing them to follow after Austin. "Come on, we can't let him go alone."

Chapter 25

Harold Bridgewater

The younger Pennel siblings packed themselves into the backseat of the Jeep, still fumbling with the seatbelts as Austin shifted into drive, spinning the wheels and shooting out a fusillade of gravel as he yanked the wheel into a U-turn. He blasted the horn until some of the trapped cars rearranged themselves to clear a path.

From the passenger seat, Kenia turned to brief the Pennels on what had happened at her apartment. All three listened, the horror on their faces occasionally lit by the headlights of passing cars. "Don't worry, I'm all right," Kenia said, trying to reassure them and head off their questions before they could ask. She recounted what she could from Austin's explanation regarding the chlortrofluorine, allowing Austin to add details when he felt it necessary, but mainly Austin drove—this time heedless of speed limits, double lines, or prohibitions against driving on the shoulder. Kenia closed her eyes and braced herself more than once for an impact that did not come.

"Don't worry, Austin is an expert driver," Stan said, his voice calm.

"The bigger question is what do we do when we get to the Bridgewater place," Shane said. "Are we really certain they are behind this?"

"Certain enough," Austin said.

Hailey said nothing, but hers was a brooding silence, her anger smoldering just beneath the surface. It unnerved Kenia.

"You all right, Hailey?"

"I will be when this is all over," she said.

"These things, they're not just 'over,'" Austin said, speeding up the road to the ridge on the opposite side of the valley. Private driveways passed on either side. Kenia knew they were in the vicinity of the Bridgewater Estate, but how close, she was not sure. None of her interviews had taken her to this section of town.

"What do you plan to do when you get there, Austin?" Hailey asked.

Austin downshifted and they rounded a hairpin turn. He gunned the engine and shifted again, "D.W.I.G.H.T. it I guess."

"Oh, that's my favorite sort of plan," Shane said, slapping the back of Austin's seat.

"Who is Dwight?" Kenia asked.

"It's an acronym: Decide When I Get the Hell There," Stan explained.

"It's code for 'I don't have a plan and I am acting recklessly,'" Hailey said, a maternal note of disapproval creeping into her voice.

"You heard Officer Keith," Austin said.

"I like to think of this more like . . . Improv," Shane said.

"Anyone ever tell you, Shane, the world is *not* a stage?" Hailey said, crossing her arms.

Anxiety made a pit in Kenia's stomach. "Is this such a good idea?" she asked, a well-illuminated gate coming up fast on their left.

"You don't like spontaneity?" Shane said.

"I like staying alive. I've already had one close scrape tonight that your bother had to save me from."

"It's basic battlefield strategy," Austin said. "Orient, Observe, Decide, Act, repeat. Even if it's the wrong decision, it's better than no decision. Whoever goes through that loop faster tends to win."

"This isn't war," Kenia said.

"You sure?" Austin said without a smile, before he hit the brakes and skidded into the driveway, the scent of burnt rubber accompanying them. The Jeep's RPMs redlined as Austin climbed the slope of the driveway.

"Gate was open. They must have been expecting us," Shane said, craning his head into the front seat for a better view.

"No, they're having a party," Hailey said.

She was right. They emerged from the wooded driveway, and the mansion appeared—at least a wing of it. It was far too large, and they were far too close, to take in the entirety of it. The design was like a Flemish castle, with corner towers topped with conical peaks layered with slate shingles. The trees of the grounds were evergreens, perhaps to evoke a Scandinavian, alpine feel. Kenia noted horse stables and trailers off a branch of the driveway. Austin drove into a parking lot with a bed of fine, cinder-like gravel. It was surrounded on all sides by crimson Japanese maples, miniature pagodas, and packed full of luxury sedans and sports cars.

Beyond the parking lot, the lawn was aglow with Chinese lanterns. A white party tent—the kind Kenia had seen erected outside for dinner parties at country clubs, Sigma Pi Phi events, and Ivy League graduations—stood in the center of the bustle of well-dressed guests.

Austin drove as close as he could and came to an abrupt stop next to teenaged boys in red jackets, black slacks, and black running shoes, standing next to a valet stand. Austin cut the engine, got out and kept his keys to himself, growling at the valets, "Don't worry, I won't be long."

Kenia and the other Pennels ran to keep up with him. They plunged into the casual elegance of the summer garden party, weaving through figures in pressed polo shirts, Burberry blazers, and Versace dresses, with the occasional Ralph Lauren sweater tied over the wearer's shoulders. By the people Kenia could see in the garden—and the tent through the faux windows—she estimated the crowd to be about three hundred people. The Bridgewaters had offered an impressive spread: a chocolate fountain, raw oyster bar, a Mongolian style grill—flames flashing as the chef in immaculate white flipped a slab of meat.

The servers were all female and looked to be moonlighting actresses and models. Their tops were formfitting button-downs with bow ties and cummerbunds that accentuated their small waists and buxom chests. They smiled invitingly at the middle-aged and older men who cracked jokes with self-satisfied smiles, as if convinced by the rented friendliness of the hired twenty-somethings, oblivious to their wives, who looked away with scowls and reached for more drinks. Many of the wives had congregated at the numerous bars where eye-candy male bartenders, two at each bar plus bar-back, shook drinks with the efficiency of soldiers and the easygoing smiles of gigolos. By the sound of the raucous laughter coming from the women, the bartenders appeared to be giving out generous pours.

Two Latino men picked at elegant classical guitars on a small stage against a backdrop of blooming hydrangeas. Beyond the flowers, children played in a section of lawn, supervised by white college co-eds in matching knit shirts and khaki shorts. A clown made balloons, and a gas generator let out a gentle hum, while it kept a row of bouncing castles inflated.

Kenia and the Pennels passed through the tent. It was lit by hanging chandeliers. A marble fountain filled with koi bubbled in the center while a sommelier with a pencil mustache moved between tables. Austin scanned the crowd like a hunter. When he did not spy his target, he continued through the tent to the far side.

The full rotunda of the mansion came into view. Every window in every room glowed with warm light, the front façade lit by floodlights and accented by flickering Edwardian-style English gas streetlamps. It formed a striking contrast in Kenia's mind, ostentation versus invasion, when she remembered the Pennels' homestead, last seen in the harsh glare of law enforcement floodlights.

Her mind kept coming back to the same word: privilege. The whole place was saturated in it, and yet even as the Pennel children looked around wide-eyed, she recognized in herself a certain familiarity with the setting. Had she not been to weddings, debutante balls, and college graduations with all the same trappings and similar guests? It was an uncomfortable realization to make, even as she felt the scratches, strains, and bruises from her recent flights and fights on her body.

On a quiet terrace of the lawn that smelled of cigar smoke, Austin homed in on his target. By now he had a great lead on them, and the four of them had to run to catch up. As they did, Kenia could not help but notice the tall, athletic men in black shirts wearing leather hip packs and earpieces with coiled wire running down their necks and under their collars. Each had the physique of professional bodybuilders or soldiers. They did not fail to notice Austin's approach, speaking into their wrists and moving to the edges of a table where half a dozen men were seated.

The seated men each had an air of distinguished pedigree. They lounged in dinner jackets and wore slacks with creases sharp as knives. Their skin was smooth and unblemished, their nails buffed. Those who folded one ankle up on their knees revealed that they wore loafers without socks. Three women, ages ranging from thirty to late fifty, sat with them drinking cosmos and apple martinis. The men let out a burst of synchronized laugher, a picture of careless, genteel comradery and mutual regard.

"Harold Bridgewater," Austin called out. A fit, tan man in his fifties, his temples flecked with gray, turned, setting down his cigar in an ashtray and picking up a scotch on the rocks. He took a sip, savoring it with an intake of breath, followed by a wide relaxed smile, "Yes, that is me. Are you enjoying yourself? I'm afraid we have not met."

"I'm Austin Pennel. You know who I am."

The other men seated near Harold were regarding Austin with suspicion. Kenia noticed the woman next to Harold, his wife perhaps—her face immobile, her breasts full and set high on her chest—exchange a subtle glance with one of the black-clad men on the periphery. The bodyguard signaled to one of his comrades and they moved in closer.

Austin did not fail to notice. But before he could speak again, Bridgewater stood and offered his hand.

"You are the war hero. *Captain* Pennel, if I recall. It's an honor to meet you."

"Mr. Bridgewater, I'm here to tell you that if you threaten my family or my friends in any way, all sorts of hell will rain down on you and *all* you hold dear."

A pause followed that the swell of music and background conversations could not cover up. The men shifted as the awkwardness grew. One of the younger women checked her phone while Mrs. Bridgewater tapped at the stem of her glass with a polished nail, painted the color of blood.

"There must be some sort of misunderstanding," Mr. Bridgewater said with a convincing display of innocence mingled with concern. "I'd never do such a thing. If you feel threatened, I'd like to know if there was anything I could do to help."

The muscles in Austin's forearms flexed, his USMC tattoo rippled. One of the men at the table took a sip of his scotch while another pulled a long drag off his cigar before blowing it in Austin's direction.

Austin was unmoved. "I'm not playing games, Mr. Bridgewater."

Then, quietly as he had intruded, Austin turned and left. Kenia thought it well-timed, for it was abrupt enough that it left Bridgewater without a retort. He was speechless and off balance. He could have tried to reply, but he would have had to raise his voice at Austin's back, calling attention to himself, diminishing himself before his peers. Instead Harold Bridgewater chose to play the benevolent host, turning to the other Pennels, but ignoring Kenia.

"And you must be the rest of the Pennel clan. You've done a lot to bring jobs to folks in Selah Station with your little . . . show. You are town treasures, true entrepreneurs." He turned to his guests and continued, "See, it's young people like this who will make America great again."

"Here, here!" the men said, rapping their knuckles on the table and raising their glasses.

"And you, young lady, I have not had the pleasure," Bridgewater said, turning to Kenia. Face-to-face with him, she took in his whitened, bonded teeth, the professional tan on unblemished skin, the svelte physique honed by professional trainers and organic food. Even poised on level ground, she could sense the way he looked down on her, her braids tousled, her clothes dirty from running through the woods, her bruises and bandages from the violence visited upon her on full display. While at the same time, it did not escape her how his eyes wandered up and down the length of her body, as if tracing her figure and noting her own physical attributes the way any sexual predator might. In that moment, she felt all the pretentions and liberties of his race bearing down on her, her people, her ancestors.

She wanted to spit.

"I'm Keniabarido Ifeanyichokwo Diambu Dezy, and I have nothing to say to you."

Bridgewater looked stricken. "Well again, I don't know what has led to this misunderstanding, but please, I want to extend my hospitality to you. Make yourselves at home."

"We should be going," Shane said.

Kenia was more than ready.

Bridgewater waved down one of his servers. "I'll have one of the girls get you to-go boxes. All this food should not go to waste."

"Thanks, but no thanks," Shane said, trying to corral his siblings off the terrace and in the direction of the parking lot where the Jeep was waiting for them. The moment had passed. Austin had left at the right time. They should have known they would not rattle a blueblood like Bridgewater any more than Austin already had with the element of surprise. It was Bridgewater's turf, after all, and he was surrounded by peers and sycophants he would be determined not to lose face around.

Bridgewater was not ready to crack, but his wife was another story. The woman with the immobile face exuded resentment; it was clear in the way she knocked back her drink and snapped her fingers at the closest bodyguard. "Brent, get these orphans off my property."

The word stung. Shane and Stan showed the injury in the way their shoulders pinched together. Hailey, by contrast, became a small fury, which in retrospect, Kenia realized she should have expected, for the anger had been building in the young woman at a slow boil all evening.

"You talk about making America great?" Hailey said, stepping towards the table of seated adults. "Great at what exactly? Great at locking people up, making weapons of mass destruction, great at exporting arms and ammunition abroad? Is that what makes us 'great'? Or the fact we produce more pollution than any other country? Maybe it's our climbing rates of infant mortality, obesity, and our failing educational system? Even while you fat-cat one-percenters get rich off white supremacy, structural violence, and mass incarceration?"

"Whoa, Hailey, time we probably should go," Kenia said, stepping forward.

But the spirit of resistance had seized Hailey—she was too quick. She swiped up a martini glass by the stem and flung the contents into the face of Mrs. Bridgewater. "And if you call me and my brothers orphans again, I will punch you in the face so hard no amount of plastic surgery and Botox will fix it."

Women were gasping. The men had stood up from the table, knocking over more glasses, spilling their contents into the laps of the other seated women. Shane and Kenia were of one mind. They picked Hailey up by the elbows while she kicked and cursed, knocking over a stand of discarded dishes in the process. The crash attracted more attention, conversations abruptly ending when the partygoers turned to stare. The men in black knit shirts were closing in while Stan blazed a trail through the crowd calling out, "Make a path, make a path, medical emergency!"

The stunned onlookers parted willingly, their faces flashing expressions of concern. Kenia kept checking over her shoulder as the men in black followed them out. They seemed content to keep a distance as long as she and the Pennels were on their way out. Kenia had no intention of testing their resolve or finding out what they carried in their hip packs.

Austin, as if he had sensed trouble in their delay, had backed the Jeep onto the lawn. Never had the illuminated taillights of a car looked so welcoming to Kenia. Hailey stopped resisting and walked-ran the rest of the way, she and her brothers scrambling over the tailgate while Kenia jumped in the front, slammed her door, and said, "Drive."

Austin dropped the Jeep into gear, the wheels ripping into the Kentucky bluegrass and flinging it up at the guests in heavy clods of soil.

"Well, that was a nice get-together," Shane said, after they had rolled down the driveway in uniform silence.

Stan let out a snort and started laughing. "I'll say."

"What the hell, Hailey! You were on fire. Where did all that come from? I need to write some of it down," Shane said, fighting laughter himself.

"Such a basic bitch," Hailey said, referring to Mrs. Bridgewater.

Even Austin cracked a smile now. They recounted for him what had transpired after he had left, as the Jeep roared down the driveway back to the main road. It was as if a seal had been broken, the tension released. All five of them laughed and shouted over one another to the point of screaming as they argued about what had been, for them, the "best part." The double line of the main road lit up before them, Austin steered them home through the tunnel of old growth trees.

In was only when Kenia turned in her seat as she attempted to share her favorite part that she saw the grill of the black SUV, its headlights off, approach the back of the Jeep, its engine revving just before the driver swerved and connected with their rear fender.

The seatbelt crushed against Kenia's torso. The knobby tires of the Jeep let out an abrupt screech before they lost contact with the road. The Jeep spun, flipped, and tumbled into the trees.

Chapter 26

Arc Haven

The series of rolls were an uncountable sequence of impacts and unimaginable jolts in which they were pelted by debris from the road, the forest floor, and the gravelly shoulder, not to mention pieces of windshield, mudguards, and whatever other items were loose in the Jeep, Kenia praying that each roll would be the last.

The Jeep finally stopped with a jolt that stunned them all. Kenia struggled through a haze of confusion and pain, desperate to reorient herself. She realized she was staring out at the forest floor though a shattered windshield before she understood that she was hanging upside-down, held in her seat by her seatbelt. She found it impossible to speak, but she was aware of other voices. One was Austin, but he had to keep repeating himself before she understood what he was saying.

"Is everyone OK?"

Blood and glass were glistening in the crown of his head, the bleeding profuse. The air was thick with the smell of gasoline, pine trees, burnt rubber, and freshly churned earth.

"Kenia. Kenia, are you all right?"

It was Stan, who had unbuckled himself, negotiating an awkward somersault and lowering his feet to the ground. He crouched on the roll bar, which had gouged itself into the leafy forest floor, plowing up ferns and saplings.

"I think so," was all Kenia could croak out.

Shane was cursing from where he hung, suspended by his own belts—taller and longer than Stan, he had a more difficult time freeing himself. Hailey was holding her head, blood dripping from cuts on her hairline, above her lip, and a gash splitting her left eyebrow into two.

"Hailey, you look bad," Shane said.

"I feel bad."

Stan picked up one of their phones, which had landed on the ground under Kenia's head.

"Shane, what is your security key?"

"3142."

"Call 911," Austin said, working his own buckle free and looking over his shoulder at the feet of the approaching men unloading themselves from the SUV. Stan's thumb danced across the screen but he cursed when he realized there was no reception. Austin climbed out of the Jeep. He gasped and let out a grunt of pain as the men outside seized him, threw him lengthwise along the Jeep, and started to kick and stomp him.

"Austin!" Hailey cried out. But they were powerless; stunned, injured, and trapped as they were. Stan hurried to unbuckle each of them but even when he had, it was too late: Austin was motionless in a pool of his own blood.

"Get out," a voice said.

What choice did they have? Kenia went first, followed by Stan and Shane, who helped Hailey. All four of them stood with their backs against the wrecked Jeep, prisoners before a firing squad. Kenia recognized the men by their black knit shirts as the bodyguards from the Bridgewater's.

"Radio in that we got them," said a man with his hair shaved short, as if he were still in the military.

The reply came back in one of their earpieces, the recipient sharing the orders, "Alpha Hotel says to take them to the icehouse entrance and put them in a detention cell."

"Right. Big one in the first truck, the other four in the second."

The bodyguards, mostly indistinguishable from one another in build and brute strength, picked up the lot of them and carried them to the waiting SUVs. The first SUV's fender was dented from where it had collided with Austin's Jeep. They opened the tailgate, spread out a blue tarp to catch his blood, and threw the eldest Pennel down over it. Kenia and the younger Pennels could offer little meaningful resistance as the men rammed them into the back of the second SUV, slamming the door behind them.

Hailey's pupils were dilated asymmetrically.

"Don't fall asleep," Kenia told her.

"Shut your fucking mouth," one of the men said, climbing into the back seat.

"She has a concussion," Kenia said.

The man turned, his head rotating on a small stump of a neck over his beefy shoulders. "So will you, in a second."

The bodyguards drove them back up the hill they had come down, taking the curves at reckless speeds that made Austin seem like a Sunday driver. Kenia felt no surprise when they turned right back into the Bridgewater driveway. This time they cut left instead of right, moving in convoy away from the mansion and partygoers. The branch of dirt road terminated in a clearing that was thickly wooded on all sides, but still had a tall chain-link fence and a perimeter where the forest growth had been cleared. An old brick building built partly into the hill waited. It looked to be colonial by the weathering of the bricks and the rusty iron door. But the debilitated exterior was only a façade. The inside had a floor of freshly poured and polished concrete. Security cameras hidden in orbs of darkened tempered glass tracked them from the corners. The space inside the structure was enormous, tunneled deep into the hill. At the far end, a massive blast door stood open. Its profile was at least six feet thick and looked to be made entirely of tempered steel. The bolts and tumblers of the locking mechanism were as wide across as bowling balls. Beyond the door was another anteroom where one of the bodyguards punched a code into a keypad and a second, hydraulic door hissed open.

More surprises were in store for them. On the other side was a reception area, expansive as an airport departure hall, complete with desks and counters with charging stations in a waiting lounge. Large bronze letters bolted to the walls read: "Welcome to Arc

Haven Luxury Living." As the bodyguards clicked on the lights—which gave a soft, calming blue-pink glow—a number of large wall screens also came up displaying images of scenic vistas, the horizon distant, creating a convincing illusion that they were not underground.

The lounge was not for them. Instead the bodyguards marched them through a series of doors and hallways into a section designed as a jail. Rows of detention cells greeted them, as well as a quarantine enclosed in thick glass, and a waiting area where each chair had a D-ring set in the floor for fastening body shackles. The place smelled of fresh paint and stale air. After bringing them through a gate and into a hallway of cells, their captors herded them through the door, slammed it after them and the gate after that, leaving them alone in a dim, sleepy light.

While they all were bewildered and battered, Austin was their highest priority. He was breathing but still unconscious. They picked the largest pieces of glass out of his scalp, his brothers tearing off the sleeves of their shirts to use as bandages. Hailey was next. Kenia sat her against the wall and told her to try to stay alert, despite her drowsiness.

"Just stay with us, all right?" she said.

This left her, Shane, and Stan to huddle in the center of the room and try to understand what was happening or where they were.

"What is this place?" Kenia said.

"Beats me," Shane said. "It's like they are preparing for the apocalypse."

"In a way, they are. It's a backup bunker living for the one percent. It's all the rage among hedge fund managers, dot com billionaires, and the like who feel like the US is headed for a complete disintegration. It's like buying up real estate in New Zealand; a backup plan for when things fall apart," Stan said. "I read about it in the New Yorker."

"So all those investment bankers who made dough with deregulation cash out and get out," Kenia said.

"That's about right."

"Bridgewater has done a good job keeping this secret," Shane said.

"Discretion is part of the draw. But we wouldn't know about it anyway. We're not exactly the folks he would advertise to."

"I don't imagine we are," Kenia said.

It was undeniable that their prison was secret and that they were not escaping. Their captors did not bother to turn on the heat either, so they were all forced to huddle for warmth in the corner. What felt like hours passed, with nothing happening except for the sound of footsteps outside the locked gate as their sentries rotated through shifts.

Kenia tried to think through all that had transpired. Clearly they had done something to shake up Bridgewater—beyond spoiling his summer lawn party—otherwise he would not have risked the crimes of assault and kidnapping. He had other tools to ruin them, as he had demonstrated with the FBI raid. This had to do with the Selah Station Coal Plant and the 1953 disaster. It was a cover up, but she felt that they were far from proving it. Everything they had was still circumstantial.

She said as much aloud, looking back and forth from Shane to Stan.

"Maybe we got too close for comfort," Shane said.

"I think that is a foregone conclusion," Kenia said.

Stan was quiet, tending carefully to his sister who rested her head on his shoulder. "I don't like that they have shown their faces."

"Why not?" Shane asked.

"Means they are not worried about being identified. Meaning we might not be around to identify them."

"Don't scare me," Shane said.

The lock in the gate to the outer hallway banged. The gate opened without a sound, the hinges still new and well oiled. A row of bodyguards entered in a line, Harold Bridgewater in the center of them, walking with all the self-assured panache of a rock star taking the stage. He stopped before the door to the cell, took a moment to stare at the lot of them, then ordered, "Open it."

One of the bodyguards snapped the lock up and the door slid aside on rollers. The bodyguards entered, lining up to flank Bridgewater on either side, and he took his place in the center of them, crouching down and scanning his prisoners over, his head slightly cocked, his lip curling, and his nose wrinkled as if he were taking in a scent of meat that might have been rotting in a sewer. Then, as if suddenly aware that they were staring back at him, he clasped his hands and rubbed his palms together.

"So, here we are," he said.

The men fanned out to his sides then remained still and impervious. Even more waited outside. Kenia jumped as one of the nearest to her slipped a telescoped baton from a holder on his belt and snapped it out, extending it to its full length.

"Not as much to say now, I see," Harold Bridgewater said. "Not that it matters. You all are a waste-disposal problem at this point. It didn't have to be this way, but you forced my hand, so to speak. Whatever possessed you to go snooping around the plant? Couldn't leave history alone?" He turned to Kenia, pointing a manicured finger her way. "Was it you? Did you want to bring back some interracial utopia you thought existed there?"

Kenia didn't owe him an answer and knew it was better if she said nothing at all. His words "waste disposal" echoed in her head. He did not wait for a reply from her.

"Let me tell you something; even Selah Station was built on betrayal, a lie. Reginald and Leonard loved the same woman, Selah Branch, that legendary negress," he said, drawing out the syllables of "le-gen-da-ry" with a roll of his eyes towards the ceiling. "It was in her interest to lead them both on and, if you ask me, I'm certain she did. It's what women do." He chuckled to himself and looked to his men and their nods of consent before continuing. "But Reginald couldn't have her. When he realized this, he played along with Reconstruction. But all the time, he was sowing the seeds of malice and revenge in his own children and grandchildren, down to my grandfather, Crowley Bridgewater."

He shook his head. "I couldn't care less about revenge or the other Bridgewaters, even if my grandfather Crowley had not killed them off in the blast. But you see, secrets beget secrets, and my father Sterling, and in turn, I, was left quite a fortune because of Grandpa Crowley's machinations. And we can't have you bringing that to light. Some things are better left . . . in the past." He looked around, gesturing at the space around them. "And I clearly have other things to attend to, things concerning the future."

"You are a dick," Shane said.

Bridgewater chuckled. "Maybe, but tomorrow I'll be alive, and you won't be."

"You'll still be a dick."

One of the bodyguards with a baton raised it, but Bridgewater lifted his hand to restrain him.

"Not yet," he said. He inched closer to Hailey. Kenia could smell his cologne, hair gel, cigars, and a faint scent of body odor. "You showed some real feistiness out there," he said to Hailey. "Too bad we met under these circumstances." He reached out to touch her chin, but Austin let out a cough and interrupted

"Don't you touch her." Austin was still prone on the tarp they had carried him in on, his blood congealed in sticky pools.

"Oh, I see our American hero has awoken," Bridgewater said, his slacks straightening, the creases making a neat, tailored break just at the calf and above his oxblood loafers as he stood. "You know, I think you imagine yourself a patriot. All of you likely do, I'm willing to bet. But let me tell you something. *We, the people* never included *all* the people. From the beginning, it was *we-and-not-them.* Back then, the *not-them* were blacks, the browns, the yellows, women, natives, the poor, whatever. We've seen that *we* expand over time, but things that expand also can contract. It's natural. And we're in a contraction right now, if you have not noticed. It's not a matter of republican or democrat, red state or blue state, or even urban or rural. It a matter of those who are willing to go with that contraction, to draw a line and say 'this is *we* now,' and those who think we can keep the doors opened and continue to add more and more. But the truth is, there isn't enough to go around to keep adding to the *we*. Some of you just don't get that. But you'll be culled. Society will see to that. It won't be pretty, but that's life."

He stopped himself, as if just remembering something. "What am I talking about, you all won't even make it until then. You have a date with a deep freezer."

"You are going to freeze us to death?" Stan asked.

"It's slow but painless. I hear it's peaceful even, like falling asleep. Makes for better clean up when we drop you into the wood chipper and fire your remains out into the river. Keeps the bodily fluids from gumming up the gears. But don't worry, we'll rinse it out with bleach first. Don't want any DNA evidence remaining. Wouldn't want to have to buy off any more federal agents than I already have. Enough of my money already goes to the government in taxes."

The bodyguards let out a chorus of laughter that echoed the sycophants that had been seated at the table with Bridgewater at his party above ground. He waved his men out after him, but they left the door open. A fresh cadre of men swept in, four for each of them. These men wore aprons, rubber gloves, hairnets, and surgical masks, like butchers or autopsy examiners. These men bound Kenia and the Pennels with zip-ties, then lifted them to their shoulders and carried them out of the detention center, back through reception, and to a set of elevators where they waited as the doors slid open. These elevators were also new, the off-gasses from the carpeting, epoxy, and fiber paneling still strong. Kenia's sense of claustrophobia grew, not as much from the sense of being in a small space—if anything the elevators and the halls they opened up to were spacious—but rather from the growing awareness of how deep they were underground and moving deeper.

Their captors brought them to a dining hall modeled after a rustic mountain cabin, complete with roughhewn logs set into the walls and pine timbers stretching across the ceiling as rafters. The LCD display screens placed where windows would have been were blank. Hundreds of empty chairs waited in the dim light at long tables. The men did not stop, but instead continued through a swinging door, into a modern kitchen of stainless steel countertops. They came to a large meat-locker door with a spring-action lever handle. The seals hissed as they opened. A blast of frigid air wafted out, Kenia suddenly able to see clouds of her breath. The men carrying her dropped her to the floor inside, where she landed, the air knocked out of her chest. They deposited the rest of the Pennels next to her then shut the door behind them, the seals and insulation squeezing shut as the locks clamped into place.

All five of them lay still, the clouds of their breath lit by the light coming in from the double-paned window set high in the refrigerator door.

"We are so fucked," Shane said.

"Come on, let's move closer together to retain heat," Stan said, trying to wiggle, despite his limbs being zip-tied.

"What does it matter at this point?" Shane said.

"We can't give up. Come on Hailey, get closer to me." Stan nudged Hailey. "Hailey. Hailey, you awake?"

"She passed out," Austin said, from the other side of her, his voice cracking.

"Let us out of here!" Shane screamed.

"God damn it, Shane, as if my head didn't hurt bad enough," Austin said.

"Someone has got to hear us."

"And do what? Have pity on us, turn on Bridgewater, and let us out?" Austin said.

No one said anything for a long while. Kenia kept her thoughts to herself, reluctant to comment on the pain building behind her eyes until she was certain what was taking place.

"Uh, guys, I think we have another problem," she said, her body already beginning to shiver.

"What is that?" Stan asked, his teeth chattering.

"I think I'm about to jump."

"What?" Shane turned himself using his elbows to look in her direction.

"It's the pain behind my eyes. I can feel it coming. I recognize it now."

"Well, then at least one of us is getting out of here," Shane said, despondent.

"No, no, I'm not leaving you. Maybe you can come with me."

"Say again?"

"All of us, maybe if were all close enough, if we all hold hands or something."

"It's worth a shot," Austin said, struggling to sit up. "Kenia, how long do we have."

"Not long."

They each grunted, shuffled, and strained, leaning against one another to sit upright, and rolling Hailey's unconscious form onto their laps. Already, Kenia could see Hailey's lips had turned blue.

"Come on, Hailey, hang in there," Shane said.

"I hope this works," Stan said.

"It has to work. God, please make it work," Kenia said.

"Please, please, please . . ." Shane droned on, rocking forward, his hands clasped with Austin on one side, Shane on the other, breath surrounding them in clouds.

Kenia put all her strength of will towards bringing the Pennels along with her. She would make it work. Her hands were out of her control now, as were her chattering teeth and the rest of her trembling body. Each inward breath was painful, the cold stinging her lungs. She pressed her head against Hailey's as Stan put his on Kenia's shoulder. The pain behind her eyes was excruciating.

Then it was gone. So was the cold. Warm, moist air closed in around her, along with the sound of crickets, tree frogs, leaves crunching beneath her, and all the scents of the nighttime forest. The sudden change of temperature and air made Kenia cough. She swallowed and opened her eyes to the darkness of night. But she already knew from the emptiness of her hands that she was alone.

Chapter 27

Redman Can Get Ahead, Man

Four by four by four.

Kenia focused on her breathing, shutting out the growing sense of urgency to act, to do *something.* Action without thought would only make things worse, she told herself. Go slow now, to go fast later.

My friends are in danger. They are going to be killed.

But she only had what was right here in front of her. And who knew *when* here was.

After a few more deep breaths, she took in her surroundings. She could feel frost melting from around her nose and mouth as she took in the forest clearing she had jumped to. The air was warm and close, in line with the season she had been materializing in with previous jumps. Was this perhaps the very night of the accident—which was clearly no accident at all. She thought it likely, but even if she could guess the *when,* she did not know her *where.*

The trees were red maple, white oak, with a number of slash and scrub pine, consistent with what she had seen throughout the region around Selah Station, but that did little to help. When she listened for it, she heard no traffic. A dog barked in a distant hollow. All that was left for her to do was walk, but which direction? She was on a slope and figured it was best to head downward, since the town itself was at the bottom of a valley. After walking a little ways, she was encouraged to see the outline of a building, its rectilinear sides standing out against the natural shapes of the forest. She made out a clearing in front of it with a road, even a turnabout in it.

Slowly, the place took on a familiar shape: it was the icehouse and driveway at the Bridgewater Estate. She felt a rush of relief, as she knew now with certainty where she was in relationship to the town, and continued down, out of the woods, into the clearing.

It was empty of cars or people. She moved to the doors of the icehouse and peered through the gap between them. In this era, it was nothing more than an icehouse, the extensive renovations not yet constructed. She felt a sick sense of powerlessness, so close to where her friends would be, but so distant in time. She shook and kicked at the doors, for no other purpose than to vent her frustration. They remained locked fast.

Focus, Kenia.

She would have to help them later. If she had been drawn back to this period, she knew it was for a reason. She had decided that reason centered on the disaster. What else could it have been? But this meant she had to get to Selah Island and that started with getting off the Bridgewater Estate and back to town. She knew traffic was sparse on the main road in the twenty-first century and bound to be even more so in the twentieth, so hitchhiking was likely not an option. But neither was walking.

She ran down the road to the main driveway of the estate and decided to turn uphill, towards the mansion. The distance was much longer on foot, as opposed to how easily they had covered it in the Jeep. But finally she reached the edge of the acreage and the long swales of grassy, well-manicured lawn. Even in the nineteen-fifties, it felt as short and well-tended as a golf course underfoot.

The mansion itself was dark, except for a single square of light on the third floor of the southern wing. The ostentatious floodlights had yet to be installed, so too the English-style streetlamps with their gas flames. Only porchlights lit the exterior, in yellow cones to either side of the front doors.

Kenia remembered a garage next to the parking area that they had passed in the Jeep. She ran in its direction, hoping it would have been built already. It was, even if it was invisible in the darkness until she was right upon it. She found her way to the door and tried the knob. It made a complete turn and swung open, without even the slightest chirp of a security system or the blare of an alarm.

So people really didn't lock their doors in the 1950s.

Inside was complete darkness, and she was reluctant to turn on any lights. But her phone and its flashlight were gone, and realizing that time was short, she took the chance, feeling along the wall until she found a switch and flicked it. A single iridescent bulb came on in a socket hanging from the ceiling. It was dim, but it was all she needed to see her salvation. Apparently old Crowley Bridgewater was a motorcycle enthusiast. These were not the motocross motorcycles she had recently learned to ride, but their mid-century predecessors. It didn't take her long to realize they were all "Indian" brand, a dozen of them arranged in what appeared to be chronological order: First were the older, military models painted in olive green with white stars on the gas tanks and copious boxes for ammunition storage on either side. These gave way to models painted in reds, black, grays, even one in auburn-and-coffee tones that seemed to be the most recent, judging by the addition of chrome features.

The Indians had fenders over most of the tires and a profile of an Indian chief on the gas tanks, frames, and motor casings. The chief looked out with a noble visage, as if unbothered by notions of cultural appropriation or the nature of white men riding polluting, fossil-fuel-powered machines across his lands, stolen through deception, murder, and genocide, under the contrived pretext of Manifest Destiny.

The keys were hanging on the wall. Kenia grabbed them all, along with a helmet which she shoved down on her head. She straddled the first bike, what she believed was the newest model and hopefully in working order. The model name on the side was "Scout." It was smaller than some of the more intimidating "Chief" models, and so better suited for her size. She tried the series of keys one after another—more appropriated Indian chief profiles stamped on each one. Finally, one key slid in with a jump of her heart. She pumped her fist and looked for the switch to open the garage door before laughing at herself—automatic openers had yet to be invented. She scrambled to the base of one of the doors, pulled it up, and allowed the spring to do the rest of the work, sending the door folding upwards into the track overhead.

If the noise of the door opening did not bring unwanted attention, she knew the motorcycle would. She secured her chinstrap and took a moment to study the bike's workings. She knew she would only get one chance. She primed the engine, checked the choke, and put her fingers on the key, the chief's head conspicuous next to her hand.

"All right, Chief, let's get ahead together."

She turned the key, gunned the engine and kicked the bike forward. The front fork wobbled as she rolled forward and careened into the frame of the garage door. The engine nearly stalled, but she kept it alive, even though it filled the garage with thick exhaust. She could hear dogs barking now. It took all her strength to stabilize the bike again. There was no longer any room for discretion, so she revved the engine again, felt the pistons fall into a steady rhythm beneath her and kicked forward once more.

"One more try . . . ."

She thanked the universe that the mansion was built on a mountainside, the slope giving her added momentum to settle the bike and test her balance. She clicked on the headlight, illuminating the tunnel of the woods, before she gave the engine another shot of gas and accelerated towards the main road.

If she was noticed, or followed, she had a good lead on her pursuers. Her mirrors remained empty as she continued down from the mountainside estate, the road gradually becoming familiar despite the passage of years. Just as she reached the T-junction where she could turn left towards downtown and the island or right onto state road 521 and on to the Pennel place, she stopped. The Scout idled beneath her. Through the trees she could make out the river gorges, those fissures of darkness separating the clusters of light and life on the opposite banks. The Selah Branch Bridge was nothing more than intervals of light suspended over a river of unknown depth. She thought of all the lives at risk, those on the campus, in the neighborhoods, and at the plant—so many people, so much to lose. The lights of the campus twinkled, like the pinpricks of fragile, distant stars, their light nearly swallowed in the menacing glow of the coal plant, burning in its aura of smoky haze.

It was too much to take on alone. She needed help. She leaned the bike northward and sped up the state road towards the Pennels'.

◊

The porch light came on first, a silent beacon that a handful of moths discovered promptly and began to circle. They were soon joined by other flying insects that buzzed in direct flights into the glass sides, pinging with graceless little pops and taps before falling and trying once more. The knob jiggled while the lock clicked and the door opened. At first Kenia could not see through the screen for the way it caught the glare of the light. So she stood exposed, conspicuous, hoping the right person had come in answer to her knocking, her body trembling, from anxiety as much as from the violent vibrations of the motorcycle.

A hand popped the hook and eye latch, leaving the hook to dangle. The screen door opened with a long creak, the light reflecting silver off the screen until the door stopped wide enough for the young man she had seen before to step out onto the porch. He was in denim jeans and a T-shirt that hung loosely around his flat stomach but was snug around his chest. His hair was standing up on the side of his head as if he had just woken from where he had fallen asleep on a couch. His eyes were the same blue blazes she remembered. What a sight she must have been to him, bandaged, bruised, bloody, her clothes ripped in places, her hair a mess from her motorcycle helmet.

Her heart was pounding and she was short of breath. She could see Austin, Hailey, Shane, and Stan—all four of them—in his face, as if he were just another sibling and not their uncle. Yet there was an odd presence to him, perhaps it was born out of the surprise of her appearance, or maybe it was the ease and confidence with which he moved within his own space. But it did nothing to overshadow the kindness and compassion in his eyes, for she had no doubt that he *saw* her. Not as black, not as a woman, but as a person. It was a rare, intangible quality she had encountered but rarely, once in a rabbi, once Buddhist monk, and once in a grammar school teacher from Trinidad-Tobago. But she knew it when she saw it.

"Listen, what I'm going to tell you may sound crazy, but you have to believe me."

"All right. You have my attention, since the last time I saw you, I think you disappeared right in front of my face. Who are you?"

"My name is Keniabarido Dezy. You can call me Kenia."

"Is this a dream?"

"No. You are Mike Pennel, right?"

"Yes."

"Your family is in danger and I need your help."

Chapter 28

Iron Mike

The muscles in Mike Pennel's jaw worked, a glint of coppery whiskers on his face, as he ran his hand over his head. "What kind of danger is my family in?"

"It's complicated. May I come inside?"

"You sure I'm not dreaming?"

"Does it feel like one?"

"No."

"Even if it is one, then what do you have to lose? I mean, you'll wake up and be fine, right."

"Right, or I'm crazy."

"I thought that a lot myself. You'll feel it a few more times before I finish."

"Well, then you best get started," he said, swinging the screen door open and motioning her to follow him inside.

She stepped into the same house that she had stepped into decades into the future. Her head danced with a sensation of vertigo and disorientation. This version of the Pennel home smelled of the same wood materials, but added to that was a musty odor from the dusty rugs and a sharpness to the varnish that was not present in the future brands. She made her way to the kitchen with Mike following. If her familiarity with the place was strange to him, he did not comment on it. Instead, as she sat at the table and took in the kitchen—this version with the original pine cabinets and laminate counters—Mike went to the sink and ran water to splash in his face before pulling out a chair and sitting down across from her.

She wasted no time telling him everything and set aside any compunctions about informing him of future events which had yet to occur, Science Fiction tropes of corrupting timelines be damned. She wanted to corrupt this one as much as possible if it meant saving her friends—his niece and nephews.

She explained the events of the summer of 2017 and what she knew about what would take place on the night of August 22, 1953. She focused on the facts she knew, those most critical to their situation, and then a few of the assumptions and hypotheses she had formed in discussion with the Pennels and the Coates brothers. She felt like her sister Chinemere, laying out a case in court, or how Kenia herself might outline the case in a journal article.

When she was finished, Mike held his fist to his mouth. His throat fluttered as he tried to take in all she had shared. "If I had not seen you disappear myself, this would be harder to take in." He paused for a beat to shake his head back and forth. "My niece and nephews, they live in this house. They are your friends?"

"Yes, and I am afraid I could not stop my jump. I left them in grave danger. Our only hope is to change the timeline, or if that does not happen, hopefully I will return with enough time to help them."

"I hope so too, even if I don't know them."

"They are good people. The best. And they take good care of this house."

He smiled, "Good to know. And good to know the old place has stayed in the family."

"Where are your parents and your brother now?" she asked carefully, worried that it might prompt him to ask about his brother and future sister-in-law. Kenia was not sure if it was right to share with him that they would die in a car accident with a drunk driver, especially when she didn't know any further details on how it might be prevented.

"My brother Jay is in the Navy. His ship docked from its last tour in Norfolk, Virginia yesterday. Mom and Dad headed down to pick him up. First time they've seen him since he came back from Korea."

"What day is it today?" Kenia asked.

Mike looked at the clock on the kitchen wall, the pendulum rocking back and forth with steady clicks. It read a quarter to midnight.

"It's Saturday, August 22, at least for another fifteen minutes. So if what you say is true—"

"We need to move."

"Right. Follow me," he said, pushing out his chair.

Mike's long stride took him across the room into the hallway. He had the body of a man, but still some of the awkwardness of a teenager. His youth gave him an energy that overcame the drowsiness of sleep. Kenia hurried after him as he ran down to the basement, his feet pounding a rapid beat on the wooden cellar steps. The lower level smelled of ashes and fuel oil. A coal-burning furnace was cleaned and closed up for the summer season. Homemade jars of preserves lined the shelves. Mike ran to the northwest corner of the house and knelt next to a wooden chest that he opened to reveal two miner helmets with lamps and heavy 1950s era batteries. He clicked the switches, but the lamps remained dead.

"No matter. We don't need the lamps to work. We just need to look like miners," he said, setting the helmets aside and pulling out two pairs of work boots followed by two sets of coveralls. They were stiff and, despite washings, were dark with embedded coal dust.

"What are these?"

"My grandfather's old mining kit."

"You saved them?"

"They're sort of family heirlooms. Those old guys, even though the mines were killing them, it was their life, their identity. That work was their purpose, keeping the lights on for the rest of the country, food on the table for their families, and babies warm in the winter. They took it seriously." He touched the cloth as one might an old battlefield flag before handing it over to Kenia. "It might be a bit big on you, but we'll need them to move around the plant without attracting too much attention."

"I like the way you think," she said, pulling the zipper down on the front and slipping the coveralls on over her clothes. Mike did the same, negotiating his with much more efficiency than she could with her oversized set. While she rolled up the sleeves and positioned the pant legs to fit over the boots, Mike rounded the corner of the cellar, opening a few more chests and drawers, and returned with a climbing rope strung across his chest and a utility belt around his waist. He buckled a second belt around Kenia and cinched it, helping with the excess fabric. She felt a bit ridiculous as she pulled her braids back and tried to arrange them in a discreet fashion beneath her helmet. Mike looked much more the part than she. But he seemed satisfied as he took a look at her and declared, "That will do."

"How will we get past the gate?" she asked. Not satisfied with her hair, she bent down to where a row of old shoes had been stored, yanked out the laces, and used them to secure her hair back.

"I figure we'll jump the train that comes in around a quarter to one."

"How do you know the schedule?"

Mike shrugged. "Whole town knows it. You hear the whistle as it crosses the trellis at night . . . at least those of us who are light sleepers do."

"Sure," she said remembering the open bedroom windows in this era without widespread AC.

"But we need to move. We will have to hop it before it gets to the trellis," he said, moving to the steps. "Can you drive that bike with a passenger behind you?"

"I guess we'll find out."

◊

The Scout handled differently with the addition of a passenger, but Kenia was able to adjust. Mike caught on that he had to lean with her around the turns, keeping his center of gravity close

241

to hers, and hunker down on the straightaways when she would shift into higher gears and open up the engine. He had to shout over the roar to direct her where to go, leading them through town and eventually into the woods along roads Kenia was not sure she had been on—or if they even still existed—in the future she was familiar with. These roads were unpaved and went from gravel to nothing but wheel ruts that shook the frame and caused the fenders of the Scout to shudder.

"Fire trails," Mike cried out in her ear. "They are better suited for a Jeep, but you are doing great."

Kenia would have thanked him, but she was distracted as a panel from one of the fenders went flying off into the bushes. The effort required to keep the bike upright was too great anyway. Had she tried talking, she likely would have bit her tongue from the clacking of her teeth. She wrestled the Scout for another half mile, until Mike pointed out a break in the trees. Kenia had to downshift and bring the bike to a stop to steer it up and out of a wheel rut and over a small rise adjacent to the fire road. The far side barely even presented a path. The bike skidded through leaves and sprayed up fans of dirt, nearly toppling over, before they came out in a flat space next to the railroad tracks. Over the idling engine they both heard the unmistakable howl of the train whistle.

"That way," Mike said, pointing west. Just before a bend where the tracks disappeared stood a signal tower, the lights burning red in their direction.

"Hold tight."

Kenia steered the Scout along the rail bed. The easement was mostly clear of obstructions, but the earth was soft from pools of runoff, causing the rear tire to spin out more than once. The train whistle sounded again. Mike didn't need to tell her to go faster. She twisted the accelerator, and they barreled towards the tower at a reckless speed. A deer carcass, the creature likely frozen in the headlamp of a previous locomotive before being struck and flung to the side, loomed up in the cone of light in front of the Scout. Kenia held her breath as they rolled over it, but they both still choked from the cloying scent of decay.

They could hear the thrum of the diesel engine as they reached the base of the tower. The access ladder for maintenance crews was outside of their reach.

"We should hide the bike in the bushes," Mike said, climbing off and pulling a steel hook-shaped wrench of some sort from his belt. Kenia turned to push the Scout into the bushes while he lifted the rope from his shoulders and looped the end around the handle of the wrench. The bike was too heavy to move on her own in the soft ground, so Kenia gave it some gas and rode it into the tall grass and bushes at the forest's edge. She cut the engine and gave the seat an appreciative pat.

"Thanks, Chief," she said to the profile, now scratched, its shine gone from a patina of mud.

"What's that?" Mike asked from the tower base.

"Nothing, how can I help?"

"Wish me luck," he said, twirling the wrench on the end of the rope. He reminded her of a pitcher winding up for a fastball, his concentration unbroken by the crescendo of sound from the looming locomotive, its headlamp appearing through the trees and reflecting off the river just below them.

Mike released the wrench. It *wanged* against the lowest rung of the access ladder, the sound like a poorly tuned drum, and fell back to the ground with a thud. Mike recovered the line, made a few adjustments with his feet, spun and released again.

This time the wrench floated right over the last rung, the line arching behind it. Mike wasted no time pulling the slack, hesitating only when the wrench approached the rung and dangled, twisting in a slow circle. He yanked it taut at the right moment and the hooked end caught on the rung. With another pull, the maintenance ladder clattered down.

"Come on, you first," he said.

Kenia jumped up, Mike kneeling to unhook then refasten the wrench so that when he followed Kenia up the ladder to the catwalk he was able to pull the ladder up back into place, shake the wrench free from the bottom, and wind it back up around his elbow and forearm.

The tracks below were lit in bright relief by the approaching locomotive.

"Hide yourself behind the signal," Mike said, motioning towards the catwalk that extended over the tracks. On either side were two sets of signal lights in black metal casings about the size of a small refrigerator: red lights shone in the direction they had come; green in the direction of the train.

Kenia crossed the catwalk, her feet banging on the metal grating. She was able to crouch and hide herself behind one—Mike the other. The beam from the headlamp brought day to night, illuminating the tracks with the searing intensity of a sustained lightning flash, even from a hundred feet away. The metal of the tower gleamed; Kenia was grateful Mike had had the foresight to hide them from the engineer's view. While they waited, Mike freed the wrench from the rope and began to fashion a complex new knot around the handrail between the signal cases.

She would have asked him what he was doing, but the train whistle sounded. It was deafening so close. She covered her ears as the cone of light around them narrowed, and the engine itself passed beneath them. The burst of withering heat from the turbines and the haze of exhaust nearly made her faint. It was like standing before a blast furnace. Mike caught her by the shoulder as she wavered.

"You all right?" he screamed over the drum of the railcars, the throbbing of the axles, and the *clomp-click-clack-click* of the wheels over the track joints. She nodded, taking a gulp of the fresh air that swept past in the locomotive's wake. The outer layer of her clothes was hot to the touch, her skin flushed and sweating.

"Yeah, yeah," she said, although she had to steady herself with the handrail as she got to her feet.

244

Four by four by four.

Mike wiped his own brow. He secured the knot and lowered the rope down to dangle just above the passing cars. The railcars were uniform, as far as the eye could see, each one a coal car, the beds empty as the train was headed to the plant to be filled. Each had its own wheel brake at the end, above the couplers. The first few to pass struck the end of the rope, whipping it wildly, one after another. Mike adjusted the length so that it hung just above them; at the same time, he kept looking down the tracks for sign of the caboose.

"You first, watch the wheel brakes."

Kenia had not considered just how dangerous the stunt was going to be. The train was indeed moving too fast to come alongside to jump on or climb aboard—so fast, in fact, that the window to drop into the bed of the coal cars was breathlessly short. A thousand last-second doubts log-jammed in her head.

"Will this knot hold?"

"My brother is a sailor. He taught me a thing or two about knots. But we got to move before the caboose comes."

Kenia nodded. She swung herself over the railing, testing her grip on the rope and the placement of her feet on either side. She tried to tell herself it was no different than the climbing wall at the school gym. The wheels of the railcars that would cut her in two, notwithstanding.

She lifted her feet and put her trust in the rope and the knot. They held. Her arms burned and she tried to give them some relief by slipping her legs around the line. She lowered herself hand over hand, watching the beds thunder past: a series of rusty bottoms punctuated by a gap where the couplings clanked together with all the weight and force of ocean freighters, completely indifferent to her soft, fleshy body. The picture of the shattered deer corpse flashed into her mind.

"Kenia, the caboose!"

She chanced a look towards the rear of the train. Two red lights were approaching. She loosened her grip, sliding down, the skin of her palms burning with the friction. She stopped just at the end, her feet running in air as a wheel brake passed just beneath her, then another, and another. When she thought she had the rhythm down, she let go.

Chapter 29

Riding the Rails

The bed of the coal car thrummed like a giant gong as Kenia smacked the bottom. The force of the impact stunned her, and she rolled backwards towards the rear of the train with her own inertia until the momentum of the locomotive caught her in its pull. Once she had regained her equilibrium, she crawled to the end of the car and pulled herself up against the side.

The tower with the signal lights—red from this side—was already distant and receding fast. She could not make out Mike anywhere. She called out his name, but it was no use in the roar of thunder from the railcars, each reverberating like a giant drum. The locomotive let out another piercing whistle. She had no landmarks close by to judge from, but she knew they had to be nearing the river crossing. The thought of entering the plant alone, without Mike, uncertain of his fate, created a bilious feeling in her gut.

She had to find him. She started to climb the set of steps welded into the railcar's side. Once atop, she looked down on the space between cars and the blur of sleeper-ties beneath. She felt the full force of the rushing air. The *click-clack* of the wheels over the rail ends was as loud as a jackhammer. The deep knocking of one coupling against the other contained all the force of ships colliding.

"Kenia!"

"Oh, thank God," she said, as Mike clambered over the far wall of the next car in line, crossed its bed, and appeared just over the near wall. He negotiated the gap with care, grabbing hold of her hand once he was close enough, before they both collapsed to the floor of the same railcar, breathing a sigh of relief.

"Oh my God, I'm glad to see you," she said, wrapping him in her arms.

"Uh, yeah, me too," he said, less sure what to do with his arms. The moment lengthened and she released him. He was blinking fast and touching the back of his neck.

"Sorry, I was just worried something had happened to you."

"Safe and sound, so far."

"So, what's next?"

"We ride. We stay low. We wait. If you don't mind, I'm going to sit down. My heart is still in my throat. Plus, we're less likely to be seen that way."

"Sure," Kenia said, sliding down, their backs against the rear wall, the vibrations sending tremors through her body. They rode like that, side by side, shoulder to shoulder, hip to hip, for some time, surrounded by a cocoon of noise—the thunder of the train and its steady progression into the heart of things. It was a strange mix for Kenia, to be riding this behemoth of industry, its movement directed by even larger forces of technological progress and capitalistic gain, forces historically willing to churn up the bodies of the poor, black or white, to serve the ultimate goal of profit. At the same time, stars blinked at them through tree branches, the nighttime forest and the celestial backdrop a reminder of grander, more majestic cycles and timelines that rendered their own strife and striving meaningless.

She took a deep breath and another, followed by another, *four by four by four,* aware of the tension rising in her as the train slowed and began to negotiate the turn towards Selah Island. The rhythm slowed. The pitch of the rumbling cars changed in tenor but, still, the train cars moved forward with the same, fateful, inexorable drift as of one continent into another. Stars blinked through steel girders now instead of tree branches as they rolled onto the trellis. A trellis she knew well by now, in multiple eras. Kenia took one last measure of comfort before the chaos. She felt to be in a liminal space. No one expected them, but these were their last breaths while in the safety of concealment. If only the world were as simple as two people, side by side, holding hands—she had not even realized she had reached out for Mike's hand but there they were—tiny and unnoticed like mice on a freighter or like cats in that box of possibility that Stan had talked about, alive and dead at once, all outcomes possible until the end of the story was written, the train arrived in the station, the period placed at the end of the sentence.

And how often did one get the chance for a rewrite?

With every inch of trellis crossed, every girder that swept past overhead in a soft *whoosh* of sound, Kenia knew she was scared. She was about to say so when it occurred to her when she had last uttered the same words, "I'm scared." It had been at the Black Lives Matter rally, to Audre. And with that she felt pulled back from the tranquil, majestic, eternal places of firmament and the principles she had projected her thoughts towards moments before. Now she was trapped again amidst pointless distinctions—distinctions humans, in their failings, were willing to kill for.

And die for, she reflected. She was willing to, because of some notion of fairness, of justice, those concepts that she hoped resonated in those eternal spaces of the stars with dreams, aspirations, and things bigger than herself. And maybe, she hoped, resonated with what this country was *meant* to be. For some reason she thought of Martha Andersen's son Joel, stewing in his hopelessness and anger. Had she, in her own way, been too harsh, turned her back on him, painting him with a brush of irredeemable, original sin that was the progressive mirror of a moral, religious fundamentalism—a secular obsession with political purity, used to the same ends: to stoke hate and foster division?

Or was she granting him a grace he would never grant to her?
We can't let ourselves be divided.

With that, her resolve returned. Her fear quieted. Even her clasping of Mike's hand was an act of resistance in this strange confluence of fissures, timelines, and tragedies. Despite it all, she was next to a white male, this most unlikely of allies, in this most unlikely of circumstances.

"I'm glad it's you," she said to Mike.

249

Even if he understood her, there was no time to say so, for the train slowed further and the trellis came to an end. The stars dimmed as they moved into the iridescence of the floodlights orbited by insects and illuminating the mountains of coal that rose up alongside them, dwarfing the train. One, two, three of the mountains marched past in a stately progression, the locomotive coming to a stop, the brakes letting out a powerful hiss, and the couplings sounding in a simultaneous *ka-chunk* rising along the length of the train as the railcars ground to a stop all at once. Kenia and Mike could hear voices in the railyard, so they remained low, Kenia keeping an eye on the boom of the reclaimer to make sure it did not move overhead to bury them in a torrent of coal.

Mike removed his mining helmet to peer over the side of the coal car. Just as he did, a steam whistle blew.

"Is that the shift change?"

"Yeah, second to third. This will give us a chance to get up, out, and wander around," Mike said.

Footsteps passed just alongside their car, sending them both back down behind the steel walls. The voices of the workers walking by were low and weary, as one might expect at the end of the second shift. The men talked of getting showered, changed, smoking cigarettes, and going home.

"We'll wait for the first wave of them to roll out, then, before the third shift starts, we'll get out. Second shift guys will think we're with the third shift and vice-versa. But—"

"But, what?"

"I'm not sure what we do next."

"Good question. The fire allegedly started at the coal stacks, so we're in the right place if we want to warn people in time to stop it. But if it was just a distraction from the truckload of chlortrofluorine, then we need to get to the truck and keep it from being detonated."

"Roger that," Mike said, standing up on his tip-toes to scan the ground alongside the train cars. "Looks clear, let's go."

They climbed over the side and jumped down to the coupling and then to the ground. "Stop crouching, you look like you are sneaking around," Mike said. "Just act like you belong."

"Easy for you to say," Kenia said, trying her hardest to look like just any other plant worker.

"That's strange," Mike said, stopping to sniff the air. "You smell that?"

"Smells like kerosene."

"Pretty dangerous to have that around coal." Mike bent to examine the base of the coal stack next to them. The rocks were shiny in the floodlights, but what Kenia had first taken for a mineral sheen was actually accelerant. Mike picked up a piece and sniffed it to make sure before throwing it back on the pile. "Whole stack is soaked in kerosene."

"Sure seems like that fire was intentional now."

They heard more voices close by. Their instincts had shifted now that they had stumbled into something sinister. They ducked between coal cars, climbing over the couplers, and hid on the far side behind the wheels. A trio of men in CCP uniforms came rushing alongside the train carrying tankards of clear fluid and dumping it on the coal, the contents sloshing loudly as they shook the last drops on the stacks. They moved as if in a hurry, watching out in both directions along the train for witnesses.

"That will be enough," one stooge whispered to another.

"I'll say. It's going to go up like Hiroshima," the other said in diction that was surprisingly familiar to her.

She peered around the corner of the railcar, but the men had already moved beyond the gap. She could hear their retreating footsteps. It didn't take her long to realize what they were running from. They had thrown a flame onto the kerosene left behind, and the coal stack was lighting up in a loud *whoosh*. Blue ripples of flame raced from one stack to the next, morphing into yellow tongues that curled into the night sky, the stars blotted out by the rising cloud of smoke. Already Kenia could feel the scorching of the heat on her face and through the fabric of her coveralls. She and Mike both reached up to cover their faces.

"We need to get out of here," Mike said, taking her by the elbow and breaking into a run.

She didn't need any more urging than that. The fire was spreading so fast, the third stack was already aflame. She felt frustratingly slow, burdened as she was by her heavy clothes, work boots, and helmet. Mike was not much faster, even with his long legs; his utility belt bounced awkwardly on his hips. and his boots clunked along like bricks on each foot.

The land ran out, dropping off into the Potomac, which swirled around the head of the island like the bow wave of a ship. They crossed behind the locomotive and ran in full view of the nearest buildings and the operating booth of the reclaimer and the tippler. All the windows were dark. They continued to sprint away from the train and the growing inferno, now entering the plant proper, running down driveways between the buildings until they came to a chain-link fence. They ran along its length to the gate, only to find it locked.

The sky over the stacks and the rail yard was red as a forge. The buildings were silhouetted in a hellish glow, the steel on the sides facing the flames popping as it expanded from the heat. Mike spotted a fire alarm mounted on the side of a pillar and moved to pull it.

"I wouldn't do that, if I were you," a voice said from the shadows. Mike and Kenia turned in unison to see six white men in CPP uniforms. They ranged in age from late teens to fifties. All of them were holding crowbars, sledge hammers, fire axes, or some other type of improvised weapon.

"You all lost?" one of the older ones said. He had a jowly, unshaven face. The patch on his breast read John. "We locked the gate after the second shifters left. So you all ain't third shifters."

"You ain't even workers here, judging by those uniforms," another younger one said in a nasal peckerwood accent. His was the voice Kenia recognized from earlier, and she studied his face, perplexed. He had a pitiless stare, pale, washed-out eyes, and a narrow angular face that seemed familiar.

"What you looking at?" he said.

"Nothing, just, nothing."

"This one's a girl!" he said, slapping his palm with his crow bar before he closed in on her, knocking her helmet off so that her braids fell about her shoulders.

"Calm down, Buzz," John said.

Kenia understood now. It was Buzz Grimsby, as a young man, who would go on to become the old guard at the Selah Branch Bridge. Buzz Grimsby, who had glared at her with such suspicion from her first visit with Octavian. The same Buzz who she knew had likely tipped off Bridgewater that they had returned with Austin for a second visit. All this time, from the very beginning, he had been one of the original conspirators charged with keeping the secrets of the plant's sabotage safe.

Mike had moved protectively between her and Buzz, but he was already backing off as John reasserted himself. "Let's take them to Mr. Dorsevage. He'll decide what to do with them."

Chapter 30

Buzz Grimsby

The conspirators escorted them at a brisk run to a squat office block building. The lights were on inside but the blinds were drawn. The fire alarm had sounded and squads of workers, black and white, raced across the grounds with fire extinguishers. Amid the rising emergency, Kenia and Mike, and their group of captors' hurry did not seem out of place, even though they were not headed in the direction of the fire.

She and Mike were pushed through a door labeled, Administration Block, then onward through a hallway and into an office. The nameplate beside the door declared that it belonged to Russel Dorsevage, Foreman. They passed through the empty, unlit secretary's office and stopped outside a door that was slightly ajar. Kenia could hear a slow, baritone voice on the phone speaking in deferential tones, "Yes, sir. No, sir. All right, I'll keep you informed."

John hesitated, waiting for the sound of the handset returning to the cradle before he knocked.

"Come in."

Russel Dorsevage was a heavyset man whose bulk filled up his entire office chair with, what looked like, an immobile presence. His hands were wide, the phone handset looking like a child's toy while his hand rested upon it. The skin on his face was lumpy and marked with splotches of rosacea. His pale eyes roved back and forth among the men, who filed in and formed a semicircle around Kenia and Mike. Kenia could read the fear in Mike's eyes.

"What's this?" Dorsevage said, an edge to his voice.

"Found them by the stacks," John said.

"Who are they?" the foreman asked, as if Kenia and Mike were not there.

"Wouldn't say."

Russel Dorsevage leaned back in his chair, the wood creaking under his weight. "You kids got bad timing. Wrong place. Wrong time. You from the college? Who you trying to be, dressed like that?"

Kenia was not sure if any answers, true or not, would help their case, but Mike tried to concoct a cover. "We just started. We're new."

"Shut up, boy. You're a damn liar," Mr. Dorsevage said. Mike's mouth snapped shut and some of the men snickered. The foreman turned back to John. "Everything else going according to schedule?"

"Yes sir, Mr. Dorsevage," John said, a jaunty tone creeping into his tone. He almost sounded relieved.

Kenia saw no use in keeping up any sort of pretense. "That was Crowley Bridgewater on the phone with you, wasn't it?" she said, remembering the one lit window she had seen in the mansion earlier that night. She pictured the Bridgewater patriarch of that era ensconced in a mahogany and leather study, nursing a bourbon and a legacy of familial and racial resentment. She didn't wait for an answer; Mr. Dorsevage, for all the power granted to him by his own masters, was not a sophisticated liar. She read his surprise easily enough. "Doesn't it bother you a bit that he wants to destroy his own plant, murder his own employees, and wreck your livelihoods?"

Dorsevage stared at her for a beat. He looked like he had eaten something sour. Finally, he laced his fingers together in the center of his ink blotter as if to pray. "Well, it don't. And you, young lady, know too much."

One of the men in the back sniffed while another shifted from one foot to the other. Dorsevage's eyes darted to them, noting their restlessness, before returning to Kenia, a hatred so great burning in them that Kenia wondered if he would get up and strike her. "Listen to me, you dumb nigger bitch. You don't know your place, but you're about to. We're setting things right tonight, and if it weren't for niggers like you, and the damn nigger lovers here in Selah Station, all this wouldn't be necessary."

The men behind them made grunts of assent.

"How much is he paying you?" Kenia asked. "I'm sure it's a fraction of what he'll make on the insurance money. You know he has at least three different policies through all his shell corporations?"

"Shell corporations, payments? Well you're right. He is paying us handsomely. It will keep our families comfortable and then some," Dorsevage said. "But you don't understand. We'd do this for free. It's our obligation, to keep you niggers in your place, ain't that right boys?"

More mumbled assents and curses about the "damn niggers and nigger lovers." Satisfied, Dorsevage exchanged a look with John and nodded. Kenia was spinning for the floor, her ears ringing, her vision blurred from the blow from John before she even realized she'd been struck. Mike moved to cover her, but the other men threw him against a filing cabinet and began kicking him, the violence shaking the thin walls of the office block so that pictures fell off the walls.

Kenia was curled on the floor, staring at the dirty and matted brown carpeting, trying to keep the room from spinning, the fragility of her body, the enormity of her vulnerability as a woman, as a woman of color, as a woman of color in pre-civil rights America, never more terrifying to her.

Dorsevage was addressing Mike now: "What is a boy like you doing messin' with a nigger like this anyway?"

"Pussy is still pink on the inside," one of the nameless men said, followed by collective laughter.

"I guess so, but not on the outside," Dorsevage said, shaking his head. "And that's what matters," he added. He *tsked* and moved to the blinds, parting them with his fat fingers, stripes of orange light across his face. "Time's running out. Things look chaotic enough out there for phase two. Take these two and put them with the truck, then make sure you hightail it out of there. If that chlortrofluorine is like Mr. Bridgewater says, this side of the island will be one big blast crater."

They dragged Kenia and Mike to their feet and carried them to the back of a waiting flatbed truck, the rear covered with a canvas canopy, military style. The two of them were thrown onto the floor while the conspirators lined up on seats set against the canvas walls. The doors slammed shut, the engine coughed to life, and they were jostled as the truck rumbled over to the garage on the far side of the grounds. The cries of workers rushing to put out the fires and the wail of sirens formed a picture of chaos outside. Mike was coughing blood onto the floor of the truck, one of the men laughing and kicking him in the ribcage again as the truck came to a stop. Someone outside opened a garage door, and the truck rolled forward a few more feet before the driver pulled the hand brake and cut the engine. While the garage door rolled down behind them, John opened the back flap of the canvas so that the interior lights of the garage lit up their grim faces, a fresh wave of sobriety settling them.

"Men, have your watches standing by."

Each man pulled a sleeve of his coveralls back to reveal identical watches.

"Carl, you have the ring?"

"Yes, sir, it's ready to go," one of the men toward the back said. On his belt were gauges, loops of cord, tape, and utility scissors. Resting in his lap was a ring of what looked like specialized blasting caps, arranged like some sort of twisted parody of a Christmas wreath, the loops of charge wire and fuse cord a macabre imitation of the bow. This was the modified detonator needed to set off the chlortrofluorine, Kenia was sure.

The other men busied themselves passing out tankards of kerosene to one another and holding them in place between their feet.

"Pete, Arnie, you two tie these two up, put them right next to the truck. There won't be anything left for their mamas to mourn. All you others, let's go. You know the drill."

With military precision the men set to their tasks, filing out of the truck. Pete and Arnie dragged Kenia and Mike out, finding rope quickly enough to tie their hands and toss them down alongside the tanker truck Kenia had seen pull in days before. She took in more of their surroundings. The garage was a vehicle service bay. Lifts and pits for maintenance abounded, as did thousands of tools hung on shelves and set on worktables against the walls and between workstations. Aside from the garage doors, all of which were shut, the only way out was a single door on the far wall between two worktables. Kenia did note, with some shred of hope, that their captors had tied their hands but neglected to bind their feet.

Drums of fuel and smaller tanks of engine oil were stacked on the near wall. Other trucks, tractors, and bulldozers waited, parked in the dim garage, but it was the tanker truck that dominated the space, the gleaming silver tank of chlortrofluorine radiant as chrome even in the dim light. The man called Carl scaled the access ladder on its side and moved down the catwalk on top while the men waited in two rows on either side. The conspirators synchronized their stopwatches, measuring out the last moments of so many people's lives. Each pinched the sides of their wristwatches, waiting for their mark.

"Set for twenty minutes," John hollered.

Carl made his way to the center of the tanker, knelt beside the hatch, and pulled on the lever to open the lock. It snapped free with a hiss from the tank. Carl grimaced as the fumes hit him full in the face, coughing with his fist to his mouth, his eyes tearing, Kenia wishing him all the harmful short- and long-term effects of the stuff. But Carl mastered himself, set a few switches and dials on the ring of detonators, double-checked a few connections, then held it out over the open hatch. With a final glance at John and the waiting men, he started a countdown.

"On my mark after a count of five: . . . five . . . four . . . three . . . two . . . one . . . mark!"

At his last word he flipped a switch on the detonator's timer. It let out a small high-pitched whine that was silenced as he dropped the ring straight into the tank. It hit with a splash before settling on the bottom of the tank with a clunk. "Fire in the hole. Nineteen minutes and fifty seconds and counting," Carl said, slamming the hatch closed.

As the men began to disperse, carrying their cans of accelerant, Mike struggled to his feet. His hands were still bound, but he used all his force to slam into the nearest man. It was Buzz. He fell, dropping his tankard.

"Run, Kenia!" Mike cried out, just before Buzz recovered himself, tackled Mike, and pinned him, knees on his chest. Buzz began to strike Mike's face with his fists. Kenia made a weapon of out her body as well, twisting up to her feet and running to ram Buzz herself. She came to an abrupt halt, choked by her own coveralls as John horse-collared her from behind and swung her against the cab of the tanker.

The impact stunned her. She was coughing from the pressure her collar had placed on her windpipe. John stood, his legs apart, watching Buzz continue to strike Mike, until Buzz slowed, the effort tiring him.

"That's good, Buzz. We're on a timeclock here. Drag him to the other side of the truck to keep them separated. Then keep an eye on them."

"Yes, sir," Buzz said, breathing hard and wiping the sweat from his brow with his forearm. Mike let out a groan before Buzz took a fistful of his hair and dragged him around the length of the truck, leaving him outside of Kenia's line of sight.

John picked up the fallen tankard of kerosene, more focused on their next task now that the detonator was running in the chlortrofluorine—that next task being setting the garage alight. Already Kenia could see the light of flames glowing in the windows up near the rafters. The corrugated metal walls were warping and expanding in the heat. More fires, more cover for the coming explosion. With all the drums of fuel and cans of oil, it would be easy to conclude that the garage bay had provided the needed heat to set off the chlortrofluorine. It was a well-planned cover, and it was everything they had pieced together in the future, but yet they had made no difference. They were too late. Even worse, they were in the center of the coming blast of destruction that would incinerate every living thing for a mile.

Perhaps history is too much for anyone to change.

Buzz Grimsby, unerringly obedient to his masters, stationed himself in front of the cab where he could keep an eye on Kenia and Mike. The door slammed as John left to join the others setting the grounds on fire. Buzz alternately shook out his fists, his knuckles skinned and bloody, and checked the time on his watch. The noise of sirens as the municipal fire department joined the fight floated inside along with the shouts of conspirators as they worked against them. A window near the ceiling cracked from the rising heat, the shards dropping down the length of the wall and shattering on the floor. Smoke began to curl around the edges of the garage bay doors. Buzz began to pace, glancing back at the rear door, waiting for his friends to come and tell him it was time to flee, abandoning their prisoners to their fate.

It was fascinating for Kenia, to see the young man while knowing the old, even more so to see his hatred displayed so brazenly, even if she could not comprehend it.

"You are all right with all this?" Kenia asked him, knowing the answer already. "All right with murdering hundreds of innocent people."

"They ain't so innocent and some of them ain't people," Buzz said, taking a few steps closer to her, his hands making fists at his sides.

"They are human beings. You are killing white men and women out there, too."

"Never gave much care for nigger lovers. Too many of them running amok for too long in Selah."

"You don't win, Buzz. Not in the long run. You'll see in your lifetime."

Buzz stalked even closer to her. She could feel the heat of the flames now. Beads of sweat formed on both their faces. Buzz's eyes gleamed red from the hellscape outside, the noise of collapsing structures, wrenching metal, and the cries of men growing louder. It was the sound of chaos, death, Armageddon. Even if she knew the future, this triumph of evil felt like the end of the world. Buzz's face was close to hers now, his eyes examining her, her skin, the shape of her body, in the same objectifying way he would as an old man.

"You just don't know your place, nigger," he said. He reached out for her. Kenia did not know if she could expect him to grope her or strike her. He did not seem sure himself, as the desire to do both played back and forth on his face. Finally, fury won out and he took hold of her neck, his hand squeezing to cut off the air to her lungs and the blood to her brain. And all she could think about as her consciousness faded was that, for Buzz, this was some sort of justice, a setting things right. His world view, his values, were mirror opposites of hers, and his identity staked on the opposition, to the point of violence, to the point of denying her continued existence. Pest control indeed. As darkness closed in on her vision, she reflected that at least death now would spare her from the blast.

It was not to be. Blind, but not deaf, she heard a loud clank, like metal striking bone. The rest of her senses and her consciousness surged back to her as the pressure around her neck released, her organs drinking in the oxygen Buzz had denied her. She fell to the floor, landing on her back. The rafters above were lit by flames, casting dancing shadows. She turned her head to see Buzz sprawled out next to her, rendered unconscious by a blow to his head, seemingly by the head of the shovel held by the tall dark figure who looked down on her now with compassion, surprise, and most of all, love and protection in his eyes.

"Kenia?"

She knew his voice, even if she had not heard it anywhere but in her memories and dreams for the past five years.

"Dad?"

Chapter 31

Nexus

Donovan Diambu Dinobi Dezy, her father, knelt down beside her, untying her wrists with the sure dexterity she had always associated with him. She threw herself into his chest, wrapping her arms around his familiar shape, the sobs escaping her uncontrollable.

Her father, however, was more clear-headed than she, his concern and confusion driving him to gently separate himself and study her face.

"Kenia, baby girl . . .what . . . when . . . you're a grown woman. How long—" He stopped himself short, taking in the rising flames. He refocused his line of questions, his face taking on a determined expression of inquiry she knew well. It was clear to him that Kenia had made a jump as well, so no dwelling on that. Instead he settled on the urgency and safety of their immediate context. "*When* are we?"

"It's just after 1 a.m., Sunday August 23, 1953. We're in Selah Station, West Virginia. There is an integrated college here and a coal plant that the owner blows up with this truck in order to destroy it all. I've been making these jumps back for a few weeks now."

"I see."

"Mom told me about you."

"She did—Kenia, you are all grown up."

"Dad, you . . . disappeared," she said, squeezing his arms as the feeling of loss resurfaced. "We thought you were dead. It's been five years."

"Five years?"

"Dad, the bomb has been set. It's in this truck. We've got—" she scrambled over to Buzz where he was still knocked cold, took his wristwatch and put in on, "—thirteen minutes."

Her father took her by the shoulders. "Baby, there is always a reason we're called back. This," he turned his eyes to the truck, "this has got to be why. We've got to get this out of here, away from the city."

"The city is on an island with river gorges on either side. We could drive it into the river."

"What about these guys, how many more?" he said, nodding to Buzz.

"There are six or eight others. They're outside now but they'll be coming back to collect their friend. That door over there."

"I'll hold them off. You've got to get this truck out of here."

"You're not coming with us?"

"Us?"

"I've got a friend here with me, from this time. He's tied up on the other side."

"Get him loose and get him out of here."

"But what about you, Dad?"

A shadow passed over his face. "Kenia, pumpkin, I don't think that's in the cards."

"What do you mean?"

"You said it yourself, I've been gone five years."

"But you are here now! You can come back, you can always come back."

"Don't you see, Kenia? The last time I saw you, it was five years ago to you, but it was just moments for me. I jumped to here. I'm supposed to help you. But our people, who have this gift, this burden, we don't always come back. Sometimes the wrong we're supposed to right is . . . bigger than we are."

"Dad—"

"Look at you, Kenia. You're a woman. You've got to go back and live your life. Quick, tell me about Chinemere?"

"She's a civil rights lawyer. She just won the distinguished alumni award from Columbia Law School for her work with the trans community."

The pride in his face was unmistakable. "Chikmara?"

"Actress on Broadway. Was the lead in *The Color Purple*, not the high school production, but you know, for grownups." She laughed a bit through her tears at her choice of words.

"Chiazam?"

"Harvard, pre-med, when he is not lecturing me on the merits of Dark Horse comics over Marvel and DC."

He touched her face. "You?"

"Georgetown, studying public health, at least when I'm not living out a Dr. Who episode."

"I always wanted a degree in public health," he said, wistful. "What about your mother?"

Kenia felt a bubble of sadness rising and expanding in her chest again. "She misses you, Daddy. We all do. Please, don't do this."

Voices were closing in on the backdoor, close to the tailgate of the tanker.

"You are my child, Kenia. And no one is going to lay a hand on any one of my children. Not today, not tomorrow, not *ever!*"

She tried to reply, but the words were stuck in her throat.

"Like I said, there is always a reason we're called back, honey," he said, his eyes filming. She had never seen her father weep. "I wish I had known you had the gift. I wish I could have told you more. But there is no time. We've got to see this through."

She couldn't see for her own tears. He clasped her by the shoulders. "You know what you and your friend need to do?"

"Yes, Daddy."

He hugged her. She felt she would drown in all the things she would never be able to say. He stood up, taking up the shovel again and testing its weight in his hand, looking for the best place to hold the handle for what he had to do. He checked over his shoulder as he approached the rear door to make sure she was getting to her feet. She was, even though the tears kept streaming from her eyes. She circled the cab and found Mike. His face was swollen, his lips split, but he was conscious.

"Kenia, you got free! Where is Buzz?"

"Taking a nap. We're getting this truck out of here and in the river."

"Do we have time?"

"We'll make time," she said, checking the watch. They had ten minutes. She succeeded in untying the ropes on his wrists and tossed them aside. "Can you get the garage door open?"

"On it," he said, limping to the bay door. Kenia ran back around to the driver's side of the cab, climbed up on the running board, and swung open the door. Before she slid inside she took a final look at her father.

He was there, standing between the door and the truck. He had already braced it with a crowbar through the handle, while the men on the other side battered against it. She could hear them calling out Buzz's name between their blows against the door. The handle was starting to give way. Her father nodded at her, then readied the shovel.

Not today. Not tomorrow. Not ever.

She swung herself behind the wheel. One of the rafters from above twisted free and came crashing down to the floor in a glut of flames. Kenia turned the keys in the ignition and revved the engine. The dash was full of gauges and switches. All she cared about was the gear indicator and the RPMs. She struggled with the clutch and the stiff gearshift, the truck lurching forward as she tried to find the friction point. She missed it and the engine stalled.

The pounding at the back door increased as the men heard the engine starting and stopping. Kenia could see the entire door shaking in its frame. Her father stood ready, in place, prepared to hold back hell if he had to.

She started the engine again. The truck settled into a steady drone. She searched the cab to make sure the handbrake was off, found the horn cord above the doorframe and pulled it, signaling to

Mike to hurry. He turned from where he was pulling at the base of the bay door and shook his head. "It's jammed. It's the heat."

A shower of sparks exploded downwards as another section of ceiling collapsed. Eight minutes on the watch. She checked the rearview mirror just outside the window; the door had come off its hinges, and her father was bracing himself against it.

No time.

She punched the accelerator down with her foot and the cab growled forward, picking up speed in low gear. Mike understood her intent, rushing alongside the cab, hopping onto the running board and grabbing hold of the rearview mirror.

"Mike, are you crazy?"

"Just go!"

She redlined the engine as the bay door neared. She shifted once, the cab bouncing, the exhaust pouring out of the stacks adding to the smoke and hellfire. "Hold on!"

The truck burst through the doors with a crack of wood and a scream of steel. The engine coughed, threatening to stall, but Kenia finessed it and kept the truck moving, the heat of the flames receding. Mike was still on the outside of her door, his hair and clothes singed, but safe. "Kenia, there's someone back there, fighting with the good old boys!"

"I know." But she said nothing else, for she was determined to make her father's sacrifice mean something. A tableau of destruction was already unfolding before them. The coal stacks were three mountains of converged fire that towered into the night sky. The plant's fire suppression teams were overwhelmed and in retreat, even as cars and fire engines clogged the entrance gate. She knew Prentice Bridgewater and so many other good men and women were likely already among the people rushing to help. But more critically, the new arrivals were blocking their means of escape.

"Mike, how do we get out?"

"Take that driveway there. There's a second gate, an access road, but it will take us through the town," he said, pointing to the north end of the grounds.

"We have less than eight minutes."

"Then drive!"

It was a derby in hell's racing ring. Kenia rolled up over curbs, tearing up grassy lawns as needed, smashing and sideswiping smaller trucks and cars in her way. The truck was powerful, hard to maneuver, but once she built up speed, its mass could knock away any obstacle. There was no point in slowing down for safety.

A police cruiser spun out as she struck its fender. A firetruck slammed on its brakes, the firemen bracing themselves against the dash as she cut them off. Another group of plant workers scrambled over a truck's bed as she careened up against it's tailgate, apologizing with a loud "Sorry!" useless as it was.

"There, that gate!" Mike said, pointing to a chain-link fence standing locked across an unlit roadway leading towards the forest.

Kenia knew there was no time to unlock it and shifted the truck into a higher gear. Mike braced himself against the door again, the distance shrinking, the gate growing as it rushed into the windshield. The cab shuddered with the impact, but the fencing popped free in a blast of sparks and tangle of wire. The gate remained lodged on the front of the cab, the windshield spider-webbed with cracks. They were approaching a tunnel of dark road enclosed by the branches of the forest.

"Lights, lights, lights," Mike said.

Kenia flailed around the cab but could not locate the switch for the high beams. Mike finally reached through the window and pulled a knob that turned them on.

"Much better," he said.

Kenia kept accelerating down the straightaway, the sections of fence and gate they dragged along sending out an apron of sparks to either side. She checked the wristwatch. "Five minutes, Mike!"

"We can make it. Get ready to slow down when you take this next turn to the left."

The road stopped at a T-junction, Mike gesturing left with a karate-chop motion. She braked, surprised at how reluctant the truck, with all its momentum, was to slow down.

"Should have braked sooner, hold on!"

"Downshift, downshift!"

"Trying," Kenia said, wrestling the clutch and gearshift. The brake pads squealed and smoked until she was able to engage the engine brake, the engine snorting, the entire cab shaking. The entire vehicle tipped to the side just before it came crashing back down on all eighteen tires. The smell of burnt rubber, overheated brake pads, and fuel-rich exhaust filled the cab.

"Oh my God, that was scary," Mike said.

"Scarier now that we are driving into town."

"Don't worry, we'll make it, just don't tip us on the turns," Mike said. Even as he did, the stoplights of the streets came into view. Kenia kept their speed steady, watching for traffic, hoping for an opening as headlights and taillights crossed through the intersection up ahead.

"You'll need to turn right on Principle Avenue, then it's a straight line for the bridge."

"Tell me when I get there," she said as they passed by the first buildings of downtown. People were out and about, having heard the sirens and been drawn by the glow of the fire. She noted black and white faces, young and old, as in previous jumps—Selah Station, before the dream was lost. The tanker truck was approaching the town square. She recognized it from previous jumps. A crowd was gathered, roused by all the commotion and waiting for news.

"That's your turn!" Mike said, pointing to the looming intersection with cars waiting at the lights, parked at the curbs, and people lining the sidewalk. "Blow the horn!"

Kenia pulled the horn line so hard that the line felt as if it would cut into her fingers. The blare stunned the people into stillness rather than flight. "Don't stand there, move!" she cried.

Mike screamed the same thing, waving them to the side as they roared closer. She kept pulling the horn, and the bystanders finally began to flee. She tried to take aim for a path around cars waiting at the light, but it was impossible. She resigned herself to crashing through them.

"Slow down, slow down!" Mike said, swaying on the review mirror. He was right, she needed to slow to negotiate the turn. She smashed down the brake pedal and even yanked up the handbrake, before downshifting, the gears grinding. Their force still turned cars up and over on their sides. Mike was flung away from the cab, the images in the side mirror dancing as he held on to it, his feet kicking in the air beyond him. Kenia fought with the oversized wheel as Mike's feet floated back to the running board. Steady once more, he reached through the window and grabbed the wheel with her.

The truck rounded the corner. It did not tip this time, but the trailer with the tank swung wide, the rear-most set of wheels screeching, sending up a cloud of blue smoke. People scattered and the tailgate smashed a series of storefront and diner windows, dragging merchandise into the street and tearing lunch counters out onto the sidewalk. A salt shaker hit the windshield, followed by a flurry of napkins. The gearbox was screaming, gears knocked out of alignment. Lights flashed on the dash, warning Kenia of overheating systems, a flooding engine, an oil leak, and other mechanical catastrophes. A cooking-pot-on-asphalt sound told her that they were likely dragging the oil pan beneath the cab. The engine let out an angry whine, just as the trailer fell back in line with them. They had slowed considerably. A red light told her the rear brake line was out. A morbid thought told her she would not need it anyway, and she shifted for more speed. She checked her watch.

"Mike, just over two minutes."

"Bridge is straight ahead."

"Is it?"

"Yeah, gun it! We can make it." Mike said, banging the side of the door. Indeed, she could see the Selah Branch Bridge and its lights, spanning the expanse of the river gorge ahead, curds of smoke from the plant fire rolling overhead. For the first time, other possibilities, new potential futures, seemed probable. She knew her purpose with a clarity that had eluded her up to this point. And she knew what she had to do next, as if she had seen it before.

Then she remembered, *she had.*

"I'm sorry, Mike."

"What?"

"I'm sorry, but you need to survive."

She was thinking about the Pennels, her yet-to-be-born friends, who she knew would need their uncle. She had put him at risk up to this point, but she could not ask him to continue any further. She took hold of the wheel with her right hand, leaned in her seat, and shoved Mike in the chest with her left. He reached for the doorframe as he fell backwards, but she knocked his arms aside, throwing him, at last, off-balance so that he went tumbling into the street.

And she was fairly certain, as she did so, that she detected the flash of a camera out of the corner of her eye—an intrepid photojournalist by the name of Oliver Andersen snapping a picture, a picture she would see, decades later, wavering on the edge of existence, where an arm, reaching out from the shade of the cab had been her own all along, in an alternative timeline that was always potential and was now becoming real.

All that was left was the straight road, lining up with the bridge and the gorge, like a rendezvous with destiny. She shifted again, thought of her father and the willingness with which he had walked towards his own fate.

Voices are calling us . . . voices that mean work, sacrifice, and death.

Her vision blurred but she wiped her eyes. The watch gave her less than a minute.

If I perish, I perish.

Flashing lights raced across the bridge—firetrucks from the next town over. She pressed down the accelerator. They could likely see the flames from the neighboring valleys, glowing like a forest fire. The island was burning, like an epicenter of conflict in the dreamscape that was America. The fire would go on, she knew, but if the truck could hold out, the island, and Selah Station—and what they represented—might be spared.

The bridge was nearing. Kenia checked the speedometer, pushing the truck up to seventy, the temperature light still burning red. She picked out a break just off to the side of the roadway, before the guardrails of the bridge started, and took aim for it.

Thirty seconds.

Time had gone faster than she had thought. Her breath seized as she looked at her wrist. She was not sure if she would make it. More gas. The warning alarms were buzzing at a frantic pitch. The practicalities of steering the truck filled her mind. She knew by now that an abrupt turn would run the risk of sending the cab off the edge but swinging the trailer outward and hanging the tank up on the bridge. To compensate, she eased the truck onto the shoulder, the frame bouncing. Tree branches struck the cab with the sound of gunshots. She pressed the accelerator down harder to keep up the speed.

Fifteen seconds.

The bridge was nearing, but more importantly, so was the cliff. She steered off the road completely for the last few yards. Trees, bushes, and branches rattled against the cab, the wheels grinding in the earth and then . . . nothing. The cab cleared the cliff and the noise of collisions ceased, replaced by the rush of air, the roaring of the engine suddenly unencumbered by the weight of its load or the friction of the road. All this was accompanied by the lightness of tipping forward, as if at the crest of a rollercoaster hill, then a pressing of her body against the seat as the cab accelerated downward with the pull of gravity. The trailer had cleared. Over her shoulder, she could see its end following, the trailer lights glowing, surreally, alongside stars. Cars were stopped on the bridge. The surface of the Potomac was dark, its obsidian surface riffled by a gentle wind and the force of the current. She had never found the seatbelt and so, as the surface of the river raced upwards to meet her, she braced herself against the wheel, anticipating the collision.

The water struck with all the force of a concrete wall, slamming the wheel into her gut and her head against the windshield. Water gushed in through the windows, the cab engulfed in an instant and driven straight down by the weight of the following trailer. The water pressure on her body was crushing as she plummeted into the depths. Her pocket of air in the cab was quickly gone. The pressure built in her ears. A cloud of her blood floated from the lacerations on her head.

It surprised her, what was suddenly important to her in these last moments of her life. She did not want to die under a tomb of wreckage. She knew that. She wanted to, at least, float free of this contraption, meant to harm, to kill, so she pulled herself through the window and kicked.

The tanker continued past her before slamming into the bottom, the bending and twisting of metal sounding close as the noise carried in the water. The blast was coming, she knew it. She felt ready, her race completed, her task at an end here in the darkness of the river. Already the sight of the tanker truck was lost, the headlights and taillights flickering out as the circuits shorted. Her head was pounding, from the impact, from the water pressure, and her body trembling. Was this the shockwave? A rushing sound filled her ears. She saw a flash of light, but to her surprise it was a drawn out and steady glow, not an explosive blast, or a wall of expanding steam and superheated water. She knew the force of it would come, crushing her internal organs. Perhaps the oxygen saturation in her blood was already playing tricks on her brain, drawing these last moments of her life out longer, her perceptions slowing.

The light neared, sweeping through the dark of the water. She regarded it with a calm curiosity, was this a heavenly light? Was that form she saw approaching an angel? Perhaps all she needed to do was to surrender, to take a breath of the water and the figure would come closer, across the veil to take her hand.

The biochemistry of drowning consumed her thoughts as her synapses slowed further. Saltwater could not cross into lung tissue but acted as a barrier for the air to reach the lungs, cutting off the exchange of oxygen, allowing carbon dioxide to build in excess. The fresh water of the river would be even worse. The daughter of physicians, she knew how it *would* cross through lung membranes to upset the balance of ions . . . leading to hypertonic lung tissue . . . ruptured cells . . . water rushing into her own bloodstream, diluting it . . . hemoptysis . . . elevated potassium . . . depressed sodium . . . ventricular fibrillation . . . cardiac arrest . . . hemoglobin bursting from cells in her kidneys . . . renal failure.

The light closed in on her, slow and ponderous, just like her thoughts. The shape of the figure coalesced: a rounded head, a bulbous tubular back, waving fins. Bubbles rose in a column alongside a reflective scuba mask.

But angels don't scuba.

Then she realized: she had jumped. One last time. A desperate urge to live surged back into her will. Her need for air was painful. The diver shone the light on her face as if seeing her for the first time. But if he was surprised, he didn't respond like it. He kicked closer, removed the respirator and placed it to her mouth.

Kenia breathed.

She took a few more precious gulps of air before the diver moved them in a slow ascension towards the surface, exchanging the air regulator between them until they neared the surface, a light as bright as the moon waiting for them as they crested.

"Found her!" the diver said, as they broke into the world above. The light was not the moon but rather a light shining down from the stern of a boat. Kenia coughed and sputtered. "There, there, hold on, Kenia. I got you," the diver said.

"Kenia, take my hand," a mature black woman in a life vest said, leaning over the stern of the boat. The diver guided her hands until she could link up with the woman, who pulled her through the water to a ladder on the side of the boat. The diver floated behind her, his arms holding her steady as she climbed up and over the gunnel. The woman immediately wrapped Kenia in a towel before she moved to help the diver aboard.

Kenia looked around, the gauges, the fixtures on the boat, looked modern. Above she could see the stars bisected by the Selah Branch Bridge.

"When—"

"August 23, just after midnight. You are in 2017," the woman said. She was in a wetsuit herself. The man who had retrieved her sat down on one of the boat's benches, slipped off his flippers, his mask, and set the air tank on the deck with a clang like a bell. He peeled off the hood of his suit, looking over at her with radiant blue eyes.

"Praise Jesus, I found you down there."

Kenia stared. He was an old man, with wild white hair, messed from the hood of his wetsuit. But he was still fit and strong, evident in the way he moved and how he had steered her up to the surface and onto the boat.

"She's confused," the woman said, putting her arm around Kenia and rubbing her back, while Kenia moved the tangled braids out of her face. The man took Kenia's hands, like an old friend.

"I would be confused, too. Kenia, the last time I saw you, you pushed me off the cab of that damn tanker truck. It was over sixty years ago for me, but just moments ago for you. I know this must be a bit . . . disorienting."

"Mike?"

"I know I'm a bit worse for wear, but it's been a couple decades," he laughed. If she focused on the sound of his voice alone, she could still hear the Mike Pennel she had met in 1953. He barely got out the words, "This is my wife Rochelle," before Kenia leaped across the deck and embraced him.

That was when she started to cry.

Chapter 32

For Us, It's Just Another Wednesday

The boat's motor bubbled and churned the surface of the water at the stern of the craft as Rochelle steered the bow downriver. The Selah Branch Bridge blazed in an aura of streetlamps while light traffic passed overhead, the hum of the wheels interrupted at intervals on the expansion joints. On either riverbank the lights of buildings, headlights, and stoplights, competed with the stars arrayed above. The hills, their eternal black silhouettes, were the same as always, but the town of Selah Station was altered. Kenia noted houses all along the waterfront, their rooms lit in warm amber glows. The bobbing of lights indicated lamps floating on docked boats, and floodlights at the end of the piers drew in the catch for those taken with night fishing.

Selah Island itself was the most remarkable to her. The brooding overgrown forest now grew in equilibrium with homes, docks, even a five-story residence hall on the edge of campus.

"That is one of the dorms," Mike said from the seat next to Kenia. As he spoke, the distinct sound of music, laughter, and voices reached them over the slap of waves on the prow. "It's pretty high demand, that hall, right on the water like that."

"The whole university is high demand," Rochelle said from behind the steering wheel.

"She's right, Selah University is thriving."

"We'll have a chance to see it; our boat slip is next to the school's Marine Science Building."

"I think I need some more explanation," Kenia said.

"I can only offer a partial one, as I belong to this timeline. It's been over sixty years," Mike said.

"That's sixty years more in this timeline than me."

Mike smiled, the creases and lines of age unable to hide the face she'd known decades before. "I've read so many novels, watched movies, even read comic books on time travel over the years, and despite authors and writers' best efforts, they got it wrong: the whole instantaneous changing of timelines. It has to do with wave function, the different possible outcomes, and universes whose potential existences influence one another in ways we're still trying to understand."

"Stan mentioned as much, but well, my physics did not go much beyond 'E equals mc squared.'"

"Sure, well, I'm self-taught myself. I've taken a few classes at the university as a night student. I'm still stumbling around in the dark here, but it seems like yours is a case of a person who somehow can stand at these nodes where different probable outcomes branch off. Interesting thing is that they don't seem to disentangle immediately. Proximity to the person standing at the node points—you—allows people proximate to the change to see or know the other outcomes, as if they are remembering things that never happened or never would happen but *could* have happened."

"I think you're losing me," Kenia said, realizing that the unexpected sight of undergrads playing volleyball in a sandpit lit by tiki-torches where once there had been a toxic Zone of Alienation distracted her. "Are you saying you can see the future?"

"Possible futures, but not clearly. It's like remembering a dream. And as we've progressed on this timeline, the other, where the chlortrofluorine rendered the island uninhabitable and killed so many people, faded. I wrote it down, journaled what I saw back in the fifties after I crossed paths with you, before I lost it completely. But I seemed to know *that* was the timeline, with the disaster and the successful sabotage, that you had come from. But I figured, you couldn't return to it after you disappeared."

"After I disappeared . . . after the truck went into the river . . . Did it explode?"

"It did, but the water contained it and neutralized most of the reaction so it was not much more than a loud 'thud.' The truck itself survived, they dredged it out, and the tank, too. It just had a large hole in it, but it was hardly obliterated like it would have been had you not driven it into the Potomac. The plant still burned down, but the island, the school, and most importantly the people, survived."

"But how did you know I didn't drown or blow up with the truck?"

"Never found a body. I had a hunch, maybe more of a hope, that you had jumped back to now. Been prepping for your return for a while. I knew I'd have to learn to scuba dive; also got this boat and some radar for sport fishing a couple years ago that I hoped would help," he said, pointing to a screen next to Rochelle that projected a fuzzy image of the depths below.

"I never met you in the other timeline. You were down in the Florida Keys, scuba diving there, too."

"Interesting."

Rochelle piloted the boat to a dock next to a glass building labeled: Marine, Riverine, and Aquatic Science Building. Most of the interior lights were off but a few burned still, where Kenia could see students in lab coats working experiments late into the night. Mike stepped out onto the dock and pulled the boat flush against the mooring tires. He helped Kenia and Rochelle off and Rochelle led her to the boathouse and the ladies' locker room where she produced a large, well-stocked first-aid kit and began to see to the cuts and bruises all over Kenia.

"I need to stop making a habit of this," Kenia said, as Rochelle pulled away the very same Steri-Strip Hailey had applied in the other timeline. Kenia winced as Rochelle cleaned the old cuts and the new, speaking to her, as tender as possible. When Rochelle finished, she handed Kenia a duffle bag of dry clothes.

"Mike tried to describe your measurements to me. Seems like they were pretty close to what I wore when I was your age. Hopefully they will fit."

"Thanks," Kenia said, pausing for a moment to look at her face in the mirror. More bruises, more cuts, more bandages. She looked worse for wear, but she was alive, and it was more than she had even dared hope for just minutes before, in another time, another era. She took the bag, unzipping it, but not really noticing the clothes. "This whole thing is so disorienting."

"I can imagine," Rochelle said.

"When did you and Mike meet?" Kenia said, stepping into a stall for privacy as she changed.

"A couple years after he met you, I believe, although he didn't tell me about his 'brush the with the time traveling sister' until we'd been married twenty years. I guess he wanted to make sure I didn't think he was crazy." She paused a moment and looked Kenia in the eye before laughing. "I still did. But well, you've proven that I was wrong tonight . . . and I'm glad."

Kenia stepped into a bathroom stall and used a towel Rochelle had packed to dry herself off. The clothes were her size, and as she stepped out, Rochelle looked pleased with the fit. "Now come with me, young lady. Let's tour this campus and see what you made possible."

◊

What had been an overgrown forest overtaking the campus ruins now appeared as a well maintained green space. The new buildings still retained a brick-and-mortar style of New England meets Renaissance Europe fusion, but there had been an additional evolution of the architecture that referenced the mosques of West Africa and the Swahili stone towns of Zanzibar. The walkways among the buildings and grounds were brick and well lit. Students—black, white, Middle Eastern, Asian—milled about talking. A few threw a glow-in-the-dark Frisbee while a couple others took turns slacklining between two red oaks. This being a warm summer night, there was a mixture of shorts, skirts, T-shirts, tank tops, even hijabs.

"I feel like I'm at the United Nations," Kenia said.

"They do call Selah University the mini-UN," Mike said, changed out of his wetsuit and into a pair of loose fitting cotton pants and a sky blue linen shirt.

"You're kidding."

"I'm not. The campus is a model of integration and diversity, religious, social-economic, racial, and otherwise. Other schools from all over the world send representatives here to learn how Selah does it so successfully."

"It's a vision of God, if you ask me," Rochelle said, now in a dress with a colorful orange-red, white, and blue East Asian print. "A tri-partite, trinitarian God. We're better off for our differences and distinctions."

"Rochelle teaches in the School of Divinity, if you hadn't guessed," Mike said.

"Uh-huh," Kenia said. They moved at a leisurely pace into the heart of the old campus, where she had come with Octavian Coates her first week in Selah. Many of the old buildings remained, preserved and refurbished. The statue of Leonard Bridgewater included his wife Selah Branch alongside him. "Mike, do you know Octavian and Morris Coates?"

"Yes, we do," Rochelle said. "Dr. Octavian Coates is a tenured professor in the English Department. His brother Morris is a tenured history professor. You all right, Kenia?"

Kenia wiped her eyes. "Sorry for all the waterworks. It's just a lot to take in, but that is great. Really, *really* great."

They walked for a while longer, coming to the town square after a few moments of quiet companionship. Like the campus, it was a mix of the historical with the contemporary. Zoning guidelines preserved the heritage of the place, keeping the low-slung brick storefronts, even if they now had coffee shop signs glowing over the doors. Live Calypso music drifted out of a night club. The sidewalks were crowded with patio sets full of the late night crowd. Kenia picked out Mexican, Ethiopian, and Cajun-Italian fusion restaurants. A sushi place was also doing a thriving happy-hour business.

Rochelle mentioned how the north end of the island, where the coal plant had been, was now the site of a sustainable energy resource center, complete with wind turbines and waterwheels turned by the flow of the Potomac and Shenandoah Rivers. Closer by, Rochelle directed Kenia's attention to the park in the center of the town square. The gazebo had been upgraded to a larger, grander one, glowing in a web of light that reflected off a shallow pool around it. A string quartet was packing up their instruments for the night while the audience remained—couples stretched out on blankets with picnic baskets and bottles of wine in ice buckets. A ring of dancing water bubbled up around the statue of David Solomon Bridgewater, the city hall building a backdrop to it all.

Mike's phone buzzed in his pocket. He checked the screen, reading the text. His voice broke Kenia out of her reverie. "Looks like we need to get up to the Bridgewater Estate."

"The Pennels!" Kenia said. "I left them—they were in danger—in the other timeline."

"Exactly," Mike said, comforting her. *"In the other timeline.* They're all right. They went up there on their own. Seems like the FBI has served old Harold Bridgewater a warrant, and he has barricaded himself in his mansion."

◊

They drove up through the winding mountain roads that had not altered much in their routes or appearances between timelines. Kenia tried to make sense of seemingly competing realities in her mind. She was firmly aware of the events of her past few months in Selah Station, the existence of an impoverished, fractured community; a historical legacy of integration that had been lost, buried beneath an industrial disaster, toxic fallout, and a cover-up.

She could easily recall her interviews for Dr. Quientela's phone app, Healthy-Bytes.

But she had a growing familiarity of this timeline, too, as if she had been here all the time.

The driveway to the Bridgewater Estate was crowded with vehicles, including news vans, police cars, and civilian cars that belonged to curious neighbors and Selah Station residents. Kenia noticed the absence of affluence in this timeline. The driveway itself was unpaved, rutted, and bumpy with washouts. Gone were the lamps spaced at even intervals, the fine gravel, and the sports cars and luxury vehicles. But the property was not lost in darkness or silence. Quite the opposite: the engines and generators of the news vans were chugging away, powering the lights illuminating the field reporters who were providing updates to the cameras. One reporter was interviewing a distinguished looking woman with honey-toned skin whom Kenia knew she had never met and yet recognized as Monique Bridgewater, Mayor of Selah Station—in this timeline— and descendant of Prentice Bridgewater—who had indeed *not* died in the chlortrofluorine explosion that had killed so many in the alternate timeline.

Kenia's head spun as the alternate branches of possibilities resolved themselves in her mind.

Mayor Bridgewater was elegant and poised, but her eyes— deep pools of sympathy—invited the reporter, a young mixed-race man, close to her. Mike parked the car, and as they made their way to the crowd at the edge of the property, Kenia could hear the mayor speaking to the reporter.

"Sadly there has not been much contact with that scion of the Bridgewater family, but we are hoping for a peaceful solution to tonight's situation."

Kenia noted men in familiar blue jackets with yellow FBI lettering. Another reporter was interviewing Agent Saavedra, who this time seemed to be investigating Harold Bridgewater and was not acting as his patsy.

"FBI agents and local police attempted to serve Mr. Bridgewater a warrant for his arrest and to search his premises at approximately six fifteen eastern time tonight," she said.

"What were the charges?" the reporter asked.

"Racketeering, bribing public officials, money laundering, attempted kidnapping, and blackmail."

"Is there evidence for these accusations?" the reporter asked.

"These accusations are the result of an investigation which the Bureau, Justice Department, and local law enforcement have been conducting in collaboration over a number of years now."

"Has Mr. Bridgewater resisted arrest?"

"When agents approached his door he threatened them with a firearm. A SWAT team surrounded and secured the premises. After that a negotiation team was called in."

Her updates trailed off as Kenia, Mike, and Rochelle approached the edge of the lawn where a crowd gathered along a strip of yellow police tape. Kenia took in the mansion, which was familiar to her through a number of eras, but this version was unique. The mansion was the same shape and size, but this iteration lacked the refinement and ostentation of the previous twenty-first-century one. The landscaping, terraces, sculptures, and fountains were gone, replaced instead by trees with years of deadfall spread beneath them and lumps of overgrown weeds and grass throughout the hillside. The mansion itself sat in darkness, without floodlights, even if the porchlight and windows glowed defiantly. A black armored van was parked close to the front door, officers and agents in tactical gear with automatic rifles and battering rams moving up the steps with coordinated caution.

"Kenia!" a familiar voice called out. Hailey turned from the crowd of onlookers, bounded over to her, long hair bouncing, and hugged her. "Where have you been? This is crazy, isn't it?"

Hailey started to pull away, but Kenia was not ready to release her. "Hailey, I'm so glad to see you."

"Kenia, everything all right?"

"Yes, it is now," she said, studying Hailey's face, rejoicing to see it free of injuries. It was the Hailey she knew, and it wasn't. Hailey, on the other hand, looked shocked to see the bruises, cuts, and abrasions on Kenia.

"What happened to you?"

"Long story."

"Kenia, come over here," Shane said, waving them both towards a spot between himself and Austin a— who nodded towards her, but was much more interested in the drama unfolding at the mansion.

Stan offered a quick, "Hey, Kenia," between tweeting updates on his phone and live-streaming his own reporter-on-the-scene briefings on Facebook, his tone as officious as possible. Hailey snorted with laughter while Stan did his best to ignore her.

Kenia put her arms around each of them, causing them to regard her with a bit of surprise—Stan with some annoyance as he tried to maintain an air of professionalism while she kissed him on the cheek.

"Kenia, you sure seem glad to see us," Hailey said.

"Like you wouldn't believe."

"Seriously, what happened to your face?"

"First, update me on what is happening here."

Shane and Hailey took responsibility for filling Kenia in, but she had learned much of the details from the news interviews lower down on the hill. The drama at the mansion drew out into a prolonged wait for news. The SWAT team entered and emerged shortly after, their weapons pointed down, their fingers away from the trigger guards, their sense of urgency drained away. They started to file back into the van while an EMS team rushed up the steps carrying a stretcher. The crowd went silent. A familiar figure walked past on the opposite side of the police tape.

"Chief Farrcroft," Stan asked in his best newscaster's voice, holding out his phone to capture any comments from the police chief that Kenia had known formally as Officer Keith Farrcroft. "Any official comment?"

"Nope, not while that is recording," he said, looking at the phone.

"Turn it off, Stan," Hailey said. Stan complied and pulled out a pad and pen instead.

Chief Farrcroft looked at Kenia, his face flashing concern at the sight of her bruises and bandages. At the same time, a memory of a 5K with his officers and staff from the Med-Dent building flooded into her mind. They had all collaborated to raise money for . . . diabetes research and prevention. Was that something that had happened in this timeline?

"You look banged up, what happened?" Chief Farrcroft asked.

Kenia realized she couldn't keep dodging questions and that she would need a cover story. She said she had been in a tumble on her mountain bike. It seemed to satisfy Officer Farrcroft, but even as Kenia shared her contrived story, she read some confusion on the part of the Pennel children, as if they were starting to experience the same flood of conflicting memories and timelines as she. Kenia pressed on, "What happened to Harold Bridgewater?"

Chief Farrcroft grimaced. "I'm not really allowed to say, but it's pretty much an issue for the coroner at this point."

"I thought I heard a gunshot," Austin said.

"Self-inflicted. Our men had not even entered the room yet."

It was Hailey who was touching her head now, right in the place where she had sustained an injury in the alternate timeline, as Chief Farrcroft was called away by one of his officers. Hailey looked confused.

"What is it, Hailey?" Kenia asked.

"Just weird, like a vision or something. It's nothing."

"No, tell me."

"We were in Austin's Jeep. I saw us getting rammed by another car, a black SUV. Then we were trapped somewhere . . . cold."

Stan lowered his phone. "I just had the same . . . and Bridgewater was there. But not the hermit we know, it was like he was . . . fancy and rich."

"And hated us," Shane said.

Mike and Rochelle, who had remained at the periphery, moved in close to gather all of them. "Time for us to go," Rochelle said.

◊

It was a retread of their conversation at the kitchen table before: the Pennel boys talking about wave function and probable timelines, with even more depth and detail than before, now with their uncle Mike present to answer questions. Rochelle and Austin prepared tea and snacks. Kenia was seized with the weird sense of déjà vu, noting that the house was as it was in the alternate timeline, refurbished, contemporary, the rooms crowded with audio-visual equipment. But she still retained knowledge of both realities in her mind. One in which the kids had a fake reality TV show, with faux news, and this one—new to her—where they had the same online presence, but the YouTube channels focused on science, tech, engineering, and math education. As she reached for memories of Klan impersonators who waved Confederate and Tea Party Flags for backdrops, with missing teeth and fat suits, she instead found ones wherein she *remembered* videos by the Pennels demonstrating chemistry phenomenon, super fluids, conductors, slow-motion videos of underwater pressure waves, and GoPro films taken from the edge of space from weather balloons.

"So Mike, all these years, you knew Kenia was going to appear in that river tonight?" Shane asked.

"Sort of. I've forgotten a lot of the other timeline I glimpsed but, like I said, I wrote it down in the fifties.

Austin was staring into a cup of untouched chamomile cooling in his hands. "This all sounds so crazy, but it's like I remember it, even if it never happened to me."

Shane and Stan argued about quantum wave function, Heisenberg uncertainty principles, and Copenhagen Interpretation, all of which Kenia remembered hearing from them before, as well as from Octavian Coates. She wondered if the Coates brothers were sitting up in bed right now, confused by their own strange dreams and competing, conflicting memories of multiple timelines.

Rochelle turned to Kenia. "You must be exhausted."

Kenia realized that she was utterly, bone tired. Hailey, also having grown weary of the discussion regarding space-time, turned to her. "I'll set up a room for you."

The girls went upstairs, Hailey providing Kenia with an extra set of pajamas, a floor fan, covers for the bed in the guest room, and towels for the bathroom. Kenia was eager to wash off the slurry of dirt, blood, and coal, mixed with river water. She sat down on the clothes hamper in the bathroom and spoke to Hailey before she went to her own room.

"There is something I didn't tell anyone yet," Kenia said. Hailey stopped, set down the lid of the toilet and sat across from her, their knees almost touching. "I saw my father."

"What?"

"In 1953, at the plant. He . . . he came back. I guess it was his last jump. He held off the men trying to stop me and your uncle Mike from taking the truck. He saved us."

"Could he have lived?"

"I don't know," Kenia said, cursing the tears coming down her face once more. "The garage was collapsing all around us. He told me he loved me. I got to say goodbye. I never got to do that before. None of us did. But it still hurts. It's like losing him all over again."

Hailey reached across and pulled Kenia to her shoulder, the two of them laugh-crying at the awkward embrace as Hailey began to slip from the toilet and the hamper tipped over beneath Kenia. They both slid down to the floor, their backs to the tub, their arms around one another, sisters in loss. Despite everything, despite the extraordinary nature of her jumps through time, Kenia still felt as if she had no control, as if so much was outside of her influence, her will, and the wishes of her heart. Then a more practical concern struck her as she wiped her eyes: her butt was cold. She said so.

Hailey got up and flipped a switch on the wall and returned, putting her arm back around Kenia. The sound of water rattling in pipes beneath the floor preceded a gradual warming beneath her.

"Heated tiles," Hailey said. "Proceeds from the channels paid for them. We can sit here as long as you need, warm butts and all."

Chapter 33
Summer Practicum Brownbag

In the morning, after a breakfast prepared by Austin and Mike including blueberry, cranberry, and chocolate chip pancakes, Kenia stepped out onto the porch with a cup of coffee and rocked in one of the chairs. She listened to a meadowlark while a robin hopped from the flagstone walkway to the porch rail. The grass blades were translucent in the slanting rays of the rising sun, drops of dew hanging on their ends like the heads of musical notes set on a staff. She held herself still and silent, as a mother deer with two fawns wandered from the edge of the woods to graze on the south end of the lawn. Kenia's muscles were just beginning to ache from the stillness imposed on them when the screen door whined open. The noise startled the mother and fawns so that they dashed into the woods, white tails flashing.

"Odocoileus virginianus," Stan said, noting the retreating deer with the cerebral intensity she had come to expect of him. He sat down in the next rocking chair over from her, pushing back and forth a few times before he said, "This yard used to be full of junked cars. Not *used* to . . . . but well . . . could have been? Man, I don't even know how to talk about all this."

"I know. It's not working like the movies."

"No. It seems like it takes longer for the timelines and probabilities to disentangle. I wonder if they ever will completely. Maybe we'll always remember the two alternative paths."

"Or not. Mike thinks I will, but you all won't. Something about proximity to nodes or nexuses of some sort."

Stan screwed his mouth up into a question. "You all right with that?"

Kenia shrugged, adjusting her coffee cup on her lap. "I guess. It reminds me of your transformers and all their different origin stories."

"We've talked about my transformers?"

Kenia laughed. "Well, I did with *one* version of you. But it's just like that, I suppose. Different possibilities, equally plausible and equally real, in my head."

"You know, I like the origin story where—"

"—Optimus Prime and Megatrons' stories are linked. Megatron's philosophy influencing the evolution of Prime's own principles. I know."

"Wow," he said, slack-jawed. "You really do. I guess we did talk."

Kenia smiled and downed the last of her coffee, tipping her cup bottom up before setting it on the railing where the robin had perched and flown off. "Let's take a walk."

Stan bounded down the steps after her. They made their way down the flagstones, past Austin's Jeep and Mike and Rochelle's Touareg, Kenia noting how much she preferred the lawn with just a bird feeder and birdhouse as lawn art—the birdhouse itself a miniature of the Pennel house that she had no doubts Austin had made. Azalea and crepe myrtles grew in abundance, without the rusting auto carcasses impinging on their space and sunlight.

She led them down the driveway, through the tunnel of emerald branches, listening to the soft crush of gravel underfoot. She and Stan reached the main road, where they could see the valley through the trees, the ribbons of the Potomac encircling Selah Island like an embrace, the sweeping blades of the wind turbines erected on the north end of the island turning in the breeze. She remembered seeing a Trailways bus in this same place on the road and realized that, in fact, that scene *had* taken place, no matter the branch of the timeline she occupied now. She thought of those students, having reached Selah University, studied there, and graduated, and wondered where they were now, and about the generation they had raised after them. They were out there, somewhere, and the thought gave her comfort, as well as some measure of hope that perhaps so was her father, maybe somewhere in the gap of time between.

She tried to move herself past the melancholy rising within her at the thought of losing her father all over again. She turned down the road, walking a few paces downhill to the next driveway.

"Where are we going?" Stan asked.

"To visit a friend," Kenia said. "And check on a hunch."

They moved down the driveway to Martha Andersen's home, Kenia slowing as she went. Not for fear, but rather for the growing knowledge surfacing in her mind as she moved closer. It was the same phenomenon she had experienced when she had first approached the Pennels and Chief Farrcroft in this timeline—the memories and history of this branch of reality taking hold.

Stan seemed oblivious to any changes, politely matching her pace as they came into the yard. This time there were no overflowing trash bins but instead dozens of tall sunflowers facing the sun, their blooms as big as Kenia's head. The boxes in the yard held dark, fertile soil with tomato plants, peppers, cabbage, and long, flowering pumpkin vines. A red pickup truck, its bed beaten and worn from use, sat low on its suspension from the bags of fresh mulch piled inside. Next to it was a cleaner hybrid sport-utility crossover.

A familiar dog—Mocha—barked as they knocked on the door, the wind chimes clanging as they waited. The door swung open. Kenia willed herself through the confusion and disorientation that followed as timelines tangled in her mind and finally the dominant one resolved into her consciousness.

At first Martha looked like a stranger. No longer the heavyset woman Kenia had known before, this Martha was a well-proportioned woman, although still buxom and generously endowed. Her skin was smooth and glowing, her eyes bright, the whites clear. Her genuine warmth, which was as familiar to Kenia as her voice, conveyed itself in an instant as she opened the door and cried out Kenia's name.

"Kenia," she said, wrapping her neck in a hug. "What a nice surprise. Come in!"

The house was airy and well lit, sunlight pouring through open windows, the curtains billowing on breezes from outside. Martha dashed upstairs, saying she needed to get someone, but Kenia did not listen carefully enough for the name to register. Instead she was entranced by the home. No smell of clogged drains, rotting food, cigarettes, or animal dander here. To Stan, it was all as expected, and Kenia sensed him studying her as she looked around, wide-eyed.

"You remember this place . . . differently," he said, a statement rather than a question.

"Quite. Who is this?" she said, pointing to a framed picture on the wall of a young man dressed in a National Park Ranger uniform next to a cheerful-looking girl, her hand on his chest, a fat engagement stone on her finger.

"Well, that's Joel, Martha's son."

Kenia smiled. Mocha was standing on his hind legs, pawing at her knees. "Hello Mocha!" she said, dropping to her knees to rub the dog's head. Tom and Tom, the cats, were also both there, lounging in the sills of the open windows, their attention moving back and forth between Kenia and a few birds outside at the birdfeeder.

Two sets of feet came down the steps. Martha came down, followed by another woman who crossed the hall to also hug Kenia.

"Hello, Ms. Jolene," Kenia said, her smile wide, her hunch at her "new" memory having been correct. Jolene's short hair was gone. In its place were long, well-oiled cornrows that gave way to locks that ran the length of her back. Her face was free of makeup as well as the scowl she had worn when Kenia had first met her "boss" at the Med-Dent building. An orange oval stone replaced the plain wood-and-metal crucifix. Martha kissed Jolene on the cheek and excused herself to the kitchen to make tea for all of them. Jolene shepherded them to follow, pulling out chairs so they could sit down at the kitchen table. While Jolene stepped away for a moment to help her partner, Kenia noticed one constant from one parallel timeline to the next: a Sports Illustrated swimsuit calendar, still hanging in the same prominent place on the wall, its pages and pictures having progressed to Ms. August, an impossibly curvy and statuesque goddess who looked East African in origin. Kenia smiled to herself.

It had never been for Joel . . . .

The two women settled down across from Kenia and Stan, Ms. Jolene asking about how work and interviews were going and if Kenia needed any help.

"No," Kenia said, her memories of interviews and surveys in this timeline catching up with her along with some of her observations and conclusions—some, however, were the same. Sadly poverty, substances abuse, and health disparities did indeed persist, even in this altered branch of possibilities, but she also harbored knowledge that the rates here were not nearly as discouraging as before.

She pushed work thoughts aside for the time being, remembering something else: a picture of a tipping truck careening through the streets of Selah, a young man rolling to the curb, a dark-skinned arm pushing him off the truck. "Stan and I were wondering if we might look at some of those old photo albums of yours."

◊

"And here is Monique Bridgewater, the mayor of Selah Station. She is descended from one of the founding families of Selah, who have long held service positions in the town. She's inaugurating the farmers' market, where local farmers can come and sell their produce at the town square two days of week," Kenia said, waiting a moment before she advanced to the next PowerPoint slide.

It was late September, but the summer heat still lingered and so the AC was turned on high. Her audience in the boardroom of St. Mary's hall wore sweaters against the cold pumped in from the rooftop HV/AC units. Her advisor, Dr. Quientela, sat eating yogurt with her colleagues alongside her, also nibbling away at their bag lunches. Students did the same—the lucky ones also at the boardroom table—and those who had come later sat in seats against the walls. Audre watched from right behind Dr. Quientela, leaning forward with the rapt attention of a best friend.

Kenia had documented the progress they had made through home visits and awareness campaigns to the health behaviors she had gone to measure in the communities around Selah Station, but she knew in her heart that the greatest intervention was the one she could not share. Changing the past, saving the Selah Island and the university, had kept the community whole, its ethos of integration, diversity, and cohesiveness intact. Furthermore, the growing university ensured jobs, and people had remained. The rural poverty that categorized so much of the US persisted outside Selah Station; the problems of coal country and the rustbelt were stubborn. Shortened lifespans, high rates of drug abuse, depression, suicide, obesity, hypertension, and heart disease, correlated with high unemployment and low education, persisted—but not to the same worrying degrees in Selah Station. If anything, Selah Station was a "positive deviant," breaking from the national trends, demonstrating traits of resiliency that Kenia had been sure to document to test for replicability in other communities that were still struggling.

Kenia advanced the slide. A few more pictures: these of Ms. Jolene conducting health trainings along with Thea Ferguson; another of Janice (no longer an employee of McDonald's or even Dawson's Hardware, but rather a drug and alcohol addiction counselor) providing advice to a client; the Coates brothers helping at a table to sign people up for health screenings; and even the Pennels, documenting it all with their cameras. Kenia added, "These teens you see here with the cameras have a thriving YouTube following for their science education channels. They volunteered to put together a piece on the health fair and the farmers' market."

"People have channels on YouTube?" an older male professor asked from the end of the table.

Some of the students stifled laughs.

"Yes, Rodger, I'll show you later," said Professor Basau, a Bengali expert on child nutrition and early cognitive stimulation.

The applause when Kenia was finished was polite, the questions general. After taking a few, Kenia sat down next to Audre, who gave her a thumbs up before standing up to give her own presentation on her summer in Haiti.

As much as Kenia wanted to pay attention to her friend's results and the pictures from her practicum, she had already heard most of the stories over shared meals, study sessions, and late night chats. Kenia found her own thoughts wandering, considering what had really changed after the summer in Selah Station. Selah was different, radically so, its potential realized, or at least building. She hoped the best days were ahead for the city.

But she had been surprised—disappointed even—at how short the waves of change rippling out from the epicenter of Selah Station had actually been. The world was still the same broken world, unjust, unfair, the country still rife with white supremacy, the same bloody foundation of slavery and genocide beneath it all having persisted. Corrupt, conmen politicians still peddled in lies, equivocation, and deceit, praying on ignorance and profiting from fear.

The indelibleness of it all had been waiting for her on her ride back from Selah, when the bus had stopped for a break again at the Junction. Awash with the triumphs of a resurgent Selah Station, she had walked to the end of the parking lot to the same historical marker, marking the murder of Ernest Cunningham. In retrospect, she could see her naiveté now, that foolish hope that the sign would not be there, that Ernest would not have been lynched and murdered.

But the sign read the same as before. Crestfallen, Kenia had wondered what purpose any of the jumps or sacrifices —the Pennels', her family's, her own—had amounted to. These thoughts reoccurred to her as Audre flipped through pictures of malnourished, stunted children in Haiti. What other proof did she need? The same phrase, "Nigger go home," had remained scratched at the bottom of the historical marker as well—despite the triumphs and accomplishments, the integrationist dream at Selah Station, just two hours away. The sun had progressed in its celestial track each day, burning a scar in the heavens, and moving time forward—in one branch of possibility or the other—shadows shortening and lengthening in a circular dance of hemispheres. And yet that damnable sign remained, history persisting, that six-letter word, with its deep gouges and pointed edges, endured.

"Kenia," Dr. Basau called her name. She realized she had not been paying attention to the discussion. "Did you hear Dr. Quientela's question."

"Oh, no. I'm sorry, I was thinking of . . . something," she said, embarrassed, coming back to herself, the room full of her professors and fellow students. "Could you repeat it, please?"

"Of course," Dr. Quientela said. "I was just saying that with this new tranche of funding from NIH, we can send both you and Audre to Haiti next summer. But considering all that you accomplished in Selah Station, I was wondering if you would want to go back there."

"I would," Kenia said without hesitation, equal parts bitterness and hope kindling in her heart. "There is still so much work to be done."

Thanks and a Promise of Change

Thanks for reading. Know that your purchase of The Selah Branch will go to support the following nonprofit organizations focused on the betterment of communities of color and opportunities for children and families from traditionally marginalized communities.

Creating Your Success Inc. (CURS)
Creating Your Success, Incorporated (CURS), based in Atlanta Georgia, has a mission to assist youth reach their post high school graduation goals, by facilitating career counseling services and life skills workshops. Through their work they hope to give youth access to information, opportunities, and resources available for them to achieve their career goals. CURS (pronounced: "cures") strives to inspire, educate, uplift, and provide tools to promote change and growth within each youth participant. You can find out more by looking them up on Facebook or at www.cursinc.org

Atlantic Street Center
Based in Seattle Washington for over 100 years, Atlantic Street Center has provided leadership in educational, school/community relations, case management services, homelessness, gang prevention and intervention, family support and mental health services to vulnerable communities of color in Seattle. The direct service staff provide a variety of academic, youth development, early literacy, mental health, and family support services to more than 3,000 children and their family members each year. For more information visit www.atlanticstreetcenter.org

Georgia State University
In the form of scholarships for African American students. Georgia State University has one of the highest rates of students who are the first in their family to attend college and has a variety of scholarships for students of color studying an array of majors in undergraduate and graduate programs. As a recipient of a scholarship to the Georgia State J. Mack Robinson College of Business as well as the 2013 MLK Torch of Peace Award, it's this author's wish to "pay it forward" to support the next generation of graduates. www.gsu.edu

Made in the USA
Lexington, KY
06 October 2017